—AGRICOLA—
INVADER

SIMON TURNEY

—AGRICOLA—
INVADER

HEAD
ZEUS

An Aries Book

First published in the UK in 2024 by Head of Zeus,
part of Bloomsbury Publishing Plc

9 7 5 3 1 2 4 6 8

A catalogue record for this book is available from the British Library.

ISBN (PB): 9781804540435
ISBN (E): 9781804540398

Cover design: kid-ethic

Printed and bound in Great Britain by
CPI Group (UK) Ltd, Croydon CRO 4YY

Head of Zeus Ltd
First Floor East
5–8 Hardwick Street
London ECIR 4RG

WWW.HEADOFZEUS.COM

To Paul and Charlene Harston, who opened up for me a whole new Roman world.

PART 1

INVASION

Non sane alias exercitatior magisque in ambiguo Britannia fuit

(Never before or since had Britain been in a more disturbed or critical condition)

Tacitus, Agricola 4

I

Agricola's blade came up sharply, Noric steel glinting in the morning sunlight, meeting his opponent's sword with bone-jarring force. The edges clashed and metal shrieked as they slid along one another until they broke free, Agricola's blade whipping up into the air, his opponent's drawing a narrow red line across his thigh. He grunted as he staggered away, looking down and then back up at the aggressor.

'You cut me.'

'I'll bloody *gut* you if you don't give me everything, Gnaeus. You're still dropping your guard when you think you've got the edge. Concentrate. Always be aware of your opponent, watch his eyes, his hands, his feet, anticipate every possible move.'

'According to you I'll need at least six eyes to fight well.'

'Yet I have only two and you've still to pass my guard.'

Breathing heavily, Gnaeus Julius Agricola stepped back a little more until he reached the colonnade that surrounded the peristyle. There, he leaned against a column and looked down at his sword. There was a small nick there, evidence of that last clash. He closed his eyes and sighed, thinking of the hours of polishing that lay ahead, working out that new imperfection. He could always use another sword of course, but he knew he wouldn't. This was the blade his father, Graecinus, had used when he'd served his own time in the army and, if family legend was to be believed, was the same blade that had been borne by their ancestor when the Saluvii fought for the great Caesar and earned the family's name with their grant of citizenship. In truth, he didn't believe that tale one bit. Swords of this pattern weren't

3

in common usage back then, especially not by mid-ranking Gallic tribesmen. Likely his grandfather had commissioned the sword at the earliest, but his father had believed the tale, and so that made it important. A weapon to be treasured.

His gaze slid slowly up the gleaming blade to the guard of finely carved walnut and brass, the grip of bone in a hexagonal form, worn to shape by three or more generations of Julian hands, the pommel a perfect sphere of walnut. It was, in fact, entirely unremarkable, especially when compared with some of the decorative and expensive blades the young hopefuls of Rome wielded, but it was more than mere glamour. This was a soldier's blade. A warrior's weapon. His father had worn it as a young tribune in the war against Tacfarinas, and his grandfather against the Delmatae. It had drawn blood from the enemies of Rome for generations.

'You're daydreaming. Stop staring at your sword and come at me again. We're going to keep practising this again and again until you pay attention and stop cocking it up.'

Agricola heaved himself out from the column with a grunt, sighing. 'You sound like a veteran training officer, Gaius. You're not. You're only a year older than me.'

'And I've spent that year with the Seventh Claudia, while you've been mooning about in Rome like a lovesick poet. Now come on. Attack me again.'

Gaius Suetonius Jovinus swung his sword in a wide circle twice and then planted his feet apart, hunched down a little, and crooked a beckoning finger at Agricola.

With a slight smile, the younger man took four steps forward, the last two at a jog, and threw his sword out from shoulder height, lancing towards his friend. Jovinus brought his own weapon up to parry the blow, and that was when Agricola stamped down hard on his extended foot. The two blades met again but this time there was no resistance, for as Agricola lifted his foot, Jovinus fell away, bellowing obscenities.

'Now, now,' the younger man grinned, taking a step towards

him, 'it doesn't do to drop your guard. Always be aware of your opponent, watch his eyes, his hands, his feet...'

Jovinus rose like Neptune from the deep, face set with an angry grimace as he tottered momentarily on his painful foot. 'Fighting dirty might be acceptable for slaves in the arena, but it's hardly appropriate for men of distinction,' he snapped.

'If I find myself facing a seven-foot German warrior with an axe the size of a man, I'll fight as dirty as I need to,' Agricola laughed.

Jovinus levelled an accusatory finger at him, but before he could say whatever cutting remark had leapt to mind they heard the voice of Glyptos, the family's chief house slave, calling them in for dinner. 'After we eat, farm boy,' Jovinus said, 'we're going to start all over again, and this time I'm going to leave you black and blue.'

Jovinus scowled again for a moment, but took in the enthusiastic sight of the younger man and shook his head, his irritation cycling back to his usual friendly smile, which Agricola returned. Few men could get away with calling Agricola 'farm boy', highlighting the cognomen his father had given him. Back at school in Massilia he'd broken three noses for that particular habit before people had learned to stop. But Jovinus was one of those privileged few who could do so without fear of reprisal. It was partly their long-standing friendship, their mutual respect, and, of course, partly that Jovinus' father was one of the most celebrated military men in the empire right now.

Still, despite their easy friendship and near-equality, Jovinus walked quickly, making sure he was ahead. It was something Agricola had learned over his years of schooling among the Roman elite in Massilia, and even more so in their short time back in the capital: Rome was all about the pecking order. Jovinus was both older, if only by a year, and more important, if only because of his father's current celebrity, and that meant he expected to be at the front of any social gathering. Agricola allowed him the conceit. His own family had risen fast and far, but neither fast enough nor far enough to shake off the faint trace of their provincial, agrarian origins.

With a smile still gracing his unmarked features, he followed Jovinus through the garden and into the atrium, seeking out the summer triclinium whence the voice had called, examining the surroundings once more as they walked. The gardens were well manicured, expensive and planted with an eye to flora that few in Rome possessed. And only someone who really knew such things would be able to see that despite the multi-hued and serene glory of the peristyle it was, in fact, comprised wholly of inexpensive parts. Their family was far from wealthy by Roman standards, and had been so since the day his father had been taken from them.

He tried not to dwell on that, instead focusing on the house as they passed into the atrium, the room still decorated rather garishly with its former owner's mosaic of nymphs doing physically unlikely things to the sea god and his cronies. In one corner stood the cupboard still full of the family death-masks of the house's previous occupant.

It had been a stroke of good fortune really, for the impoverished widow and her son moving back to Rome from the family estate in Forum Iulii. They had sought a modest town house, and been stunned by just how modest the options had been with the gold they felt they could spare. Then this prize had dropped into their laps, Agricola's uncle the one to send hurried news of it their way. The bloated hedonist senator who owned the house had foolishly lampooned the emperor's new poem at a formal dinner. Nero was not a man to take artistic criticism lightly, and the poor bastard was dead before the cock crowed. The emperor had been merciful and let the man's family live, and so it was his widow who had sought to sell the place and leave the city as fast as her feet could carry her, before Nero changed his mind and had the whole family exiled to some barren atoll. She had willingly accepted a very low offer and fled Rome for provincial obscurity. Now, slowly, Agricola's stoic, reserved mother was replacing the graphic and appalling décor of the place with something more in keeping with their own staid Gallic roots.

The atrium was next on her list, for she still made sure not to look at the floor as she passed.

Jovinus was considerably more traditional in his manner, and sniggered wickedly at some of the images underfoot as they passed through towards the dining room. Agricola rolled his eyes, stepping over a mosaic image of Priapus fondling his enormous appendage as they joined their elders for the meal. He straightened as he crossed the threshold, bolting to his face the rigid impassiveness of the Roman nobleman.

The banquet was already in progress, though only just. The room held a U-shape of three lines of tables laden with food of all varieties, surrounded by comfortable couches, each occupied by a man of note and his wife. Within the open space at the centre stood a wide marble table that bore a huge krater of mixed wine and water, slaves darting to and fro, serving drinks to the guests in expensive glasses. In an alcove still decorated with nymphs sporting pendulous breasts, a pair of slaves issued old Gallic melodies on a soft drum and a set of pipes.

Agricola moved towards his seat, nodding to his mother. In another world, one of imperial clemency, it would be his father sitting beside her at the head of the gathering. That world would never be, thanks to cruel men on thrones of gold. Instead, it was Agricola who made his way around to the couch that would have been occupied by the father he had never met, and sank to it, arranging his tunic carefully enough to hide the red line of Jovinus' sword blow.

'You reek of sweat, dear,' his mother hissed. 'If you must practise, you should keep such things to times when the result will not embarrass us. This is a very important occasion, you may recall.'

'Yes, Mother,' he replied, with exaggerated obedience. 'Though I wonder whether the great general over there berates Jovinus for his own battle scent.'

'Yes, well, Jovinus has nothing to prove.' She gave him a withering look. 'Besides, Jovinus is probably not bleeding liberally into his best tunic.'

'A scratch. Watch him limp and you'll see that my wound was bought and paid for in full.'

'I am so grateful to have a son who prizes war above peace.'

'Without war there would *be* no peace, Mother.'

Her eyes rolled again. 'I paid good money for you to learn such things in Massilia?'

He chuckled. 'Every man here values those sentiments. Is that not precisely why they are here?'

Her silence was all the confirmation he needed. It was so. The room was filled with men who had won glory and power under the eagle of Rome's legions, bringing the light of a civilised empire to the dark corners of the world. It was the very reason for this dinner they could only afford by selling three of the slaves back in Forum Iulii. More than that, even. It was the entire reason they had abandoned his family's heartland and returned to the viper-filled cesspit that was Rome. A huge outlay of money and a vast upheaval of family and home just in order to arrange one expensive night to petition these people.

'I would secure a tribuneship anyway, you know?' he murmured. 'Even if I'd stayed with a friend in the city and we'd spent nothing.'

Without looking, she huffed, eyebrow arching dangerously. 'You may have secured a place, but it would have been with some obscure provincial unit where the greatest chance of glory is building an aqueduct or playing honour guard for some barbarian chieftain. No. You are the son of Julius Graecinus, a true nobleman of Rome, heir to the name of Caesar, and you should be with the grandest of legions, earning a place in the heart of the empire. I will accept no less.'

With a nod of acceptance for all she had done for him, Agricola looked around the room again. He'd been to dinner parties with Rome's elite only twice, and both had been the most awful engagements. The men had generally been purulent, avaricious politicians, trying to outdo one another in both word and deed, while the women had been harpies, shrieking calls at one another from behind their white-lead, mask-like faces. This gathering at least was different, as anyone who knew his brilliant, forthright, noble mother might expect. *This* room was filled with the earnest conversation of soldiers, and the polite chatter of ladies who were comfortable with that sort of man. Indeed, Agricola marvelled at the men his mother had managed to assemble for one dinner, the only event they could really afford without selling up entirely in Forum Iulii.

Two tables to his right sat Jovinus with his new bride, a voluptuous beauty with a sultry whisper, and on the couch in between, his friend's father, the great Gaius Suetonius Paulinus, along with his wife, now entering her dotage and yet striking and witty. Few men in Rome could match Paulinus for reputation, with the exception of the famed general Corbulo, of course. Corbulo would not be attending, given that he was currently out in the east, cutting the Armenians and the Parthians into ribbons for the glory of the empire. But if there was one man whom Rome might currently hold in similar esteem to Corbulo it was Paulinus – and here he was, in pride of place at their banquet.

Off past Paulinus and Jovinus was the couch of the former general Vespasian, a jovial-looking fellow until you saw his eyes, which spoke of a man far too familiar with steel and death. Vespasian, like Paulinus, had been a colleague of Agricola's father almost two decades ago. That he had agreed to attend should not really be a surprise. Eighteen years is a long time to maintain a family friendship after the pater familias has died, but men such as these had long memories and few true friends, and it was the memory of the quiet but capable Graecinus that drew them to this banquet more than it was money or food. That, and the eloquent request of his mother, of course, whom everyone respected.

Beyond Vespasian and his wife, Quintus Petillius Cerialis

sat with his own spouse, Vespasian's daughter. The man spoke infrequently, and when he did it was either an outlandish boast of military prowess or a cutting and insightful comment. Such was Cerialis: a genius and a fool combined in one unpredictable mind.

The other side of the room, past Mother, held an equal scattering of luminaries. Gnaeus Hosidius Geta, hero of the Mauri wars, the general who had joined Vespasian in the first landing in Britannia, former consul and well-known strategic genius. His wife was a tall, thin, elegant black woman who, rumour had it, had come all the way from Mauri lands with him.

Beyond Geta sat Gaius Caetronius Miccio, a war hero like the rest, but a man so old now that he seemed already half-mummified, and occasionally squinted as he put a hand to his ear to try to make out what was being said. It made Agricola smile to see the octogenarian's wife beside him, a buxom beauty of no more than twenty summers, who clung to his arm with wide, devoted eyes.

Finally, at that far side sat the other great warrior of Rome to match Paulinus: Aulus Plautius, Claudius' favoured general, conqueror of Britannia, or of its coast at least. He had been an associate of all the older men in the room in his time, and of Agricola's father, and few men were as respected as he. The man's wife was the picture of Romanitas, and both of them spoke only when they had something of value to say.

Quiet and intelligent guests all, so far removed from the normal Roman dinner party.

'Do tell us,' murmured a sing-song voice, 'why you invited us all tonight.'

All eyes turned to Cerialis. As he took a glass of wine from a slave, his face bore a half-smile that suggested he knew the answer already.

'Blast you, Quintus,' barked Paulinus. 'Can you not even accept a dinner invitation without pulling it apart to see what's written beneath the wax? I'm aware there is a purpose, but can we at least enjoy ourselves first?'

'Eh?' asked the venerable Miccio, hand going to his ear as he swung from Cerialis to Paulinus.

'I fear the answer is clear, given the presence of the youngest of the Julii,' Aulus Plautius muttered, swilling wine in his glass as his eyes rose to Agricola.

'The lady seeks a favour?' Vespasian offered.

'Eh?' repeated Miccio, head snapping back and forth between speakers.

All eyes now fell upon Agricola, and then slid inevitably from him to his mother, Julia. She neither moved nor changed her expression as she spoke.

'Our family has no patron, since the day Caligula took my husband from me. We have no clients, despite our respected history and our eminence. But what we do have is ties to your eminent selves. To the great men of Rome. You ask what favour I seek? I ask nothing for myself, nor for my poor, fallen husband. I seek only what is due to my son, who prepares for his first step on the ladder of public service. And now that you are gathered here, you will not deny him it, I know.'

There was a strange, pensive silence. His mother's voice had taken on a hard edge at the end, like a sword, and it remained so as she continued. 'You are Rome's glorious, the conquerors, the heroes. But I will know any man who denies us now to be but a shadow of his reputation. You, Aulus Plautius. Where would you be without my husband's father defending you in the basilica? Vespasian, whose appointment to the praetorship my husband sponsored? Paulinus? You, I know, owe a near miss on your life only to a timely word from my Graecinus. Each of you owes my family. And if it be that I must clear all those debts, I would call them in to see my son given a chance to fulfil his family duty.'

There was a strange silence again, as each man around that table recalled their connection with Julius Graecinus, rolling it over their tongue to see how the memory tasted.

Oddly, it was the ancient Miccio who broke the peace.

'Say what you mean, Julia Procilla. You wish a favourable appointment for your son, for with the lyre-player on the throne, only those in a position of eminence might rise to the top.'

Beside him, his painted young wife drew a sharp breath. 'Darling, you must not speak of the emperor so. He has ears everywhere.'

'Then he must look a fucking fool,' Miccio laughed in his ancient, scratchy voice. 'Anyway, I am ten years past the boatman's bell already, and every day is a bonus. I say what I think, and I do what I like, as you well know, my beauty,' he grinned, giving her a pat on the behind.

To Agricola's astonishment, the old man's young wife blushed, which set Miccio to cackling.

'It does not do in some regimes,' Geta noted, 'to rise to the top. From the top a man can fall a long way. There are fears already that Corbulo is being a little too successful for his own good.'

'And so a man must strike a happy medium,' Vespasian said, 'between eminence and obscurity.'

'Gentlemen, you are quite correct,' Julia confirmed, 'and the respected general is most astute. In the current, rather unpredictable, reign of our beloved emperor, it is good for a man to rise high enough to be honoured, and yet remain low enough not to be a threat. As such, I seek the advice, aid, and even patronage, of the great men whom my husband called friends and colleagues. You will help me?' Not really a question, despite the way she said it.

Agricola held his breath. He'd said nothing throughout, holding his tongue carefully, for this was his career that they were discussing. His future. He was eighteen. In the coming days, he would either secure a place as a senior tribune among the legions of Rome and begin the climb that would take him to the dizzy heights of the cursus honorum, and perhaps even the consulship, or he would disappear into obscurity, never to rise again. A lot rode on the decision of these eminent men.

The first to speak, and a blow to his hopes, was the capricious Petillius Cerialis.

'I'll not take him, I'm afraid. I'm bound for Britannia, for the Ninth Hispana, as its legate. The Ninth has a reputation as an insular unit, and if I want them to accept me readily I will need to become one of them, rather than attempting to mould them into my force. If I bring my own officers, it will make that much more difficult. Sorry, my good lady, and in the future I will owe you a boon and see it out, but at this moment, to take your son would be to endanger my own position.'

A blow. A nasty one, too. Britannia was a troubled province, a place where names could be made and glory won. He glanced at his mother. She was nodding her stoic acceptance.

'I can do little,' Vespasian added. 'I have been unpopular with our beloved emperor for some years, since that unfortunate incident at his recital. It has taken me everything I have to get my own son Titus appointed to the German legions, and I have no strings left to pull. Had I the option, I would, such is my respect for your departed Graecinus and the friendship we shared. And like Cerialis, I will hold in my heart your request. When times have changed and I have power to grant it, I will readily do so.'

Another blow, and a bad one. Still, Julia Procilla seemed to take it calmly, with a nod.

'I have already granted a favour for a friend,' ancient Miccio said with an air of resigned sadness. 'I have a nephew commanding a legion in Aegyptus, and I have managed to place a friend's son as their senior tribune. I can promise the very same for your young Gnaeus Agricola, but I can only do so when that appointment opens up once more in two years' time. I know this helps you little now, young lady, but at least, if all avenues close, there will be something in his future.'

Agricola threw a thankful glance at the old man. It was something. Of course, in two years a lot could change and, without the income of a man of means, their family might once more be relegated to provincial obscurity. But at least the old man was willing to do something, even if only in the future.

'I am in similar straits,' Geta replied. 'I am all but removed from the circles of such appointments these days. I may be able to be of help in due course, but not yet. Not yet.'

Agricola winced. Every door was closing, and they would not afford such a meal for a second tier of Roman heroes to try again. Not without selling the estates to which they may yet have to retire.

'Father?'

His glance shot to Jovinus, who had spoken. His friend was looking to Suetonius Paulinus. The great man looked troubled.

'No.'

'Father, you have to. You will *govern* Britannia. *Four legions*, Father.'

Paulinus turned to look at Agricola. 'It is difficult.'

'Oh?' his mother murmured conversationally. 'How so?'

'I have already granted every position of note to men I trust, for I am almost ready to depart.' His eyes slid to Cerialis, whom he'd clearly already pulled strings to appoint to the Ninth. 'I have four legions, but I have put men in command and in all the tribunate positions in each. I cannot change them without creating bad blood with someone who is already my client.'

There was a silence once more, broken eventually by Jovinus. 'What of the Second? You said they were unimportant?'

Paulinus shot his son an irritated look, then turned to Agricola and his mother. 'The Second are based in the south-west of the island. Since the day Vespasian resigned his command and left the island, the Second have really done nothing of note. They sit in Isca and monitor mining activity, occasionally kicking angry tribesmen. I will have a war of conquest while I govern Britannia: I will take the border north, but the Second will not be part of it.

They will sit back in the south-west and keep the miners under control.' He leaned back and folded his arms. 'I have vouchsafed the tribunate of the Second to someone anyway.'

'But not someone you care about,' ancient Miccio grinned, 'else you would not have landed them with gloriless caretaking.'

Paulinus cleared his throat in a worried tone. 'That might be true, but to grant such a poor position to the young man over there would hardly do his bloodline justice, while similarly damaging my relationship with another client,' he finished at a hiss, eyes meaningfully on the old man.

'So assign him to the Second Augusta, and second him to your staff,' Plautius said, placing his glass back down on the table with a clack.

'What?'

'You know as well as I do that it is a general's prerogative to select his staff. He draws the most capable officers to his standard and takes them with him on campaign. You should know, Paulinus, since once it was *you* who stood at *my* campaign table scratching your crotch and thinking of the girl back home.'

The silence that followed was tense, and Agricola held his breath. Paulinus' face had coloured a little. To embarrass one of Rome's greatest men could cause trouble, even for another such figure. So much rode on this conversation.

The tension evaporated as Paulinus exploded with laughter. 'Sometimes,' he said, wiping his eyes, 'I am so taken with my own legend, my own importance, that I forget how once I was a lad in an ill-fitting tunic hoping a general wouldn't notice me and ask me a question.'

Plautius chuckled at a shared memory, and Suetonius Paulinus, newly assigned governor of Britannia, turned to Agricola. Not to his mother – for the first time during the exchange, he directed his gaze to the young man.

'Alright. I will lose a contact in a very nice wine trade when I tell Suro that he's out. But he *is* out. And you're in. I will take you to Britannia. You will be assigned tribunus laticlavius of the

Second Augusta. Their commander has a reasonable reputation as a strategist, and I'd already decided to bring him onto my staff. You will come with him. The Second can manage under the command of their camp prefect for a while. They've nothing to do but keep control of backward mining regions after all. Very well, young Gnaeus Julius Agricola, you're on my staff. But I expect great things from you, since I'll annoy a long-standing client to grant you this.'

Agricola threw a relieved smile at the general. 'I shall not disappoint, sir.'

'I know you won't,' he said with a sly look. 'You cannot afford to.'

As he smiled, Agricola could feel eyes on him, and not the general assessing gazes of the gathered luminaries. Eyes burned into him, and he turned to see Petillius Cerialis frowning in his direction. Something had got to the legate, but the conversation had moved on already, and there was nothing he could do right now about whatever had irked Cerialis.

'It seems,' Paulinus was saying, 'that the Silures are causing trouble again.'

'The Silures?' Agricola asked, turning to him.

'A tribe that lives in the western hills of the island,' Vespasian clarified. 'I left the province before we came into contact with them, but they've started wars with several governors over the years since then, and harboured the most dangerous criminals.'

Paulinus nodded. 'My predecessor thought he'd dealt with them for good, but it appears not. It seems that no matter how hard Rome kicks these people, they keep getting back up and throwing rocks at us. I will need to settle them myself, but they are not alone in the region. There are four main tribes in the mountainous west, according to sources, and it is my intention within my term as governor to subdue them all, which will draw our border north to a neat line between two estuaries.'

'Four legions should be more than enough,' Geta murmured.

'We had only a little more than that when we invaded in the first place.'

'I shall take only two legions into the hills, though,' Paulinus replied. 'The Second are useful in their quiet garrison role, and the Ninth are based on the far side of the island, between two of the most warlike and dangerous tribes. Cerialis will have his work cut out keeping the island calm with his legion while I advance. I will take the Fourteenth and Twentieth on campaign.' He turned to Agricola. 'Along with my staff and sundry other units, of course. It is a good chance for a man of action to prove himself.'

Agricola smiled, but his eyes slid back to Cerialis. This, then, was the reason for what felt like a touch of enmity on the part of the headstrong commander. Agricola had come from nowhere and would be taken on campaign, while the older warrior was to sit in garrison with his legion and make sure the conquered tribes of the island stayed quiet. No wonder the man was irritated. Agricola tried to throw the legate a look of apology, but it did little to change the other man's expression.

'What do you know of these tribes, Father?' Jovinus asked.

'Not a great deal of detail, in truth, beyond the geographers' works and the reports of previous governors kept in government records. We'll have to learn most of what we need on arrival, as there's no one really to ask in Rome. Plautius over there only knows the southern tribes, as he returned to Rome before the advance moved north, and the same is true of most of the former legates who retired back to the city. Since then, both Veranius and Scapula died while in office in Britannia, and Gallus passed away within months of returning to Rome.'

'Sounds to me like being governor of the place is a death sentence,' Cerialis grunted.

'I fully intend to serve my three years successfully and retire to Rome in triumph.'

'Doubtless Veranius, Scapula and Gallus said the same, right until the boatman came for them.'

The conversation began to devolve then into a general discussion of past campaigns between the great warriors around the room. Agricola listened politely, asking occasional pertinent questions, but none of it seemed likely to have much of a bearing on his own coming appointment. Plautius, Geta and Vespasian occasionally spoke in passing of their time in Britannia, but only of tribes that were now settled under the Pax Romana, and who would be in the care of Cerialis and his Ninth. He sat quietly and, as the meal came to an end, the various luminaries filing out, issuing their thanks and praise for the evening, waited patiently. The last to leave were Suetonius Paulinus and his son, the governor turning to his new appointee as he rose.

'I will be taking ship for Britannia in three days. By Tubilustrium, I will expect all my officers in attendance at the campaign headquarters in Viroconium. I realise that you will have much to do in preparation, but you should have ample time to join me there, after making an appearance with the Second at Isca and joining their commander. I shall see you on the edge of empire, young Julius Agricola. Do not be late.'

As the great man departed, Jovinus gave him a grin. 'Seems you've escaped the beating I promised you. I'll save it for when next we meet. Good luck, and don't piss off Father.'

The two young men shook hands, and the last guest departed. Julia Procilla waited until the slaves began clearing the dishes, and then strode with her son out into the peristyle.

'Remember everything I have taught you. Be reserved, respectful, brave, and careful. *Especially* the latter. Paulinus is a great man, but a jealous emperor can turn on a great man with astonishing speed, as our family knows all too well.'

Agricola nodded his understanding. 'I think I have almost everything I will need. I'll have to take several of the slaves, of course. But there is one thing I lack, and I think I must attend to that before I go. I'm afraid I will need coin for it.'

'What do you need, Gnaeus?'

'Knowledge,' Agricola replied.

2

The Graecostadium was eye-opening. Agricola had been to the slave market in Forum Iulii as a boy, and the larger one in Massilia in his teens, but neither held a candle to the great market of Rome. Rounding the Basilica Iulia, he was faced with the exterior of a huge porticoed complex, the outer facing walls rather plain, punctuated only by small windows, just two portals in the entire, massive complex. To the west stood the heavy, iron-barred double doors that admitted slave wagons, and to the east lay the rather more decorative door for admitting customers. To this latter, Agricola strode. He was alone, one hand resting permanently on the coin purse at his belt, wary of the many thieves to be found in the city's streets.

His mother had been insistent that he take at least one slave with a stout cudgel for protection. It was not done, she argued, for a noble of Rome to travel the streets alone and unprotected. He was a tribune now, after all. He had argued in response that he was bound for military service in a warlike province. If he could not handle himself in the city streets, what chance did he stand against barbarian tribes? He'd left the house before she could wear him down, though, as she inevitably would. In truth, his motives for anonymity were somewhat different. Firstly, he wanted a slave from this place, if he could find the right one, and he wanted to do so without said slave having any preconceptions of what lay ahead. Secondly, his budget was tight, and traders always marked their price up heavily when they knew they were dealing with landed families. And thirdly, as he had decided during his educational years in Massilia, it was often much more rewarding to listen to people when they were not being deliberately guarded around their betters.

Unfortunately, without a toga or a military tunic, he was rather miscellaneously attired, and found that he was nudged and bustled among the crowd as he followed the general flow of humanity towards the door. At this time of the morning the market had only just opened, and the majority of buyers came early in the hope of a bargain, before the best stock was sold.

Fighting his way through, he passed the doorway and entered the enormous complex. Inside was, if anything, even more crowded. He paused to take stock of his surroundings as people knocked him repeatedly this way and that. A senator passed by, with a small gathering of guards and a priest with a thoughtful look in his wake. Agricola's decision was borne out as he watched, for the merchants began to close on the man hungrily, spying a fat purse in a rich toga. Thieves, too, were gathering.

The wide-open square was surrounded by a portico, behind the columns of which he could see numerous offices of slave dealers, each labelled with its own sign. All around the square, platforms displayed the latest acquisitions, ragged figures standing tied to posts with placards around their necks bearing an inventory number and some pertinent details about the wares. Some of the platforms were revolving, another shabby remnant of humanity pushing the thing around, face grimed with sweat, a slave helping his master sell other slaves. By each platform stood the salesman, rattling off their patter to anyone who would listen.

Agricola craned to look over the heads, peering at the dejected figures, still or slowly revolving. Many he dismissed in an instant. He had no real idea what a Briton looked like, but it seemed highly unlikely, living in the cold, damp north, that they would be dark- or olive-skinned. Germanics tended to the pale end of the scale, and so did the northern Gauls. The Britons would likely be similar. Thus he walked past the tall Nubian with the shaved head, white teeth and eyes gleaming from an ebony face marked with ritual scars. He barely glanced at the Syrian with the oiled black hair, the girl with the olive complexion that spoke of African summers, the Spaniard.

Some halfway across the square he finally stopped beside a podium. Standing with an air of defiance atop it was a tall and broad man in a ragged loincloth, skin almost white, hair in wild red locks, braided down one side, a whorl tattooed on one bicep. The salesman was busy in deep conversation with a prospective buyer, so Agricola craned close to the stand and peered at the sign around the big man's neck. He didn't bother reading beyond the first word: SUEVI.

A German tribesman, then, and consequently of no value to him. Frustrated, he moved about the square from podium to podium, heaving between people, examining placards with increasing disappointment. Every man or woman he thought possibly a Briton turned out to be Germanic or Gallic, or even from some land north of the Danubius.

After a fruitless half hour, and becoming increasingly irritated, he reached the far end of the square and leaned against one of the columns, looking back across the crowd. Here and there, slaves were being taken down from the podiums, sold on, while new merchandise was raised in their place. If he waited just a little there would be a whole new selection to peruse on his way back, but this was futile. He could browse all day and come no closer to what he wanted.

A new tack was required. Turning, he strolled over to the nearest office, peering at the sign. A trader from Lugdunum with an office in Rome. There were possibilities there. Lugdunum would be on the most direct route for a slave convoy from Britannia, and so he entered, hopeful. A woman was busy making some final arrangements with the merchant at a table laden with tablets. Agricola waited patiently just inside the door until one of the merchant's men bowed to the woman and led her out, telling her that her purchase would be delivered by sunset that day.

As he finished with his documents, the trader glanced up, noticing Agricola for the first time.

'Can I help?' he asked as he continued to make notes.

'I'm looking for something specific.'

'Isn't everyone. That's the market these days. What do you need? Work or house?'

That was a good question. He hadn't really thought beyond geographical origin. 'It's more a case of source. Do you have any Britons on your rolls at the moment?'

The trader sucked on his lip as he lowered his pen to the desk and snapped the tablet shut. 'Depends what you want. I have a few. Not the best stock, I'm forced to admit. All girls, but not a looker among them, and not one of them speaks even remotely passable Latin. They are, on the other hand, quite cheap, and I might be prepared to strike a deal for bulk.'

'I need only one. But I need someone fairly bright and who can talk to me.'

The trader sighed. 'Then I have little of interest for you, I'm afraid. There's not been a lot of stock from Britannia since Scapula's time. The last governor doesn't seem to have done much campaigning. Even the ones I have in stock were just suppressed tribesmen that sold their young.'

'Where are they from? Do you know their tribes?'

The man clicked his tongue a couple of times, then began to search the desk for a tablet. Finding it, he snapped it open and ran a finger down it. 'Trinovantes, Durotriges and Atrebates, the lot of them. Any use?'

Agricola shook his head. All three were names he'd heard last night, tribes that the old warriors had ground beneath the heel during the initial stages of the invasion. Nowhere north enough to be of use.

'I'm looking for someone familiar with the western hills.' He cast his mind back to the conversation. 'The Silures, perhaps, or the Ordovices.'

'I've nothing in stock. As I say, there's been not much since

Scapula's campaigns half a decade ago. There was a flood of Silures then, but they only come in in bits and pieces these days.' The trader frowned for a moment. 'I did hear the Silures mentioned yesterday, mind. If I could only remember who it was.' The man tapped his lip in an exaggerated fashion, one eye rolling towards his visitor.

Agricola had trouble not snorting at the rather transparent demand. He fished out a small silver coin and rolled it across his hand from finger to finger, looking meaningfully at the trader.

'Toranius, I think it was,' the man said. 'Fifth office from the gate on the north side. I can't guarantee he has any stock, but he did mention the Silures in passing yesterday.'

The young nobleman flicked the coin across to the trader and nodded his thanks. Leaving the man to it, he made his way around the portico, keeping out of the main crowd in the square as he closed on the fifth office. The name TORANIUS beside the door confirmed he was in the right place. Inside, the trader was clearly identifiable. Toranius was apparently doing rather well for himself. The heavily built man with the two-day growth of beard and the ringleted hair wore more jewellery than Agricola was used to seeing on even ostentatious matrons. His four clerks were busy making notes as he rattled out lists and prices to them, and it took him some time to notice the visitor in the doorway. He flicked a finger at his staff, and they stopped their work and fell silent, stepping back.

'Good morning, sir. Perhaps I can be of assistance.'

Deference? Interesting. Agricola adjusted his thinking. From his appearance, Agricola had formed a certain opinion of the man, but in a single glance Toranius had looked past the ordinary tunic and seen a nobleman in his presence, something the other trader had missed completely. Toranius was observant and clever. Perhaps that was the key to his obvious success.

'I am looking for something specific,' Agricola said. 'I have relatively limited funds, but what I seek should not be overpriced, I think, no bedslave or gladiator.'

'Go on,' the man urged, steepling his fingers.

'I understand that you may have in your stock a Briton or two. Perhaps even of the Silures.'

Toranius smiled over his fingertips. 'My, that *is* specific. I have a few bodies that might fit your bill. It depends on what, precisely, you require them for. I'm guessing not field work or kitchens, else their origin would be unimportant. And nothing academic, for I have yet to find a Briton who, if you gave him a copy of the *Aeneid*, would do more than wipe his backside with it.'

Agricola let out a light chuckle. 'Quite. I'm seeking information on the lands and tribes of western Britannia. One of the Silures, or any of their neighbouring tribes, would fit the bill nicely. Preferably one with more than a passing word of Latin, though I realise that might not be easy.'

'My dear young sir, your words are sweet melody to my ears. I may have one that would fit your needs, though I might point out that such specifics tend to drive up the price. A Briton with a command of a civilised tongue is a rarity, and one from the tribes outside our control is even rarer. That I even have such a thing can only be the will of the gods made manifest. Might I ask with which noble house I am dealing? I like to keep account of my connections, should I ever have anything else I think might interest you.'

'What makes you think I am a nobleman?'

Toranius laughed. 'A toad may wear a tunic with a broad stripe and still be clearly a toad. In my experience you cannot take a man whose family can afford to have him educated in Massilia, unless I misplace your accent, and dress him down enough to appear a pleb. No, sir, I think you are of senatorial stock, especially from the quality of your footwear. Calfskin, with a stitching pattern of Sicilian design, I think.'

'I am impressed. I am Gnaeus Julius Agricola, formerly of Forum Iulii.'

'Nephew of Lucius Julius Graecinus? Son of the famed and

noble Marcus Julius Graecinus? Then I am greatly pleased to make your acquaintance. Your uncle and I are acquainted and have done business on a number of occasions.'

Again, Agricola shifted his thinking. The man had an unparalleled memory, clearly. Few would remember the father who had stood for justice against the cruel whim of Caligula and fallen for it, and few knew that the man's family had returned to Rome from their self-imposed exile. As for connecting the two...

'Perhaps I could view your stock?'

The merchant tapped his lip. 'Such slaves are kept in my warehouse. If you are in no hurry I can have them brought here, though it may take some time. If it is more urgent, then I can take you there, but you must prepare yourself for the conditions.'

Agricola nodded. 'I am happy to take a little walk to speed things along.'

Toranius turned to his clerks. 'Keep the office running. I shall be out for half an hour.' Then, to Agricola, 'Come, young sir.'

Striding from the room, he moved towards the public gate. Agricola was impressed. As Toranius stepped between the columns of the colonnade, three guards with heavy clubs suddenly appeared at his side, shouting for the crowd to clear. In moments, the clubmen carving an open path for them, they were out of the gate and in the street. The crowd passing in and out had thinned a little as time went on, and they had no difficulty moving to open space.

'I presume from your rather incognito attire,' the man said, 'that you did not arrive in a litter?'

'No. On foot.'

'Then we are lucky, for my warehouse is close by.' With a smile and a sweep of the arm, Toranius led the way along the street for two blocks and then turned left, his guards making sure to keep the ordinary folk of the street out of the way. Past the storehouses of Germanicus, high brick buildings rose, built into the lowest slopes of the Palatine. As they approached, one of the guards called out ahead, and a door was opened. Two more of the man's staff emerged and stepped to either side.

'I must apologise in advance for the smell. I do not usually bring customers to the warehouse. Our only running water is a small channel drawn from the supply of a nearby bath house, and that is not nearly enough to keep such a number of slaves clean.'

As he approached, Agricola was hit by a strange smell, a combination of sewer and human sweat, mixed with roses and spicy perfume.

'That is... cloying.'

'We do what we can to alleviate the worst of the stench. Hold your breath for a few moments, good master Julius.' And with that, Toranius led him into the building. The place was a high and open hall with three storeys, open from ground to roof. All around the edge were endless cages, with walkways and stairs leading between the floors. Near the rear of the ground floor were a number of ordinary doors, and as they neared he could see them labelled as offices and storerooms. Despite the warnings, he was forced to take a breath before they reached the far end, and gagged. All around him, hundreds of tongues cried from three storeys of human misery, plaintive and desperate voices calling out in dozens of languages. He paid them no attention as he was led through one door at the far end, and heaved a relieved breath as he found himself outside once more. This was a small colonnaded square with a number of comfortable couches beneath the portico and five of the rotating podiums at the centre.

'My private viewing area. I have been attempting to purchase land to the side, in order to have an approach that does not require passing through the storeroom itself, but sadly negotiations keep falling through. Land prices even this low down the Palatine are horrifying.'

Agricola took several breaths until he felt considerably better, and then allowed himself to be led to one of the couches. A servant brought him a cup of wine and water and a plate with a small pastry, while Toranius gave instructions to another.

They sat quietly and made small talk about Agricola's family and the state of the slave trade in these troubled times, and before long two of the guards reappeared in the courtyard from the rancid atmosphere of the building. They were escorting a man of middling height with a short beard, badly clipped, and dark, almost black, hair down to the shoulder. He was not large or well muscled, but there was a leanness that suggested there might be more to him than was immediately apparent. The man was soaking wet, presumably having been hurriedly bathed before display. He was clad in only a loincloth, his bare feet grubby.

Agricola looked him up and down. If he was a warrior in his former life, he'd either been a very good one or very lucky, for the young Roman could see only two small scars on the man's body, one just below his left eye and the other on his right forearm. Neither looked like sword wounds. The man was looking at him rather insolently, and Agricola was unsurprised to see an echo of hatred there.

'Examine him,' Toranius urged, gesturing as the man was tied to the post on one of the podiums, hands behind his back.

Agricola put his wine down on the table beside him and stepped up towards the slave. The man's eyes, sharp and bright, followed his every movement. He circled the man twice, looking him up and down. He was perhaps thirty years old, or a little younger. His skin was good and clear, and his hands thin-fingered and agile. He was bound and still, but Agricola could picture him having the grace of a hunter were he free to move.

'I would like to speak to him alone, if that is possible?'

The trader frowned. 'He is bound, sir, but it would be extremely remiss of me to leave you in his presence without a guard. Your safety is paramount, and many of these men are little more than animals when it comes down to it.'

'Still, I would like to.'

With a shrug, Toranius rose and gestured to his men. He cast a last look at Agricola. 'Stay well out of his reach, young sir, or at least his reach if he had his hands free. And if there is trouble, run for this door. It will not be locked.'

Agricola waited for the others to leave, judging himself far enough that even a desperate kick would not reach him. He locked gazes with the man. Still there was nothing but spite in the slave's eyes.

'I am led to believe you can understand me,' he said, slowly and clearly.

'I understand all Romans,' the man said in good if strongly accented Latin. 'You are a punishment sent to us by the gods for some slight of our forefathers.'

Agricola chuckled. 'Do you know, that is not at all impossible. I studied the origins of man under very clever Greeks at Massilia, beyond the tales of Aeneas and Troy. I have had my own lineage linked to the goddess Venus through our familial connection to Caesar, though I will admit it is an adoptive connection, and not by blood. But for all the divine links, none of them ever propounded the notion that we were a divine punishment inflicted upon the non-Roman world. I find that quite fascinating, and not a little amusing.'

'Romans also talk too much.'

'As do you, for a slave.'

'Whatever you seek in a slave, I am not it.'

'I think that might be rather for me to decide. You are breathtakingly insolent. I wonder if that is why you languish in your cell rather than being in some nice household with baths and a kitchen. The aroma of your captivity lingers despite the quick wash. I fear you have been in there some months.'

'That cell and others.'

'You are of the Silures, I understand.'

No answer seemed to be forthcoming.

'What is your name?'

'That has yet to be decided,' the man grunted.

'I do not mean your given slave name. I mean the name you had among your people.'

The slave's eyes narrowed as if he were trying to work out how such information could be used to further damage or degrade him. Apparently unable to see any danger in it, he shrugged, a difficult thing with his hands bound behind him. 'I was called Luci.'

'I am bound for Britannia, Luci. For your own homeland, in fact. The new governor intends to put down the latest rising of the Silures and then continue the conquest through your neighbouring tribes.'

'He will fail.'

'I'm not so sure. Suetonius Paulinus is a great man.'

'Great men die in our hills.'

'I do not wish to go into such a new and unknown land unprepared. I must make a name for myself in these two years. This is my one opportunity to become noticed and climb the ladder. If I achieve nothing in Britannia, I will be relegated to obscure posts and unimpressive commands. I will become noticed, though, and you will help me.'

'No.'

'Oh, you will. I will buy you from Toranius, and you will come with me to Britannia. You will tell me all about your tribes and your land, your rivers, your towns, your history. I will know who it is I face before I face them, and it will be you who tells me. I will use that knowledge to stand out among my peers. And you? You will gain from this in two ways.'

He waited for an argument but Luci remained silent, his calculating gaze still on Agricola.

'Firstly, as long as you serve well, I will pay you a reasonable stipend, beyond that of a low house slave. Should you save your money, within a decade it might even be possible for you to purchase from me your freedom. This is the only way you will ever legally find yourself free again, and you will not find a master in Rome, I'd wager, willing to meet such generous terms. Secondly, you will be out of this place, in clean air, dressed properly, well fed and even given small moments of independence if you warrant it. Given the choice between that and...' he gestured to the door and gave a sniff of distaste, '*that*, only a fool would argue.' He waited for a time again, in silence, and then said. 'And I do not take you for a fool, Luci of the Silures.'

He realised that the slave was sizing him up, learning things about Agricola even as he was himself interrogated.

'Tell me why I should.'

'I just did.'

'No. Not why I should allow myself to be bought. That is beyond my control. Slavery is nothing new to me. Romans are not the only people to enslave their foes, you know? I have owned slaves myself, in times past. No. Tell me why I should help you conquer my own people. *That* is something within my control.'

Agricola nodded slowly. 'So you account yourself a hero? You would stand tall and die for your Britons? Laudable. Or perhaps you are not so noble, and simply test the water? Very well. I can think of two good reasons. Firstly, if you really do care about your people, then you have to understand, to recognise, that Rome has come for good. Britannia is no longer a free land. It is a province of the empire, and any part of your island that has yet to feel the weight of imperial taxes is only passing time until that happens. Your people – the Silures, and any other tribe you can name there – will become part of the empire, and they will eventually even come to think of themselves as Roman. If you care for these people, then help me conquer them with the least bloodshed and disaster possible. Caesar conquered Gaul over a century ago, and some parts of the land are still depopulated and unfarmed, such was the damage done. I do not want that for Britannia, and neither, I suspect, do you.'

He stood back, and folded his arms.

'Secondly, I understand your tribes, even if I do not yet know them. My own people were the Saluvii once upon a time. We lived like you, in long huts and farmsteads. We had chiefs and warbands. We even prayed to the same gods as the Britons, from what I understand. Now we are Roman. *I* am Roman. But in the time of my ancestors, when we were free like you, we cared little for Rome, because we were too busy fighting and feuding with our neighbours, the Massilians, the Segobrigii and many others. You owned slaves, you say? But they, of course, were also Britons. From which tribe, I wonder. The Ordovices? Well, perhaps if you are not so noble, you will get some small satisfaction from seeing your childhood enemies conquered. Any way you look at it, it is better for you to have some influence upon the war on your island, no matter how small, than it is to languish here in your own filth, bitter and alone.'

This time the silence dragged out until finally Luci coughed and cleared his throat. 'I will bow my head to your slave collar, Roman, but not because of these theories of yours. I care little for you or your career, and you do not understand me half as well as you think you do. I will submit because of a man. Have you heard of Caratacus?'

Agricola shook his head. 'Who is he?'

'He was one of the great war leaders when you landed on our island, chieftain of the Catuvellauni. He fought you, and he failed, losing his tribe. So he fled beyond your control. He fled to the Silures, and my people took him in, for we had no love of you. And then you came north, and he was no longer beyond your reach. He had a silver tongue, though, did Caratacus. He could persuade a corpse to march to war. It took him no more than a season to get my people whipped up into a battle frenzy and drive them to war. Do you know what happened?'

Again, a shake of the head.

'*Scapula* happened. Rome's governor. We had thought him weak like the others. One season it took for Caratacus to make us hungry for war. It took Scapula less than that to make us desperate for peace. We lost the battle and we lost the war. We lost so many people that starvation threatened all the hill tribes. I watched our people sue for peace with Rome. They put the slave collar around their own neck, willingly. But Caratacus survived, and fled again. He went north once more, to the Brigantes, but they already coveted those slave collars, and their queen sent him back to Rome in chains. I know this, for I was with him when they handed him over. Him, and fifty warriors who had survived the war. And now we are here, those proud warriors, spread across your city, serving your wine, ploughing your fields, washing your feet. And what of Caratacus? I hear he somehow talked his way into a pardon from the emperor. It is said he lives like a prince in this city, eating sweet treats from gold bowls.'

There was a silence again. Then, '*That* is why I take your collar. That is why I will come with you to the land you call Britannia. That is why I will help you. Because my people are finally at peace, after decades of misery. Because I will not let you destroy what is left of my tribe for the resistance of others, like the accursed Caratacus. Because men like him and the other tribes who rallied with him or sold each other out deserve everything they get.'

Agricola nodded. 'You help me, teach me and tell me of all I need to know, and I will live up to my word. I will be a better master than you will find elsewhere. But heed this too: if you think to join me and flee back to your wilderness a free man, then think again. That will not happen, and attempting to do so will only blacken your name. I live by an old Massilian idiom: to forgive once indicates clemency. To forgive twice indicates weakness. I will give you one mistake, and only one. Do you understand?'

Luci simply nodded.

'Try to look worthless. I don't have that much money.'

Leaving the slave watching him with narrow eyes, he strode back to the door. A brief knock brought forth a guard, and soon after, Toranius. 'You are still interested, young sir?' the trader asked.

'I am, depending on your price.'

The trader opened a tablet he'd been carrying. 'I do not wish you to think I had tweaked the price at this sign of interest. This is my Briton stock, with their standing sale prices.'

Agricola looked down the list. There was a IX on the chain around Luci's neck, and the corresponding entry on the tablet gave a breakdown of the price. He was listed as *Work slave, grade two. Additional skill: Latin. Price 1,500 denarii.*

It sounded expensive, but a quick glance at the other entries on the list showed a base price of a thousand denarii with a varying rise in price depending upon their skills. Of course, Toranius had likely written up this entire list while Agricola had been in conversation with the slave, no matter what he said. Agricola nodded, calm, expression blank. 'I will give you eleven hundred.'

The trader raised an eyebrow. 'The price, good sir, is fifteen hundred.'

'But you and I know that your price would have been considerably lower had I not been looking for something so specific. Take the eleven hundred, and an offer of ongoing patronage from my family. Now that you know we are back in Rome, you know the value of that. And I myself am bound for a military tribunate in Britannia. I may have slaves of my own to sell in the coming days. I suspect your shortfall will soon be paid back.'

After a brief pause, Toranius laughed aloud. 'Good master Julius, you should be in the trade yourself. You would be rich in no time. Very well. In a spirit of goodwill and the hope of future endeavours, I accept your offer. I will have him delivered to your town house this very afternoon.'

Agricola nodded. 'I have four hundred here in coin,' he said, unstringing his purse and handing it over. 'The rest you will have upon delivery.'

As Toranius marked the details on his records, Agricola turned and looked at Luci. The slave was clever, and fast. Might he regret taking such a man with him? Only time would tell.

3

The journey from Rome promised to be relatively easy for the time of year – the waves low, the winds calm enough to quell the fears of the sailors, yet strong enough to fill the sails and save the oarsmen work. Agricola departed the domus in Rome with Luci at his side. Three more of the house slaves followed on: one leading the pack horse, one carrying his master's more valuable personal effects, and the third gripping a stout club against unwanted attention. They boarded a naval vessel – a swift liburna used by couriers and scouts – at the navalia on the left bank of the Tiber, and sped down the great river to the sea at Ostia, turning north and hugging the coast with a plan to overnight in Italia's more impressive port cities.

The first day revealed a clear distaste at their mode of transport on the part of Luci, who glared resentfully out at the open water, shivering. Agricola frowned as he gathered his cloak around him.

'You realise there's far more danger on land than at sea. Piracy is extremely rare, and the omens for the weather all month are good. By land we'd have to cross mountains and travel roads frequented by bandit gangs. This really is safer.'

'But the road does not change and flow and tend to swallow travellers,' was Luci's sullen reply.

That put an end, more or less, to their discussions. The slave was taciturn at best and, with his loathing of their journey, became little more than a grumbling figure in an unimportant corner of the deck. Agricola fretted over the matter for a time. He really needed to probe for information about where they were going, since that had been the whole purpose of buying Luci in the first place, yet the man seemed unwilling to issue even a word. He owned other slaves of course, including the three who sat huddled by the rail, keeping guard of the horse and bags, but they were always cowed creatures that went about their tasks with a sort of automatic servility. He'd never owned a slave upon whom he would have to rely, and was coming to realise that there needed to be a fine balance struck here between control and respect, else the man would clam up completely. Oh, he could beat Luci, of course, but he knew instinctively that such treatment would only make matters worse, while coddling him would send entirely the wrong message. He thought about the problem all that first day, and had come no closer to a solution as they pulled into the harbour at Cosa for the night.

The first evening was no easier, even back on dry land. The ship's trierarch directed them to the city's mansio, used by visiting dignitaries, which was perhaps half a mile from the port, by the north-east gate. With his entourage in tow, Agricola climbed the streets wearily. As they moved, he caught out of the corner of his eye a subtle change in Luci, and not one based on the solidity of the ground beneath his feet. The Silurian was alert now, eyes darting into every side street, every doorway, noting every figure, especially the armoured ones here and there. In anyone else, Agricola might have thought the man wary, suspecting trouble. In the case of Luci, it was likely the slave that would *be* the trouble. He was not watching for danger, but for opportunity.

On the assumption that while Luci had a solid command of Latin he would be baffled by Greek, Agricola spoke quickly over his shoulder to the other three in the eastern tongue, warning them to keep a close eye on their new companion and to be ready for trouble.

His mother had always insisted that all their house slaves be versed in both tongues. 'An ignorant slave is only half as useful,' had been her motto. Now, her son was grateful for her decision, for as they moved ever closer to the mansio, his other slaves changed their pace so that they more or less surrounded Luci. The Silurian threw him a look that suggested he knew precisely what was going on despite being unable to comprehend the command.

They reached the mansio and settled in for the night, Agricola spending his meal, and the short stretch of the evening for which he could stay awake, in silence. His mind turned over the problem again and again. How to draw Luci out and make him useful without either stamping down on him and risking complete antipathy or pandering to him and appearing a weak master. There had to be a way in. His eyes strayed throughout the evening – and during occasional wakeful periods in the night – to the Silurian slave, who sat close to the window, cross-legged, bathed in moonlight. It was hard to tell whether he was asleep or awake at any given moment, so still and silent was he. Indeed, on the occasions he did move, he was so swift and so quiet, Agricola barely caught it. By careful arrangement, though, the other slaves would take it in turns during the night to keep guard, so he felt comfortable that Luci would try nothing. If the worst came to the worst, Agricola carefully kept his sword and dagger by his bedside, while Luci remained unarmed, so any fight would be to Agricola's advantage.

An early morning saw them back to the port and boarding their liburna once more. The horse and gear secured, the five of them returned to their usual positions and settled for the day's travel. Once again, Luci was silent. So, of course, were the other slaves, but that was to be expected. They were supposed to be silent around their owner unless spoken to. Luci, on the other hand, was only here to talk. The coast of Italia slid past throughout the day, and three times on that cold journey Agricola began to spark a conversation, variously choosing as his subject the Silures, sea travel, and wars both Roman and barbarian. He made a little progress. Luci began to reply to direct questions, though with short, clipped answers that were less than illuminating. Still, it was better than nothing. Agricola was forming the opinion that the man was only humouring him while he continued to look for a way out.

That evening they landed at Pisae and made their way once more to the mansio, where the military documents Agricola carried saw them to a comfortable room and a warm meal, all paid for by the state. Again, as they travelled through the town, Luci watched their surroundings like a hawk. This time Agricola had no need to warn the others, and they gathered more protectively for the journey.

That night Agricola started awake sometime in the early hours and blinked open his eyes to find Luci, as usual in his cross-legged place near the window, but looking intently at his master. It was rather disconcerting, though he could see no clear intent of malice in the man's eyes, and there was little chance of him making any move with one of the other slaves watching him, and Agricola's weapons within ready reach.

Still, as he woke the next morning he was all the more determined to get Luci talking. The day was less conducive, though, for they woke to a light drizzle that settled into their clothes and left them sodden even before they boarded their ship for the next leg. They climbed the ramp to the deck in glum silence, and it was approaching noon as northern Italia slid past on their right before even Agricola felt remotely like conversation. During one lull in the drab weather, thinking ahead over their next few stops, a thought occurred to him and he focused on Luci.

'You lived far from the sea, didn't you?'

The question came enough from the blue that it made Luci frown, as though trying to work out what the underlying meaning was. Unable to see anything other than the obvious in the question, he shrugged. 'In the hills. There is a river we call the Usg, which you call Isca. Near my home it can be crossed on a horse, and that is the most water to be found for days in any direction.'

Agricola almost blinked at the statement. It was not only

the most talkative Luci had been since they'd met, it was more informative and more personal too. It was, in fact, exactly the sort of thing he wanted to know. Unwilling to let this crack in the slave's armour close up once more, he drove a wedge in, suddenly seeing a possible angle.

'I understand why you hate the sea.'

Luci's eyes narrowed. 'You do not understand.'

'I think I do. But feel free to prove me wrong.'

The slave chewed his lip for a moment, as though trying to decide whether to clam up again. After a while, he straightened a little. 'I do not hate the sea. I am not frightened of the sea. I just do not understand the sea. It is not that I fear it, but I see no point in it, and no point in travelling across it.'

Agricola smiled. 'I think that in an odd way, Luci of the Silures, you have more in common with the Romans than I.'

The slave's lip twisted and he snorted. 'Foolish words.'

'Hardly. You've travelled with me these past two days. You spent those first few hours on the ship from the city's navalia sailing down the Tiber until we reached the sea at Ostia.'

'So?'

'So how do you think the Romans feel about the sea? Rome began, and still lies, fifteen miles from the sea and, no matter how great the empire grows, in the Roman soul they remain fifteen miles from the sea. I do not think any Roman truly understands the sea any more than you do.'

'You are a Roman,' pointed out Luci dismissively.

'I thought you listened better than that,' Agricola laughed, feeling that he had just played an important move in the game they contested. 'I've told you before that my people were the Saluvii. I am from Forum Iulii in the province. I am Roman in that Rome governs my people, in the same way as is beginning to happen to your own.'

Luci frowned. 'You are a complicated man.'

'Thank you. But importantly, and something you do not know, Forum Iulii is a port. It has been a port since the day Caesar founded the city on the site of my ancestors' village. More than this, Forum Iulii is the home port of Rome's navy. I was weaned on brine and grew to manhood by the sea. I have known its call and the power and grace of ships all my life. You realise then that it is I who is the outsider here?'

Luci's frown remained in place. 'But what of the sailors? *They* are like you.'

'Perhaps some. But remember what I said. They may pull oars, furl sails, and steer ships, but in their heart they will ever be fifteen miles from the sea. They do what they must, but it is not who they are.'

The slave seemed to take this in for a time.

'I still don't understand it.'

'It may take time for you to do so. Or you may never make a sailor. But if you seek to make your way in the world as it changes, it is important that you try to change with it. Those who do not grow with the empire get left behind.'

And that was it. The floodgates apparently had opened. Despite the dispiriting drizzle, Luci talked then, throughout their journey. It was not quite on the subject Agricola had hoped, but over the hours they explored the nature of the sea and of the souls of Roman and Briton. At one point during the afternoon he caught a sullen look on one of the other slaves, and realised they were beginning to resent the emphasis he was placing on this difficult new companion. Damn it, but it seemed there was destined always to be a problem. Finally he appeared to have cracked the issue with Luci, only to cause a new problem with the other slaves. He had to keep control of them, keep them in their place, and yet he could not afford to relent with Luci and allow him to slip back into silence.

This new issue preyed on him as they docked in Genua the third night. However, as they climbed through the streets in search of the mansio, another problem caught his attention. They moved through a market in a small square on their walk, and suddenly there was a commotion at one of the stalls they had just passed. The stallholder was barking at a passer-by and accusing him of stealing a cooking knife from the table, where there was a clear gap in a display of similar items. The indignant shopper was denying responsibility.

As they walked on, Agricola glanced sidelong at his four slaves. The three who led the horse, carried the kit bag, and wielded the club were all paying attention to the furious argument in their wake, which looked set to boil over into violence at any time. Luci, conversely, had his gaze set upon the path ahead.

The silent Silurian had stolen the knife in passing.

The question was what to do about it. It seemed clear that there was only one reason Luci could want a hidden weapon. In any ordinary situation, Agricola should stamp on the man right now, push him to the ground while the others beat him a little, find and remove the knife and then have Luci battered to within a breath of death. That would be the sensible way to deal with a slave who seemingly harboured violent intentions towards his master. And yet confronting him would likely undo the progress they had made today, and probably any hope of such in the future.

It was a knotty problem.

To allow Luci to continue blithely the way he was going was to invite revolution and violence. Had Agricola made a fundamental error in buying and bringing the man? Had Luci already become too dangerous to keep? More trouble than he was worth? He was going to have to make a decision, and soon. Tonight, in fact.

He pondered this all the way to the mansio, gaze always on Luci, weighing up the man and his intentions. He'd made a decision by the time they reached the place, and as the four slaves paused to catch their breath, Agricola spoke with the manager, showing his papers, and added one unusual arrangement to the evening.

They ate in the main room with the other visitors, then retired to the room upstairs. As always, Luci sat by the window, the moonlight gleaming between the shutters, playing lines of silver across him. The other three were curled up by the door, while Agricola lay in bed, sword close by his side. After a while he allowed his breathing to regulate and deepen, as though in deep sleep. He couldn't say why, but he felt certain that Luci was planning something more or less immediately, and he had to force himself not to move every time he heard a slight shuffle.

In fact, it was in a moment of utter silence that he knew the time had come. His eyes snapped open. Luci was on his feet, and had somehow managed to overcome one of the other slaves in silence. The hapless man was locked in Luci's grip, the stolen knife just below his chin, resting on his neck. The pair were by the window. Agricola's mind flashed back to that first night, when Luci had moved so quickly and quietly he'd hardly noticed. Moreover, the slave had managed to lift a knife from a busy market stall without breaking his pace or being seen by anyone.

'Think twice,' Agricola said, rising slowly from his bed.

'I do not like breaking my word,' Luci hissed. 'But as you said, Romans are in their soul always fifteen miles from the sea, and so in my soul I am a free man, not a slave.'

'The man you are about to kill is my property. *You* are my property. I told you from the start, "to forgive once indicates clemency... to forgive twice indicates weakness." You had one chance. You've spent that chance tonight. Draw blood with that knife, try for the door or window, and that will be as far as you go.'

'I think you underestimate me, Roman,' Luci said. 'By the time you draw your sword and move, this man will be dead and I will be gone.'

'You make a move, and you will waste your life and my money. This is your moment to decide. Live or die. Think hard.'

Luci's brow furrowed. Perhaps he had seen something in Agricola's eyes, for a moment later he let go of the other slave and pulled the knife away. The clubman staggered back and lifted the weapon, his face contorted in anger.

'No,' Agricola told him. 'Back down.'

As the man dropped the stout haft and crossed the room to the others, Luci lowered his own knife.

'Why did I not run?' he asked, more of himself than of Agricola, judging by his expression.

Agricola gave him a knowing smile. 'Because you're brighter than you look.' He slid from the bed, unarmed and in just his tunic, and crossed the room towards the slave. Luci stepped back out of the way, and the Roman reached the window, flipping the catch and swinging open the shutters. Outside the window stood two of the mansio's guards with clubs of their own. 'Always remember, Luci of the Silures, that though you may be brighter than you look, I am brighter still, and I'll always be a step ahead.'

Luci turned to look at the pair outside the window, nodding slowly to himself, and then flipped the knife in his hand, grabbing the point and holding it out to Agricola, hilt first.

The Roman shook his head. 'Keep it. But bear in mind that if it ever comes my way, the sword that comes in return will be meant to kill.'

Luci nodded, reversed the blade and tucked it into his belt.

'And we'd best get you a sheath for it before you gut yourself accidentally.'

Oddly, he felt then as though some important corner had been turned, and as he returned to bed, Luci dropping to the floor and sitting cross-legged once more, Agricola fell asleep, confident now there would be no further attempts at escape.

When they rose the next morning, he had made another decision. It was a gamble, he knew, but it would resolve at least one problem, and hopefully two. The weather was better once more and a pale sun shone in a sky the colour of Noric steel. The crew of the liburna seemed in better spirits with the improvement in conditions, and as the passengers settled into their accustomed places, Luci leaned on the rail, watching the boarding ramp raised and the water slip past as the oars rose and fell, taking them away from Genua. He turned to Agricola.

'How many days of this shit until we get there?'

Genuine interest was a new thing. A corner had been turned, indeed.

'Another day along the coast and we have a brief stay. Then another two days across the south coast of Gaul. From there, five days overland to the coast of Aquitania and a new ship at Burdigala that will take us seven days to Britannia. That is the plan, anyway. I'm hoping to move slightly faster. That will leave us just seven days to pick up the commander at Isca and ride north for Viroconium before the festival of Tubilustrium, when the general is expecting us to be present. Timing is quite tight, and we have only two days to spare.'

Luci nodded. 'So altogether, nine more days of water. I can survive that.'

They spent that day in conversation, which was a whole new experience. And while, once again, the subject was not quite what Agricola needed, it touched upon Luci's past with the Silures, while also making enquiries as to Agricola's own history, and comparing the now-Romanised Saluvii with the not-so-Romanised Silures. By the time they slid towards their next harbour late that afternoon, Agricola had given Luci something of a potted history of Caesar's wars and of the Gallic peoples who had lost their fierce independence to the great general. In return, he had learned one particular thing that seemed to be of importance. The way Luci spoke of the Silures suggested that they were more a collection of sub-tribes than one straight tribe. It was Rome who had labelled them the Silures and bundled them together, giving them more of a singular identity than they would naturally feel. That, Luci told him, was why Rome was having so much trouble keeping the Silures conquered, because there would always be groups among them who thought themselves separate and not bound by any agreed settlement.

In addition, there had been tantalising hints about Luci's

past, despite the fact that the slave generally avoided the subject. Sometime, Agricola decided, he would like to know the full story. Luci had such a good grasp of Latin that there had to be more to his story than just that of a captured warrior.

'Then to the west, the Demetae...' began the man, propounding on a new subject, his voice trailing off as they moved towards the port and his gaze strayed from the open sea to the harbour.

Agricola let out a soft chuckle. 'Now do you see why *I* understand the sea.'

Forum Iulii's harbour system was huge, bigger than any they had visited so far, even Rome's port at Ostia. More than that, there were in fact *two* ports here. The liburna on which they travelled slid through the waves towards the civilian port, a vast basin before the town, enclosed with quaysides and dotted with shipyards and warehouses, a huge lighthouse tower rising from the end of the mole, guiding them in with its blazing fire, lit in preparation for the dusk. Luci's eyes were wide, for certainly he'd never seen so many ships of all shapes and sizes ploughing through the water in every direction.

And that was only the civilian trade. Just half a mile along, within javelin distance of the city walls and built on the edge of a huge lagoon, the military port dominated the coast, as big as the civil harbour, with a fortress the size of a legion's base controlling it. The home of the Roman fleet. It even impressed Agricola, and he'd grown up here. He could only imagine what it was like to see the place for the first time.

'Welcome to Forum Iulii,' he said with a grin.

'This is your home?'

'Is. Was. Will be.'

Luci said nothing in reply, simply staring in astonishment at their surroundings as they slid towards the wharf. He would have experienced such a culture shock when he first arrived in Rome from his provincial origins of course, but even now, he would never have seen anything like this. He was still dumbfounded as the ship tied off and the ramp was run out.

'Tonight we stay in our town house,' Agricola said as he led them down to the wharf. 'I have a few things to attend to in the city, so we'll stay two nights. It will be good to sleep in my own bed, even if briefly.'

He turned to take in the other three as they led the horse down onto solid ground. 'And then, the day after tomorrow, the three of you will remain at the house and prepare for Mother's return in the summer. Luci, you and I go on alone from here.'

The other three slaves struggled with their expressions at this news: part relief at not having to accompany their master on campaign in a northern island, part disappointment at being so relegated, and part distrust of their new peer who seemed destined to take over. Luci, on the other hand, was watching him now with glinting eyes.

'What makes you think you'll be safe, travelling alone with me?'

Agricola shrugged. 'I think you're bright enough not to make the same mistake twice. And I think you know you underestimated me. You won't repeat that either. No, I think we'll be fine travelling on alone from here. Faster, too, if you can ride?'

'I can handle a horse.'

Another hint of something more in his past. Something to discuss in the days ahead. Turning, Agricola looked out over the home town of his youth with a sigh of relief.

'Come on. Let's go home.'

4

The sojourn in Forum Iulii was short, but busy. Agricola had visited neither the town house here nor the rural family estate along the coast in a number of months, since their return to Rome, yet everything had been kept in good condition by the staff and really there was not much to do. He collected a few more items that might come in useful on campaign in the north, and left behind some of the things he'd brought from Rome that now seemed excessive. He deposited the three slaves back in their accustomed place and had a sober, small-scale meal before visiting the mausoleum of his ancestors and paying respect to his grandfather and the others. His father was buried in Rome, the only one of the family thus far: the majority of the family's cinerary urns sat in shelves in the modest brick building on the edge of the town.

He'd taken Luci with him throughout. It probably looked, to the slave, as though his new master was keeping him close, keeping an eye on him, but there was more to it than that. Agricola's mother had taught him even as a young boy that quid pro quo was the way of the world. If you wanted something, no matter the circumstances, you had to be prepared to give something up. Men who did not understand that simple law of the world suffered for it. Men like Caligula and Crassus, who had thought only of acquisition and themselves, and who inevitably fell because of it.

And so Agricola had decided to take the same approach with Luci. He needed to understand the slave, his people and his world, and if he wanted Luci to be forthcoming, it would help if the slave understood more about the man who was doing the asking. Thus he introduced Luci to the city, its port, the navy, the manner of Roman burial. He went through the history of his family and his people, from their service with Caesar, through the founding of this city, the raising of the Julii first to the equites set of society and then further to the senatorial class, Agricola's father the first to reach such a height.

Luci was his usual quiet self, yet he could see the Silurian taking it all in as they moved about, meeting people and visiting places. Though it seemed a visit of mere moments before they were back on board the liburna and putting out to sea once more, looking back it was clear just how much information Luci must have absorbed about his master's world and family. The hope – especially the way Agricola had presented it all – was to show that, despite being Roman, the Julii were in many ways still the same Gallic tribesmen who shared a cultural bond with the Silures. A bridge half built.

Indeed, once aboard and at sea again, the Silurian actually initiated a conversation for the first time.

'You focus much on ships.'

Agricola shrugged. 'I told you, I grew up with them. I see the value in them that most Roman officers overlook, I think.'

'They will have no value in my lands.'

'You may be right. I've never taken a ship up a hill before.'

Luci snorted.

'But,' Agricola added, 'there is more to a navy than warships on the open waves. Rivers can carry goods and men into the heart of the most forbidding land, and there are things sailors know that escape others.'

'I wish them luck in the hills of my people.'

That just made Agricola laugh. They indulged in sporadic conversations throughout the day, in similarly small snatches. He could see the sailors watching them with disapproval, and realised he was going to face a lot of that in the coming days. No Roman of rank would ever be seen talking to a slave on an almost equal basis, which was how their relationship now seemed to work. But then Luci had shown no sign of disaffection nor any desire to run since that night. And, he kept reminding himself, this was not an ordinary slave. In some ways he was a teacher, in others a student, but above all he was a companion. And there was something about Luci that he had yet to uncover, for the man was also no ordinary captured tribesman.

The next night they put in at the ancient port of Massilia, and he continued the Silurian's education with a potted history of the place, recalling his own days of learning here, where wealthy Romans sent their sons to prepare them for the world of Roman politics. He told Luci of the siege of Massilia by Caesar and his lieutenants, an action in which, according to family legend, his own ancestor had distinguished himself and come to the great general's attention.

Then they were off again. And by the time they were bearing down on the port of Narbo things had changed again, if subtly. Agricola liked to think he was good at reading people, and he noted a slight relaxation in Luci's manner, as though he were coming to terms with their positions, accepting where he was, even *what* he was.

Of course, that was quid pro quo in action, again. Agricola had made concessions in their relationship, treating the man more like a travelling companion than a slave. In return, Luci's manner had become more that of a confidante and client. Not a friend, though. No matter how much their relationship eased, it seemed unlikely that would ever happen, *could* not happen, of course, as long as the man was a slave. You could go too far, after all.

His curiosity over the man's past peaked as they travelled overland from Narbo to Burdigala, using high roads and stopping at official mansios as they went.

'You ride a horse with the expertise of a cavalryman,' Agricola noted the first afternoon. 'Better than me, in fact, and I was taught by experts from boyhood.'

And it was true. He'd rarely, possibly never, seen a man so naturally at home in the saddle. The horse had been one of the three they kept on the estate back near Forum Iulii, a good Roman pony, which Luci had never ridden before, yet the man had the horse mastered within a mile, and the two of them moved like one creature. It was very impressive.

'Yes, I can ride,' was Luci's enigmatic answer.

'Strabo makes no mention of your people riding,' Agricola mused. 'But then he said you were all huge, and the implication was perhaps that you were too big to sit a horse easily.'

'Strabo also said some of us are cannibals,' Luci grumbled. 'Don't believe everything you read.'

Agricola frowned. That the man spoke good Latin was surprising enough, without him being well read. Luci gave him a sly smile, perhaps noting the surprise. 'Besides,' the slave laughed, 'Caesar mentions our cavalry.'

The mystery of Luci seemed only ever to deepen. Despite a number of subtle attempts at probing questions, he learned nothing more of the man's past by the time they reached Burdigala, and there, somewhat frustrated with himself, he pledged inwardly to put aside his fascination and stop trying to unwrap Luci's history. After all, he was focusing on that to the detriment of his whole purpose in acquiring the slave.

So, once they were settled onto a new ship, a trireme of the classis Britannica, he began to ask about their destination.

'Tell me about Britannia,' he began.

'Firstly, stop calling it that.'

'Why?'

'Because Britannia is a Roman invention. If you want to understand my people you have to stop thinking like their conqueror. To my people it is just "the land" and we are "people of the land". We have mostly come to think of ourselves in the tribal groups you acknowledge: the Silures, the Ordovices, the Demetae and so on. But here and there you will find small tribes that Rome considers Silurian while they themselves think otherwise. Indeed, you will find tribes who are part of the Silures and are content to recognise the fact, and yet still call themselves by their own ancient names.'

'No wonder you could not mount an organised defence of your island when we came.'

Luci narrowed his eyes. 'From what you tell me of your people's history, you were no different.'

'I'll give you that. Perhaps Rome would not have taken Liguria and Gaul if we had managed to overcome our own hatreds and differences long enough to turn them on our enemy. Speaking as a product of their conquest, though, I'm not sure we would have survived without the order that Rome brings.'

A grunt was the only answer to that.

The journey up the west coast of Gaul was filled with such titbits of information, all somewhat randomly given, and yet all precisely the sort of thing Agricola had wanted to know. In the few days before leaving Rome he'd read Strabo, and Caesar, and half a dozen lesser accounts of the island for which they were bound, and even delved into the public records office to peruse the campaign reports of the various generals and governors who had campaigned there. But they were dry reports on the whole – or highly suspect, as in the case of Strabo, who had clearly never been within a hundred miles of the island. They were largely geographical treatises or military reports. Luci was beginning to put flesh on their bones and build him a mental picture of 'the land'.

Then came Osismis, on the north-western capes of Gaul. As they put in there the winds were whipping through the port and streets like a mine overseer, billowing black clouds sitting threateningly on the western horizon, and the sailors were making warding signs against disaster and dark magics as they looked out to sea.

'At least five days of storms,' said a ship captain as they sat at a table in the mansio that night.

'Do we stay in this place for the duration?' Luci muttered.

'Because we left much stuff on the ship. I'll have to go back and get it.'

'No,' Agricola answered. 'We sail at dawn as planned.'

'What?' The slave stared at him wide-eyed.

'Brave,' murmured the ship captain. 'For me, I'm port-bound until it clears.'

'I have a schedule to keep,' Agricola said. 'We need to be in Viroconium in time to depart with the governor. My career may never recover if we are late.'

'Perhaps we shouldn't have spent a day choosing your underwear and saying hello to your ancestors, then?' his slave snorted.

The young Roman turned a hard-eyed look on Luci. 'Despite that we have become closer these past few days, perhaps you should occasionally remember your station?'

'Oh, I remember it well enough, even without an iron collar round my neck.'

Agricola kept up his glare for a moment, then allowed it to soften as he saw the wildness in Luci's eyes. The man was not a good sailor, and the prospect of a storm at sea had him more than a little jittery. It was fear that was behind such ill-chosen words.

'In a perfect world, I would stay here until good weather. But we have few enough days' leeway as it is. I cannot afford to stay put.'

They settled in for the night, Luci back to his old quiet self, though this time through nerves more than anger. Indeed, despite his own familiarity with the sea, Agricola was starting to feel the touch of nerves himself, made worse by exposure to the slave's mood. He took some time to get to sleep that night, listening to the sound of Luci's gentle breathing, as usual uncertain whether the man was asleep or awake. When he did finally succumb to slumber it was a difficult sleep, punctuated by dreams of drowning, the last of which woke him before dawn, wreathed in sweat and wrinkled sheets.

'I think we dreamed the same thing,' Luci murmured, looking across from his place by the window as Agricola sat up, shivering.

'Come on. Let's break our fast and then get to the baths. We have time before sailing for once, thanks to being up so early.'

'No point. You'll be cold, wet and covered in salt in half a day. Probably dead half a day later. Why bother with a bath?'

'Because it is healthy to be clean. In Rome, or at home, I would bathe twice a day, and have at least one massage. The last time I visited a baths was in Burdigala, and the last time I got to do so in the morning before we travelled was at home.' He gave Luci a cursory look up and down and wrinkled his nose. 'You could do with it anyway, just on principle.'

'I am fine as I am.'

Clearly the Silurian's familiarity with the finer points of imperial life had not stretched as far as bathing. When he'd left the slave market he'd been bathed and dressed in better clothes. Since then he had visited the baths only once, back in Forum Iulii, a small establishment that did not balk at the lower rungs of society using its facilities as long as they had the coin. Since then, Agricola had offered him further opportunities, but the man seemed unimpressed by the whole bathing ritual, and had plumped twice for stripping down to his loincloth and throwing himself into a river.

'Then find a river to dip in, but meet me at the baths at the top of the street in an hour. We have something to do.'

Leaving Luci to it and, as usual, praying that the man was still there when he came back and there would be no need to employ slave hunters, Agricola made his way to the small public baths. There was a private balneum at the mansio, but since he had the opportunity it seemed a good chance for a proper massage, and to have his hair clipped and face shaved.

He spent the next three-quarters of an hour doing just that, relaxing despite the days ahead, and listening to the general conversation around him. The baths were still warming up, having only been open a short time, but already they were full of sailors and shopkeepers preparing for their day. The usual tales of Nero and his mother Agrippina were spoken, likely blown out of all proportion, news of Corbulo's successes in Armenia that were well behind time, for Agricola had heard such things many days ago in Rome and, here and there, voices worrying over the storms coming to Osismis.

Finally, looking neat and Roman once more, he stepped out of the baths into a howling wind that carried the first pattering of drizzle. He blinked into the glum weather and spotted Luci leaning against a wall under a portico nearby, cleaning his fingernails with his teeth.

'You didn't run then?' Agricola said with a grin as he ducked under the roof.

'Ran. Came back. Nothing here worth running away for.'

'Ha. You look clean, at least. You could do with a shave.'

'I shave when my neck gets itchy.'

'Well, you look like a barbarian. Come on.'

With Luci in tow, he turned a few corners and passed along a handful of streets until he brought them to the columned frontage of a building on a bluff.

'What's this?'

'This,' Agricola replied, 'is the temple of Neptune. Here we can give offerings in the hope of an easy voyage.'

'Neptune's your sea god. I've heard of him.'

'Yes. Who is *your* sea god?'

'Don't have one. Never saw the sea until Rome took me away from home.'

They had to knock and wait for the temple attendant to let them in, for it was still only shambling towards dawn and the place was not properly open to the public yet. With a few words of encouragement, he got the attendant to admit them and light a brazier and a couple of lamps. As the temple came into view in the golden glow, Luci looked up at the great statue of Neptune at the rear of the temple, behind the collection of altars. The god of sea and waves was naked, folds of cloth draped over the shoulder of an arm that held a trident as high as a house. His beard and long curly hair needed a touch-up, and the paint of his face was flaking with the corrosive sea air, but he was imposing nonetheless.

'All your gods look alike,' Luci murmured. 'Take that weapon off him and he looks just like all the others. And none of them look Roman, anyway. Never seen a Roman with hair and beard like that. Few even with a short beard.'

'If you're done with your fascinating exposé of religious statuary, perhaps we can do what we came for?'

He stepped forward and raised his hands high, looking up at the god. 'Great Neptune, Father of the Deep, I pray you take a small offering this day and grant us safe passage across the strait to Britannia. In gratitude I pledge, before the closing of the year, an altar in your name.'

With that he fished in the purse at his belt and pulled out a dozen gleaming coins, dropping them into the bowl on the top of the central altar. Bowing his head in respect, he backed away. Luci said nothing, but stepped forward regardless, fishing out two of the three coins he owned and dropping them into the bowl. Roman or not, a god of the sea was to be respected when you made your way across his domain.

'Feel a little better about it?'

'About two coins' worth. That's all.'

With that, the two of them strolled back down the hill, keeping under the shelter of porticos where possible, pulling cloaks around them against the wind. At the mansio they picked up their gear once more, and then made their way to the port in the first gleaming of dawn, such as it was – little more than a paleness glowing through cracks in the dark grey sky.

The trierarch seemed surprised to see them.

'I was about to unload your horses, tribune.'

'That won't be necessary. We sail as planned.'

'No, young sir, we don't.'

Agricola fixed him with a look. 'You told me it would be five days from Burdigala. It's been three up the coast of Gaul. I need to be in Britannia in two more days. I don't have time to wait.'

The trierarch shrugged. 'Better late than sunk. That's an old sailor's adage, but I suspect you can work out the meaning.'

'I need to sail,' he hissed through bared teeth.

'No one in port will try today. Two days across open water in early spring with a storm coming in? You'd have to be mad.'

Agricola felt the beginnings of helplessness. He was of a distinguished family and of military rank, but his bloodline meant nothing here, and even a senior tribune was outranked by a trierarch. He had no authority to demand –

A thought occurred. It would be a bluff, and if it failed, the man would take him no further even if the weather broke. But it was a chance. The weather was poor, and perhaps he could just pull it off. Without a pause, he turned and gestured to Luci for his pack. Rummaging inside, he found his letters of authorisation to use ships, mansios and horse relay stations on his journey. It was starting to look a little travel worn, but still it was a roll of parchment in a leather scroll case sealed with the official stamp of the cursus publicus, the imperial department that ran the postal and travel system. He had seen couriers carrying official dispatches. They looked remarkably similar.

'Do you see this?' he asked, turning and brandishing the scroll case. He made sure to keep it moving slightly, so that the trierarch could only get a cursory look at it, enough to register its official nature and the seal, but not that it had already been opened and used a lot.

'I do.'

'This is a dispatch of import for the new governor. He is in Viroconium and about to embark on campaign. If this does not reach him before he leaves, there will be repercussions. You are beholden as servants of the emperor to aid a courier in any way possible when upon official business, are you not?'

The trierarch glared at him, but nodded. Before there could be any cross-examination, Agricola dropped his letters back in the pack and sealed it. 'Neptune is appeased, and so will I be when you give the order to cast off.'

The ship's captain chewed on his lip for a moment, but finally nodded again. 'When you meet the governor, you'll drop in the name of the trireme *Celeritas* with respect, yes?'

'I will. And I will also personally remember the favour. After all, I won't always be a tribune.'

'So far I've been sailing fifty oars short to make room for you and your horses. If we're to face this, I'll need at least thirty of them back. You'll be cramped.'

Agricola nodded. 'We'll manage.'

'You are very determined,' Luci muttered as they found their usual place near the rear and began to gather their animals and gear closer, clearing some of the seating for fresh oarsmen.

'A man in my position gets one chance to show his strength. Many are happy to take their tribuneship as a sinecure and just a stepping stone to a post back in Rome. But if a man wants a real place in his future, a multi-legion governorship, a praetorship of note, even a consulship, he wants to stand out and be recognised. I refuse to let my chance slip away because I was late due to a little rain.'

Within half an hour the trierarch had sourced the extra rowers he needed from the military bunkhouses in the port, and all was made ready. The new rowers found their seats, uncomfortably close to the passengers and the two horses, which whinnied and nickered nervously.

'I hope your sea god was listening,' Luci murmured, moving himself into a position where he was braced against the hull and pulling his cloak tight around him.

'We'll find out soon enough.'

As the slave shivered, wild eyes darting this way and that, Agricola found his money pouch on his belt. It was looking a little thin, but he was almost there, and once he'd taken up his posting at Isca he'd be on the legion's payroll. Then he should be fine. Locating a spare pouch in his bag he divided the remaining coins in two, filling the second pouch and, when he pulled the drawstring tight, tossing it across to Luci, who caught it instinctively then frowned at it, casting a silent question at Agricola.

'Call it hazard pay. Danger money. If we get to Britannia untouched, you'll deserve it. And if we drown I won't need it anyway. Call it an advance on your freedom.'

The slave looked at the pouch for a while, then tucked it away safely, nodding his appreciation at his master. Moments later there were calls, the grinding of the timber ramp being pulled in, then the clunks and bangs as the ship pushed itself clear of the dock. Once there was room, the oars fell into the water and began their rhythmic roll and dip. There was no need for an aulete here, keeping time with his pipes, for these were professional sailors of the Roman fleet, men like Agricola, who had grown up with sea air in their lungs, and their sense of timing was innate.

The *Celeritas* cut an easy way across the harbour and past the mole, out into the open waters. The difference was clear in an instant, for the moment the ship hit the waves of the sea it began to buck and sway, throwing them this way and that. Luci wedged himself ever more carefully into place, while Agricola shuffled with difficulty across to the horses, which were looking increasingly restive and nervous.

With a thud, the sail dropped and was tied off, immediately bellying with wind, driving them north-east, worryingly close to the rocky promontories and inlets that characterised the coast of the region. Luci looked with anxious eyes across to the sail. Agricola smiled. 'I know. But it will move us much faster than the oars, and the trierarch hopes to stay ahead of the worst of the weather.'

The slave nodded, still looking unhappy, then glanced past Agricola at the two horses. Biting down on his own fear, Luci seemed to pass through some barrier and into a serene state, only the whites of his eyes betraying the appearance of calm.

Seeing the bemused face of Agricola, he shrugged and pointed at the horses.

'Nostrils flared. Ears forward. They're scared. They pick up on our moods. We need to be confident.'

'I *am* confident,' replied Agricola with a smile.

'Speak in hushed and calm tones – what the *fuck*?' He finished at a shout as the ship lurched and slammed to starboard.

'Ah, like that?' Agricola laughed, then reached up and stroked the horse. He was having trouble keeping his own footing, so he was half calming the beast, half using it for support.

The next hour passed with little difference, the full light of day rising, such as it was behind the black rolling clouds. Luci tried hard to maintain his calm for the horses, though with periodic explosions of cursing as he was thrown about. Agricola held his place carefully. The horses remained nervous, but no worse than that. Then, sometime around noon, they left the coast behind, and everything changed.

If he had thought the ship wild before, he learned something now as the *Celeritas* was hurled this way and that, battered by waves that swept easily up and over the deck, drenching everyone. At times the deck seemed too vertiginous to survive, held by Neptune at an unfeasible angle so that ropes and tools slid this way and that across the timbers; at other moments the ship would lean horrifyingly to one side or another, to such an extent that it seemed the sail must touch water at any moment.

Yet still they travelled.

Luci had fallen silent in open water and now sat, head down, lips moving in a constant, silent beseeching of any and all gods that they survive the trip. Agricola managed a certain stoicism for a time, but as the night closed in, still out in open water and a day from land, and the crew failed repeatedly to light lamps that simply could not withstand the conditions, even he began to wonder at the wisdom of his insistence they sail.

He tried to sleep. He failed. He had no need to wonder this time whether Luci was awake, and indeed no man aboard slept, each trying to maintain a pace with his oars, hoping against hope that they were still on course, for there were no stars, moon or coast to confirm such a thing. The tribune finally fell asleep a little after what he thought must be midnight, but an hour later was jolted awake as the storm hit.

He'd imagined they'd already had the worst the sea could throw at them, but he was wrong, for in the deep of the night the ship was tossed here and there, slammed and battered, things tearing and breaking, sailors shouting in panic, a man crushed by an uncontrollable oar. Within half an hour they had lost two men over the side to the waves. Luci never even looked up, so terrified by it all that he remained almost insensible. The horses would have long since leapt overboard had not one of the sailors helped Agricola tether them tighter.

He had no recollection of falling asleep, and must have done so during the worst of it. He awoke with the first light of dawn filtering through high, steel-grey clouds and falling across a ship that had been battered but remained remarkably intact.

He shivered. He was soaked and freezing cold, but the ship was doing little more now than roll and yaw through the waves. The storm had passed, and they had survived. He rose and looked about. Another great bank of black sat threatening on the horizon, south he reckoned, at an educated guess.

'Worry not,' the trierarch said, apparently noticing his activity. 'That storm is passing west-east across our stern. It'll miss us. Whatever you promised Neptune seems to have got us through the night.'

The loss of a total of five men might have soured the crew against the man who'd forced them to sail, but the simple fact that they were alive was enough of a balm for every man aboard to feel gratitude rather than resentment. Throughout the day the wind picked up, threatening the return of bad weather, yet even as a deep grey roiling mass rolled its way across the sky, the call came that land had been spotted.

Agricola waited with bated breath to find out how far off

course they were. They might well have added a day or two to their journey anyway. Finally, as he saw the spit of green ahead, a sharp peninsula jutting out from some unseen coast, he turned to the trierarch.

'Well?'

'Hades' point,' the man said with a grin. 'We're twenty miles east of where we should be, that's all. We can make that up in hours.'

'And that?' Agricola asked, pointing at the grey sky rolling towards them.

'Half a day away. We'll make it to port first.'

The young trireme heaved a sigh of relief as he watched the coast of Britannia slide towards them.

They'd made it.

5

Agricola was not sure what he'd expected, but whatever that might have been, Isca was not it. The fortress of the Second Augusta, only established a few short years ago, had the appearance of something rough and temporary to his eye. Moreover, it seemed a little small to house a full legion, no more than maybe two-thirds the size of the fortress by the coast back home – certainly a cramped installation for more than five thousand men.

Isca sat on a low hill overlooking the river down a gentle slope, surrounded by defences of shabby timber and turf, further protected by ditches. A small settlement had begun to grow outside the walls to the north, but that too was of rough timber, while the streets as yet were little more than mud and jumbled rock.

If there was an edge of the world to be found anywhere in the empire, it was clear that Britannia was that frontier. Something about that sent a small thrill through the young tribune, and made him immensely grateful for his mother's work in securing him this position. Without her, he would probably be counting supply records in a headquarters somewhere so thoroughly Romanised there would be little chance of excitement and glory.

Isca's frontier appearance promised both.

'Magnificent,' he murmured as they rode their horses at a walk up towards the east gate.

'Really?' Luci snorted.

The young tribune shrugged. 'I was raised in Forum Iulii and Massilia, then Rome. Everywhere, the marble trappings of empire, every foot of space occupied by something, everything planned, owned, maintained, nothing unknown, nothing new. *Look* at this place. This is the edge of the world.'

'Hmph,' grunted the slave, a sharp reminder that this wilderness was his home.

'There cannot be many places in the world where the land is so raw and unspoiled, where the grasp of the emperor has yet to reach.'

'He's grasped quite enough here, believe me.'

'But it's still a new world,' Agricola insisted. 'You've been to my home, to Rome. You must see the difference.'

Another grunt was all. As they approached the gate, which was resolutely closed, a small group of men gathered above it on the wooden walkway. The two riders reined in, twenty paces from the defences, on the causeway over the ditches.

'Who goes there?' a man in an optio's crest called out.

Agricola was momentarily taken aback by the lack of respect in the man's voice, but then remembered that he was wearing just an ordinary travelling tunic and cloak, his cuirass wrapped in leather covers on Luci's horse, his helmet and crest carefully tucked away in his own kit. He could be anyone, and most certainly would not look like the second most senior officer of the legion.

'Gnaeus Julius Agricola, direct from Rome, assigned as tribunus laticlavius of the Second. Here are my papers,' he added, fishing out the battered container and holding it forth.

The manner of the men on the wall changed a little, though not as much as he expected. The soldiers straightened somewhat, and the optio threw out a shoddy salute. Moments later the gate opened and the junior officer descended two steps at a time, coming out with hand held forth. Taking Agricola's documents, he examined them. As his gaze ran down the papers, Agricola looked past him. The rudimentary nature of the fortress did not stop at the walls. The rows of barracks, workshops and stores inside were uniformly of rough-dressed timber with tile roofs, the roads between them topped with gravel that had already been churned down and mixed with the mud below.

'This all seems to be in order, sir,' the optio said with a slightly more professional salute. 'And this is your slave?'

Agricola nodded. He wanted to ask the man why everything looked so half-finished, why the men seemed slovenly and unprofessional, why this was not the great Second legion Vespasian had led to military success across the west of the island. It had been only a little more than a decade, after all, since those glory days. Somehow, though, he didn't think this was the place or time for such a query.

'Where do I report?'

'Legate's office, sir, in the headquarters building. That's—'

'I know where to find it, soldier.' He swiped the documents from the officer and urged his horse on, Luci at his side, leaving the men behind with suspicious gazes as they closed the gates once more.

'How do you know where it is?'

He looked at the slave. 'It's at the centre of the fortress. They always are. The optio took me for some uninformed politician on a sinecure, but I do not intend to fulfil that role. I have the honour and reputation of my family to live up to. Whatever we do, we do it to the best of our ability. My father started the vineyards on our estate half a century ago, and already they are renowned for their quality. Never do anything at less than your full capability. These are words to live by, Luci of the Silures.'

But as he looked this way and that, passing through the fortress, it was becoming apparent that the men of the Second were not living by that axiom. There was a dejectedness in the very atmosphere, an air almost of defeat that hung over the fortress.

Beside the headquarters – which was of timber but had at least been painted – stood the only structure of stone, a bath complex belching smoke from the vents at the roofline which did little, when combined with the grey cloudy sky, to lift the atmosphere of the place.

Despite his lack of uniform or armour he must have been projecting an aura of importance, for as they approached the large doorway into the headquarters, the soldiers to either side straightened to attention and did nothing to bar his entrance. In the courtyard, watched over by statues of Minerva and of the emperor, Agricola handed his reins to Luci.

'Stay here with the horses. Try not to engage anyone in conversation and try not to sound outspoken. It will reflect badly on me if you do, and I fear I will have my work cut out here anyway.'

Luci nodded and took the reins. He was somewhat out of his depth here, a native Briton surrounded by the might of the Roman military, albeit not at its best. Leaving him to it, Agricola strode purposefully over to the door to the great cross-hall, then located the offices. At the centre stood the chapel of the standards with its guards. The office of the legate would be one of the adjacent rooms. Likely Agricola's own office would be the other.

Only one seemed occupied, from the drone of conversation within and the guttering lamplight, so he walked across to it and stood in the doorway. The legate's desk was strewn with maps and tablets, two clerks discussing details of cartloads of leather that were late, while a man with saggy jowls and a noteworthy paunch nodded his agreement. His face was drawn, bags beneath the eyes and lips that fell into a natural pout, as though the very ground was pulling his face downwards. Agricola's eyes lowered to the man's torso and noted with interest the tunic of an officer of equestrian rank. This was not the legate, apparently. He cleared his throat loudly.

The three men fell silent and turned to look at him. Again, his manner must have carried authority, for the two clerks straightened a little. The officer did not – he leaned back in his chair and waved the two men away.

Agricola did not move as the clerks edged around him and disappeared out into the fortress, careful not to brush him and with murmured 'sir's.

'Can I help you?' the officer said, once they had gone.

'I am seeking Lucius Valerius Geminus, legate of the Second, to confirm my appointment as senior tribune of the legion.'

The man sighed. 'Then you're out of luck, tribune.' He rose with some difficulty and held out a hand. 'Poenius Postumus, praefectus castrorum of the Second.'

Agricola looked at the extended arm, not at all sure he liked how this was going, but stepped inside and took the hand, shaking it anyway. The man's grip was tight, suggesting that perhaps his appearance belied something. Certainly a man who had reached such a position, third in command of the legion, should be a solid veteran, having served a full term as a senior centurion.

'What puts the camp prefect in the legate's chair?' he said.

Postumus sighed. 'The legate is not a well man. He is spending half a month at Aquae Sulis, taking the waters for his illness.' There was something about the way he said 'illness' that put Agricola on his guard.

'He is not aware that he is required by the new governor?'

Postumus shrugged. 'I have a small pile of messages for the legate, awaiting his return, but he made it quite clear before he left that they were not to be opened in his absence. If he's not back in a couple of days, I'm going to send a vexillation up to Aquae with them.'

Agricola frowned. 'This place seems... less than ready for war.'

He stared as Postumus burst into a derisive laugh. 'The Second is not at war, tribune.'

'It may be soon.'

'Then there will have to be some major reworking by the governor. Come. Look.'

As Agricola followed him to a map on the wall, Postumus

stabbed a finger at a small symbol near the south coast. 'This is Isca. Home, such as it is. Here you'll find just four cohorts.'

'I had noticed the reduced size of the fortress.'

'That's because we are babysitters and prison guards, not soldiers. Look at these markings,' he added, stabbing his finger at small symbols all over the area. 'Each one is a mining settlement. That's all this region is, really, just a source of tin and copper, covered with grass and uncooperative natives. Every one of those mining areas is held by a concession with rights granted by Rome, worked by slaves, but thanks to the agreements made, each one has a century of the Second assigned to it to keep control.'

He began to move his finger. 'Then there are strategic forts in places where the natives have a tendency to become restless, each manned by men from Isca. Then there are all the depots that line the roads to protect the ore convoys as they leave the region at the port you must have landed at, four miles away. Every one of them has a small number of men from the Second. It's a bloody full-time job just working out who's assigned where, which units need to be rotated, who's due for retirement, the sick lists and so on. I'm sure you can imagine how much of a headache my work is, especially when I'm doing both mine and the legate's jobs.'

Agricola's frown had not fled but deepened as he listened. 'I would have thought such deployments the job of auxiliary units.'

'In a perfect world, but the auxiliary units are trained purely for war and pacification, so they've always been kept on the front line of the advance north. A legion like ours is trained for construction too, and it was assumed that we would be of value here in the ongoing civilisation of the region – aqueducts and roads and the like. But who wants to Romanise a tin mine or a shithole pond surrounded by hovels? Hence what you see here.'

Agricola found himself starting to feel a little sympathy for the man. As third in command, his remit as camp prefect should end at the fortress walls. He was expected to maintain the Second's base, not control all their activity.

'I'm afraid, then, that my arrival is not going to ease things for you, Poenius Postumus. I have orders to join the governor at Viroconium by Tubilustrium, and for the legate to join us also. Command of the Second will continue to fall to you, Prefect.'

Postumus' brow furrowed. 'Tubilustrium?'

'Yes.'

'That's five days away.'

'Yes.'

Postumus drummed his fingers on the map. 'Viroconium is five days away by fast horse. I don't think you're going to make it.'

'I have to. I'll manage.'

'I'll detail a detachment of our cavalry to escort you. They know the roads and the settlements. They'll get you there as fast as you can manage, but I think you'll be lucky to get to Viroconium on time, especially picking up the legate.'

Agricola frowned, peering at the map. 'This Aquae Sulis is something of a detour?'

'No. Actually, it's directly on your route, but I told you, the legate is not a well man. He'll not travel fast. He will slow you down and you'll be late. And to be honest, he really should not be going on campaign. Better to send him back here or leave him where he is and make his apologies to the governor.'

Agricola took a deep breath, held it for a moment as he looked at the map again, and then let it out slowly. 'I have my orders. So does he. I will leave it to the legate to decide whether he wants to ruin his own career. It's not my call. But I won't be late. What ails the legate?'

Postumus paused for a moment. 'It's not really a thing to announce publicly. Let's just say his liver isn't what it was.'

Agricola nodded. A dependence upon the grape was not unknown in the army, he'd heard, but it seemed strange that a man in the legate's position, easy as it should be, would require such a crutch. 'Give me eight riders, and spare horses for each man, including myself, my slave and the legate.'

'And the legate's slaves,' Postumus added. 'He has three and they go everywhere with him.'

'How long do we have before dark?'

'A good eight hours.'

'Then we will not tarry in Isca. I will leave immediately, as soon as you can furnish me with an escort.'

Postumus nodded and called for his clerks. The two men who'd sidled out round Agricola returned, looking worried, and the prefect issued the orders through them, sending them to make arrangements. He then looked at the map. 'You'll find no towns or comfortable mansios yet in Britannia. There's a growing site at Aquae already, but most of what you'll find are native settlements or our forts. If you can bear a sore arse, eight hours of solid riding will bring you to Lindinis, where we built a fort last year to protect the crossing. There's two centuries of the Second there now. You could overnight there, and another good ride the next day will take you to Aquae Sulis. After that, you're at the mercy of the legate, and your future's in the hands of the gods, tribune.'

Agricola continued to study the map as soldiers came and went, confirming arrangements with the prefect. Two of them appeared with a meal of cold meats and cheese and bread all wrapped up and bagged for a journey, for which Agricola thanked them. The prefect dug through the collection of messages awaiting the legate and located a case bearing the gubernatorial seal, passing it to Agricola, whose eyes returned to the map. From what he could see, Aquae Sulis was roughly halfway to Viroconium. Just above it and to the left, almost on the line of their route, was written the legend SILURES, which was a troubling notion.

'If Aquae is halfway, how can it take five days, not four?'

Postumus sighed. 'Because we've laid down some good roads from here up to Aquae, but beyond that you're in the border zone. No roads, frequent threats of ambush and brigandage, rivers without bridges where you have to detour via fords. You get the drift. The going is slower. All I can say is good luck.'

Agricola nodded, continued to peruse the map, and waited until a soldier appeared and announced that all was ready. With the same sagging dejectedness that seemed endemic in Isca, the prefect escorted him from the office and back out to the courtyard, where Luci was busy sitting on a statue's plinth, drumming his fingers on his thigh, while the horses stood tethered to the arm of a great bronze of Nero.

'We're leaving. Come on.'

He brushed past Luci, leaving the man to gather the reins and walk the horses on behind him. Through the archway and out into the open street he found eight riders already armoured and in the saddle, each of them with a spare mount, several others roped together. Postumus crossed to them.

'The decurion there is Iventius Sabinus. He'll escort you right the way to Viroconium. It will be up to the legate and yourself whether he stays with you or leads his men back to Isca. I put him under your direct command.'

He turned to Sabinus. 'A full day's ride for all of you. Get the tribune to Lindinis by nightfall and to Aquae Sulis tomorrow and find the legate there.'

The decurion bowed his head to the prefect and then to Agricola. Luci handed over the reins and the two new arrivals pulled themselves up and into the saddle. The tribune looked about himself. His visit to Isca had been as brief as could be, but he had learned a great deal in a short time. His sense that they had entered an untamed wilderness at the edge of the civilised world had only grown with what he had seen and been told. Truly they were far from the comforts of empire now. And though he felt more than a little trepidation at the days ahead, the sense of having set out on a great adventure was undeniable. He had to fight to maintain his composure and not grin.

With a farewell to Poenius Postumus, a man in a truly unenviable position, Agricola gave the nod to the decurion, and the small party trotted down the murky street towards the fortress gate and the open land of Britannia. Thus far, all he had seen of the island was the four miles of grassy terrain between the small port and the fortress. As they began to ride at a steady, mile-eating pace north-east, Agricola looked at the men around him. The legionary cavalry seemed better kept and exhibited less gloom than most of those he had met. Had they been chosen specifically by Postumus to put forth the best impression he could? That didn't really seem the prefect's way. He gestured for the decurion to join him and the officer fell back from his position as vanguard and dropped in beside Agricola, opposite Luci. The man was tall and thin with an angular face and a single, heavy brow impressive enough to stand out even in the shadow of his helmet.

'Iventius Sabinus, you sit straighter and more professionally than some of your colleagues back in the fortress.'

'Sir?'

'You may speak freely.'

The man clicked his tongue in his cheek and answered in a careful and measured manner. 'There is little call for legionary cavalry in the Second's current duties, sir. We are used almost uniformly as couriers and wagon escorts. The opportunity to do something different is hard to play down. The lads prize days like this, sir.'

Agricola let the smile free now. This was refreshing to hear. 'Good man. Good men. Alright, unless the legate counters my orders, I'm assigning you and your men as my bodyguard. You'll come with me and stay at Viroconium and then join me on campaign. This sits well with you?'

'It does, sir. The chance to do something useful.'

As they rode, the miles passing them by in a kaleidoscope of wide fields, low hills and woodlands, all nestled below a dull grey sky, Agricola quizzed the decurion on his history, the Second, their current situation and everything he could think of. Unfortunately the man's knowledge of events and conditions north of Aquae Sulis was limited to the basic geography that permitted him and his men to act as couriers. Indeed, it seemed that Luci had a better grasp of the north than this man. But the professionalism and attitude of Sabinus and his men pleased the young tribune, and by the time they reached the fort of Lindinis in the fading light of the day he was comfortable that the decision to assign them as his bodyguard unit was the correct one.

Lindinis was a new place, more so than Isca. A timber and turf fort still showing the signs of construction and yet to acquire the usual civilian settlement around its perimeter, Lindinis sat beside a small river in an area of uniform and uneventful flatness. As they approached, the gate was swung wide, the garrison recognising their comrades from the legion, and they were admitted and introduced to a veteran centurion who commanded there.

They passed the evening with the commander, who was already showing signs of the same bored resignation and stress that had been visible at Isca, his daily duties little more than watching occasional ore convoys pass and dealing with the complaints of local farmers. As they saddled up the next morning for the second day of their journey, requisitioning adequate supplies for the day, Agricola had begun to form the distinct opinion that the Second was being ignored and underused, and that the result would destroy what was left of morale and discipline in the legion unless they were reassigned soon.

Despite their clear professionalism, he kept his opinion from the riders accompanying him, even the decurion. Moreover, he felt that he might have to build the relationship between Luci and their escort somewhat. The slave's position clearly put him beneath the social rank of everyone else by miles, and none of them seemed inclined to speak to Luci at all. It took him an hour of paying attention as he spoke with both Sabinus and Luci to realise that it was more than the stigma of slavery. They had discovered that Luci was of the Silures – the Second had had only peripheral dealings with that tribe, but they'd been enough to make Luci quite unpopular, especially given fresh reports of Silurian trouble to the north. If he was going to get the most from both the cavalry escort and his slave, he needed to somehow bring them closer together. That was a problem to solve.

It was a relief to arrive at Aquae Sulis towards the end of the second day of their journey. There were still two hours before dark as they neared the settlement, and Agricola began to hope that perhaps they might even be able to pick up the pace and reach Viroconium the day before their appointed arrival. That hope was crushed the moment he mentioned it to the decurion.

'Sorry, sir, but even if we can persuade the legate to leave with us, he won't go before dawn, so the rest of the day will be spent here. And even if we did move on, we're reliant upon military sites to put us up, so we'll still be a solid three days.'

Postumus' 'growing site' of Aquae Sulis was less impressive than Agricola had anticipated. A fort sat on the far side of the river to their approach, on the higher ground – such as it was – and between it and them, a native settlement sat beside the river where a recently constructed timber bridge granted access. Between the fort and that settlement a small huddle of stone buildings had been constructed, though they were nothing grand, the bones of a new, partly constructed temple jutting towards the leaden sky.

'Where will the legate be?' he murmured. 'I cannot believe there's a mansio here.'

Sabinus pointed to the cluster of stone buildings. 'That is the thermal complex. They have hot springs here. The legate will be there.'

They rode across the last stretch of open road and into Aquae Sulis, a collection of shambling native huts gathered around the bridge and on both banks of the narrow but deep river. Suspicious native gazes followed them as they passed doors and windows, and Agricola noted that even such places, which had now been under Roman dominion for a number of years, still held grudges against their occupiers. It led him to wonder how long it had taken his own Saluvii to accept that they were Roman now and not a conquered tribe.

He was unused to feeling so unpopular, despite having picked up something of a reputation as old-fashioned and stiff among his peers in Massilia, and the atmosphere that gathered around them among the natives made him shiver. He was grateful to pass the last of their houses and approach the new thermal complex, which was growing and expanding even now with a new great temple at its edge. As they neared what was clearly planned to be a monumental entrance, with plinths and niches for statuary that had not yet found its way into place, Agricola spotted two men standing by the entrance, each in a plain tunic, but each with a good solid length of timber in hand. The managers of this establishment were clearly keen to keep out the riff-raff.

The decurion trotted out ahead and leaned forward in the saddle, speaking to the guards, who nodded, one dipping inside for a moment and then returning with a well-attired fat man with a shaved head, several slaves hurrying in his wake. The man glanced at the arrivals and his gaze fell on Agricola as their leader without pause, an obsequious smile breaking out across his face, making his chins wobble.

'Good afternoon, sir. Have you come far? How many for the baths? Are you here for the general public bathing area or for the private spa? We can comfortably accommodate four overnight at this time if the latter, while the rest can be made comfortable in guest accommodation. If you would like to hand your reins to my staff I will see you into the complex and explain what we have to offer and how everything works.'

Agricola blinked. The patter had rattled out of the man with barely a breath between sentences, so fast that he'd spotted no convenient moment to interrupt. Indeed, without waiting for an answer, the man was already waving his slaves forward towards their horses.

'No,' Agricola said, giving an approaching slave a hard glare, then holding a hand up to halt the others. Then, to the host, 'I'm afraid we're not here for leisure. I'm looking for the commanding officer of the Second legion, who I believe is staying here. We will need basic accommodation and meals for ten men for the night. Nothing more.'

The portly host was not taken aback by the refusal. He gave an easy smile. 'Then I will have that provided for your men and your slave. I am sure that yourself and the decurion, as officers, would not refuse to partake of our delights gratis, for free and with absolutely no conditions attached. Indeed, if you wish to visit the legate of the Second, who is currently in our relaxation suite, you will be required by house rules to disrobe of your travel clothes and take a towel. As such, it would be a dreadful shame not to make the most of your time.'

Agricola, new to the region and not entirely keen on this approach, looked across to Sabinus. The decurion gave him a nod, and the two dismounted. He looked across and gestured to Luci. 'My slave comes with us.'

The look of distaste on Sabinus' face was echoed for half a heartbeat by the host's, before he wiped it away and replaced it with another toadying smile. 'Of course, sir.'

Sabinus gave instructions to his men, who were displaying clear disappointment at being denied the baths, but were somewhat consoled with the promise of comfortable lodgings, a meal and drinks, all far removed from their usual garrison life. Once the men and the horses had been led away, Agricola and his two companions followed the wobbling host off into the complex.

Once more, he was struck by how the whole place was a work in progress, as yet very plain and unfinished. The main hall into which they passed was unpainted and again full of empty niches, though a mosaic floor had been recently laid. Here there were personal slave attendants awaiting customers, though they did not rush to the three men being led by the host, who indicated a large doorway ahead, beyond which they could hear splashing and voices.

'The public pools. Gratis, obviously. The private part of the complex is usually bookings only and rather exclusive, but as we are currently in a period of flux and growth, we are offering free use of the facilities to military officers and to government officials.' He glanced sideways at Luci. 'And to their staff, of course.'

The man led them off to the left and to a smaller door. As they approached, Agricola could feel the heat emanating from the rooms ahead.

'There are steam rooms, and we have underfloor heating in several rooms. The pools and basins, though, are unheated, fed by a naturally sulphurous and warm flow. Variations in temperature are controlled through distance from the source spring, so you should find it easy to locate the perfect temperature. We also have the facility to offer the water as a tonic. The locals here have been drinking the Sulis water for many centuries, and medical academics have confirmed the healthy and beneficial qualities of the water.'

'Just show us to the legate,' Agricola murmured. He was aware of Sabinus and Luci occasionally exchanging glares, and that boded ill for the coming days.

'Of course. But first, the changing room.'

It was not the most ornate of rooms but, once again, there were signs that it was only partially complete – though at least here the walls had been painted, with images of fish and of improbable sea monsters. Slaves now approached, each bringing with them a large towel and a pair of wooden clogs. Luci gave the man nearing him a hard look, but shot a quick glance at Sabinus and took the proffered items. Agricola allowed himself a small smile. Luci hated Roman bathing, he knew, but the Silurian was damned if he was going to appear less civilised than Sabinus, who was already shrugging out of his cloak. Agricola followed suit, stripping out of his travel gear. He'd fully intended to simply march in, find the legate, and leave, but now that he was here, the lure of the warm pools was almost physically pulling him forward. Once the three of them were wrapped only in towels and clacking around in their clogs, the slaves handed them each a tin medallion with a number on and then scurried away with their gear. Others took their places and followed the three men at a discreet distance, ready to help in any way as required.

'Please,' the host said, gesturing for them to follow him.

They did so, Agricola in the lead, the other two trying not to walk side by side at his shoulders. They followed the portly man through a series of chambers and corridors, past basins of steaming water and across sizzling floors, beneath paintings of sea nymphs and past statues of heroic-looking naked Greeks indulging in a variety of sports.

Finally, they were shown to a room and asked to wait for a moment. As they did so, the host entered the next chamber and the murmur of conversation filled the echoing space before he emerged once more and beckoned them with a smile. Agricola led the others into the room, and into the presence of Lucius Valerius Geminus, legate of the Second Augusta.

The commander sat in a circular basin, wisps of steam rising up around him, a pewter cup in one hand, the other stretched out languidly along the edge of the bath. He focused on the three of them, apparently writing off Luci as lower class and Sabinus probably through at least faint recollection, and focusing on the man who was clearly a visitor, neatly clipped and shaved in Roman fashion, but with the complexion of a man of Italia or Cisalpine Gaul.

'You come from Isca?' the man said, and a flicker of a wince crossed his face for a moment as he moved. Agricola frowned. The steam had hidden some detail at first, but now that he looked more properly at the naked legate, he could see an unhealthy pallor to the man, his flesh carrying more than a hint of jaundiced yellow. As the man moved, he winced again, and the cup of wine sloshed slightly, a drip falling into the water where it rippled out in pink waves.

'Yes, legate. I am your new senior tribune. I apologise for disturbing your convalescence, but I carry orders that were awaiting you in Isca from our new governor. He is now in

Viroconium, preparing for the summer campaign. Both you and I, sir, have been called onto his staff this year. I have left Poenius Postumus in command as he has been, and rushed here with all haste. The prefect does not believe you are well enough to travel, and yet the governor is expecting both of us in three days, and Suetonius Paulinus is not a man to rest and wait. I believe he will mean to move as soon as the trumpet festival has passed.'

Back in Isca he'd insisted that the legate should come, but as he watched Valerius move and wince with a grunt of pain again, he was rapidly coming to agree with Postumus' assessment. Yet as the man rose, water cascading from his form, despite his pallor and apparent physical condition, and despite advanced years too, Valerius had a body that spoke of a military past and his eyes, as they focused, were sharp.

'Then we must move, my young tribune. When a governor calls, we answer, whether we be in the bath or standing on board Charon's boat waiting to set sail.'

And that was that. It appeared that the legate was coming with them after all. Three days. Three more days of travelling, and then war was afoot.

6

It was on the fifth day of their three-day journey that the young tribune was starting to truly despair. Back in Isca he'd readily brushed aside the prefect's concerns over their commander. Legate Geminus might be ill, but if he was well enough to consider campaigning, then surely he would at least be able to ride a horse. Indeed, when he'd met the legate in the steaming waters of Aquae Sulis, the man had seemed alert and ready, almost eager.

Then they'd set off.

Lucius Valerius Geminus walked like an old man, slowly and carefully, and paused every twenty steps or so to clutch his side, groan and curse. When Agricola had a horse brought round for him he'd shaken his head and instead summoned a wagon, padded, cushioned, and bedecked with rich drapes, of a very modern design with excellent suspension that made the vehicle almost float, despite the roughness of the bumpy road they followed. The wagon was, of course, slow. That alone had added an extra day to their journey.

The other additional day had come through Geminus' apparent need to stop every time they passed even a hint of civilisation. They called in at forts, fortlets, watchtowers, local hamlets and even occasional farms. Each time, Geminus consulted with the owner or commander of the place on the local situation regarding the Silures, who seemed, according to reports, to be inactive in this region. Such enquiries might appear to be a perfectly sensible thing, but by the time they'd stopped half a dozen times in the same area only to hear the same news, the pauses had clearly become redundant. It did not escape Agricola's notice that on each occasion, when he attended upon the legate, the man had a cup of wine or beer in his hand, offered by the respectful locals. At least, despite what was an impressive intake of intoxicating liquid, the man was showing no clear evidence of being drunk.

The whole thing didn't seem to affect Luci, but then why should it? He had nothing invested in all of this, and his status as a slave removed any responsibility from him. Besides, now they were on the edge of Silurian territory he seemed endlessly distracted, constantly looking out over the land to the west as they travelled. Sabinus, the cavalry decurion, and his men seemed similarly unperturbed. In their case it was not so much a matter of distance from responsibility, but more a familiarity with their legate. Clearly this was exactly what Sabinus had expected.

At Burrium, two days into the journey, they had found the fortress of the Twentieth manned by just three centuries of men, the rest gone north a month ago to join the assembling army ahead of the governor's arrival. As on all their other stops, the centurion there confirmed that he'd seen no trouble among the Silures, though he admitted he'd heard concerning reports filtering down from the north, where the force was gathering.

Agricola had pulled Luci aside that night.

'I thought the Silures were supposed to be causing trouble. All evidence suggests otherwise.'

The slave shrugged. 'Remember what I told you. The Silures are more than just a tribe. Each clan within the tribe has its own chieftain, its own needs, opinions and goals. Of course there's no trouble here. These people have had a decade of being kicked in the head by men like Scapula. They've accepted their lot and now they look to a Roman future. But there will be pockets among them, further from the influence of the empire, who stand proud and defiant, and it's *them* who cause the trouble.'

Agricola nodded then. 'But to Rome, the Silures are the Silures.'

'And so when Rome marches, it will be these poor bastards... *my* people... who suffer.'

'That's why you're here, Luci. That's why I went to all this trouble. With knowledge like yours we can direct our spears to where they're needed and not stick them in our own foot. If we can manage to persuade command of the need to take care and be precise with our campaign, perhaps you can save your people and I can save lives among mine.'

They set off with more of a sense of purpose the next morning, though that enthusiasm flagged with every slow mile and unnecessary stop.

The journey had been particularly galling last night as they slept at a small fort that overlooked a stream with a rickety wooden bridge. Bitterly, he'd watched the soldiers throw a small celebratory party in honour of the ritual unveiling of the trumpets, the main ceremony held in Rome to mark the start of the campaigning season, a small echo marked with a sacrifice in every fort in the empire. It should have been a glorious moment, and would have been, had he watched the celebration in Viroconium in the presence of the governor. Instead, the deadline by which he'd been ordered to attend had passed in some nameless military installation on the way.

The commander of the fort, a centurion with a scarred, misshapen face, had told him they were but a single day from their destination, though in his head, Agricola had naturally added a day to that thanks to the legate's need to stop every half hour.

Thus their one extra day had dragged on, and by nightfall they were still three or four hours from Viroconium. He had braced himself and tried to persuade the legate that they could travel through the hours of darkness in order to at least be only a day late, not two. The legate would hear nothing of it.

'Travel in darkness here in the borders? Where the Silures could swarm over us in the night? Never. We move in daylight like civilised men.'

And that was that, for the legate's word was law, even when it was clearly idiotic. They'd heard nothing of unrest among the Silures at any of the stops. The last morning, Agricola was almost fuming as they paused in some local hamlet for half an hour, with Viroconium so close he could almost smell it.

A little short of midday they crested a hill and the might of Rome came into view. Despite everything Agricola had been expecting and anticipating, the sight stole his breath. The rough, recently constructed military road from the south crossed the slope and descended towards a wide river, which snaked with glittering white-blue scales off to both east and west. Here, the route led down to a massive timber bridge, wide enough to permit two-way cart traffic, which led across to a wide plain in a huge loop of the river where an immense timber fortress stood, easily the largest installation he'd seen in the province. The fortress was packed with men and horses, smoke rising from half a hundred cook fires, and smaller temporary camps were clustered on the gentle slope beyond the fortress, which could easily hold a legion. That alone was the most soldiers the young tribune had ever seen in one place outside the headquarters of the fleet back home. But that was not all.

A new stretch of road, so recent that it gleamed with white gravel, ran off to the north-west along the far bank of the river, and more small auxiliary units were encamped along its length. At the far end, perhaps two miles away, he could see the main concentration of the army. A new fort, small at this distance, stood by another bend in the river, and there lay so many camps that there could hardly have been a blade of grass visible. He tried to estimate the number of men at the gathering, but his experience with such matters left him with little more than an educated guess. Two or three legions and the same number of auxiliaries, so maybe thirty thousand men all told. And then, of course, all the ancillary groups, the camp followers, the supply units, the medical detachments. It was a temporary city of soldiers.

Beside him, Sabinus whistled through his teeth. Oddly, the one who looked neither impressed nor fazed was Luci, and the memory struck Agricola with a lurch. Luci had fought with this Caratacus rebel, along with his Silurians. He must have faced an army such as this in the field. Brave man. Something of the steel in the slave's manner made a little more sense with the realisation.

They moved on down the slope, and the tension almost tore Agricola apart. He wanted to ride ahead, fast, to find the commander and hope that his career could be recovered, yet he had to potter slowly on alongside the legate's plush carriage. Sabinus rode in front now, clattering across the bridge and approaching the pickets, asking directions to the headquarters of the general. Following instructions, the party crossed the river and followed the new road past a dizzying array of military units of differing types, each beneath its own standard, towards that new fort. Reaching the gates, they were admitted swiftly and directed towards the principia at the fort's centre.

Reaching the place, Agricola dismounted and was about to instruct Luci to wait with the horses when he realised that the legate was busy telling his gaggle of slaves to look sharp. If Geminus was taking his personal slaves in, then Agricola was content to follow suit, and beckoned for Luci. 'You'd better join us, decurion,' he added, nodding to Sabinus.

Leaving the horses with the weary cavalrymen, they strode into the building. Naturally, Agricola let the legate lead the way. It was his place as the senior officer, but more than that, it put him first in the face of any criticism or anger coming from the governor.

Suetonius Paulinus was standing with his arms folded in an office cluttered with maps and records, two clerks busily scribbling orders. As they entered, the man's eyes took on a hard edge and he dismissed the clerks. Once they were alone, the general also ran his eyes over the assembling visitors, noting the presence of the slaves. There must have been something about

Luci's manner that made him appear military, for the disapproval in the man's gaze was reserved for the three oiled characters bowing obsequiously in the shadow of Legate Geminus.

'You are late.'

Geminus nodded and affected an apologetic expression. 'Troubles in the south-west, general, and then a journey through dangerous lands. The Silures are disaffected. They could rise at any moment. We travelled with care. I take full responsibility for our lateness, unavoidable as it is.'

The hardness did not leave Paulinus' eyes as they shifted to Agricola. The tribune carefully kept his gaze neutral, while inside he raged, wanting to gainsay his commander, to denounce his words as fallacies and blame their lateness on the man's habits. He'd forgotten how clever and perceptive Paulinus was, but that was made clear as the man's eyes now changed. Somehow he saw in the two men before him at least some of the truth, and all the blame slid towards Geminus.

'You have missed all the briefings, which is inexcusable in a senior officer. As such, your subordinates will need to fill you in on much of the detail. I am a very busy man and the army departs in two days.'

'We will do what we must to be ready, General,' Geminus said, straightening impressively, given the fact that he was probably already drunk, and as he snapped straight he winced, but managed not to clutch his side this time.

'You have a reputation as a tactician and a successful commander,' Paulinus said, eyes still locked on the legate. 'I understand that you have in your time made something of a name for yourself. Given your lateness I would normally assign command of the force I had reserved for you to another senior officer, but I am new to this province and do not know many of the men under my command. Moreover, the officers I brought from Rome are all assigned already. Thus, I can only hope that you live up to your reputation.'

He huffed, glancing briefly at a map of the western hills, a lump in the form of Britannia the shape of a backwards C. 'In a perfect world I would have three legions for my campaign, but I am told that the Second cannot be safely removed from the south-west without endangering mine production, and that the Ninth must remain in the east lest we see a rising from the tribes nominally under our control. I have drawn two cohorts from the Ninth, much to the disgruntlement of their commander, but that is all I dare remove. This leaves me with a little more than two legions for a three-pronged campaign, and that is how it must proceed, I am certain. Thus I am pulling vexillations out of the Fourteenth and Twentieth legions to form a third force of heavy infantry, and dividing the auxilia three ways in order to create three advances.'

He turned and pointed to the map, stabbing with a finger and drawing lines by dragging it across the vellum. 'I shall personally lead the Twentieth in the northernmost advance. My army will march north from here into lands we have only thus far ventured into on rare occasions. The tribe there, the Deceangli, have yet to feel the true power of Rome. We will subdue that tribe and then move west along the coast into the lands of the powerful Ordovices, who continue to resist Rome's advance. It is my understanding that at the north-west point of the region is an island sacred to the tribes. We may be required to secure that to be certain of their submission.'

His finger dropped back to Viroconium and this time drew a new line. 'The commander of the Fourteenth, Servius Didius Costa, will lead the second advance directly into Ordovices territory, pushing control west. His is anticipated to be the slowest advance, and I am hoping that my activity in the north of their lands will divide their strength and make the Fourteenth's job easier.'

His finger returned to the start.

'That leaves the third force with the mopping-up. A mix of centuries from the Fourteenth and Twentieth, along with appropriate auxiliary support, is hereby assigned to you, Lucius Valerius Geminus. Agricola, of whom I have high hopes, will be your second in command. Of the three advances, you have the furthest to travel, but I anticipate yours being the quietest one. You will secure the Silures. I am aware of rumours of risings among them, though we have yet to actually see it or identify any source.'

As he said this, his expression made clear just how little he believed of Geminus' excuses.

'But no matter how small, there is clearly something going on among the Silures. You will make sure they are settled. Then you will move into the south-west, where a tribe called the Demetae lie. They have yet to come into full contact with Rome, but we have received overtures from them, and it is possible that they can be incorporated into the province with the status of a client kingdom without the need for a fight, or leaving more than a small caretaker garrison. From there, your force will move north along the coast.'

He stepped back and folded his arms. 'I give you one season to suppress the Silures, treat with the Demetae, and fight your way up through Ordovician lands. It is my intention that by the time we are hit by autumn, which I am informed can be dreadful in those hills, all three forces will be converging in the north-west. We will winter in garrison and then next spring we will finish the job, crushing the last of their resistance and securing the entire region. By the time my governorship ends, I want to be able to send a letter to the emperor confirming that we control all territory up to a line drawn between the rivers Seteia and Abus. Any officer who is instrumental in the completion of that achievement will be mentioned in dispatches and their reputation will be gilded. Any officer who fails in his task or duty will regret being part of my campaign. I expect nothing but the best from all my officers.'

He let his mouth curl up at the corner into a smile. 'Corbulo continues to gather fame in the east, but I have a mind to eclipse the great general's reputation before he can return to Rome. Fly with me or fall behind. That is all I have to say.'

Agricola snapped to an attentive stance, as did Decurion

Sabinus. Geminus managed something similar with just a hiss of discomfort, while his slaves fawned and scraped. Luci stood impassive, meeting the general's gaze in a most unservile manner. Paulinus gave him a brief glance, but nothing more.

'Very well. Report to your own command. Back by the main bridge is the old fortress from Scapula's campaigns. You will find your rather unorthodox command quartered there. They are currently under the command of the Fourteenth's senior tribune and a junior tribune from the Twentieth. They will be able to give you more detail. I forgive you your late arrival, but it will not happen again. In two days, when the army marches, you will be ready, or your commission will be resigned and you will return to Rome in shame. Do you understand?'

'Yessir,' they all snapped in unison.

'Good. Dismissed.'

The gathering departed. Agricola had half expected Paulinus to call him back, to take him aside and question him over their tardiness and Geminus' condition, but no call came as they emerged into the pale grey day.

'That could have gone worse,' the legate said with an air of satisfaction.

'And better.'

'True. But we will just have to prove ourselves, will we not, Agricola.' As the tribune mounted, the legate climbed up to his carriage, rolled his shoulders and winced at the pain in his side. 'We shall begin with the Silures. The governor seems to think they are no great trouble. We must demonstrate their strength and resistance, for only by emphasising the danger can we truly claim glory when we defeat them.'

Agricola frowned. 'Most of the Silures are settled and peaceful. We can root out the trouble, though, and attack it as a surgeon would cut out the rotten meat around a wound while saving the body.'

Geminus snorted. 'If the Silures are quiet it is because they are up to something. You do not know them the way I do.'

Agricola glanced sideways to see Luci giving the legate a withering look. Trouble was in the offing. Geminus may have a reputation as a solid military man, but he was also clearly a political animal. The tribune could read between the lines. He feared the legate intended to provoke the Silures into a major conflict just so that he could defeat them and look good to the general. Foolish. And wasteful. But mostly foolish, especially when there were two tribes to deal with after the Silures.

'My slave here is of the Silures. His intelligence will be critical to our activity, I think.'

Geminus waved the comment aside. 'That's what we have scouts for. I would sooner trust their word than that of a slave.'

As the man slid into the carriage seat and closed the door, Luci stepped his horse a little closer to Agricola.

'Your commander is a fucking idiot.'

'Be quiet. Remember your place. And yes. Absolutely.'

'And not all scouts are so trustworthy.'

Before Agricola could question that last rather enigmatic comment, Luci had stepped away again, and to speak to him would mean raising his voice to a level that Geminus might hear.

As they began to move, heading from the command post, leaving the fort and setting off along that riverside road to their own command, Decurion Sabinus fell in beside him. 'I hate to agree with your slave, sir,' he said, 'but he's right. The Silures are bastards. They've been cowed by a generation of war with Rome, and right now they're as calm and peaceful as they've been since we arrived. But they're a warlike lot. It won't take much to push them back into open revolt. I'm not afraid of going to war with them, but it strikes me that we've got two seasons of war coming, and creating extra aggravation right at the start is just asking for trouble.'

Agricola nodded. 'We must somehow steer the legate in this campaign, rather than being led by him. You've served with him since he was assigned. You know him better than me. Any ideas?'

Sabinus was silent for a while, looking troubled.

'You can speak freely, without fear of punishment, decurion.'

'The legate is erratic, sir. When he's lucid and in full control, he's brilliant. Honestly, he could have been a Corbulo himself, I reckon. But if he's too sober he gets maudlin and black, and he's in too much pain to be particularly active. When he's in his cups the pain recedes, but his common sense is replaced with a wine-fuelled bravado. I have yet to work out how to manoeuvre him into the correct state.'

'Thank you for that rather frank précis, worrying as it is. We will have to work on it. I trust I can rely on your support in doing so?'

Sabinus saluted. 'Anything that saves lives among the lads gets my vote, sir.'

'Good. And in that vein, I would like you to bury the hatchet with Luci. I know you find it distasteful to consort with a slave, but he is no ordinary slave. He is a man of the very land we move into, and has a history of warfare here. He has a knowledge of the Silures and their neighbours that outstrips anything our scouts can manage. I am convinced that his involvement will be critical to our success.'

'Can you trust him, sir?'

'What?'

'He carries a knife. I do not think he is safe. These are *his* people. The moment we blow a trumpet and start to charge the Silures, one denarius gets you ten that knife will be in your back.'

Agricola gave him an odd smile. 'I don't think so. There's a lot to Luci. And these peoples are far more complicated than a simple tribe facing Rome. There are groups among the Silures that I think Luci detests, just as much as there will be others he loves. Gods, but I suspect if I gave him the cap of freedom today, he'd stay by my side.'

'I hope you're right.'

They rode on in silence along that road beside the river and approached, finally, the gate into the great timber fortress. Admitted, the legate now moved ahead, approaching the headquarters at the centre. As they neared the building, a small group of officers emerged from the doorway, including several tribunes and prefects. They lined up at attention as the wagon trundled to a halt, and Geminus opened the door and descended to ground level with a series of rhythmic grunts. As he turned to them the officers all snapped off a salute, which he returned rather sloppily.

'Lucius Valerius Geminus, legate of the Second Augusta, assigned as praepositus, commanding this vexillation force.'

Among the gathered officers, a man in a broad-striped military tunic identical to Agricola's stepped out a pace in front of the others.

'Tiberius Claudius Emeritus, sir, senior tribune of the Fourteenth. It is my honour to pass command of the force to you in the name of the emperor and the senate of Rome. Might I introduce you to my officers?'

Agricola frowned at the phrasing of 'my officers', though Geminus seemed to miss it entirely.

'First, allow me to introduce my second. This is Gnaeus something-or-other Agricola, senior tribune of the Second and my sub on this campaign.'

The look Claudius Emeritus shot Agricola was loaded with spite, to an extent that made him blink and lean back in the saddle. Quite clearly he'd been assigned above this man, his equal in rank, while Emeritus had expected to step into the role.

'Watch that one,' Luci murmured from his shoulder, echoing his own thoughts.

Fabulous. *Another* obstacle to overcome.

7

It had taken mere hours for Agricola and Tiberius Claudius Emeritus to discover that they did not like each other one bit. Agricola was proud of his lineage. A lineage of Gallic and Ligurian blood, with a grant of citizenship from the great Caesar for their service to the republic. A lineage raised to the equestrian order by Augustus and to the senate by Tiberius; a father who had served as a praetor and who would have gone on to great things, maybe even the consulate, had his morals not set him against the emperor Caligula. Agricola's was a history of which to be proud. Emeritus, conversely, had not acquired the name Claudius as a gift of citizenship. In fact, his father's line carried the distant blood of the Julio-Claudian emperors, and the man seemed intent that everyone should know as much, and as often as possible.

He was, in fact, everything Agricola despised. Emeritus had not needed to lobby for position, walking into an important senior tribuneship on the back of his lineage, with a near-guarantee of future power, position, and probably even friendship with the emperor. He'd never done a day's hard graft with his fingers, never worked. Agricola had spent his youth tending the vines on the family estate, learning the craft that had made his father popular. He knew the soil, the land, the meaning of work. He had prepared for army life not only by studying his histories and his tactics, but by swinging a sword and blocking a blow. Emeritus, conversely, had barely learned a thing, his tutors too afeared of putting a foot wrong to give him a clip round the ear and tell him to concentrate. In short,

Emeritus was here on a sinecure like so many of Rome's top classes. And, as Agricola's uncle used to tell him, sloppy shit always floats on the top.

Agricola had, he'd have to admit, goaded the man in those first few hours. Once it had become clear that Emeritus' knowledge of military history and strategy stretched only as far as stories from epics and poems, Agricola had manoeuvred him during every conversation into betraying his ignorance. Emeritus did little in response but glare, hard-eyed, at his peer. That, and repeatedly drop the word 'provincials' into conversation with the inflection usually saved for describing something you'd trodden in on the street.

It had been something of a relief when the legate assigned roles to the men and put some distance between the two tribunes. Agricola was to remain with the commander as his second, Emeritus was to take sub-command of the cohorts from the Fourteenth, while a junior tribune with a pleasant moon-face and an easy smile called Lucius Cornelius Pusio would command the vexillation of the Twentieth. At least that meant he and Emeritus would only really see each other at briefings.

Emeritus had enlightened them as to the details of the invasion, none of which had much bearing beyond the main plans that Paulinus had laid out in brief. They were all matters of logistics, and Agricola noted that the tribune had to be handed written lists to jog his memory.

'The Silurian lands, such as they can be defined, mostly lie to the west of the Isca River,' Emeritus had said with an air of self-importance. 'The border used to ebb and flow between them and the Dobunni until we took control. The Silures seem on the surface to be peaceful and obedient. This is a fiction. All we see is their border, where they are careful not to provoke us. Beyond the border, it is our belief that they remain a defiant mass. As such, strategists suggest that we install minor garrisons along the Isca to keep that situation as is and then march the army into their heartland and install a more major garrison somewhere central. To the north of them, the Ordovices are an even more troublesome tribe, but they are not our problem.'

Cornelius had chipped in when silence fell.

'Our only real problem is a delay. We can march to the edge of their lands immediately, but we are still waiting for a number of shipments of equipment and artillery that are coming from across the island, as well as a part-mounted unit of Batavian auxiliaries that should have been with us days ago but is late. It would be premature to move into enemy territory without them.'

'That,' Emeritus grunted, 'is the legate's decision. Personally I believe we have sufficient baggage for now, and I cannot see what difference five hundred savages from Germania can make.'

The junior tribune straightened, and Agricola braced himself. The man was about to gainsay his superior, and that was clear from his stance. 'In fact, sir,' he said, 'the Batavi are a very flexible force, capable of crossing water even in armour, at home in hills, forests and swamps alike, and afraid of nothing. They have proved to be the most effective and useful of all the auxiliary units since the invasion began. That is why the governor has assigned a cohort to each advance of this campaign.'

Agricola almost chuckled as Emeritus glared irritably at the junior tribune, and forged there and then the opinion that Cornelius was worth ten Emerituses.

It was the legate who settled the matter, wine slopping from his cup as he used it to gesture at the men. 'We will march to the edge of Silurian territory and make temporary camp there, I think by the Sabrina River, safely ten miles away from enemy territory. We will then wait for all the supplies and units we are missing. We will leave a small cavalry detachment here to escort them on to our new position, and to keep in touch. While we wait by the Sabrina, the days will be useful for scouting. We can use our time sending forays deep into the Silures, giving us a better picture of what we face.'

That had been a balm to Agricola. His worries over Geminus' condition and habits had not been allayed, but here was perhaps a glimpse of the renowned tactician of whom Paulinus had spoken. Perhaps he might be a boon after all.

As they rode out at the head of the army, leaving Viroconium for unknown and unsettled lands, Emeritus rode with the legate as much as possible, as duty allowed, a clear attempt to inveigle himself into the man's circle and undermine Agricola's authority. It would be fruitless. Geminus knew that the governor had personally assigned Agricola to the staff, and he would not overturn such a decision readily. Thus, Agricola left Emeritus to his machinations and spent most of the ride with either Tribune Cornelius or Luci for company.

'This, I think, is our opportunity,' he said to the slave that first day of travel.

'Oh?'

'We will have a few days waiting at the border while the scouts investigate the Silures. The legate is sharper than I thought. He wants to know more before he moves, while Emeritus would have us crack their border like an egg and plant a flag in the yolk. You and I have some work to do here. You know these people, and if we want to prevent a bloodbath and settle the land with the least losses to both sides, we need to get more information and then persuade the legate.'

'Will he listen?'

'I don't know. I think so. It depends on how much influence Emeritus has gained.'

'I don't know how he can ride with a stick so far up his arse,' Luci grunted.

Agricola fought down a smirk. He really had to stop Luci being so outspoken, but the problem was, the man was right.

Two days out of Viroconium they arrived at a site the scouts had reported back as ideal for the army. Across the river lay the remains of one of the massive campaign camps of Scapula's advance a few years earlier, but the scouts reported it as lying in partially flooded land, and identified a site on the near bank as being preferable. By sunset the army was in place and defences were being raised. Emeritus had questioned why the only defences raised were a small fort while the bulk of the army camped in the open with pickets out at appropriate distances.

'We are here for but a few days,' the legate replied, 'and large parts of the army will come and go on duty. The river protects us from the enemy in the west. But we build some defences, for I intend to leave a caretaker garrison here to guarantee our supply line.'

That had blessedly shut the tribune up. Agricola had waited until camp was fully set, but not long enough for the legate to be in a stupor, and then attended upon him in his tent. Admitted by duty legionaries after securing Geminus' permission, Agricola made his way inside.

Already, as the fortifications were still going up, animals being corralled and supplies distributed for the evening meal across the army, Geminus' tent spoke of luxury. That rather foxed Agricola. A legate would expect home comforts on campaign, he knew – but when he'd picked Geminus up at Aquae Sulis, the man had only three slaves and what they carried on their horses. Where he had acquired tables, chairs, rugs, wall hangings and even a writing desk in the intervening days, the young tribune could hardly imagine.

'What is it?'

He straightened and snapped to attention, hands behind his back. 'Sir, I would like permission to use the coming days to join the scouting missions.'

'Highly irregular. And foolish. It is not the place of a tribune, or any officer, to scout or to take part in any of the army's front-line activity. It is as unprofessional as having a scout sit with the staff and decide strategy.'

'And yet, sir, is that not what they have done in selecting this site?'

Geminus frowned. 'You would engage me in rhetoric?'

'If it gets me what I want, yes, sir.'

'Then tell me why it would be anything other than foolish.'

Agricola nodded. 'My time here would be wasted. There is nothing for the staff to do that cannot be done by you, and the day-to-day work will be handled by the centurions. I am at a loose end. However, when we do move, you and I, sir, will be relying upon the reports of the scouts for our strategy. As such, it can hardly hurt for one of us to have first-hand knowledge. Moreover, my slave is of the Silures. He knows these lands and these people. We have only rumour and peripheral reports to go on. I would like a better outline of the true situation before we commit to anything where we might lose men. And while there is an element of danger, I will have my cavalry bodyguard from the Second with me.'

Geminus sucked on his teeth and poured himself a cup of wine. 'Your slave will sell you out the moment you're across the Isca, and run home to his people. I told you before to trust in the scouts.'

'I do not believe he will, sir.'

Another pause. 'I want repeated updates. No disappearing for days.'

'Yes, sir.'

'Very well. I will have the officers notified.'

Agricola left the tent with a smile on his face. Back in his own quarters, he summoned Sabinus and set both him and Luci across a small table from himself. 'I have gained us permission to run our own scouting mission into Silurian territory.'

Luci's face betrayed no emotion, though Sabinus' was filled with surprise and worry. 'Is that a good idea, sir?'

'Only time will tell. But if we wish to prosecute a campaign here that settles the Silures with the least destruction, I would like to be able to aim our blows precisely, and we cannot do that blind. Tomorrow morning we ride for the Silures, the three of us and your cavalry. I want every man to keep his weapon sheathed at all times unless we are in danger. I want respect for the tribes in every voice and on every face. If we are to embrace these people into the Pax Romana, it will be easier with gold and toga than with sword and fire.'

At this, even Sabinus nodded.

That night as Agricola lay quietly, unable to sleep, the anticipation of what was to come coursing through his veins, he became aware that Luci, near the tent door, was similarly restless.

'You can't sleep?'

'No.'

'You're worried?'

'I'm the closest I've been to my home in half a decade.'

There was a long pause.

'Will you run?'

The silence dragged out for some time. Finally, Luci's voice came quiet and dark. 'I do not know.'

'I will not let you do so unchallenged, you realise?' There was no answer to that, and the two men were asleep before too much longer.

The next morning they rose with the buccina calls of the legions, washed in bowls of cold, clear water, dressed, and stepped outside to meet the day. To Agricola's satisfaction, Sabinus and the cavalry were already gathered waiting. Grabbing skins of water and packs of bread and salted meat, they rode to the edge of the sprawling camp and headed south, making for the known ford across the river. Some three miles south the Sabrina was easily crossable, with a narrow island occupying the centre of the flow, a route used by the legions over the years as evidenced by the flattened and back-filled remains of the enormous campaign camp they found not far from the river. Luci eyed it blackly.

'This was where your Ostorius Scapula launched an assault that drove Caratacus and his rebels north. Eventually he brought us to battle by the river a long way from here. But the Silures still hang corn-doll effigies of the governor from their huts and, on the anniversary of the battle, they burn him in their fires. They may have accepted their lot, but Scapula cost them dear, and the Silures have long memories.'

Sabinus did not look highly impressed at this snippet of information, but even he could hardly deny the value of local knowledge on their mission. As they sat in the remains of Scapula's camp, Agricola scratched his chin. 'Alright, Luci. If we want up to date information on the Silures, what now?'

The slave rolled his shoulders. 'To the south-west, past the Isca River, the Silurian tribe is the Brithii. You will find no resistance from them. A little resentment, I suspect, but no trouble. Less than a decade ago they lost more or less every man of fighting age in the revolt of Caratacus. The land is all greybeards, children and women who are scratching a living, trying to survive. Any trouble will be to the west, towards Ordovician lands. The next Silurian tribe above the Brithii is the Cantri. They are a little more warlike, though again they lost most of their warriors in the Caratacus debacle. We can gain our best understanding of the current situation there.'

'Very well,' Agricola nodded. 'The Cantri it is. Lead on.'

They rode slightly north of west for some time, Agricola watching his slave from the back as he did so. It did not take long for a suspicion to occur to him. Leaving Sabinus with the others, he trotted forward to fall in beside Luci.

'The Cantri are your people, aren't they.'

'Yes.'

'Is it good or bad to be going home?'

'I'll tell you tomorrow.'

'There's something I don't understand.'

'Oh?'

Agricola shifted in his saddle. 'From what you've told me, your people are still angry at this Caratacus?'

'Yes. He was not even one of our people. He was a rebel from the south of the island who came here and used the Silures to build a second rebellion. When he fucked that up as badly as the first one, he abandoned them to their fate and ran north to try a third time. None of those tribes who gave their menfolk to fight for a foreigner remember him with kindness.'

'And it was Scapula who defeated Caratacus, yet you seem to suggest your people hate Scapula's memory even more than the rebel who led them to disaster.'

Luci threw him a dark look. 'There being one arsehole does not preclude the possibility of another.'

'Tell me.'

'You wouldn't understand.'

'Try me.'

'Scapula did not stop with Caratacus. Having won the war and sent his enemy fleeing to the north, before any chance of pursuit, he turned his attentions to the beaten tribes. He said – and these words are *his*, remember – that the only way to stop such a thing happening again was to exterminate the Silures entirely. To remove even their name from history, as a warning to other tribes.'

'Carthago delenda est,' whistled Agricola.

'What?'

'Nothing. Something someone once said. So what did Scapula do? He died in office a year or so later, and the Silures are still here. Did he die before he could finish them?' *And how do you know his words…?*

'He started it. He had his scouts identify all the droving routes for our animals down to low pasture, and all the trackways to good farmland, and he fortified each of them. Look at one of your maps. You'll find one of his forts everywhere the Silures could turn for food. A year, maybe two, and we'd have begun to starve. He would watch the remnants of the tribes fade away without a blow struck. He would starve us to death. Fortunately he dropped dead in office, as did his successor. I've heard it said that both were the work of druids. Personally I like to think so. I *hope* so. They deserved it. So yes, my people hate Scapula's very memory. Had your gods not taken him, he would have seen every man, woman and child of the Silures dead.'

Agricola sagged in the saddle. It was all too easy to see history repeating itself if Geminus and Emeritus were left to launch a war of annihilation on these people. The Silures were beaten. They needed now to learn the other side of Rome, the one that built and grew, that included and encouraged. They needed the toga and the coin, not the sword and the flame.

'Help me find where the trouble lies so we can direct the army where it needs to be and save these people.'

They rode on for two more hours before a ribbon of high hills grew on the horizon, and Agricola called to Luci again. 'We'll have to turn back in an hour or two if we are to return before dark. When will we be in Silurian lands?'

The slave looked over his shoulder. 'You've been in them for an hour.'

Startled, Agricola frowned. 'We crossed no river.'

'Not all the Silures live across the Isca. The river turns west into the hills.'

Looking around, Agricola followed on in silence once more. As the highlands came ever closer, Sabinus and his men gathered around, the party falling into a tight formation. After a time, they turned in a northerly direction and into a narrow valley of brown wild grasses around a narrow stream, rocks towering above the slopes on both sides.

'Perfect ambush ground,' noted Sabinus quietly.

And it was. The longer they rode away from the army and into Silurian lands, the more Agricola felt his nerves beginning to jump, his imagination populating every crack and rock with unfriendly eyes.

'I feel like we're being watched,' he said eventually.

'Be certain you are. We'll have been watched for some time, especially where I'm going.'

If he'd thought things would become easier when the valley ended, he was wrong. A couple of miles further on, they followed a muddy, rocky track that curved to the west and climbed into the hills. The path entered a gloomy stretch beneath thick trees that kept out much of the daylight, and still they climbed, the track narrow now and passing between rocks hung so thickly with moss and foliage that it appeared a green drapery of nature. The track broke out into open country only once they had climbed a considerable way, and now they could see vast forests stretching out to both sides below them like a carpet covering the land. Ahead lay another valley and they began to descend slowly towards it, the trees closing in once more. As they moved to lower ground once more, a small farmstead came into view on the right. It had to be occupied, for animals were in evidence – chickens in coops, a small, fat pony tethered – yet there was no sign of human life.

'Ride on,' Luci advised, and they did as they were bade without argument.

Back down out of the trees into the narrow, barren valley, they passed a stone that stood to shoulder height beside the path. Shapes were scrawled upon it in some dark pigment. To call it writing would be a kindness. It was perhaps stylised pictograms. What they were drawn in did not bear thinking about. It could have been mud, shit or any dark, brownish pigment, but Agricola's mind was suddenly filled with the words of Caesar and Diodorus, of druids plunging blades into their victims, awash with human blood. He shivered.

Luci seemed to pay no attention to the stone. He rode on past, a man with a purpose now, clearly knowing precisely where he was going. They followed the valley for some time as it narrowed, then took a side dale that climbed alongside a stream which dropped in regular falls, like a ladder down the hillside. Atop the slope, he reined in.

'Come,' he said, and as the others began to dismount, he held up his hand. 'Just the tribune.'

Sabinus began to argue, but Agricola waved him down. 'I will remain in sight, or call for you if we go any further.' And with that he slid from his horse and handed the reins to one of the riders as Luci had done, turning and following the slave.

Ahead, he couldn't see anything impressive. He'd been expecting a village, or a hillfort, or some such. Instead there was a small stand of three trees, impressively defiant on the bald slope, challenging the elements to remove them. Indeed, as they approached, a frisson of some unexplained energy passed across Agricola's flesh, puckering it. There was something strange about the trees. It was not the plants themselves, though he was interested how they seemed to be roughly of an age, yet they stood one tall and slender, one short and wide and the other between the two in both respects. Only as they approached did he realise what was truly odd. Trees in open ground almost always had a lean in the direction of the prevailing wind. These three, conversely, stood on a hilltop in the wide open, yet all three were straight as a die, reaching up to the heavens. He glanced about. Down the slopes he could see more copses, and then the woodland, and other trees in less exposed places, all leaning. His alertness grew at the sight of a large, flat rock before the three trees, nestled in the wild grass. There were no stains of dried blood he could see, but the vegetation here was suspiciously lush, as though better fed than most of the region.

'What is this place?' he muttered. 'This is a nemeton?'

'If you wish to call it that. Stand. Be quiet.'

They stood there, shivering in the breeze beside the trees. The world was silent apart from the whirr of the winds and the distant shush of trees swaying, the mournful call of some sort of hawk circling high above in the light grey sky.

'What are we waiting for? *Who* are we waiting for?'

'The keeper of this place. Hush.'

They stood silent for a while. Agricola was about to question the slave again when Luci snapped round, looking past his shoulder. The Roman spun and blinked at the sight of three figures. A woman stood leaning on a long staff, her dress plain grey, a cloak snapping at her shoulders. Beside her were two men. One was an old fellow with a wild beard, back crooked, eyes milky and face drawn, the other a tall, gaunt man in brown with a bow across his shoulders.

Luci asked a question of the trio in a strangely melodic tongue. There was a moment's silence, and then the hunter answered, his eyes falling on Agricola – almost a challenge, if not quite. The tone of his words did not sound encouraging, and Luci replied in a hard manner. This time it was the old man who spoke. His voice was so reedy and hollow it was hard to determine the tone, but clearly it was more helpful, from the sound of Luci's own response.

Agricola stood silent for some time, arms folded, as the exchange went on, all four now involved. The Silures did not seem particularly happy to find them here, but their tones no longer spoke of challenge or violence. Briefly, Luci glanced at Agricola, then back as he asked something. There was a nod from the old man, and the slave beckoned. Agricola crossed to them.

'The keeper of this place – you would call him a druid – has gone. Apparently all his kind have gone from these tribes in the days since Caratacus fell. In truth many of them came with us to fight for him, spitting bile at the Romans. But the rest have also left, apparently.'

'Fascinating. But where does that get us? Have you other news?'

'Oh, that was a simple thing. The Brithii to the north are the people you're looking for. It seems that last year at the meeting of the tribes, the Brithii renounced their allegiance to the Silures, who they say are cowed now, and have thrown in their lot with the Ordovices. It was not hard to draw out of these three. My people have never trusted the Brithii, and the bastards' current actions put all the Silures in danger.'

'Like you said back in Rome, they are more endangered by rebels from their own than by the presence of the legions.'

'That's a simplification, but yes. The fact is Rome has nothing to fear from a rising of the Silures, but these Brithii are your enemy. It is they who stand against Rome. If you move against them, my people will not get in your way. None of the Silures will.'

Agricola gave a guarded smile. 'This is exactly what I'd hoped, Luci. Can we reward these people?'

'Only by leaving.'

'Then let us do that at once. Thank them for me on behalf of Rome.'

There was another brief exchange, and then Luci gestured and led him back towards the horses. They reached Sabinus and the others and mounted.

'Did you learn anything?' the decurion asked.

'Exactly what we wanted. I'll tell you all about it on the ride, or maybe Luci should. We need to get back to the camp and call a meeting of the staff. The legate needs to know all this.'

Sabinus nodded as they turned their horses and put heels to flanks, beginning the long trek east once more.

'There is something else here,' Luci murmured to Agricola as the riders led the way.

'Oh?'

'The druid has gone. Not just him. *All* the druids are gone.'

'What does that mean?'

'I don't know. It's unprecedented. It takes a lot to drag a keeper away from his place. He risks the disapproval of the gods. And he will feel... wrong. They are tied to their groves in a way no Roman could understand. For them to leave there must be something important, something dreadful. They are our leaders, our teachers, our priests and our lore, but they are something else.'

'Oh?'

'They are our heart, our mettle and our war-banners. Even silver-tongued Caratacus would never have whipped the tribes into such a frenzy had the druids not gathered to his standard and proclaimed him the champion of the people. If they are not here, then it begs the question, where are they?'

Agricola nodded his understanding. It was a worrying question. They certainly wouldn't have gone south and east into Roman lands, into the world of the 'cowed' Silures. That left deeper into enemy territory, to the Demetae or the Ordovices.

He considered the problem all the way back to Roman lands, never coming any closer to understanding or a solution. Once again, at least until they were back in the flatter lands towards the river, he swore he could feel eyes on them as they travelled, and it was with a certain sense of relief that they passed Scapula's deserted camp and splashed across the ford in the failing light of the day, returning to their base. As they passed pickets and scouts, Agricola girded himself. Legate Geminus might be open to suggestions, but he had a feeling that Claudius Emeritus would do his best to get in the way. This was not going to be an easy conversation.

And a lot rode upon its success.

8

'It already begins to look familiar,' Agricola murmured, peering into the misty morning ahead.

'We're not far from the pass,' admitted Luci, and the two of them tore their eyes from the way ahead and turned to look back.

The army stretched for some distance, far enough for much of it to be hidden by the billowing white of the cold fog. Only the army's commanders on their prancing horses and the legionary cavalry were visible, the fog enveloping even the first few ranks of legionaries, the main force lost to sight, let alone the supply wagons at the rear. They turned to face forward again, only a troop of Batavian horsemen out front, playing the part of both scouts and vanguard for the army.

Another glance back, this time aimed at the officers, eyes hard, regarding the arrogant Claudius Emeritus, who rode as always as close as possible to the legate, his very presence a constant attempt to snatch some authority from Agricola's grip.

The meeting had not gone well.

Looking back on it, Agricola could see precisely what Sabinus had meant when he'd noted the difficulty of finding the perfect balance between maudlin sobriety and audacious inebriation with the legate. Agricola, Sabinus and Luci had reported back with their findings from their scouting mission to find with some relief that the commander had yet to unstopper his dinner, his eyes yet to take on their familiar pink vagueness.

They had described everything they had found, gone over

the information they'd received, unpacked one of the rather sparsely drawn maps of the region and used it to highlight their intelligence.

It had come as little surprise when Emeritus had frowned and cleared his throat, a look of dismissal already crossing his features. 'All you have is the word of one group of these warlike savages that another group is responsible for the trouble. You are too trusting, Agricola.'

He'd clenched his teeth, fought the urge to point out that though they were of equal rank, Agricola was the senior officer here, as adjutant to the legate, and due a lot more respect than this. Confrontation right now would detract from the matter at hand, and that was more important.

'We have also the evidence of our own eyes, Claudius,' he said with belaboured patience. 'From Aquae Sulis all the way to Viroconium and then here, we have seen only peaceful Silures, settled under the Pax Romana.'

'Or so they would have you think.'

Fighting down the irritation once more, 'The wars with Scapula, the revolt under Caratacus – these struggles have stripped the Silures of a generation of fighting men, especially those bordering lands we control. Even if they felt like rising, most of the Silures couldn't raise more than a handful of women and greybeards with pitchforks. Our intelligence is good.'

'I'm not sure "intelligence" is the word here,' snapped Emeritus, with staggering insolence. 'Maybe gullibility.'

As Agricola fumed, teeth grinding, unable to find the words for a reply without dragging himself down to the man's level, Luci stepped in.

'We deliver you the information that can win your war without a disaster, and all you can do is find fault.'

Emeritus' eyes bulged, his face slowly turning puce. 'If your fucking slave dares to even open his mouth in my presence again, Agricola, I will have him scourged until you can see his liver.'

'Damaging another man's property is a criminal offence,'

Sabinus said, moving forward to stand shoulder to shoulder with Agricola.

Emeritus took a deep breath, a finger rising to jab furiously in their direction, but before he could utter another word, the other tribune in the room, Cornelius, hurried to fill the tense silence.

'Gentlemen, we are all tired. I think emotions are running high and we should take a break before something is said that cannot be unsaid.'

The room fell silent once more. Emeritus, the momentum torn from his ire, wagged his finger angrily. Agricola was still trembling with a fury of his own, a slave and a decurion at his sides in support.

'Quite right,' the legate said finally, his words a sort of sagging sigh followed by a grunt as he shifted in his chair and then reached down to his side, massaging it gently. 'Everyone out. To your own commands, and do not allow your paths to cross until you can behave like officers.'

The word had been given, and Agricola threw a last look at his counterpart before turning and leaving the tent, his companions at his shoulders. Emeritus made the mistake of loitering for a moment, turning to speak to the commander.

'No, Claudius Emeritus. You too. Go.'

And with that they left the command tent and, exchanging a last evil glare, separated. For two hours, Agricola and the others sat in his own quarters and marshalled all their arguments ready for the next round. Some time after they had finished a light meal of pork and turnip stew, one of the guards asked permission for Tribune Cornelius to enter, and the man delivered the message that the legate was ready to see them, to resume the discussion. Crossing the camp, they made their way into the tent to find that this time Emeritus was not present, nor did Cornelius stay with them, departing once he'd delivered them to the commander. In fact, aside from the three of them and the legate, the tent's only other occupants were the three slaves, one of whom was massaging his master's feet with warm oil, one tending to a brazier that warmed the room, the last playing a quiet, pleasant melody on a lyre.

'Tell me,' was all the legate said.

Agricola looked at the man. That delicate balance had gone. The sobriety had slid away with the evening, and whatever the moment Sabinus had hoped for looked like, they had clearly missed it, for the man was trembling, his eyes bloodshot, two empty wine jars lying on the floor and a third making a distinctly hollow sound as the man filled his cup and replaced it on the table, no sign of water in evidence.

'In truth, I said it all earlier, sir. The Silures we face here, to the south and the west, are a people ripe for integration into the empire. They are beaten and weary of war. They are hungry and poor. They need to be exempt from taxes for several years while they begin to rebuild, and could do with the support and aid of our engineers and administrators. With a little work they could be a productive part of the province in a matter of years, paying their taxes and their respect to the emperor. But if we draw blades against them, we risk starting it all over again. We risk annihilation of their people and a war to the bitter end.'

'So you would have me make peace with them?'

'With the ones we see settled, yes, sir.'

'And where is the glory in that, tribune?'

Agricola winced. Damn it, but that was an unhealthy direction to take. 'Sir?'

'The governor assigned me because of my military record, which is, I might point out, excellent. We expect the Demetae to treaty with us and assimilate peacefully. Then we face the Ordovices, but by the time we reach them, having travelled to the godsforsaken corners of this land, they will already have been at war for months against two other Roman advances. Any hope of victory there will be but small, and even then shared with other commanders.'

'Sir—'

'I am not well, Agricola. I know it. I hope to recover my health, I really do, but even *when* I do, I will not be a young man anymore. This is my last command in the field, and we all know it. When I return to Rome, I hope for the consulship. My wife begs me to raise our line to such heights. If I want the emperor to notice me and even consider me for high office, I need something noteworthy. Scapula had himself victory honours in Rome for his campaigns against these people. Even if I have to wipe them from the world, I need that victory. Against the Ordovices, I would have to share it, and I've been given specific instructions to bring in the Demetae peacefully. This is my only chance.'

'Sir, I am not suggesting that we do not fight any rising here. I am merely suggesting that we be precise, and target where the trouble really lies. This one tribe of Silurians which stands against us and sides with the Ordovices can be the victory you want.'

'Yet they lie on the northern edge of the Silures?'

Agricola nodded, glancing at Luci for conformation, who joined in the nod. 'Yes, sir.'

'Then if we skirt around the lands of your vaunted settled Silurians in order to come at your rebel tribe from the north, we will be in Ordovician lands and run the risk of interfering with the advance of another general.'

'Sir, if we—'

'No. I agree with your summation in principle, Agricola, but I will not interfere in the northern pushes. What we do must impact solely on the Silures. I see a compromise.'

He threw out an arm, wine slopping from his cup, and then winced and rubbed his side gently with his free hand. 'A compromise, yes. You will select a small party of engineers and pioneers from your force under a solid centurion. You will dispatch them to the Silurian tribes south and west of here. They will make plain their orders, which are to help the locals, to improve their infrastructure, to build roads, secure water sources and the like.'

'Thank you, sir.' A moment of relief. But just a moment.

'Then we march west, through the lands of the Silures, directly at these Brithii. I will have my victory against them, and then we will move into the Demetae.'

Luci cast his master an imploring look, sensible enough not to speak in the legate's presence without being ordered to do so. Agricola gave him a tiny nod.

'Legate, we have good reason to believe that the majority of Silurian tribes will not get in our way if we march against these rebels, but it would be safest to move *around* their lands. If we bring the army directly *into* their territory, we must be careful not to provoke them or appear to be a threat.'

Geminus snorted. 'I will not cast the red spear of war into their midst, tribune, but neither will I sneak through barbarian lands like a nervous trader in bandit country. The army marches with swords on display and banners of war high. Rome's might visible to all. I will have it no other way. If these tribes melt out of our way there will be no trouble.'

And that was it. They were dismissed, for better or worse.

The next morning, as the army prepared to move on again, Agricola caught a glimpse of the smug features of Claudius Emeritus. The tribune was clearly pleased that the legate had only partially accepted Agricola's recommendations, and the prospect of wholesale war remained a possibility.

'Will we meet resistance?' Agricola asked of Luci that morning.

'Who knows? Marching an army through their lands is provocative, after all. We will just have to hope. It would have been better to skirt those tribes, but I got the impression your legate was not in the mood for listening.'

During that day, there was one other occurrence that intrigued Agricola and lent him a new suspicion. The legate had called for additional scouts, added to the irregulars of the Cornovii and the Batavian auxiliaries, and a number of hunters and riders from nearby Silurian settlements had been brought in, offered a considerable sum for their services. Of course, ravaged by years of war and half-starved, even the most jaded of Silurians would consider such a proposal in order to relieve their burdens.

As the score of ragged locals was gathered in a corner of the camp, briefed and given additional equipment, Agricola had been at the corral, checking over his kit while a soldier brushed his horse. Nearby, a group of regular cavalrymen from the Twentieth were busy shoeing three mounts, unaware of the presence of a senior officer.

'Look at 'em,' one of the cavalrymen spat.

'Last fucking thing we want. More of the bastards to watch over.'

Agricola frowned, gaze moving from the Silurian scouts to the legionary riders, and then dropped his harness back to the table and strolled over to the men. The riders noticed the approach of the tribune at the last moment, snapping to attention and falling silent, one of their number smacking his thumb with a hammer, missing the horseshoe by some distance in his panic.

'Stand easy,' Agricola said in a calm tone. 'I couldn't help but overhear.'

'Didn't mean nothing, sir,' one of them said defensively, his expression suggesting that he wasn't quite sure precisely what he was apologising for, but was determined to do so anyway.

'Oh, but you did. I know that mistrust of the Silures is going to linger in the army for some time. You've spent a decade fighting them, I know. I accept that trust is going to have to be earned by these people, and over time. But it was not what you said that drew my attention. It was the way you said it.'

'Sir?'

'Not that you didn't trust Silurians, but more as though Silurians were *innately* untrustworthy. That no matter what they did, you would have to keep an eye on them at all times.'

The soldiers looked at one another, sharing some unspoken thought.

'Tell me,' Agricola said. 'Unless you've done something wrong, you have nothing to fear from the truth.'

The silence persisted for some time until finally one man cleared his throat. 'It's a case of "once bitten", sir.'

'Explain.'

'The last time the army had any reliance on Silurian scouts, sir, we really lived to regret it. That was before the legate and yourself were on the island, I reckon.'

'Under Scapula?'

Nods all round. Agricola frowned. 'Scapula had Silurian scouts when he campaigned against the Silures? That seems unlikely.'

'No, sir. We had Silurian scouts when Scapula led our first move against the Deceangli to the north. It was considered a sure thing. The Silures and Deceangli hardly knew one another but for a scattered history of feuds and conflicts. They certainly weren't allies.'

'So what happened?' Agricola leaned on the fence, arms folded, interested now.

'The fucking southern rebel happened, sir.'

'The southern rebel?' Dots connected in his head. 'You mean this Caratacus. I keep hearing his name. Seems he's been at the heart of a lot of this province's troubles.'

The soldier who'd been talking nodded. 'Certainly has, sir. He was a right devious bastard. Clever and wily. Managed to slip the noose twice, having led revolts. But when he fled west the first time, we didn't realise he was busy raising the Silures against us, and there was us relying on Silurian scouts for our intelligence. We walked into a dozen fucking disasters before we realised the scouts had turned on us and were working with Caratacus. They destroyed supply dumps, led units into ambushes, killed several quite senior officers, burned the granaries. It was chaos for months. And they mostly got away to join their new chief and fight us in the field, too.'

'Of course, they got what was coming to them in the end,' put in another rider, 'when we kicked seven shades of shit out of the rebel's new army. But, as I said: once bitten...'

Agricola nodded. 'I understand. Thank you for enlightening

me. I don't think you'll have any trouble this time, but I agree that keeping a close eye on them might not be a bad thing.' He allowed some steel to enter his voice as he straightened. 'But that's as far as it goes, understand? If anyone deliberately insults or provokes these scouts without good cause, I'll have that man discharged without pension and sent into the wilds alone. You understand me? I won't give the Silures a reason to break their peace now. We go to war against one of their tribes, and only that *one*.'

'You'll have no trouble from us,' one of the soldiers confirmed, and the tribune nodded and walked away, but as he crossed back to his own gear, his gaze fell upon those Silurian irregulars, and he couldn't fight the feeling that he was piecing together Luci's history without the effort of digging. The man rode like an expert horseman, knew the land and the tribes, spoke Latin almost like a native, and seemed totally unfazed by the close presence of an immense Roman force. It seemed almost certain that the man was one of those very scouts who had turned on Rome and rebelled with Caratacus, only to end up in the slave markets of Rome, to be bought and brought back here.

He mentally folded that information up and filed it in his mind for further consideration.

Now, two days later, the army was on the move in Silurian territory, scouts from that very tribe out ahead somewhere in the mist. For the past hour they had passed through lands that looked familiar to Agricola from their scouting foray. And with every pace of the journey now, the tension was increasing, the hair proud on the back of his neck. There was no reason to doubt the loyalty of these scouts, but still Agricola found it hard not to think of the tales of those veteran cavalrymen, and looking across at Luci did little to ease that. They were being led into dangerous lands in an enveloping mist by men who could possibly be their enemies in a false cloak of service.

It was, as Sabinus had noted the last time they were here, perfect terrain for an ambush.

Indeed, the land's familiarity only heightened as they entered the valley with the rocky heights to either side. He was not alone in repeatedly looking up the slopes, expecting howling barbarians to pour from between the rocks at any moment. That they did not did little to reduce the tension.

'I don't like this,' Sabinus said from one side, where he rode with half his horsemen.

'I know. I can feel it too.'

They rode on, closing on the end of the valley. They couldn't see it for the mist, but he knew the narrow path up through the trees was looming ahead. Thus far they had seen no one on their march, just the odd farm off in the distance, either abandoned or with its occupants hiding out of sight. Now, they were nearing the valley, the place with the stone and the three trees. Last time they had been here, the hills had *seemed* silent and empty, and then three people had appeared seemingly out of nowhere. Not a calming thought.

The tension had become so thick they were almost wading through it when he heard the hoof-beats ahead. With a glance around, it was clear the others had heard it too, for all the riders had reined in and their hands had gone to their sword hilts, even Luci reaching towards his small knife. Sabinus threw up a hand in warning and, behind them, the officers and then the rest of the army drew to a halt.

Agricola turned back to the wall of white ahead, between him and it a hundred Batavians sitting astride their horses, ready for trouble, shields up, spears gripped in white knuckles.

He could hear just one horse, though. One horse approaching. How much trouble could it be?'

The rider emerged from the white mist at speed and it took Agricola a moment to identify him as one of the irregular Silurian scouts who had so recently been recruited. His sudden appearance did nothing to reduce the tension enveloping them all just as easily as the cloud of white that shrouded the world. The gaze of most of those visible in the valley roved around their surroundings, peering into the mist, half expecting a threat to suddenly coalesce all about them. Nothing happened, though, and the Batavians separated into two groups to allow the rider, who was unarmed, to pass through their midst.

The scout, probably unfamiliar with the command structure of the Roman army, made directly for the most impressive uniform and brightest plume in evidence, which were Agricola's, towards the fore of the army. He reined in ten paces from the tribune, his horse dancing nervously. The man's face was pale, which did little to lessen Agricola's nerves.

'What is it?'

The scout rattled something off in his own tongue, and Agricola turned and frowned a question at Luci.

'He's not making much sense. Something about gods being angry, something about a sacrifice. And he mentioned the Brithii.'

'Tell him to show us.'

As Luci translated to the frightened-looking native, Agricola beckoned to one of the Batavian riders. 'Go back to the commanders. Inform the legate that we may have a situation ahead and that I am going to investigate. I recommend the army waits here on high alert until we return. Watch the slopes, just in case.'

With that, the rider was gone, delivering his message. Luci had finished speaking to the scout, who was now moving off ahead again, though not looking at all happy about it. Moments later the vanguard moved off after him, Agricola and Luci surrounded by the other seven riders from the Second legion, the Batavians following on, a strong force in support in case of trouble.

It was all very familiar to Agricola as time crawled by. The curve, the road up into the trees between the rocks, then the tops. Here, things became all the more weird and unsettling, for as they exited the treeline onto that high slope, they seemed to have passed through the mist and emerged above it, where a pale blue sky greeted them. Instead of the carpet of trees stretching in all directions, this time the world all around below them was white, the bleak hilltop clear above it all.

'Did you get anything more from him?' he asked Luci as they rode.

'Not really. He's terrified. Frankly, I'm surprised he came back. I have the distinct feeling the other scouts have all run away.'

Then they were down into the valley once more, the mist creeping back over them and then surrounding them, dampening all sound. They passed several more sites that looked very familiar, and then the stone with the markings on. For some reason Agricola was entirely unsurprised to see new designs on it, and his suspicion as to the nature of the reddish-brown pigment deepened.

'What does it say?'

'It's not really words,' Luci replied. 'But it's definitely a warning. Or a threat, perhaps. A little of both.'

'Wonderful.' He turned to the leader of the Batavian riders. 'Be ready for trouble.'

'We always are,' the man grunted in German-inflected Latin.

It came as no surprise when they found themselves atop that slope once more. He could not see the trees for the blanket of fog, but clearly this was where they would find what they were looking for, since the Silurian scout was wide-eyed, ashen faced, and had come to a halt with a clear refusal to go any further. Agricola looked at the others and then gestured to the Batavian officer. 'Leave twenty men with him. The rest of you, follow me.'

With that he rode forward, heading for the small sacred grove. Luci was close, and now Sabinus and his riders had moved to protect them, slightly ahead and to each side. As they walked their horses slowly into the all-concealing mist, he looked down. The turf of the hillside had been churned with hooves recently, and plenty of them. He cursed himself for not having watched the ground earlier for such signs.

Gradually, the scene coalesced in the drifting white. First came the ghostly dark figures of the three trees, reaching up into the unseeable sky, black boles in the white. Then the stone. And then the rest.

Agricola reined in, face set in a rictus, as the others did the same, a number of the men murmuring charms of protection from magic and wicked gods. Hands were uniformly on sword hilts now. The tribune slipped from the saddle and dropped from the horse, handing the reins to Sabinus. Luci did the same, and the two men walked, master and slave side by side, into the nemeton, trepidation evident.

The executions were more than that. They were not merely deaths, but warnings, threats, displays, sacrifices, offerings. All that. All at once.

The three figures were as recognisable as the rest of it. An old man, a woman and a lithe hunter. They could not have been dead more than half a day, but it had probably taken another half day to do all this. Swallowing down the bile that rose in his throat, Agricola stepped around the stone and approached the bodies. The three locals who had met them a few days ago, people of Luci's own tribe, had been bound to one tree each, their arms pulled back around the trunks and bound tight, pulling the shoulders out of joint.

He fought the urge to turn away. He was no stranger to violence, of course. Violence was part of everyday life in the city, from the bodies of unfortunate mugging victims in the backstreets to the occasional bandit hanging from a cross, broken and crow-pecked by the side of a main road. But this was different. This violence was a spectacle that had personal meaning for him. He could not look away. Could not walk away. He had to look, for if he couldn't face this, what would happen when he met the perpetrators in battle?

Each of the three had been smacked in the forehead, just above the eyes, with some narrow-headed weapon or tool, for in each case it had smashed the bone and driven the shards into the brain, a neat circular wound just a finger-width across. Agricola was no expert in things medical, but he'd be willing to bet that the wound had been agonising and debilitating, but not fatal. It would have left them weak and disoriented, unable to struggle as the rest was carried out. Each of the three had a thin cord of metal, a wire of some kind, around their neck, also looping around the bole of the tree, holding their head up. The wire had cut deep into the neck, severing the blood vessels and the windpipe together. The sheer quantity of blood that had soaked down all three, leaving their faces a pale grey, was astonishing, though by now it had soaked into their garments and into the disturbed ground. A quick glance around the other side of a tree confirmed his suspicion. A stick jammed in the wire had the metal looped round and round it. The wire had been slowly tightened, suffocating the victim and then, finally, after a long, slow, agonising time, scything into the flesh.

They had also been eviscerated, their innards hanging down their fronts from opened bellies, like strings of purple sausages, looping in a sticky pile on the ground before them. Again, this probably had not been enough to kill them. They had endured all these wounds at the same time. When finally the wire had cut their throats, it must have been a blessed relief.

He walked back, face sombre, and blinked in surprise at the sight of Luci. Soldiers all around them were holding down the bile, looking horrified as one might expect, but Luci had gone very pale, the only time Agricola had ever seen the slave unmanned so. Agricola was still green to all this, and he had held himself sturdy against the horror – and Luci was both older and more inured to warfare than he.

'What is it?' he murmured.

'The threefold death,' Luci answered, his voice little more than a whisper.

'Never heard of it.'

Luci turned a look on him that was a mix of hate, fear and shock. 'Wherever the druids have gone, either not all went, or they have not gone far. This is their work. We need to take them down. Bury them. Cleanse this place.'

'Why?'

'Because, subdued as they are, if my people see this they will rise again. They will turn on you. This is the druids' call to war. This is their version of your "red spear". Clean it all away.'

As Agricola turned, telling the Batavians to do just that, his eyes fell on the stone amid the lush grass, and he spotted something he'd not seen in passing. A bird had been laid out on the stone, wings widespread. That it was an eagle was clearly yet another part of this great statement. The glorious animal was transfixed with a long iron spike through its middle.

'I take it I don't need an explanation of the meaning of this one,' he grunted, closing his eyes and picturing the eagles that wavered aloft at the head of the legions. Luci simply nodded.

'Right.' Agricola straightened and clapped his hands, seemingly breaking the spell and drawing the eyes of all, bar the score of Batavians who were moving to cut down the bodies.

'Sir?' Sabinus asked.

'I am a soldier of Rome, beloved of Jupiter and Minerva. I am an educated man, and no fool. I will not be cowed or dissuaded by such shows. If these Brithii and their druids think to frighten me with torture, then they understand nothing about me or about Rome. They will pay for their actions, and will soon learn that their druids are not the only ones capable of such displays.'

He looked meaningfully at each of the others.

'This will be cleaned and the bodies buried. When we return to the column, no one here speaks of it. I will present the basic facts to the legate, drawing no attention to the intent to raise the tribes. If the legate hears that, he will expand his advance to obliterate those very Silures the druids seek to recruit. It will undo all our work. We will continue as planned and take the war to the Brithii.'

He allowed a vicious smile to reach his lips as he gestured to the hoof-churned ground beneath him.

'And they have made their first mistake. They left us a trail.'

9

'What's happening?' Agricola said.

Valda, the commander of the Batavians, peered off into the distance. 'Looks like a small group is leaving the place, some mounted, some on foot,' he rumbled in his Germanic tone.

'Do you think they know we're coming?' Sabinus murmured, shading his own eyes to peer across the wide open land at the hillfort.

'Be certain of it,' Luci replied. Agricola found time despite himself to smile. They were a motley collection, his consilium, and nothing highlighted that like a slave speaking to army commanders as though he were one of them, let alone those commanders paying heed. A slave, a veteran legionary rider and a German horseman. Yet they were each good men, and each clever, and he had come to trust them all.

'But if they're abandoning the place because we're coming, why are only a *few* leaving?'

Luci nodded. 'Someone important. They're preparing to fight, but someone is being led away to escape our clutches. I don't know. Their chieftain? An honoured foreigner? A druid?'

'Whoever it is,' Agricola said quietly, 'if they want him out of our clutches, I want him.'

And if he is the man responsible for that display back at the trees, he needs to pay.

Beside him, Valda nodded his agreement. 'But how to go about it?'

Agricola looked behind him. He had the seven other riders from the Second, and a hundred Batavian horsemen. Another glance at the land ahead. This would be his first battle. The first time he had ever drawn a sword in war, yet he had a good grip of what he was facing. He had read his histories and his treatises, knew every battle and siege of Caesar and of Germanicus inside and out, could judge forces and defences like a seasoned general, despite his youth. Or at least, he hoped so.

The hillfort to which the trail had led them occupied a long ridge with forbidding steep slopes on three sides. Atop it, a cluster of huts occupied the summit, which was divided into an upper and lower enclosure by a heavy gate. The whole thing was surrounded by a palisade and the only realistic approach, from the north-east, was protected by a triple wall of earthen banks, each with their own palisade and protected gate, each tier drawing the attacker higher towards the summit while within the reach of defenders above. It was a troublesome proposition, though not enough to withstand the legions for long.

There were maybe a thousand fighting men in the hillfort, and some two hundred gathered at the lower gate, preparing to depart. Of course, the Brithii would be no match for the army when it arrived. The fort was a strong one, but the legate's force numbered some three thousand legionaries and as many auxilia. Six to one odds rather made the fight something of a foregone conclusion, despite the ramparts, but there *would* be losses.

'I reckon that party outnumber us two to one,' Sabinus said. 'I don't like the odds.'

'But if we wait for the army, they'll get away,' Valda pointed out.

Agricola sucked on his teeth, deep in thought. He couldn't let whoever it was get away. That had happened repeatedly with the rebel Caratacus, and had led to repeated risings against Rome. If they could end Silurian resistance here, they should do so – letting anyone in authority escape ran the risk of a protracted war.

The bulk of the army was an hour further back at their standard pace. An army is only as fast as its slowest unit, and in the case of most Roman forces that unit was the wagons that carried the artillery and the supplies. They had been travelling at reasonable speed across the flat lands from the east, but since the grisly nemeton they had been forced to traverse mountain tracks, and the army had slowed by necessity. Agricola, somewhat frustrated, had taken the vanguard ahead, with the legate's permission, to track the enemy, leading them some ten miles north and west. Luci had warned them that they may well actually be in Ordovician territory now, but Agricola was content that the legate, determined not to interfere with the other pushes, would not realise that, and so he wouldn't call attention to it himself.

'We can't challenge them as they leave the place,' he said. 'Two to one odds will become twelve to one if we're too close to the Brithii in their fort, and if we try to contain them we have the same problem. Our only hope is to let them get far enough from the hillfort that we can take them unmolested. The question, then, is where they will go?'

'Not towards us,' Valda replied. 'East and south are out, or they'll walk into Roman arms.'

Luci pointed past the fort, off to the south-west. 'See the flatlands that way? That is the Caron Bog. Miles of ground that can only be crossed slowly and carefully.'

Agricola nodded. 'So we can rule that out. That leaves north or north-west, both towards the Ordovices.'

'You miss the point,' Luci murmured, pointing. 'If you were wanting to stay out of the reach of pursuers, where would you go?'

'Into the bog,' Agricola said, silently cursing for not having thought of that himself. 'Clever. I think you may be right.'

'I reckon it to be two miles from the hillfort to the bog,' Luci said. 'Is that enough distance?'

'Yes. Timing will be tight, though. We want to be far enough from the hillfort that they don't have time to come to the rescue, but ideally we'll catch them before they're in the bog.'

'Only a few of them have horses,' Sabinus noted. 'They'll be moving at walking speed. And the ones in the fort are mostly on foot, while we're a fully mounted force. We can outpace them all easily. We wait until they're nearly there and then break cover. I think we can cross two miles and take them on fast enough that those in the fort will have no chance to catch up. The next question is whether two-to-one odds is realistic.'

The Batavian gave a nasty, gap-toothed grin. 'They're poor odds, but we don't have time to let them get reinforcements.'

Agricola chuckled lightly. He liked the German. Some might think his manner smacked of dangerous overconfidence, and in another unit that may well be the case, but these men had been core to Rome's success in Britannia ever since they'd landed on the island. As he glanced down at the sword by his side, his hand on the pommel, once again he was struck by the fact that the next time he drew it, he would likely have to kill with it. This was no sparring session in the gardens with Jovinus, but real war. He swallowed a touch of nerves. It was moments like this that tested a man. He was determined not to be found lacking.

'Alright, Valda, you're the most experienced combat rider here. We go on your word. In the meantime, detail a man to warn the rest of the horse, and then to ride back to the legate and update him on everything we've found and what we're doing. Try not to mention that we may have strayed into Ordovician lands, though.'

The Batavian called for one of his cavalry and passed on the orders, and then the four men sat silent for a time, hidden from the hillfort's view by the treeline that they melded with like shadows, the rest of the riders even further out of sight beyond the trees. The morning was grey, but bright and dry, the mist of yesterday having disappeared in the evening as they'd made camp nervously in some bleak valley.

The small force at the hillfort's gate were assembled around a single man, though his nature and identity remained hidden beneath a cloak. He was on a horse, though, one of only a dozen in evidence among those departing the hillfort. Agricola felt a pinch of nerves when the group set off as for a time it seemed they were going to take an easy path north instead. The Romans would still follow and catch up, but they would have further to go, and timings would be harder. Then, to his relief, they changed direction, making for the great bog and their plan fell back into place. Four riders took the lead, moving at a brisk walking pace, two hundred warriors following on foot, with another pair of riders bringing up the rear. The rest of the mounted men rode in the centre, clustered around whoever it was they were protecting.

Tension rose with every passing moment. The departing force grew ever more distant, making for the bog, while at the hillfort it became clear that the occupants knew that Rome was coming, for they were barring and reinforcing the gates, manning the walls and preparing fires here and there.

'I had not taken the Brithii for fools,' Luci said quietly, watching.

'What?'

'They are warlike, but I've never found them to be stupid. They have to know the might of the force that is coming for them, yet they stay. They save one man, but are they foolish enough to sacrifice every fighting man of the tribe to protect him? They will make the fight hard with their defences, but they must know that they are doomed and will be overcome. So why stay? Why not run north to join allies?'

Agricola nodded. It did seem foolish. 'Then they must believe they will win. But how? Outnumbered as they are, how can they hope to win?'

'Perhaps they do not know how many Romans they face? Perhaps they have tricks up their sleeve? Maybe there are reinforcements we don't know about? Or even the dead that lie scattered in these lands. Perhaps the Morrigan will call them back from their graves to face us. Maybe the gods are with them,' Luci said. 'Maybe I have sealed my own fate by riding with you, and the Brithii are destined to win here and restore the land to my people.'

Agricola narrowed his eyes at the slave. Luci shrugged. 'Just a thought.'

'Try not to think it.'

'We should go,' Valda said.

Sabinus frowned. 'They're still some way from the bog. We have time.'

'Against those on foot. If the riders decide to run, we may not catch them. We need to go now.'

And with that, and a nod from Agricola, the Batavian put two fingers in his mouth and blew a shrill whistle. The riders behind the trees gave a loud whoop in answer. As the Batavians burst clear of the treeline, a savage hunting party riding full pelt from the off, whooping and shaking their spears, Agricola and the others kicked their own horses into action and joined in, shouting curses for the enemy and pleas to the gods as they hurtled down the slope.

They raced past a long-abandoned cluster of roundhouses, eyes darting back and forth between the hillfort and their quarry, the small force already approaching the edge of the great bog that was visible at this distance only as an oily smear on the horizon. Already, even as they began the chase, the alarm had gone up among the Brithii on that ramparted hillside. Figures were hurtling this way and that, abandoning their fortification work with the sudden knowledge that whoever they'd devoted such effort to saving was in danger. They would not be trouble, though. Agricola and his men would be long past, racing around the southern slope of the hill, before the Brithii could do anything to intervene. They might just catch them on the return, when it was all over, but it would be too late then.

Another flutter of nerves at that thought. To be trapped. Caught between the bog and the Brithii. And given what they had seen back at the nemeton, he could only imagine the fate that awaited a Roman officer who had the ill fortune to be captured.

He found that he was having to push his animal to keep up with his men. His horse was fast, but the mounted section of the Batavi cohort all but lived in the saddle, and they swept across the low grasslands, parallel with a glistening, clear river, with the speed of a diving hawk.

Then they were past, any danger presented by the hillfort forgotten as it shrank in their wake, the panicked occupants only now beginning to pour from the gates in pursuit, mostly on foot and with no hope of catching them.

Ahead, the two-hundred strong party had now realised they were being pursued and had begun to pick up their pace. Agricola willed them to slow, silently implored the gods to throw some impediment in their way. Once the escapees realised they were never going to make the bog without being caught, for Valda's timing had been perfect, things changed once more. He could see their force separating and knew what was happening. The cloaked figure and his small party of mounted men would continue to ride as fast as they could for the perceived safety of the bog, while the infantry would turn and defend them, buying them time to escape. It was clearly their intention, for it was precisely what Agricola would do in their position. He looked about him. They had to get past the infantry and take those riders before it was too late, and he was their commander. It had to be he who led the advance, no matter that he'd yet to be tested in battle. Every warrior would have his first time at some point. The Batavians would have to do the bulk of the killing, then.

'Valda, you and your men take on the infantry. Buy us time.'

The Batavian frowned, but nodded. It was not that he misunderstood, nor even disagreed with the plan, but more that the Batavi disliked being kept from the heart of any fight. It was said of their men that if they drew their blades, they had to be bloodied before being sheathed again, and if they couldn't sink steel into an enemy's flesh, they would take their own in shame. Still, the Germans would be outnumbered even by the footmen alone, so there was little chance of them missing out on the fighting, even if they were not to chase the riders down.

As the orders were bellowed in the Germanic tongue with all its growls and sharp edges, Agricola motioned to Sabinus. 'Apart from our quarry, there are eleven riders. There are nine of us. We will have to fight hard and fast. Take half the men around the left, and I'll take the rest around the right. Don't get bogged down with the infantry. Leave them for Valda and his riders.'

Sabinus nodded. His eyes momentarily slipped to Luci, who was riding at Agricola's back but who, being a slave and unarmed, had not been included in the number. Then he was off, jabbing a finger at four men to follow him. The other three closed on Agricola and Luci.

'Can you use a spear?' he asked the slave.

Luci seemed to weigh this up for a moment. 'I *can*,' he said, filling the stressed word with the unwritten message that he might not want to.

Agricola looked ahead. They had only moments. He gestured to one of the riders and then looked back to Luci.

'These are not your people, remember. They will not think twice about killing you. If you won't fight for me, at least defend yourself. I paid a lot of money for you,' he added with a grim smile.

Luci kept his glare up for a moment, but then grasped the spear one of the legionary cavalry was holding out to him. As he took it and couched it ready for a fight, the donor instead drew his long sword and hefted it.

They reached the enemy force at the same time, the two outlying sets of legionary cavalry and central force of Batavians, and the carnage began. The Batavians, weapons brandished ready, hit the unmounted Brithii like a hammer, smashing into the mass and sending bodies scattered this way and that, blood from a score of brutal wounds fountaining into the air, only to fall again as a gentle, warm mizzle. Swords scythed into unprotected flesh, most of the natives equipped with only a woollen tunic and perhaps an old shield. Spears impaled men, snapping as often as not, and their wielders simply let go of embedded weapons and drew their swords, or struck again with the splintered shaft of a part-broken spear, driving the jagged wood itself into men's chests, bellies and backs.

As the Batavians became bogged down in the battle, Agricola's attention shifted from them, for he had his own problems. He and the regulars raced around the periphery, but the Brithii were desperate to stop them and protect the fleeing riders, and so, heedless of the danger they placed themselves in with the Batavi, a number of the warriors turned and tried to stop the outlying riders. Two of them leapt for the officer in his attention-drawing cuirass and plume. He was not going to be able to stop both. The fear fluttered back into his heart at the realisation. He was on his own. He could not rely on Luci or the other riders, for each of them was in a similar situation. He had only his own arm, his own blade, his own mettle. A time of testing.

He swallowed down his fear in that blink of an eye, a momentary prayer to Mars, and then he made his move. Without time for any grand plan, he selected the most dangerous-looking of the pair and swung wide with his sword, smashing it into the side of a man's head, crushing his cheek bone and eye socket, sending a mess of blood and bone flying through the air. The man fell away, shrieking. He felt a numbness flood up his arm from the impact, but it seemed also to grasp his heart and clutch it. He had killed a man, but had no time to reflect on it, for to pause now was to risk following the warrior to the grave.

The second attacker had tried to sink his blade into the belly of Agricola's horse and, though he'd failed in the press and with the speed of the animal, he'd not *entirely* missed. His sword had drawn a line of red across the horse's side before he was thrown down and tumbled, broken and pulverised beneath the beast's hooves.

Then Agricola was out, free, racing past them. His mount

was whinnying, and its side had to be sore, but the wound was far from fatal and in moments the horse had recovered its composure. He looked about him, shaking. The initial clash was done, and he'd not been unmanned by it. There was something in the numbness of his heart that suggested he may pay for it later, but for now he was suddenly confident that he could do this. He could lead them, and he could win.

One of the legionary riders with him had lost his shield, his left arm hanging by his side, soaked with blood, but his sword was still gripped in the other, and his expression was determined as he continued to steer the animal with his knees.

He gave the seething mass of Briton warriors a wide berth now, his eyes locked on the fleeing riders ahead. Twelve of them, eleven with spears, several wearing shirts of chain, the central figure wrapped in a thick cloak, still obfuscated even now. Agricola fretted. He had to head them off, though the enemy were already moving into the edge of the bogland, visible where the green of the fields gradually and patchily gave way to the brown fens. He frowned for a moment, realising that the fugitives had turned slightly southwards, angling across ahead of him at a tangent, and cutting them off would be easy enough and would save considerable time. The others had had similar ideas, and the riders from the Second uniformly turned their mounts, angling to head the enemy off, though of them all, Luci kept his original course, bellowing for them to stay with him.

Agricola realised why only a moment later. His gaze still on their prey, he saw one of the fleeing riders arc out a little too far left of the party. He saw horse and rider stumble as they sank into the fens and the deep water beneath, the animal screaming in panic, the rider thrown clear into the reeds, where he slowly began to sink, desperate hands grasping at reeds and long grass in an effort to keep himself above the surface. His chain shirt was heavy, though, along with his wool clothes and the sword belted at his side, and the man disappeared soon enough, arm still desperately flailing above the surface, looking for some way to pull himself back up, then finally stiffening, going limp and following its owner under the stinking, stagnant water.

The young tribune felt a whole new icy grip of fear now, far beyond the mortal peril of war.

'Fuck,' bellowed one of the legionaries with feeling, echoing Agricola's own sentiments as the entire unit turned and formed once more on Luci, following the path their quarry had taken and not risking diverting from their trail.

They reached the bog, the safe route visible only because of the churned tracks of the riders in front, and pulled into a line two abreast, each of them horribly aware now of the fate that awaited the careless.

They were going to lose them. That was unpleasantly clear straight away. The enemy were going at a good pace, and Agricola and his men could realistically go no faster without risking their own demise. Still, with no other choice, he ploughed on, Sabinus at his side, Luci and the other riders close behind.

'Damn it,' Sabinus said, turning to Agricola. 'Permission to do something stupid, sir?'

Agricola, puffing and panting from the exertion of the ride and still shocked at the fresh danger of the fens, nodded. Whatever it was the man had planned, they had to do *something*.

The decurion took a deep breath and then turned his horse towards the fleeing enemies, who had continued to turn and were now travelling at right-angles to their pursuers. Before Agricola could shout and tell the man to stop, Sabinus was off, racing across the unmarked land, ignoring the tracks they were following and risking wet, sucking death with every pounding of the hooves. Agricola watched in horror and astonishment. Every moment, he expected Sabinus to vanish with a cry, or his horse to break a leg and throw him. One of the other cavalrymen made to follow his commander but Agricola bellowed hoarsely for the man to stay where he was. Sabinus was almost certainly doomed, and he wasn't going to risk a second cavalryman to the same fate.

Yet even as he watched, panic and horror filling him, he found a kernel of hope. The decurion seemed to be almost there. The bog had not claimed him yet, and he continued to angle more and more left now, a route that would put him directly in the path of their prey.

'Jupiter, Mars and Minerva... and Neptune,' he added as an afterthought, eying the dangerous waters, 'an altar to each of you if you let him live.'

He was, of course, acutely aware that he already owed Neptune for their crossing to Britannia. The amount of work he was going to be giving stonemasons the moment they settled for the winter would be costly at this rate.

But the gods were apparently listening. Even as Agricola watched, his heart in his mouth, Sabinus reached the path right in front of the fleeing Brithii, where he brought his horse to a halt, settling his shield, sword up and ready. The enemy slowed, their path blocked.

'Now we have a chance,' Agricola said, kicking his horse into increased speed. It was dangerous to go so fast, though not so dangerous as the idiotic bravery of Sabinus, for at least they had a trail to follow. They were closing on the rear of the small party. He felt the success of their chase now, where moments ago it had seemed they must lose the fleeing figures. Around him men gripped swords, held forth high, ready to strike. They were still riding double file, keeping carefully away from the margins of the path where the dangerous fens lay, and Agricola was dividing his attention between the enemy ahead and the path he followed when he looked up and realised that they were no longer alone.

'What in the name of Jove?'

Luci, riding behind him, had apparently seen it too. Whatever he said was in his own incomprehensible tongue, but it was most definitely a curse. Ahead, past the fleeing riders, and even past Sabinus where he sat like a Titan of old awaiting them, shapes had appeared on the horizon. As Agricola's eyes focused on the distance, he realised what they were. Many flat-bottomed craft were snaking through the wet and clearly coming their way, slowly coalescing, each loaded with figures.

'Who are they?'

'I don't know,' Luci said. 'Ordovices maybe? Or another western tribe of the Silures? Whoever they are, they've come to help the Brithii, I reckon.'

Agricola felt things fall into place. That was why the Brithii were staying, preparing to fight. The odds would not be as bad as it seemed, for they had allies on the way. His memory furnished him with a moment from Caesar's war diaries. Alesia, his greatest victory, which had almost been his greatest defeat, trapped as he was between the Gauls on their hilltop and a reserve force that had come up behind them unexpectedly. How history repeats itself. He couldn't yet make a reasonable count of them, many still emerging in the distance, but they would number sufficient to make the battle a much harder fight. *That* was what this figure was doing. Not fleeing, but meeting their allies.

Agricola clenched his teeth. And if one man was important enough to send to meet them, then his demise might be enough to change things. He urged his horse into a gallop, heedless of the sucking morass that lay to either side of the path. One slip, one wrong move, and it could be him sinking beneath the surface, just a questing hand rising from the water to show where he died. He shuddered. The path between him and the enemy was more or less straight now and, gritting his teeth, he put his fate in the hands of the gods, taking his eyes from the trail below and locking them on his quarry.

The enemy had slowed, the implacable decurion blocking their path, and now stopped, their vanguard facing Sabinus. The enemy were happy to bide their time and wait for the boats to reach them, at which point Agricola and his men would be hopelessly outnumbered. There was a fresh moment of doubt, then. Everything he'd done so far had happened too quickly, too instinctively for him to worry too much about it. This? This was a moment when he may just face insurmountable odds. They could still withdraw. Still escape.

The gods gripped the dice. Shook. Cast.

Agricola's jaw hardened.

'To battle!' he bellowed, urging all his men to the fight.

Ahead, he just had time to see Sabinus start to move before he was on them himself. The rear riders, aware that they were in extreme danger, turned, and Agricola watched in grim satisfaction as one of them slipped during the manoeuvre, his horse's leg finding no purchase as it met the wet slope. The animal lurched to the side with a scream and both it and its rider disappeared into the mire with cries of panic.

The warrior's companion barely had time to register the man's demise and his own danger before Agricola was on him. The trepidation he'd felt with that first kill was gone now, the unknown nature of battle torn away with brutal experience.

He hit the man hard, their horses colliding, pushing the rider back into his own allies. As he did so, his sword came round, slamming into the warrior's arm just above the elbow, cleaving a deep wound, smashing the bone. Nothing this time. No shock. No numbness. Just the need to win. Even as he finished the man off, one of the legionary riders was beside him, slamming into the mass of Brithii. Their combined charge had a startling effect. Pressed together, trapped between the implacable Sabinus and their pursuers, there simply was not enough room on the causeway for the riders, many of whom were turning their horses this way and that, trying to face one of the threats. Two more of the Brithii fell away to the sides, disappearing into the morass.

They were thinning out and, even though they were now ready, weapons out, preparing to fight off their attackers, they had gone from outnumbering Agricola's riders and irretrievably ahead of them to being outnumbered and trapped by them. Another warrior was suddenly in front of Agricola, heaving his previous victim out of the way. The man's spear thrust out and narrowly missed him, tearing a corner from his saddle horn before whipping away into open air to be batted aside by another rider. Agricola's sword came down hard in an overhand blow that landed on the man's shoulder, near the neck. The warrior shrieked as blood fountained up from the wound, his head turning away, arm falling limp. Agricola, taken by the adrenaline of battle now, did not give him a second thought. His eyes had fallen upon a figure slightly ahead instead, and he pushed on past the injured rider, leaving him to the others. The cloaked man was almost in reach. Beside the man another rider fell, fighting off one of the legionary horsemen and toppled, wounded, from the saddle to disappear into the fens.

They were almost clear. Their assault on the Brithii had been brutal and fast, and they had carved a bloody path through them now that they had caught up. The figure in the cloak turned, then, somehow aware of the danger, his eyes falling on Agricola. The man had curly hair, almost gone from black to ageing grey, odd flecks of dark here and there. His face was pale and age-worn, the skin mere parchment. He wore a circlet of gold on his brow, just visible beneath the edge of the hood.

Agricola made his move. Ignoring someone trying to swipe a long Celtic blade at him, ducking away from the swing, he barged past to reach the cloaked man, his sword coming up. In moments, he had the tip of his blade at the old man's throat.

He had to be a druid. Or a king, perhaps – but from what he'd read, this would fit that dangerous class of priests and teachers who drove the tribes of the north. All around him the fighting stopped, the few remaining Brithii riders aware that their master was in peril. Agricola had him now. One push of the blade and the man would die, and both he, the druid, and all present knew it.

'You can live,' he told the druid. The man's eyes narrowed, confirming that he'd understood. The man knew Latin, at least enough to grasp this. Agricola looked up past the man at the approaching boats full of warriors, each navigating carefully through the dangerous bog. What would they do if the druid died?

'Tell them to depart. We don't want a war of annihilation.'

This time the man didn't seem to follow his words, but Luci was there now, translating. The cloaked man reached up and pulled his hood back, looking into Agricola's eyes. The Roman saw there only defiance, and realised in that moment this was not going to end well. He took a breath to try again, this time focusing on the survival of the tribe as an objective, but before he could speak, the old man pushed himself forward onto the blade, the metal slashing into his neck. Blood began to spray and gush as he fell back away. A cry of dismay went up from the Brithii all around them, but they were done for. Agricola's riders finished them off swiftly now as the boats closed on them.

The druid, for that was surely what he had to be, lolled in the saddle, dying by degrees as the blood drained from him, lifted his arms to shout something, turning to face the approaching boats. Somehow, Agricola felt certain anything the man said to the reinforcements would be bad for the Romans, so he stepped his horse two paces forward and struck again, this time driving his sword into the man's back. The druid stiffened, letting out a reedy breath, and sagged.

The tribune pulled his blade free as the druid slipped sideways and slid from the horse. This time, there was no indecision, no worry, only an implacable realisation that he'd done what he'd had to do. There was a strange pause, a silence as though the world was holding its breath. The Brithii riders were all down now, two riderless Roman horses demonstrating that the fight had not been all one-sided.

Agricola's gaze rose from the body of the druid, almost certainly the man who had performed the grisly sacrifices on the Silurians at the three trees, to fall on the approaching boats. They had stopped, their oars raised and dripping into the water.

'Go home,' he said loudly, then gestured to Luci, who translated in a booming voice across the water. No one moved.

'The Brithii have chosen to die. The might of Rome even now closes on their fort, and by nightfall only the crows will live within its walls as they pick over the bodies. But that does not have to be *your* fate. The Silures are part of the empire now, and we protect our own. Choose wisely.'

He fell silent. There was no sound but the occasional drip of water and gust of wind. The tension flowed through him. If those boats came on, the army rushing to the aid of the Brithii, this could turn into a real struggle. For a moment, he considered a conciliatory approach, an appeal to the Pax Romana, but then his eyes fell on the body of the druid and he remembered the threefold death. These people would respect only strength.

'Choose to live, or choose to die. That is all.'

More silence. The riders sat there on the causeway, the tension high for a moment until, almost in unison, the boats splashed oars into water, turning slowly and retreating into the bog, like some nightmare fading with the light.

Agricola heaved a sigh of relief as he watched the tide of vessels and unidentified tribesmen that had emerged from the horizon swiftly disappear from view once more, leaving, after no more than fifty heartbeats, just an empty marsh and the distant, faint sound of splashing oars. When they were finally alone, he turned. Far back, beyond the edge of the bog, he could see the Batavians finishing off the last resistance of the infantry.

They'd done it.

His gaze slid past them to the hillfort beyond. Somehow, from here it did not seem half as difficult a proposition, although perhaps that was more a response to the euphoria of personal victory than to a different geographical perspective.

His exhilaration was almost his undoing for, focusing on the future, he had failed to notice that one of the downed riders close by was not quite dead after all, and had managed to grip a fallen spear and lift it. Fortunately, the man was lacking in strength, close to the end, and the tip of the spear failed to strike home properly, instead clanging off Agricola's cuirass and scratching a narrow red mark across his forearm. He hissed and turned his horse, the hoof stamping down on his would-be assassin, finishing him off.

Agricola looked up. Luci was watching, spear in hand.

'You decided not to help?'

The slave shrugged. 'I have been unsure. Sometimes it is good to know who the gods favour before deciding. It seems they favour you, domine, and so perhaps I have not chosen wrongly after all.'

Agricola snorted. 'I am pleased, then, to have been so *chosen*.'

Gesturing to the others, he pointed down to the druid's body. 'Bring him with you.'

Seven riders remained of the ten who had pursued the Brithii into the bog, which Agricola had to acknowledge was an unexpectedly positive result, and highly suggestive of divine favour. Luci and the staunch Sabinus rode with him, behind them the four cavalrymen, one with the druid's body across the saddle in front of him. Back on solid ground, they approached the Batavi, and Valda pulled his horse out from the press, stepping forward to meet them. The man was liberally coated with blood spatter, and it was hard not to focus on the severed head tied by the hair to his saddle horn, bouncing around with every movement of the horse, trailing tendrils of unpleasantness.

'The gods favour us, tribune,' the German called with a grin, white teeth amid the red.

'My slave said much the same. Losses?'

'Negligible, all things considered.'

'And that?' he asked, pointing at the head.

'I find trophies like this take the fight out of other enemies. We'll put them on spears for the Brithii to see.'

Agricola nodded. 'I had a similar idea. We have the druid. He was on his way to usher in some friends to help the Brithii, but the reinforcements rather lost heart when he expired in front of them.'

Valda raised an eyebrow, looking past him into the bog, then nodded. Joining forces once more, they rode back towards the hillside where they'd waited and watched. Aware that they'd failed to save the druid, the hillfort's occupants had abandoned their chase and returned to their defences, bolstering the gates ready for trouble. Still, rather than tempt fate, Agricola and his party skirted them in a wide arc on their way back, and then settled before the treeline once again.

'Shall we show them our prizes?' Valda said.

Agricola shook his head. 'They outnumber us heavily, and that might provoke an unexpected response. Let's wait until the army gets here.'

And so they sat and watched the Brithii prepare for perhaps half an hour before the vanguard of Geminus' army appeared across the hillside, the drum and rumble of thousands of men behind them. The men and officers nodded their respectful greetings as they passed and fell into position, forming lines on the hillside facing the hillfort across the open ground. The legate was close to the front, now on a horse, having forsaken his carriage, and there was a look of extreme discomfort about him from the activity.

'Tribune,' he greeted Agricola, just a curt nod from Emeritus. 'You have a report for me?'

As the army slowly assembled around them, Agricola ran over everything that had happened, from their arrival and their pursuit of the druid to the man's death and the retreat of the unknown boatmen. As he finally concluded, he sat back in the saddle. 'I do believe that this is the last resistance we will face among the Silures.'

Geminus' brow creased. His eyes glittered. 'I am disappointed in you, Gnaeus Julius Agricola.'

'Sir?'

'What glory is there in this?' the legate sneered, indicating the hillfort facing them with a sweep of his arm. 'A few hundred fugitives shut up in a glorified farmyard? The men will barely notice them underfoot. We'll be done and moving on by mid-afternoon.'

'Sir, whether it be a thousand men or a dozen, they are defiant and they are the last resistance among the Silures. Their destruction will be of note to both the governor and Rome, no matter how it comes about.'

'If you had let your boats come, we would have had a *proper* victory.'

'Sir, it took only three hundred Spartans to make a military legend that has lasted five hundred years.'

The legate simply grunted as a reply, then rubbed his sore side and gave a little groan. 'You have done enough. You may sit this one out, tribune. See to the disposition of the supply train. I will take personal command of the storming of the Silurian fort.' Beside him, Emeritus said nothing, but it was hard to mistake the smugness in the man's expression. Agricola turned to his men as the commander rode off. 'Have the druid's body crucified. I don't care whether it's part of our strategy or not, it's the least he deserves for what he did at the nemeton.'

Sabinus saluted. 'And you, sir?'

'Me?' Agricola said with a bitter smile. 'I'll be with the baggage.'

IO

Agricola glanced to his side with a certain bitterness. Claudius Emeritus was the last man he would ever choose as a companion, yet here they were, side by side, sharing a task.

And yet, in a way, he was lucky to be included back in the staff at all, so he should be grateful.

The fight at the Brithii hillfort had been short and very, very brutal. Agricola had missed almost all of it, of course, watching the action from the hillside in frustration as the various teamsters and quartermasters badgered him repeatedly with questions over supply minutiae. He answered each query as best he could, naturally, despite his frustration. His mother and his teachers in Massilia had drilled into him that one principle above all: if you do anything, always do it to the best of your ability. But still, he had longed to be involved in the action. Luci, similarly, had looked rather frustrated. Not so the Batavi, for despite Agricola being sidelined with his personal cavalry, the Germans had been required for the fight.

The legions had swept up at the fort in droves, and it had not taken long for them to take the first and then second gates, beating back the enemy with, Agricola suspected, more significant losses than were truly necessary. The third gate took a little more work, for the Brithii fought hard and to the last. But of all the brutality, the worst was what came when the last defender had fallen.

With a good four hours of daylight left, they could easily have buried the dead and moved on, away from the charnel smell of the place. But not this time. Agricola had been party to the legate's decision when there had been a lull in the supply situation and he'd managed to spend a little time with the other officers.

'We have control?' Geminus had said.

Emeritus, given direct control of the fight and returning, spotless and untouched, from the front lines, had nodded. 'The place is ours, sir. Not one voice cries out for mercy.'

'Good. How many did you kill?'

'Sir?'

'How many, man?'

Emeritus, somewhat nonplussed, had turned to the fort. 'We did no headcount, sir, but I would say somewhere in the region of a thousand.'

'Five thousand, you say?'

There was a pause. Even the smarmy tribune was a little baffled by this. 'No, sir. A thousand.'

'I would say it was *six* thousand, even.'

Emeritus looked about in confusion and caught sight of the other senior tribune, Cornelius, behind the legate, miming a laurel wreath about his head and prancing around in a chariot. As the legate realised Emeritus was looking past him and turned, Cornelius had just stopped larking about and was standing at attention. He glared at the man suspiciously. Understanding dawned upon Emeritus. By ancient tradition, a triumph could only be awarded to a general who had slain more than five thousand enemies of Rome in a single battle. To his credit, even Emeritus looked rather unimpressed by this.

'Sir, everyone here has seen the butcher's bill. It would be rather hard to support such a number.'

'Would it?' Geminus said, his voice a little high and squeaky. 'Would it really?'

There was an uncomfortable silence. Finally, the legate harrumphed. 'We will camp here tonight. I will pen a message to both the governor and to the senate back in Rome, notifying them of our glorious and *final* victory over the dangerous Silures, who fielded *seven* thousand warriors this day. You do what you have to do, Claudius Emeritus.'

Emeritus watched the commander leave, clearly troubled by his words. He did not look happy, but finally he gestured to Cornelius and to the gathered senior centurions.

'Have the men begin digging a grave for the dead. Detail a work party of men who can be trusted to keep their mouths shut, and offer them a healthy bonus for their work. They are to move around the hillfort and gather the bodies in sacks for burial. If there are less than seven thousand of them, cut them into various pieces and bury the parts separately. I don't care how many souls perished here, there will be no less than seven thousand burials. Do you understand?'

They did. They were not happy, but they went about their work. As the officers vanished, Emeritus caught sight of Agricola.

'What?'

Agricola shrugged. In actual fact, he was rather impressed by the man's ingenuity. 'Nothing. An elegant solution to a thorny problem.' He sighed. 'You know he's mad, yes?'

Emeritus fixed him with a look. 'No. He is the commander. His word on the battlefield might as well be the word of Mars himself. You would do well to remember that, my provincial friend.'

Agricola bridled, but at that moment another of the endless stream of quartermasters' assistants approached him with a question about grain storage.

And so there, that night, they witnessed the burial of seven thousand bags, some no larger than a head. Agricola had broken his own code of campaign conduct and drunk himself to sleep that night, but if he'd needed any confirmation that such an act was appropriate, it was that Luci did the same and made no attempt to run.

His sleep was not to last, though, for an odd situation arose that night. Alerted by one of his bodyguard, Agricola had pulled himself from quiet oblivion, wrapped himself in a cloak over his sleeping tunic, and hurried out into the night of the camp. Between small units of worried-looking officers and past Cornelius, bearing a strange expression, he reached a strange tableau. The legate, still in his daytime uniform, crumpled and worn, swaying a little and clearly still drunk, was standing before the cross upon which hung the corpse of the druid they had caught. Half a dozen legionaries were at work with their unit's priest, scoring prayers and curses into lead tablets and then nailing them to the body of the druid, who was already decorated with a dozen such items, each one hammered into bone, no blood welling up, for it had long since drained from the body.

'Sir?' He'd approached the legate with care, and when Geminus turned, the man's eyes were a strange mix of dark anger and panic.

'It's the druids,' the man hissed, as though that explained everything.

'Sir?'

'My illness. I realise it now. Two years ago I was hale and hearty, but then I was assigned to this benighted island, and now here I am with the shades of Hades clawing at my feet. I should have realised earlier. It's *their* doing. Their magic. It *has* to be.'

Agricola shared a look with Cornelius, for each of them had their own more realistic idea of the source of the commander's ailment. Still, it did not do to gainsay a superior officer, even a drunken and slightly moonstruck one.

'Their magic is infamous,' Agricola said, noncommittally.

Geminus nodded as though this was confirmation. 'I am told that they all talk to each other, even over distances. That their magic allows them to speak from beyond the grave, and so I am taking action, tribune. I curse all druids and seek protection from them through the rotting body of this specimen. And when we find another, I shall do the same. Again, and again, and again, until I—'

He never got any further, for the pain in his side gripped him again and he hissed and clutched his liver, glaring at the body on the cross. Telling his clerks and priest to continue their work, he slunk painfully back to his tent.

'What do we do?' Cornelius muttered, pulling him aside away from the soldiers.

'What *can* we do? He's the commander. At least his madness is aimed at the enemy,' Agricola added, gesturing to three legionaries carrying bags of body parts for burial even this late into the night. They shared another look, this time helpless, and retired for the night with a new set of worries.

The next day they had moved on. The battle was over, the defences slighted, the dead buried, the lie maintained. They travelled south, along the western edge of the lands of the Silures. It was clear, to Agricola at least, that it was these people, the western tribes of the Silures, who'd yet to meet Roman steel, who had been the occupants of those boats that had turned back in the bog. Now they watched the arrival of the passing Roman army with glowers of beaten resentment. There was not a hint of insurrection or resistance among them, though. They knew how the land now lay, and they had accepted it, no matter how badly it sat with them. It would be the governor's next job, once the west was under control, to make sure the tribes were fully integrated into the empire as content, tax-paying individuals. But for now they would sit and grumble, at least causing no open dissent, while the army rolled on.

As they marched south, Agricola began to fear more and more for the legate.

Lucius Valerius Geminus was in a visible decline, and the matter escaped the attention of no one who came anywhere near him. His drinking had only increased since they had left Viroconium, and had now reached the point where Agricola had yet to see him awake without a cup of unwatered wine in hand. He'd even been approached in a worried manner by one of the legate's body slaves, who'd been in attendance upon Geminus at his bath where the man had fallen asleep with a cup of some locally distilled nightmare in his hand and had slid beneath the water and almost drowned.

Yet it was not the drinking that bothered him, per se. Let Geminus drink, if he wanted, for the commander was no longer a young man, and this would be his last great stand as a soldier. But the problem was twofold. Firstly, it left the man in physical pain and in an increasingly common state of delirium, as was becoming more and more manifest with every passing day. Secondly, because Geminus was pained, drunk, and made less sense than a forum puppet show, the legate was increasingly delegating duties to Emeritus as the other senior officer in the force. Thus, as they moved south, more and more often they found that the legate would not leave his tent or wagon, attended by physicians, local herbalists and sycophants, leaving Agricola and Emeritus in effective command of the force.

And that was how Agricola now found himself riding side by side with the man at the head of the army, approaching the Demetae. In fact, they had been in Demetae lands for the last day or so, according to Luci, and the small farms and villages they had passed had watched them with more interest than fear or hatred. Rome was a new thing to them, a thing of which they had only heard from their neighbours.

This, though, appeared to be some important settlement, the first such they had found. Many days south and west, far from the site of their 'great victory', they found themselves looking up at the lofty earth ramparts and timber palisade of a hillfort that rose beside a river. As they approached, a mounted party appeared in the fort's gateway, a group of some thirty figures, and began to make their way, slow and stately, down the slope towards Agricola and Emeritus. Batavians and legionary cavalry fanned out protectively, but it was clear from the manner of the Demetae that this was no attack. They were armed, all, but their weapons remained sheathed, and they were unarmoured and without shields. Three men were clearly nobles of some sort, the rest their retinue.

The two tribunes reined in and let the natives approach.

'An easy peace, yes?' Agricola said, eyeing his companion.

'If they are amenable.'

As they came closer, Agricola was impressed. 'Royalty, perhaps?'

The three men were dripping with gold, gleaming arm-rings wrapping their biceps, ornate golden bracelets on their wrists, torcs, circlets, rings, belt buckles. In truth, Agricola had never seen so much gold on one man, even in the senate.

'The Demetae are rich, it would seem,' Emeritus mused.

Agricola turned to Luci, at his shoulder, a question in his gaze.

'They have gold mines,' Luci confirmed. 'We will have travelled not far from them on our approach for they are close to Silurian lands. It was always a cause of trouble between our peoples.'

Agricola nodded. A rich people. And if they could be brought into the empire without suffering in war, they would be ready to pay taxes and become a source of wealth for Rome almost straight away. And the land hereabouts looked like good agricultural ground, too, so it seemed likely there would be plentiful grain. There was much to gain here for no real outlay. The Romans waited as the Demetae chieftains approached, reining in their horses some twenty paces from the tribunes. A man was summoned from among their retinue and he rode his horse out close to the three leaders.

'Kings Bellicianus, Sualis, Hisavus, greet Rome,' the man said in a loud voice and in rather cracked and very heavily accented Latin.

Agricola bowed his head. 'On behalf of the governor, Suetonius Paulinus, the emperor, and the senate and people of Rome, I bring you greetings. The governor has been informed that the Demetae have an interest in coming to favourable terms with Rome?'

The man on the horse seemed to struggle with this, and so Agricola glanced at Luci, who translated clearly in their native tongue. The three kings listened with interest, and Agricola was relieved to see nods. They had not been misinformed. A peaceful assimilation of the tribe would save a great deal of time and bloodshed, and would be better for all concerned.

The local interpreter was sent back into the crowd, and the central chieftain looked to Luci as he spoke.

'It is said,' the slave translated, 'that there are tribes in the east of the island who live as they always have, with their kings and their families, in their ancient homes, with their own gods, their own nobles and their own peoples, whom Rome respects and does not wish to crush. This is the truth?'

Emeritus nodded. 'Tribes such as the Iceni have been allied to Rome since we arrived and have continued without trouble, in return for certain guarantees and concessions. Indeed, the Brigantes to the north have positively *prospered* with our alliance. Rome offers peace. All we ask is your people pay a tax in return for many benefits offered.'

Agricola winced. Concessions? Was the man deliberately trying to sabotage their chance of peace? One of the kings looked suspicious, too. 'There are bandit chiefs who offer security for a tax,' the man said. 'How is Rome different?'

Agricola leaned forward. 'All a bandit offers is safety from his men. Rome brings builders, engineers, traders. Houses with warm floors, clean running water even in high places. Temples and markets.'

'And miners,' Emeritus said, eyes narrowing.

Agricola frowned and shot him a look. 'What?'

The other tribune gestured to the three men. 'Your people mine gold, but I can assure you that Rome's mining companies will be far more productive and efficient. You sign over your mining to Rome and we will install professional concerns that will bring gold from your hills in quantities you could only imagine. You can receive a cut that equals anything you have produced yourselves, with the excess going to Rome and to the mine owners.'

The Demetae had acquired once more that guarded look

they'd had when comparing the Pax Romana to the protection rackets of bandit chiefs. Agricola could see the hope of a speedy and easy deal crumbling before him and leapt to halt the decline.

'Such matters are for discussion later between yourselves and representatives of the governor, but rest assured,' he added with a sidelong glance at Emeritus, 'nothing will be imposed upon you without your freely given consent. Rome seeks peace and mutual prosperity with the Demetae, not an imposition of imperial control. This will be alliance, not conquest.'

There was a long silence as the three kings murmured among themselves quietly in their own language. Agricola was aware that Emeritus was glaring at him, but he ignored the man. The lure of gold was not going to get in the way of peace. Finally, the three separated and the central man straightened in his saddle.

'Peace is a thing to be sought,' he said, through Luci. 'Our people are tired of generations of war with the tribes around our borders. We three cannot speak for *all* the tribes of the region, the ones you call Demetae, but we at least will accept the friendship of Rome, on certain conditions. Your arrival has been noted, and the kings of all the tribes are being summoned to council at Morida. The matter will be discussed there, and any deal struck. Will you and your leaders come to Morida?'

Agricola bowed his head. 'To pursue a beneficial peace, we would travel far and wide.'

The men nodded with smiles of satisfaction. 'Then come on the full moon. Morida is one day's ride south. Scouts will be provided as guides. Your nobles and princes will be welcomed to the council of kings and there the future of our peoples decided.'

And with that, they turned their horses and began the slow ride back up the hillfort.

'Peace, freely sought and easily won,' Agricola said with a sigh of relief.

Emeritus shot a glare at him again. 'They could have met and made their decision with the notion of Roman mining in mind. We could even have made signing over the mines part of the initial condition. We could have asked for hostages from the rich kings. We are in a position of strength. We could have applied almost any condition we liked. You gave all that away when you gainsaid me.'

Agricola returned the look with a fierce one of his own. 'We are in the very west of the land. Behind us the Silures are beaten, but not fully cowed. Remember there were many boatloads who were ready to fight, but stood down. It will take wily negotiation to settle them fully and not cause another rebellion. To the north the Ordovices await us, and we know that they remain defiant to Rome. We have potential enemies to east and north, and the sea to the west and south. I submit that it would be foolish to do anything that might anger the tribe among whom we travel and who could be our allies. Let's treat them well and at least have *one* tribe we can rely upon in the region.'

'I wonder if *their* druids are still here,' Emeritus said, with a wicked smile as he glanced back towards the legate's carriage.

Agricola shivered at the idea of what the tribe might think if the legate ordered their priest crucified.

'Let's not find out,' he said.

II

The amount of time they spent with the Demetae preyed on Agricola's mind. Spring had rolled through into summer almost unnoticed during their travels through Silurian lands, and everyone involved in this campaign knew that the governor intended all three forces to be in the fiercely independent north-west by the time the military season ended in autumn.

Yet as summer drifted past them, they sojourned with the Demetae as though there were no pressing matter in the world. Even Emeritus, who ever cleaved to the legate in the hope of achieving more prominence, was beginning to tire of it.

Officially, they stayed at Morida for two months working through the details of the alliance and the installation of the Demetae as clients of Rome. Clearly it involved a great deal of minutiae, although Agricola was sure that peace treaties between vast empires had been hammered out in half the time. Lucius Valerius Geminus had clamped down on any suggestion of deliberate delays whenever anyone brought it up. The last time he'd made it clear to Agricola that asking again would not be good for his career.

'I will tell you this once more, tribune,' the legate had grunted. 'The Demetae are a rich people. They control gold mines, thriving ports and very good farmland. They have much to offer Rome, and the more advantageous our treaty is, the more acclaim it will garner from both the governor and the central administration back in Rome. And you may think it vain for an old, sick man to seek such acclaim, but if you hadn't robbed me of a glorious victory against the Silures I might not need to spend so long replacing military victory with political success.'

And that had been that. Agricola was not favoured enough by his commander to push his luck.

If he had been unpopular with the legate after sending away the boats, his reputation with Geminus had plummeted to an all-time low when a weary courier reached them, half a month into their time here. The governor had received the legate's report of his victory, and had written in reply that, according to *his* sources, the battle had been considerably smaller than Geminus claimed. He had, consequently, prevented any overstated report from reaching Rome, and had issued a barely veiled threat that if such self-serving occurred again, he would consider removing the legate from command. Geminus had immediately accused Agricola of being the source that had undermined his lie, but with no proof and the tribune having been assigned personally by the governor, he could not reasonably remove him.

And so they had stayed.

The Demetae were a careful people, and with the aid of Luci and one of the local princes, Agricola began to get used to their ways. He learned the names of their gods – which were, naturally, the same gods Rome prayed to, but with odd names and rather misshapen statues. But he could see how the people worked, and was even beginning to learn a few words of the language.

Luci was as content as he'd been since they met, too. Here, among the Demetae, it was the closest thing for him to being at home, yet they were far enough west that his own Silurian tribe had never had disputes with these people. He'd been treated as a strange case throughout the campaign: clearly more than a simple slave, yet not quite a free man. Here, though, he seemed freer, almost one of the Demetae they were visiting, and was treated carefully by even those who distrusted him, for no one wanted to offend the Demetae by abusing a Briton slave during negotiations.

The real reason for the delay, and though it was not spoken all knew it, was Geminus' health. The man's decline had continued as they had moved west. He no longer rode a horse, for even climbing into the saddle was far beyond his capabilities now. His skin had a waxy, colourless look, and he tended to drop off to sleep with little notice. He could hardly walk without pain, and his slaves were in constant attendance trying to keep him comfortable. Of course, he drank more and more wine to dull the pain, which only resulted in more pain and discomfort and therefore more wine, ad nauseam.

The Demetae had offered him a healer, and the woman had mixed up concoctions for him, but Geminus would not take them. For the sake of keeping their hosts happy, he accepted them with a false smile and let the woman leave, and then tipped them out on the grass. He would have no more 'Briton magic' working its evil wiles on him.

Indeed, he had asked upon their arrival, almost conversationally, about druids. He'd noted, without any malice in his tone, that they had seen only one druid in their time here, and that the man had expired in a swamp before they could speak to him, which was true, after a fashion.

'The druids are gone,' one of the kings had said.

Agricola had been on the alert immediately, for while most of those present had their eyes on the speaker, the tribune had been watching the warriors behind him, and the way they exchanged glances made it clear there was a lot more to the matter. Geminus had done his best to draw more information from them, enquiring almost casually where they could have gone.

'This is a holy year,' the man replied, waving an arm. 'Some years are holy, when the sun goes dark, and the watchers gather in their great sanctuary at Mona to commune with the gods. They will return when they deem it appropriate. By winter they will come home, I'm sure.'

But there was so much he wasn't saying, and Agricola could see it in both his eyes and those of the warriors behind him. The days went on until finally, as summer peaked, even the legate had to admit to the worrying march of time and the distance they still had to go before winter quarters if they were to be in the north-west, where the governor expected them. He wound up the negotiations, logged a copy with the Demetae, as though anyone among them stood a chance of reading it, and then sent copies off to both the governor and back to Viroconium for forwarding to Rome.

The morning they made ready to depart, Agricola watched Geminus appear and wondered how long the legate was going to be leading them. The man could hardly move, appearing skeletal and half dead already. As he was helped out of his quarters and bundled into his carriage with the excellent suspension for the journey, even the ordinary legionaries were beginning to mutter about their commander, wondering how long he would last. And though any such speculation brought a centurion's vine staff down on them with a barked command to shut up, the concern continued to spread.

And the worry gnawed at Agricola in two ways as he mounted and rode ahead to join the Batavians in the vanguard. If Geminus fell too ill to move, or perished, it caused several problems. The first was the matter of overall command. Agricola was his second officer, and it should be his place to step into the role of overall commander, despite his lack of experience. But Geminus had already deputised the other tribune, Emeritus, a number of times now, leaving the two peers working together, no matter how much they might hate it. As such, Geminus might well place Emeritus in command, and even if he did not, Emeritus might well see it as his right now, and a weird and dangerous power struggle could ensue.

And then there was the army. Few creatures are as superstitious as soldiers. Something about putting your life on the line repeatedly, according to Sabinus at least, led to an increased reliance on portents, signs, divine powers and simple hearsay. The morale of the army was already faltering. It had been high both before and after their battle at the Brithii hillfort, but the decline in the legate was worrying them, and their extended period of inactivity among the Demetae had bred idle chatter and nerves. Some, even unit priests, had linked the decline in the legate to an impending decline in the army itself. Agricola was coming to the conclusion that only a fight, and a victorious one at that, would raise morale once more.

But a fight was unlikely in Demetae lands, for they were now allies and at peace. And though the army reached the sea within three days and pressed north along the coast of a great curving bay, they remained in Demetae territory, moving with agonising slowness, partially due to the supply wagons, and partially to the legate's need to stop ever hour or so. The weather continued to warm on their journey, too, making life all the more uncomfortable for the men, marching in their full battle dress and carrying their kit. The sun beat down day after day now until finally, one morning, one of the scouts the Demetae had sent with them reined in and pointed ahead.

With Luci translating, the man defined their boundary.

'The river ahead is the edge of Demetae lands. Beyond it lie the Ordovices. The Demetae have a shaky peace with their northern neighbours, and will not cross the river for fear of breaking it.'

Agricola nodded. Part of the endless haggling over the alliance with the Demetae was an agreement that Rome would respect their ties and feuds with other tribes and not interfere. Rome could war on the Ordovices while maintaining a peace with the Demetae, but could not call on them to fight.

Agricola looked ahead. The terrain on the far side of the river looked very much the same as this. The land in the region consisted mainly of green, rolling hillsides, dotted with occasional woodland and cut through by a number of small, winding rivers. But there was something looming on the horizon, quite literally. For two days now they had been able to see far across the waters of the great curved bay. To the north, so far ahead it was little more that hazy grey humps, they could see the coastline curving out to the west, and beyond it the unmistakable shape of distant mountains. This, then, was what they would have to face in the north-west.

They said farewell to the Demetae at the border, without the legate bothering to put in an appearance from behind the curtains of his carriage, and prepared to cross the river into Ordovician territory. The river that formed the border was neither wide nor deep, and the Batavians simply rode through it, the water coming up to the horses' bellies. The infantry lifted their packs onto their shields and hefted them aloft, slogging through the water without complaint. The only trouble came, as usual, from the legate. It took some time for the driver to find somewhere along the bank with a gentle enough slope for the vehicle, and similar conditions on the far side. And even then it was difficult. The carriage lurched, bounced and jolted, each sudden movement raising yelps and curses from its occupant. It took an hour, all told, for the legate to cross the river, and in that time half the army had managed the crossing.

Setting off once more, Agricola tripled the scout parties and gave them a wider area to cover. They were in enemy territory now, and nobody knew precisely what to expect. Luci had described the Ordovices as a warlike people, more so even than the Silures, but also a more scattered one, their individual tribes less part of the whole than their more southerly neighbours. As such, they might suddenly field an impressive warband, or they might be unable to pull together fast enough. It was all an unknown, although the Ordovices must already be dealing with at least one – if not two – other Roman armies in their lands, to the north and east.

A hillfort atop a high slope, overlooking both the river and the shoreline, stood empty and eerily silent. The scouts searched the place and reported that it had been unoccupied for no more than a couple of months. The amount of time, Agricola noted, that they had been in Demetae lands. It seemed likely then that their presence in the south-west had been noted, and their intention to move north against the Ordovices anticipated. They passed beneath the silent ramparts, keeping a wary eye on the place, for all the silence.

The first sign of life came not more than a mile from the river. The scouts reported in, noting just a hamlet of natives, no great fortress or army awaiting them. As they approached, Agricola eyed the small gathering of circular huts, the animal pens around the edge, a crude granary, and decided there and then that these people, at least, needed to be left alone. They were to crush the Ordovices, but these were simple farmers, not crazed warriors. The Batavi scoured the area and confirmed that there was nothing amiss, and so the officers rode and trundled on past the village. Agricola pulled close to the carriage of the legate and called out, respectfully.

'What is it?' came a reedy voice, and the sallow, ill face of Valerius Geminus appeared at the window, wincing as the vehicle bounced slightly.

'If we pause here for a few moments, sir, we might be able to gain a little information from the occupants about what awaits us ahead.'

Geminus nodded and gestured nonchalantly. 'Beat it out of them if you have to.'

With that he started to lean back, letting go of the curtain, and then suddenly stopped, fingers gripping the material once more and pulling it wide, face creasing into a new expression. Fear? Anger? Perhaps both. He seemed to be looking past Agricola. The change was so sudden and odd that the tribune turned instinctively. There seemed nothing amiss. A small farming village, the occupants mostly hiding or sitting in doorways, watching with nervous interest.

Then he noticed what Geminus was looking at.

A stone, perhaps shoulder height, was carved with shapes and the rough, crude image of a male figure. Behind the stone stood a single tree, with something hanging from it. He realised with slight distaste that the thing was a headless pig, its innards opened, almost as though hanging in a butcher's shop, though this one had been left to drip to the ground, forming a dark patch beneath. A sacrifice, apparently. A boy of perhaps ten summers was standing nearby, close to the stone, whittling the top of a long stick with a tiny knife.

'Druid!' snapped Geminus, pointing, eyes wild.

Agricola frowned. 'It's a boy, sir.'

'A *druid*, I tell you. Look how he carves his staff, how he tends his grove. Look, tribune, how he dares to meet my gaze, for he knows his barbarian magics are busy killing me.'

Agricola shook his head. The boy *was* meeting the legate's gaze, for sure, but it looked a lot more like simple interest to him. The boy would never have seen a Roman before, probably never seen armour in his life, let alone a rich man's carriage.

'Sir, he—' but the legate was waving him aside and gesturing to Emeritus. Agricola ground his teeth. The situation was becoming untenable.

'Have the boy crucified,' Geminus said, his eyes dancing madly.

Agricola stepped his horse forward a little. 'Sir, he's a farm boy.'

'He's a druid and a sorcerer, and all druids will be killed on sight. Understand?'

Agricola turned to see Emeritus already gesturing to a party of legionaries and issuing the orders. He gripped the reins tight, fighting the urge to intervene. Geminus was never going to listen to him, and Emeritus was the man's sword-arm now. Nothing would be achieved by trying to stop this. And, he told himself coldly, these were the enemy, after all. As justifications went, it was quite poor. So Agricola watched as the boy was grabbed by soldiers. A panicked father ran to the boy's aid, but was smacked in the head with an optio's staff, knocked to the ground and held there, two legionaries' boots on his back. The man watched, helpless, as his screaming, crying son was held tight, more legionaries hammering, nailing a sudis from the supply wagons to the tree of the grove, forming a wide crossbar. The boy was lifted to it and his wrists bound to the stake, then dropped so that he hung there against the tree, screaming, his shoulders slowly separating.

Beside Agricola, Luci was muttering something in his own language. A prayer, perhaps. They tarried in the village long enough for the army to eat a light noon meal while the boy slowly died on the tree, his father, a heap of emotion, being held back by legionaries. Geminus only looked at the boy once, and it was with an expression of wary satisfaction.

As soon as he'd eaten a little and filled what small appetite he still had, Agricola approached the grove, took a pilum from one of the legionaries and drove it into the boy's suffering heart, finishing him off. Emeritus, as soon as someone warned him of this, stormed across angrily, waving a finger, but Agricola turned to his fellow tribune and something in his face must have warned Emeritus not to push the matter, for he stopped sharply.

'The legate will be unhappy,' the man said, eyes hard.

'I don't care,' Agricola replied. 'The boy is dead. He was never a threat anyway, but he *certainly* isn't now. And we're marching against the Ordovices. How long do you want to delay in a farm, watching a boy die, while the real war waits ahead?'

There was no answer to this, clearly, and Emeritus simply glowered at him as he walked away, giving the order to have the men finish and pack, preparing for the off once more. The moment the boy's father was released, he launched himself at the nearest legionaries, a rock in his hand. He was smacked in the side of the head with a shield and collapsed to the dirt, unconscious, where he was left as they decamped.

The army moved on. By some unspoken mutual decision of Agricola and the Batavi, they carefully avoided contact with any more villages or farmsteads, keeping to open countryside. The territory of low green hills remained relatively easy, though they soon met another river and suffered the same lengthy rigmarole as the legate's carriage sought the best way across. As the afternoon slid towards evening, they passed another deserted hillfort, and decided to make camp beneath it.

Agricola turned in for the night in his tent, only to be assailed by unpleasant dreams. Among the varied scenes that played out in his sleeping mind, he came back more than once to the boy hanging on the tree, and found himself wondering even in slumber whether maybe there *had* been something magical about the lad to so insinuate himself into Agricola's mind.

He had no time to dwell on it as he woke, though, for he blinked open his eyes to a shout of alarm. Rising sharply he slipped from his bed, hand going to his sword baldric. Though he was dressed only in his sleeping tunic, he hung the baldric over his shoulder, settling his sword on his hip, and slid his feet into unlaced boots. As he emerged from the tent, one of his few remaining riders from the Second bowed his head, almost at the tent and ready to knock.

'What is it?'

The man simply pointed and Agricola followed his gesture.

Atop the deserted hillfort a fire was blazing, a golden inferno in the night.

'My horse.'

As he threw on a cloak against the night chill and tied his laces, an equisio brought round his horse. Behind him came Sabinus and Luci, each with their own mount. 'A turma of Batavi to me,' Agricola called, and Valda's men scrambled for their horses. Across the camp, he could see Tribune Emeritus in a similar state, but Agricola was ready first and, with the horsemen gathering to him, trotted his mount over to the gate in the camp's fence of stakes. As the legionaries pulled the barrier aside to allow them out, he kicked his horse into speed and raced for the slope, cavalrymen all around him drawing their swords, ready for danger.

The hillfort's south and east sides were formed of a precipitous slope too difficult for a horse, and so they circled round and approached up the shallower gradient, making for the double-ditched enclosure with its single gate. Sparks danced up into the dark from behind the ramparts and ditches. As they made their way round the hill they passed several picket stations, for one of the army's first acts as they'd settled in for the night was to position men all around the hill, keeping watch. No one wanted to stay *inside* the deserted hillfort, for there were tales of ghosts and monsters summoned by druids in such places, but watching it from outside was still safe. Especially since the place had been checked as they arrived and declared empty.

How had they missed someone?

As he approached the gateway into the hillfort, a simple gap in both ramparts with a causeway across the ditches, he allowed the Batavi to pull slightly ahead. Unknown dangers awaited them in there, and only a foolish commander led from the front at such a time. The Batavi charged inside, peeling off left and right, racing around the perimeter of the place. As riders circled and searched, others hurried over to the half-dozen dark and empty circular huts, jumping from their mounts and running to the doors in pairs, covering each other as they ducked inside and searched further.

Agricola, with Luci and Sabinus and the legionary riders, made their way through the huts and searching men towards the blaze at the hillfort's centre. The source was immediately clear. The natives had set fire to one of the huts, a timber and dried mud structure with a thatched roof. It had gone up a treat, but should already be burning low. That it was still blazing strong lent a heavy suggestion that the house had been packed with combustible material to form a simple and very solid pyre. The heat from the fire was immense, the column of flame rising into the black some twenty feet, sparks dancing even higher. Even as he stared at the blaze there was a shout of alarm. Snapping his head round, he realised that an errant spark had caught in the dry straw roof of another building, which was already beginning to burn.

There would be no water here, atop a high hill, unless it was in barrels. They would just have to let it burn, and perhaps get his men out of the huts before they were caught in another inferno.

Who had done this, how and why?

The soldiers were gathering now, having searched the whole hillfort, while others had ridden their horses up onto the ramparts, looking down outside.

'No one here, sir,' a passing rider called. 'Whole place is empty.'

'Fires do not start themselves. Someone *was* here.'

Another voice called, and past the blaze he could see a rider waving at him from the northern rampart. With the others in tow he trotted across, skirting the fire, and converging on that rider at the northern slope. As he reined in, he was about to ask the man what he'd seen, but as his eyes scoured the darkness he remained silent, for he could see it himself.

Another fire. A good distance away. At an estimate, he would put it perhaps five miles just east of north, inland from the coast. As his eyes adjusted, the afterimage of the blaze at the fort's centre still glowing in his sight, he could see another, just beyond. In fact, blinking a few times to bring clarity to the dark, he could see a series of small golden pinpricks marching off into the night in high places, disappearing off to the north-east, into the heart of Ordovician lands. Even as he watched, another in the line burst into life, little more than a distant star now. At least fifteen miles of beacons, if not more. A warning had gone out. If the Ordovices hadn't been aware of the third Roman army coming in as part of the trident from the south, they clearly were now.

'Do you know those lands?' he asked Luci.

The slave shook his head. 'This is far from my home. But the Ordovices do not often fight together as one force. If they are using such warnings, they are being unusually organised. The distances covered make it clear that we are dealing with more than one Ordovician tribe.'

Agricola rolled his shoulders. 'Someone is preparing for us. That means we will have a hard fight to look forward to.'

He became aware of thundering hooves and looked round to see Emeritus slowing nearby, a turma of legionary cavalry at his back.

'Beacons,' the man said, looking out into the distance.

'Yes. Someone is being warned of our approach. It looks like the legate might get his triumph-worthy battle after all.'

'Who set the fire?'

Agricola shrugged. 'We've found no one. And I doubt you will. We have eyes on the hillfort, but all it would take is one man in dark clothes to sneak in and he could do this. By the time the blaze was up, he was probably already halfway back down the hill, long gone before we reacted.'

'He probably lives in one of these barbarian villages nearby,' Emeritus snarled. 'When the sun rises, I shall have every settlement within an hour's ride burned in reprisal and every man, woman and child tortured until we find the bastard responsible.'

'What's the point?' Agricola sighed. 'What's done is done. We'll learn nothing from these people, and you'll never find the fire-setter. It would be a wasted day. Knowing who the warning was for would be useful, but we can probably find that out on the way.'

Emeritus' jaw acquired a twitch. He knew that Agricola was right, but he didn't like it, and he certainly was not going to admit it.

'Then perhaps I'll just burn them all with the inhabitants inside, on principle.'

'Do it quickly, then. I'm going to recommend to the legate that we leave all but the fastest supplies to follow on with a rearguard so we can move quickly. I think we want to reach the end of that line of beacons before they expect us to.'

And then: a fight.

12

The column had marched north and slightly east when they broke camp the next morning. The vanguard had been tripled, now consisting of three different auxiliary cavalry units and a turma of legionary cavalry. No infantry, to allow for speed and manoeuvrability among the gentle hills and valleys of the region. The number of scouts had also been vastly increased, their watchful eyes scouring the landscape up to seven miles ahead of the army, checking every village, ruin, woodland and defile for trouble.

They found the burned-out wreckage of the next beacon on a ridge some miles from the sea, and then descended to a wide valley where they found a sizeable hillfort overlooking a wide, shallow river teeming with fish. The fort had been deserted for days at most, everything of value taken when it was abandoned. Nearby, however, they found the first warning. Very simple, very eloquent. A legionary's helmet sat gleaming atop one of the standing stones that seemed so prevalent in this land, crusted blood marring the bronze, a jagged dent in the bowl ample evidence of how its owner had perished. The Ordovices, it seemed, were everything Luci had said they were. They moved on, all the more warily, crossing the river and driving north-east now, along the line of the lights they had observed last night.

The next beacon was located on a high peak on the far side of the valley, once again a pile of cooling ashes with no sign of life remaining. It seemed only reasonable that the beacons had followed the line of the hills along the valley side, and so the army pushed on along that wide vale, following the river on its north bank.

Just a mile further along, they paused when their scouts returned, ashen faced. When questioned, the riders detailed a scene of horror. Agricola and his consilium followed them, along with Emeritus and Cornelius and their escort, to the source of their distress.

Back across the river, and perhaps half a mile along a side valley, the scouts led them up to a plateau overlooking the river. Bleak and stark amid the ferns and brown reedy grass, yet another native standing stone rose, defiant. This one was only chest height, but broad and heavy and set at an angle, or perhaps fallen with time, so that it pointed off to the south, the direction from which the army had marched. A coincidence? But it was not the stone that had drawn the scouts' attention.

A man knelt in death below the pointing angle of the stone. The moment Agricola saw it, he knew what it was. The scouts had only said 'mutilated', but the man was attached to the stone, leaning forward, held to the surface by the cord around his throat that had bitten into the flesh and killed him, but not before the wound to his skull that had soaked his face in blood, nor the ritual disembowelment that had his guts curled like a pile of discoloured sausages beneath him.

Luci took one look and retreated, pale.

The weather chose that moment, rather portentously, to herald a change, a distant crack of thunder announcing storms nearby.

'This is the threefold death,' Agricola said. 'This is what the Brithii did to their neighbours just for talking to us.'

But this was different in one important way: the victim was no dissenting Silurian. He wore a Roman military tunic, stained and blood-soaked, and was clearly identifiable as a legionary, if only from the belt still around the tunic and the hobnailed boots on his feet.

They paused long enough to cut down the body and wrap

him in cloaks for transport to the wagons, where he would travel with the sick until they stayed anywhere long enough to cremate and honour the man. As they returned to the army, a quick check confirmed that no legionary century was mysteriously missing a man, which, of course, made the poor bastard a soldier of one of the other campaigns into Ordovician lands. It did lead to fears that at least one of the two other prongs of attack had failed, though the officers stamped down on those rumours as fast as possible. There was no proof, and such talk shook confidence army-wide.

Every soldier's eyes followed the ridges to either side of the valley now as the army moved on, finding the sites of two more burned-out beacons as they travelled. The storms grumbled and echoed around the hills inland, constantly threatening but never quite reaching the marching force. After the second beacon there was much discussion, for the valley divided, forks marching both west and north-east. As they debated, setting up camp for the night, scouts ranged along both valleys and returned with the rather unhelpful tidings that beacons had been found along each route, suggesting that news of their approach had gone to more than one group of Ordovices.

Legate Geminus made a rare appearance at the briefing that night, and his visible decline sent a ripple of worry through the officers. Slaves had to aid him into the tent, one under each shoulder, helping him walk. His skin was sallow and sagged from the bone, his face grey, eyes yellow.

Agricola had opened the discussion, trying not to draw attention to his condition.

'While there are two possible routes, we have been angling more and more to the east in our travels, and we know that it is in the north-west the general wishes us all to winter. With only a month or so until the campaigning season ends, surely we should do what we can to move in our assigned direction.'

Predictably, Emeritus took a contrary position. 'If warning has gone north-east, it is possible that it has gone to a group that is now *behind* the general's army, cutting off or threatening his supply lines. Surely it is more important that we do what we can to support Paulinus' and Costa's pushes.'

'If those armies still exist,' Cornelius added darkly. 'Given that we found a mutilated soldier from one of them.'

That brought an uncomfortable silence to the tent, for no one wanted to think too deeply on the possibility that two-thirds of the Roman advance had met the same fate as Varus' lost legions in Germany, and that their own force was now the entire Roman strength in the west.

The debate raged for over an hour with very little change, Agricola and Emeritus arguing their own points over and over again, just from slightly different angles each time. Finally, Geminus pinched the bridge of his nose and held his other hand up, motioning for silence, which he swiftly achieved.

'You are giving me a headache, and my head is the only part that doesn't hurt these days.'

'Sir—'

'No. Quiet. Show me the map.'

Cornelius unfurled the vellum hanging on the wall and let the rather sparse and uninformative map drop down the tent, opening wide. The coastlines were pretty well defined, for ships had mapped them in earlier years, and certain larger features and known settlements were marked, but a lot of it had acquired detail from the unit scribes as they'd travelled, and huge blank areas covered the region into which they were moving.

'The island.'

'Sir?'

Geminus pointed to the large island off the north-west coast. 'My sources tell me that this island is the sacred place of their druids, a sort of Capitoline temples for their priests. That must be our ultimate objective.'

Agricola blinked. He'd not thought of looking so far ahead. He had focused on the current season, with its ending as they went to winter quarters. As such, he had thought only of securing what territory they were in, assuming that the governor would have fresh orders for next year. Here, he could see perhaps a hint of the strategic genius that was Geminus' reputation of old. The man was looking far ahead, to their *ultimate* goals.

And suddenly something fell into place. Mona. The Demetae had said their druids had gone to some great sanctuary called Mona. Mona was the island. The druids had fled the Roman advance and gathered on Mona. And if they were the great driving force of resistance among these tribes, there was a good chance they had not gone there alone, but had taken strong warbands with them. The three armies might meet strong resistance among the Ordovices, but it would be on that island that the true fight would be fought, and that was now clear, thanks to Geminus' insight.

'We take the western route,' the legate said firmly. 'It takes us more generally in the direction of our ultimate goal. However, I want a single turma of our best riders to take spare mounts and sufficient supplies for four days. Send them along the other route to the north-east and set them to locating the forces of the governor and of Legate Didius Costa. Before we set up our winter quarters I want to confirm the ongoing existence of both other forces. They are to move with all haste, and return quickly. In the meantime, we move west. With luck we can locate and overcome whoever controls these beacons before the winter comes, and then look to finishing resistance on their holy island next year.'

Emeritus threw Agricola a sour look, as though he had somehow influenced the legate's decision. Geminus returned to his tent with the aid of his slaves and again nothing more was seen of him for the night, with the exception of one of his slaves drawing a hefty wine ration from the quartermaster.

The next morning, a fine mist playing on their faces and the air cold as the breath of Hekate, they turned west along the wide valley. Some four miles along the route they found the next pile of ash that had announced their approach to the tribes, and here the scouts reported that the valley led to a saddle in the hills. That afternoon, on approach to said saddle, the scouts drew their attention to another grisly find. Three legionaries had been treated to the same dreadful fate as the last one, each with a hole in his skull, each garrotted and disembowelled on different sides of a pile of stones thousands of years old. They made camp for the night nearby, and burned and buried the dead once again.

The morning brought a clear reminder that the season had changed. The past few days had nodded to the memory of summer, with blue patches in the sky despite the damp and the chill, but a further drop in the temperature, especially in the hour before sunset, had now come, with a general feeling of chilly blusteriness to accompany the change in the colour of the leaves. As Agricola rose that morning, he dressed and pulled open the tent doors to find a gentle drizzle set in and the world a uniform and gloomy grey from horizon to horizon.

Luci, standing in just his tunic and boots outside the tent and cleaning down a plate, gave him a strange smile. 'Welcome to my land. You've seen it at its best. Now get ready for the rest.'

As they ate a light breakfast and Luci squared everything away for travel, the camp in the usual chaos of departure, the scouts returned from a fresh foray. They had located a trackway that the locals had clearly used for countless years, driving their flocks and even wheeling rough carts. The importance of the trackway, which climbed a slope into the hills, was clear from the fresh sign they had found.

As the army followed on, slogging up that slope to the ancient road, Agricola rode ahead with the vanguard to examine that sign. It was less grisly than the last few, yet in its own way far more portentous and dark.

He had seen Roman trophies before. After great victories and glorious campaigns, tall trophies were made from the standards, flags, armour and weapons of the enemy. When he was seven years old, the entourage of Aulus Plautius had passed through Forum Iulii on its journey to Rome following his successful initial invasion of Britannia. He was bound for a minor triumph in the city, an exceptional thing, and along with various spoils of war and gifts for the emperor, there had been a trophy rising high and proud in one wagon. Standing a good twelve feet, it was formed of a great pole decorated with the shields, helmets, chain shirts, swords and spears of the defeated Britons, draped with their kings' apparel. He'd seen similar in Rome during his brief time there, still stored on the Capitol, reminders of old victories.

To see one made of Roman armour and weapons, all attached to a legionary standard with its clenched fist gleaming at the apex, was heart-stopping. It suggested that at least the majority of a cohort had been defeated. The gloom of the thought was hardly improved by the fact that the rain seemed to be getting heavier and the grey of the sky darker as the day wore on. Luci's comment on the weather that morning seemed all the more foreboding now. Agricola pulled his gaze from the trophy, looked up briefly, blinking into the pouring rain, then shivered and looked ahead once more.

On reflection, he decided as they tore the trophy down and moved on, it was more encouraging than he'd first thought. The message suggested, in fact, that the other armies were still intact and operating, for every legion's pride was its eagle, and surely, if the Ordovices had overcome an army, it would be the eagle that topped their trophy, and not a cohort standard.

Still, it was a statement that was hard to misinterpret.

As the army settled into their journey along that ancient route, Agricola found himself chilled to the bone. Partially, of course, it was the weather. No amount of oiled wool cloak was going to keep the weather of this island out for long. By the time they were settled into the journey, the cloak that was so vaunted by his mother for its waterproof nature was a sodden, lead-heavy garment that weighed him down and sank icy water into his very marrow. At one point he squeezed the water out of his hair and tried his helmet from the pack behind him as a covering, but when he'd taken it off again to adjust the strap he realised that the grand horsehair plume had settled into a sort of soggy bowl-cut, wilted and weighed down with water, plastered to the metal bowl of the helmet in every direction from the crown. It looked utterly ridiculous, and so he shook it out as best he could, replaced it, and resigned himself to simply being wet.

The track ran along a valley, but a valley that was already high in the range of hills, and after a few miles they passed a lake edged with fens and full of reeds. Off to the right stood yet another hillfort, though the scouts reported that it was again empty. They plodded on into the grey west, cold and sodden and becoming increasingly unhappy with every step.

The journey that day was a truly unpleasant one. They passed three hillforts, all rather close together, all recently abandoned and with all goods of use stripped away. There was no shelter in this dreadful place, and the rain drove into their faces for most of the day as though Neptune himself had cast his seas at them sideways. Worse still, the Ordovices' little signs were becoming extremely frequent. As well as the closeness of hillforts up here, there seemed to be other reminders of their religion all over the place. The standing stones were so common now it seemed like the army was following a line of calcified trees. Around them, here and there, were cairns, piles of rocks, or strange little rings of uneven stones that seemed to serve no purpose.

But with every one, they found a message. Here and there a strangled and disembowelled legionary or auxiliary soldier, the threefold death of which Luci had spoken. Each time the soldier was cut down and added to a growing pile of unpleasant corpses in one of the carts. Other displays were more imaginative. A wolf had been killed, its throat cut, and had been propped against one of the cairns, two dead soldiers positioned as though they were suckling from it. Agricola was impressed in a way that they knew enough of Rome's imagery and origin myths to be able to parody them so. A Roman soldier stripped naked and laid face down in the centre of a circle of stones with a stylised eagle carved into his back was another such example. More common were trophies of stolen armour and weapons. But the regularity with which such sights greeted them suggested they were coming close to their goal.

Of course, one thing that gnawed at the tribune was the question of whether that was a good thing. Yes, they needed to find the enemy and bring them to battle, but they now seemed to be playing the Ordovices' game, following a trail of breadcrumbs left for them, and that meant that perhaps they would not like what they found at the end. Still, they persevered. Autumn was closing in, with the necessity of finding winter quarters, and they needed to secure what they held by then.

Going was slow, and as light started to fade, the scouts began to search for an appropriate camp site. Finally they glimpsed, through the seemingly endless wall of grey, the sea, ahead and far below, down a sharp slope. But that was not to be their destination. They camped that night in soggy, coarse grass, between swamps and weathered rocks, overlooked by deserted hillforts and with the sound of birds on the lakes nearby. It was a horrible, uncomfortable night, one of the worst Agricola could remember, and he was immensely grateful when they rose once more and Luci opened the tent door to find that the rain had stopped.

It was, he suspected, only a temporary reprieve. There was not a hint of blue to the sky, and though it was pale grey, he could see a deeper and darker horizon out to the west that seemed to be growing, bringing fresh unpleasantness their way. Later, there would be rain that made yesterday's drizzle look like mere mist.

The scouts found numerous paths that morning, but the main trackway they were following remained clear, and they climbed another slope, moving into a woodland that had everyone alert and nervous, skin prickling on the backs of their necks. They managed to traverse the woods without hordes of Britons falling on them, naked and screaming with swords in hands, and emerged from the far side at the top of yet another slope. This one, though, led down into a wide, flat, lush valley. The more eagle-eyed among them pointed out the sea, off to the right in the distance, suggesting that they had turned southwards again, somehow, on the track and in the rain.

They were beginning their descent when one of the scouts hurried up and called for a halt. Agricola and the other officers, all bar the legate, who remained in his carriage throughout the journey, cursing with every jolt, hurried to the scout's position.

Signs of life.

For the first time since they had been in southern Ordovician lands, they could see a sign of habitation. It was not encouraging, though.

The path they were following descended to that low, flat valley, and another range of hills arose on the far side. Directly opposite, one hill stood proud of the others, and the sight of it made Agricola's breath catch in his throat. The rock was more mountain than hill, rising above all its surroundings, sheer rock on two sides, vertiginous slopes everywhere else. And atop that dreadful rock, where birds circled, almost close enough to touch the gods, stood a hillfort.

It was a whole different proposition to those he had seen before. This was more mountain fastness than simple hill. The fort was divided into an upper and lower area, each with its own solid stone wall and heavy timber gate. And this fort was occupied. Smoke rose from the roofs of several buildings that were visible as little more than shapes on the hillside.

Finally, having been made aware of the situation, the legate was brought forward in his carriage, manoeuvred and positioned so that he could see out of the window without disembarking.

'We have them.'

Agricola peered at it. '*Some* of them, sir. It cannot be the whole tribe, from all the abandoned settlements we've seen. Some perhaps went north-east, and I suspect many followed the druids to Mona. But yes, we have found... someone. Although I rather think that was their idea. We were lured.'

'Someone powerful, though,' Emeritus said. 'They've led us

here with their signs, and they are quite numerous, from what I can see. They fill that fort, and they think it impregnable. They think we will wilt beneath it.'

'And well we might,' Agricola added, eying the slope.

'No,' Emeritus sneered. 'I admit to your success in bringing us here. You were right to choose west. But now we can teach them what it is to stand against Rome.'

'Quite right,' Geminus muttered from the carriage. 'See to it.'

'Sir?'

'I place the two of you in charge of the assault. By nightfall I want that rock in our hands and all survivors crucified.'

Agricola chewed his lip, looking again at the hillfort, and then out west at the deep grey sky that had moved worryingly closer. 'I'm not sure we can take it with an assault, sir. I think this is a siege. We have the winter on our side. We can starve them while we sit in garrison.'

Geminus gave him a hard look. 'A siege is not as easy as you think, tribune. You are new to all this. No, I think a single assault can give us that rock in an hour. Two at the most. See to it.'

As the carriage was wheeled away, Agricola looked to Emeritus and to Cornelius.

'There is no way to take that quickly. *Look* at it.'

'The rear slopes are not rockfaces,' Emeritus said. 'We have an army twice the size of whatever they could fit in that place. We can overwhelm them with numbers.'

Agricola shook his head. 'Don't be stupid. You have to help me persuade Geminus to another course of action.'

Emeritus bridled. 'Call me stupid again, you provincial piece of shit, and you'll regret it.'

'We haven't got time for this. Even the lowest slope up to that place is more than half a mile of climbing. By the time our men are even halfway up that slope they're going to be out of breath and tired. By the time they have to engage the enemy, every one of them will be at their poorest fighting condition. The cavalry are useless on a slope like that. Artillery couldn't get anywhere near it. It will have to be taken by simple brutal force, and all they have to do is roll rocks down at us. It's going to be a disaster. We have to besiege them, to draw them out and make them come to us.'

'The legate has made his decision.'

'The legate can barely see his hand in front of his face now, tribune. He's not thinking straight.'

'I don't think you understand the military, Agricola. Orders come from the top down, obedience comes from the bottom up. Geminus wants the hill taken, so we take the hill.'

Agricola shook his head. 'No. I'll have none of it. It's wasteful and foolish. We must persuade—'

'Do what you want, Agricola,' Emeritus snapped, 'but *I'm* taking that hill.'

Agricola stood still, fists clenched, as his counterpart stormed away. After a brief pause, he turned, finding Luci standing close, as always. 'Your opinion?'

'Unless you're an eagle, leave the place alone.'

'My thoughts precisely. The fool will take the army up there and we'll lose hundreds of men at least before he gives up. And he *will* give up. Even Corbulo would think twice about that.'

With a sense of frustration, he moved away from the column as Emeritus had his orders passed down to other tribunes and centurions and disseminated throughout the army as it slowly descended the hillside into the valley. He saw Tribune Cornelius at one point bellowing orders and called him over. 'You don't have to do this.'

Cornelius gave him an apologetic look. 'Sadly, I do.' And with that, he was off again.

'What will you do?' Luci asked quietly. Agricola shot him a meaningful look, albeit bearing no real admonishment. 'What will you do, domine?' the slave asked again, tacking on a little respect in everything but actual tone.

'Watch.' Agricola sighed. 'Watch and then try and pick up the pieces when it fails. I have an idea, but unless they're willing to accept the notion of a long siege, it will never work.'

With Sabinus and his riders, Agricola moved away from the descending convoy. Careful to stay close enough to the army to not invite trouble, he moved along the hillside above the valley, above the army massing in the bottom, until he found a small knoll where they could stand and watch, with an excellent view of all approaches from three sides. One of the riders hurried off to the supply wagons at the rear of the army and returned with men in tow bringing everything they needed to erect a sizeable awning that would cover several seats and a table. Sabinus arranged things and then offered them wine. Agricola waved it away, but did take one of the seats with some relief after another day in the saddle.

They settled in. The bad weather rolled on relentlessly, but their attention was on the army in front of them. Agricola spotted what he considered the first mistake the moment the army was in position and a force began the climb, along the easiest route, around to the left and up behind an outcropping. Emeritus had marched his legionary troops straight out, leaving the auxilia standing on the wings. That was the conceit of a man of centuries of superiority: the notion that because the legions were citizen troops they were automatically better than the provincial auxilia. If there was one thing Agricola had learned from months of travelling alongside the Batavi, it was that every type of soldier had his advantages and disadvantages, and in troublesome terrain, lighter-equipped and faster auxiliaries had the edge over the heavy infantry of Rome.

His fears were quickly borne out. He watched the climb slow gradually as it ascended, formation breaking down as men were forced to find easier ways around. By the time they had climbed half the slope, they were simply staggering and lurching up the hill as individuals, with no sign of unit tactics. They had also dropped to a crawl. He could imagine them all, even from his perch across the valley, heaving in exhausted breaths, slipping, tripping, weighed down by armour.

Weary and slow, the lead figures of the advance had disappeared being the outcropping, and now reappeared, a little higher and facing the last, slightly easier, slope up to the walls of the outer, lower fortress. Something was happening over there, and Agricola had to squint and peer into the distance with considerable difficulty for some time before he realised what he was seeing. Men were disappearing, dropping to the deep ferns and undergrowth, as traps or pits or some such brought them down and crippled them. Every fourth or fifth man fell to such a trap, and Agricola began to wonder whether they would ever come anywhere near the fortress.

They did. Despite their losses and exhaustion, the legionaries persevered under the bellowed encouragement of their centurions. The first man to come anywhere close, indeed, was one such centurion, visible from this distance as a brighter, more colourful man without a shield. As the centurion wheeled his arms to accentuate his orders, he was suddenly thrown aside.

He was not the last.

The defenders had finally made their first move. Slingshots and arrows and simple thrown rocks hurtled out from the walls of the lower enclosure, and pulverised man after man. The Romans struggled on in the deadly hail, yet not one even reached the position that unlucky centurion had attained.

The attack faltered, then, and it took only a moment further to fail. All it took was one man, struck in the shoulder with a stone that broke his arm, shield falling away, to turn and bellow his pain, running back down the slope towards safety. In moments the entire force was with him, bellowing as they ran from the disaster that had been their failed assault. Even centurions were running. Arrows and stones followed them for some distance.

In half an hour the hilltop was quiet once more and the Roman force had gathered at the bottom. Agricola turned slowly to the others. 'With luck, the legate will now listen to sense.'

The small viewpoint was quickly taken down and packed away, and the officers, men and slave rode down the slope, converging on the huge camp at the same time as the last survivors of the attack at the far side of the valley.

As they dismounted in the camp and passed the reins of their horses to the equisio and his men, a scream attracted their attention, and Agricola turned back towards the lofty hillfort towering over the rocky crags above them. As the second scream rang out he realised what it was. The Ordovices were scouring the field below their walls for Roman bodies and casting them out from the clifftop into the open air to plummet hundreds of feet to the ground. Not all of the bodies were dead when they let go, either.

Agricola, stony faced, turned away from the spectacle and walked into the command tent.

Legate Geminus may have been only a breath from crossing the final river to Hades, but he'd summoned up a small reserve of strength from somewhere, for anger seemed to have pushed pain and weakness into the background.

'You did not take part,' he snapped, glaring at Agricola.

'I saw no way to win. I do not like to start a contest I know I cannot win.'

Emeritus gave him a horrible look from across the tent, but Agricola ignored him. 'Perhaps now common sense can rule. Legate, there is a solution, but it is not instant. It will take months, but the weather has closed in and winter is coming. We need to set up winter quarters, and now seems like the time to do it. We *can* defeat these people, over the winter.' He gave a wry smile, remembering those camps he had seen on his first days out in this land, where a former governor had blockaded the Silures from their good grazing and agricultural land. 'Ostorius Scapula showed us what to do.'

The winter would see everything change.

PART 2

REBELLION

Inter quae nulla palam causa delapsum Camuloduni simulacrum Victoriae ac retro conversum quasi cederet hostibus

(Meanwhile, without any evident cause, the statue of Victory at Camulodunum fell prostrate and turned its back to the enemy, as though it fled before them)

Tacitus, *Annals* 14.32

13

They had played it Agricola's way in the end. The failure at the rock fortress had tarnished Emeritus in the commander's eyes, and the man had lost sufficient credibility now for Agricola's voice once more to rise to the top. He'd laid out his plan using that map, following the very same strategy with which Ostorius Scapula had suppressed the Silures: starvation.

The winters in these western lands were known to be hard, and the evidence of the advancing cold months backed that up. To survive such winters, Luci had explained, the tribes harvested their crops and stored them in granaries, just as Romans would. Their livestock would either be brought to high winter pastures where they would rely upon stored fodder until spring, or turned into lowland pastures where they would find sufficient food. The problem was that they'd had too little notice of Rome's intent to invade, and the other two prongs of the attack were in Ordovician lands long before any attempt could be made to stockpile. The tribes had been forced to do what they had done here, retreating from their villages and lesser forts and taking refuge in their most defensible places, leaving behind most of the supplies they would need to carry them through the winter. They had taken what they could carry, and had driven their flocks before them.

But as autumn turned to winter, the meagre stocks they had brought to their refuge wore thinner and thinner. With Luci's native insight, the various routes of passage the tribe could take to any reasonable food source had been identified. Small garrisons had been installed at the entrance of every valley, across every useable trail, blockading even the roiling grey sea. The Romans sat tight in their garrisons during the hard winter, eating well, fed by both a regular supply train from the southeast but also by seizing all the stored comestibles and animal fodder that the Ordovices had been forced to leave when they retreated to the rock.

That the plan was working became more and more evident as winter progressed. The defenders from the rock began to probe the Roman garrisons, looking for ways to known storehouses, to good pasture, to the sea and its abundant fish that the Roman invaders were enjoying. Each time, they were fought back and contained. Occasionally, patrols would locate small groups of farmers driving their flock along tiny hillside tracks, seeking ways to get them to good grazing land. They too were turned back or destroyed outright, their animals taken.

By the time Saturnalia came, a rather drab affair held in camp in the rain and snow, the Ordovices of the rock fortress were becoming desperate. Agricola had made his position with the garrison nearest to the fortress, and watched the place daily from a small, rocky viewpoint. He knew the effects of starvation were becoming pronounced when the Ordovices began to eat the sheep and cast the remains from the rock. By mid-Januarius even that had stopped, for they had gone through their livestock and none remained. They'd run out of food for the flocks and so they had eaten the flocks, but then there was nothing left except forage. One day a body was cast from the top, and Agricola, fascinated and horrified at once, had wondered whether they'd turned to cannibalism for survival, but it seemed the woman had died of starvation and been cast out before she rotted in their home.

Forage.

The rock seemed to teem with bird life – the soldiers had named it Bird's Rock now – and the desperate defenders had come down to eating what greenery they could find and using their crude arrows to shoot down cormorants, gulls and even falcons for their sparse meat. Agricola had done what he could to remove even that source of nourishment. Laughing parties of legionaries scattered food for the birds on the nearby hillside twice a day, attracting creatures that would be within the Ordovices' bow range, and bringing them within Roman reach instead.

Agricola was confident that by the campaign season's start, the thousand or so Ordovician warriors up there would be desperate enough to abandon their rock. And that was how Rome liked a fight: in open ground, where they were at their best.

It had come as more than a little relief, not long after they settled into garrison, when word had reached them of the other Roman pushes. There had been losses, which they'd known of course from the bodies they'd found, but not significant ones. Didius Costa and his Fourteenth had ravaged the enemy far into their lands and had settled into winter quarters deep in the hilly territory, some twenty miles north of Geminus' army. The governor and his Twentieth had secured all the coastal region and had reached the edge of the mountains another twenty miles north of Costa. When Agricola plotted this on their map it looked as though Paulinus' plan was succeeding. They had full control over all the tribes with the exception of the mountainous region of the north-west, a long narrow peninsula, and that island called Mona that was the focus of druidry.

Simple logic now told them that not only had the druids fled to their sacred island, but that they had taken a large part of the tribal populations with them, leaving behind warbands to fight a brutal rearguard action and hold off the Roman advance. It seemed inevitable that the next season would see them reach the island and be forced to take it.

Throughout that long winter, Agricola had seen the warriors of that tribe on Bird's Rock many times, if always from a distance, but he had never seen a druid, at least presuming they all wore the same white robe as the one example they'd met. What he *had* seen, twice now, had interested him. No venerable bearded priest in white, but a woman in black. He had been close to the fortress with one of the scouting parties. It had been a dry day, and the soldiers were coming as close as they dared to the rock fortress, seeking out whatever edible forage could be found and destroying it to further diminish the defenders' supplies. A commotion had drawn his attention, and they'd looked towards the fortress itself.

On the outer wall, above the gate, a woman in a long black robe, her face marked with some sort of pattern of paint or tattoo, was waving her arms and dancing as though in a frenzy. She held a dead crow in one hand and a knife in the other as she bellowed at the Romans. Agricola cursed the absence of Luci who could have translated, but the slave was deep in the mire of a cold – something that had caused much ribbing, given that he was a native of this land – and remained in the tent in camp, wrapped up warm. The woman had broken the dead bird, crushing it in her hands and then cast it from the wall in their direction. Some sort of curse, presumably.

They had left the fortress, a little unsettled, and returned to camp.

He'd seen her once since then, only from a huge distance down in the valley, as she stood on the very edge of the precipice up in their fortress, again waving and dancing. Whatever she was doing, it would not help. Her people had to be close to breaking point. He'd quizzed Luci about the woman, and though the slave claimed to know of nothing like her, Agricola harboured the suspicion he was holding something back.

Februarius rolled around, and with it came a new worry. The legate was clearly dying. His illness had progressed swiftly, aided by the winter hardships, and he was more or less bedridden now. He rarely rose, never left the tent, and often failed to supply adequate warning to his slaves to get a pot under him before he shat himself. Consequently, his tent smelled like a cross between a latrine and a hospital, a sickly smell that made the stomach lurch. It had become clear to all that he was never going to leave the camp alive. Emeritus had visited Geminus a few times, despite the commander's position being on the southern edge, guarding access to the tidal river that bounded this whole area on one side. Agricola was grateful for the distance, for it prevented the man spending too much time lobbying Geminus for more control. When the commander died, there could be a power struggle in the vacuum that was left. He was reasonably content that Cornelius, as the next most senior officer, would support him over Emeritus, but he doubted that would stop the man from trying anyway.

It was Cornelius who was responsible for finally breaking the Ordovices on their mountain fortress. In a moment of cruel genius, he managed to find a small flock of goats, had them poisoned, and then let loose into the land around Bird's Rock. The result was predictable. It took only a few hours for the goats to be found by desperate hunters from the fortress, and they were taken inside and consumed with gusto.

Agricola watched with grim satisfaction as the effects began to show. It was two days before the first corpse was cast from the rock to fall to the valley below and explode like an overripe melon. When the body was checked by scouts, the corruption and decay among the scattered remains was clear from the smell alone. The poison had done its work. Over the following five days more and more bodies were cast from the rock, carrying their rot with them. In terms of manpower, the damage was relatively small – just over a score of men had died – but it was not death that was Cornelius' objective. Fear and desperation had been his goal. And he had achieved it.

Two days before the kalends of Martius, the Ordovices finally broke.

Having been watching the place for almost five months now, they knew the general routine of Bird's Rock, and so the morning the Ordovices prepared for war, they were aware of it early.

Agricola was seated in his tent at the time. Before him, Luci gave the military dagger a last scrape, adding to its already keen edge, and then straightened. 'You're sure?'

'I am starting to look like a Greek philosopher. I've tried cutting my own hair and shaving myself, but the results were, let's just say, unimpressive. One thing the noble life in Rome does not prepare a man for is self-reliance in personal hygiene.'

'I told you your bath houses were stupid.'

Agricola snorted. 'Far from it, but they do lead to a certain reliance upon having your hair and beard dealt with by professionals. The common soldiers do their own, or shave each other, and that's fine. They're used to it. But an officer should not be reliant upon his men for such things and, quite simply, I never learned to shave myself. We always had a slave for it, or I visited the baths. You'll remember the last time I shaved, just after we settled in here?'

Luci laughed out loud then. 'I've never seen so much blood off the battlefield.'

'Quite.'

'Of course, I might draw blood too. It might not even be an accident.'

Agricola gave him a steady look. 'What do you think your chances would be if you cut my throat and left this tent?'

'It might be worth it. A martyr to the cause of freedom for my island.'

Now it was Agricola's turn to laugh. 'You've taught me too much about this place now to play such a bluff. A wily general could probably conquer this island without an army. All it would take is to persuade one tribe to war with another time and again and before long the island would conquer itself.'

'True. It is said that if a Silurian were left alone in a room long enough he would probably go to war with himself.'

'You don't believe in the freedom of your island any more than I do. Freedom for your people is just freedom to kill each other. Rome might come with swords, but those swords buy you peace and prosperity in the long run. Rome conquers, Luci, but in doing so, she civilises. Conquest for greed is inherently wrong. Conquest for the common good, though, is a morally acceptable goal.'

'Where did you learn such drivel?'

Agricola chuckled. 'In Massilia. Greek tutors. They love to examine the philosophical angle of all things. Had I not had duties for the family, I might have liked to be a philosopher.'

'Maybe you should let the beard grow, then?'

The Roman sighed. 'Sadly, for better or for worse, a son of a patrician line has duties to both family and the state.'

'Then try not to move, and I'll try not to rid your family and your state of one would-be philosopher.'

The Briton leaned in, tongue poking from one corner of his mouth as he brought up the soap and began to lather Agricola's chin and neck in preparation.

'I thought you Romans used oil,' he grunted. 'That's all I see in bath houses.'

Agricola answered carefully, trying not to move too much as the slave reached for the razor-sharp dagger. 'Soap is an invention of the Gaulish tribes. Many Romans don't trust it, but the tribes from the south of Gaul make the most exquisite soap. Smell it.'

'Smells like a whore.'

'I know. Glorious, isn't it?'

Luci paused to laugh before concentrating again and scraping a line of wiry dark hair from Agricola's cheek. He repeated the process and denuded the left side of his face swiftly, leaning in to start on the right when there came a hammering on the tent door.

'Yes?'

'Tribune? Activity on Bird's Rock.'

Luci leaned back, lifting the knife away from Agricola's face as the tribune straightened a little. 'War footing?'

'Fairly sure, sir.'

'Then we'll be hit first. We don't want to warn them off, though. No beacons or horns. Just have every man equipped for war as he goes about his business. Send swift riders to the nearest garrisons, down at the coast and up past the lake. I want it to look like we're unprepared, since we need to draw them out, but we will also need those garrisons if they're going to hit us in strength.'

'Yes, sir.'

The soldier disappeared, and Luci frowned. 'Hadn't you better get ready, domine?'

'Half-shaved, I would look rather foolish. Let's finish the face and worry about the hair later.'

Luci grinned through his own beard, untouched in months, and went back to work.

A quarter of an hour later, the tribune wiped his face and neck with a towel and examined his warped features in the rather crude bronze mirror. He looked a little more like his old self now, though his hair still looked like a hedge. With Luci's help, he dressed and pulled on his cuirass, fastening it tight, then settling his belt and baldric and pulling on the helmet, its crest returned to its dry and fluffy glory. Once he decided he looked like a tribune again, he stepped forward. Luci belted his small, sharp knife around his middle, then found his waxed cloak and pulled it on. It hadn't rained in days, but the weather was still chilly in the mornings.

In moments they were out of the tent. The centurions had done their job perfectly – he could see that with just a single glance around. Among the lines of tents, legionaries were crouched together around cook fires with their bowls in hand, auxilia tended to their horses, men played dice, sang songs, all the many ordinary sights of camp life, but with one subtle difference. Every last one of them was ready for battle, weapons at their sides, shields within reach, helmets hanging from straps ready to jam on in a heartbeat. By the time a horn had blown twice every man in the camp would be prepared to fight and falling into position, yet from the lofty viewpoint of Bird's Rock it would look as though nothing had changed.

Each of the garrison camps around the encircled area held some three hundred men, a mixed force of legion and auxilia, of infantry and cavalry. But two of the camps were outsized, holding twice that number, those being Agricola's, so close to the enemy, and the one just five miles away by the seashore, where the legate had been installed for the winter. Emeritus was on the far side of the mountains, and Cornelius in a high valley to the north-east. Neither would be able to reach them in time to help, but with the force from the sea and the one from above the lake, they would number one and a half thousand men, which should be sufficient to deal with the Ordovices. Estimated odds of three to two very much tipped things in Rome's favour, especially when the army was well fed and the natives starving and weak.

It took but moments to reach the best viewpoint, a place where he had stood, on and off, for five months now, watching the lack of activity on the rock. The ennui was gone this morning. Even as he climbed the rocky knoll to look across the valley, the Ordovices began to pour from the gate of their mountain fastness. They moved in a shapeless mob, rolling down the slope from their fortress like an avalanche, and he tried to estimate their numbers. It was difficult. He'd little experience of such fights, even after the last season of campaigning, and was having difficulty saying more than simply 'a lot'.

Sabinus, standing nearby, cleared his throat. 'Seven or eight hundred, I'd say, sir,' he estimated, as if reading Agricola's mind.

'So they're leaving some at the fortress. This is not an attempt to flee, clearly, because they must know now there *is* nowhere to flee. They can't get to Mona, for Rome stands in the way. And they're not intending to simply fight to the death, or they'd have left no one behind. I think they hope to break us here and take our supplies, to weaken our cordon and relieve their famine. They've watched us as we've watched them. They know our numbers, and they commit just enough to give them the edge. Of course, they don't realise that we have reinforcements on the way. How long would you say we have?'

Sabinus harrumphed. 'The enemy will be on us within half an hour. It will have taken the riders perhaps a quarter of an hour to reach the other camps. On the assumption they marched immediately, they'll still be around three quarters of an hour away.'

'So we either have to win swiftly or hold them until the others arrive. Perhaps a quarter of an hour of battle alone. Whatever happens, I don't think we want them to retreat to their fort again. We need to take advantage of this and defeat them while they're in the valley. Pass the word. We have two centuries of the Twentieth and two centuries of the Fourteenth, as well as four centuries of auxilia. I want the men of the Twentieth to form as the centre line to face and hold the enemy. They should be able to do that. Place all the auxiliary infantry on the wings, divided equally. Bring the Fourteenth around to the flanks behind them, as though they're reserves, and send the cavalry with them. The moment we engage, I want the Fourteenth to move in and encircle them, cutting off their escape. The cavalry can play guard and make sure that anyone who breaks out is hunted down and stopped.'

'That'll leave us dangerously thin, sir,' Sabinus said.

'Yes. So we'll have to fight well and hold them. It won't take long for the reserves to arrive.' He glanced across the valley. 'They're halfway down already. They know we've seen them, now, so there's no point in further subterfuge. Have the men fall in ready. Let's beat the Ordovices today.'

He stood there, on the knoll, watching the tide of warriors slide down the slope of Bird's Rock towards the valley floor. Behind him he could hear the horns and whistles blowing, calling various units to action. They would win. He was confident of that. Until reinforcements arrived, they were slightly outnumbered, but the enemy were half-starved and poorly equipped, while the Romans were well fed and in good spirits. That had been one advantage he'd noticed over the winter months. With the absence of the legate, who remained by the sea, and able to relax in camp with good supplies, the men of this garrison at least had very much recovered their spirits.

Were they on form enough to finish this without the other garrisons, he wondered, with a twinkle in his eye.

'What are you thinking?' Luci asked.

'Trying to decide whether to be a sensible, if somewhat aloof and noble, commander, sitting on a horse on a high spot and directing the flow of battle as I watch it unfold, or to be a suicidal lunatic like Caesar and make my way down among them, getting a bloody sword and quite possibly a bloody nose.'

Luci snorted. 'If our chiefs did not fight they would not be chiefs for long.'

'If they fight Romans they probably won't be chiefs for long either,' Agricola replied pointedly. 'The men's morale is quite high. I am inclined to common sense.' There was a loaded silence. 'What?' he said, without looking at Luci.

'You've already decided to fight. You're just trying to convince yourself why.'

'I sometimes forget how bright you are, Luci. It's a good job you *are* a slave. As a freedman, I suspect you would be very dangerous.'

That made Luci laugh, although with a sharp edge. 'You seek a reason to do what you want to do? Then here: if you stand back, you are no better in your men's eyes than Emeritus or the drunken old walking corpse in his command tent.'

Agricola winced at the description. It was a good job they were alone. If any other officer had heard that there would be trouble.

'If you fight, or even take part and look like you're involved, your men will respect you all the more, and we both know that the time is coming when having the respect of the army might be important – when it comes down to the matter of succession, if you get my drift.'

Agricola nodded slowly. Of course, Luci was right. Not only about that, but also about the fact that he'd already decided and was simply trying to justify the decision.

'And, of course, if you died, I might be more inclined to run and be free,' Luci murmured. Agricola's head shot round with a frown, trying to decide whether the man was entirely joking. His expression was hard to read.

'I would not have you fight your fellow islanders this time. You can return to the tent.'

Luci snorted. 'I'd sooner grab a spear and put it up the nearest Ordovician arse,' he said quietly. 'They're no people of mine.'

'Then this time, if you see me about to be skewered, I'd take it as a personal favour if you didn't just sit and watch.'

No answer was forthcoming. Agricola looked up and down the valley. He could see west as far as the end of the hills, which was, he reckoned, halfway to the sea, and east for about the same distance, maybe two to three miles. No relief army was visible in either direction, but that was hardly a surprise. Had it been high summer, the grass parched and the mud tracks dry and cracked, a cloud of dust would readily betray the position of any army larger than a century of men, but now, on the way out of winter, with grey skies and a slight haze, there would be no dust cloud. They were at least a quarter of an hour away, then.

Glancing back across the valley, the enemy were finally on the lower slopes, and did not pause to form into any kind of line, but ran like a cattle stampede across the wet grass. Between there and here, the army was forming just as Agricola had ordered, heavily armoured legionaries in segmented plate with huge body shields as an immovable wall of men at the centre, their chain-clad ranks behind, backing them up, with lighter, more manoeuvrable auxiliaries to either side, and the centuries of the Fourteenth on the wings, waiting to close the trap.

The horsemen, mostly Batavian and Asturian auxiliaries, with a few legionary cavalry among them, were waiting off to the side, where they had open ground to use to their advantage.

'Come on, then,' he said, hauling on his reins and leading the horse back down towards the army that was gathering before the camp. Less than two cohorts' worth of men. Did that classify as an army? It did here, and now. It had to.

As they passed a small group of reserves handing out weapons, he gestured.

'A spear for my slave, soldier.'

The auxiliary did not look particularly happy to be arming slaves, but he kept his disapproval safely to himself and passed the spear up to Luci, who took it and shifted his grip, weighing and testing it. Taking the lead, Agricola rode down among the men, lines of legionaries moving aside to allow him access. In moments he was among them, and the men fell into a hush. The result was odd, with the distant bellowing of the Ordovices as they hurtled across the grass towards them. Agricola realised the men were waiting for him to speak. Of course. It was traditional for a general to address his army before battle. He may be only a tribune, and a recently appointed one at that, but he was also in command here. He glanced at the approaching warriors. Better make it a rather brief speech, he decided.

'We fought them on their terms, and we lost,' he called out across the serried ranks. 'Now we get to change the game and have our revenge.'

This caused a roar, and he glanced at the approaching enemy again. Almost time, but he had a few moments. 'They outnumber us, but they're tired and hungry. The next two camps are coming to pull our backsides out of the fire. I don't know about you, but I'd quite like to have won before they get here, eh?'

If the last commotion had been a roar, this one was deafening. The notion of defeating an enemy was pleasing to the men, but the idea of being able to brag about it to their mates was even more so.

'Ad signum,' was his last command, and at the call, the men turned back and stood, implacable, in their places. Agricola and Luci sat in position, behind the first three lines of men, but among the fourth: present, but in no immediate danger. As the enemy pounded across the grass, one of the centurions cleared his throat.

'Pila at thirty paces.'

At another centurion's whistle, the front line of massive, heavily armoured men took four paces forward and hunched down, bunching behind their large body shields. The second row took two paces forward, opening the ranks slightly as they lifted their pila, the iron-tipped, weighted javelins of the legions. Only the second row was so armed. They waited. The enemy closed, howling. Now, their expressions of fury, hate and desperation were clearly visible, though they didn't seem to be fazing the Romans, whose morale was at an all-time high this morning.

Fifty paces.

Forty paces.

At a triple blast from the whistles of two centurions, the second rank of the Twentieth legion let their missiles fly, forty heavy javelins soaring up into the air, arcing out towards the advancing warriors. Agricola had tried to throw a pilum once, back in the garden a world away, in the company of his friend Suetonius Jovinus. He'd been astonished at how hard it was, for in a whole morning of throwing, not once had the javelin reached its intended distance, and more than half the time it had bounced, butt-end first, or slapped sideways into the target. Not so for the men of the Twentieth, who'd trained with the weapon time and again over the years, who'd used them in campaigns since the day the legion had first set foot upon the island.

The result was impressive. Few of the pila missed, and most delivered a killing blow immediately, given the lack of armour and shields among the Ordovices. Many of the front rank of the barbarians fell with screams, pierced through, wounded or dying, their plight made all the worse as their own mates ran over them in their hurry to get to the fight and avoid being the victims of a second hail.

There would be no second hail. The javelins were spent, and

even as they had been cast, the front ranks braced themselves, the second drew their swords and took another two paces forward, supporting their mates once again as the third rank shuffled up to close the gaps.

The Ordovices, howling with fury, hit the Roman forces.

The fight had begun.

14

The first time Agricola had drawn a blade in battle had been chasing down the fleeing druid in the bog. That had been a relatively small-scale fight, just a dozen or so men on each side, clear and straightforward despite the strange conditions of the conflict, bounded by fens and sucking swamp. *This* was a whole new world. Battle joined with a noise like none Agricola had ever heard, the roar of a thousand furious and desperate throats, the clang and crash and thud of iron, bronze, wood and flesh. The Ordovices hit the line of Roman legionaries like a rampaging bull, and now Agricola understood why the legions were organised thus. The biggest, most brutal of the soldiers with the heaviest armour, some even with laminated plates down their sword-arms, took the brunt of the charge, large body shields covering their torsos, wedged tight with their shoulders pressed into the board, the bronze lower edge resting against the single greave on their left leg for this very purpose. The sheer power of the charge should, in Agricola's opinion, break just about any obstacle, short of a city wall.

And yet the front line held, with just a little bowing at the centre that was quickly pushed back and corrected. The lines were relatively open order, one pace apart, to allow just such a thing to happen without causing a ripple effect that could force back the whole army. After the initial crash and the counter-push, once the danger of any breakthrough was past, the centurions' whistles blew and the ranks closed up, adding their own strength to the front line. Agricola and Luci, of course, were not involved in all this, mounted and behind the third line as they were. But even with the initial clash, he could see native warriors noting his crest, identifying him as a senior officer and marking him as a target.

The slaughter began in earnest, and, as Agricola watched the flanks move in to enfold the enemy, he leaned a little closer to Luci to make himself heard over the din.

'Some of them seem to have spotted me and marked me.'

'Of course. You're the officer.'

'I would not have thought them so strategically minded as to consider removing the command structure. I have read of such things, but not among the northern tribes… no insult intended, of course,' he added, remembering that these were Luci's fellow islanders of whom he was speaking.

Luci gave a dark chuckle. 'No offence taken. They *don't* think like that. Our warfare has never worked like yours. Our leaders fight with the warband, and there is no command system. They single you out because for them, the most glory and honour to be found in battle is in facing the greatest enemy and killing them personally. You are at the top of the Roman heap, so in their eyes you must be the greatest warrior on the battlefield. They all want to be the one who can brag about killing you.'

Agricola swallowed a lump that had formed in his throat at that. Suddenly being in the fourth line did not seem half as safe as it had. As his eyes played across the enemy lines, he saw them in a different light now. They were not an army, guided and commanded. They were a collection of individual warriors, each sharing a goal and a purpose, but each with his own personal agenda and each his own idea of how best to fight his battle.

That gave the Romans a particular advantage.

'They don't use signals.'

'No. Once the word is given, they charge. The battle will be over for them either when they win, or when everyone is dead. Or, of course, when they break. There will never be a signal to retreat. They do not think like that.'

'This is good. Such chaos will prevent them from breaking out of our trap, I think. How do I identify their leader?'

Luci frowned. 'He'll have the most bronze and the most gold. The brightest clothes. Don't do what I think you're about to do.'

'They outnumber us, and though they're tired, they're fierce. We need to break them, to take the heart from their fight. What will they do if I kill a chieftain?' As he spoke, his gaze played across the enemy, looking for visible riches.

'It will be a bad omen for the rest of the fight, certainly. But the Ordovician leaders are not in charge because their daddy was rich. They are in charge because they're stronger than anyone else, and have killed any challengers.'

'I'm quite well trained.'

'You're new, domine. Untried.'

Agricola flashed the slave an angry look. 'Then wait here, and if I die you might be free.'

With that, he locked his eyes on one man, a bear of a warrior in the front line. He had a helmet that looked suspiciously as though it had been hammered out of a captured Roman one, adorned with horns that had been welded on and a great plume. He wore a shirt of fine chain, not dissimilar to the ones the Roman auxiliaries used, and his tunic was a bright blue, already spattered with dark stains. His face bore an expression of utter fury, his eyes glinting like obsidian, his beard braided and filled with beads. He had a hexagonal shield on his arm that bore an image of an oak tree painted around the boss, its branches and roots entwined in brown across the green face, and his sword was long and broad, larger even than the Roman cavalry swords. He was a truly terrifying sight, and clearly fearless, the way he was wading into the fray, bloody teeth bared, pushing his own tribesmen out of the way with the need to fight. Even as he watched, that huge sword came down and split a legionary's shield, shattering the arm behind it.

'You,' Agricola bellowed in the native tongue, one of only a dozen or so words he'd learned in their time among the Demetae, lifting his sword and pointing it at the chieftain.

He had to repeat the cry, not, he thought, because it was lost in the din, but probably because his accent made it sound strange, and it took the man a few moments to realise what was being said and that it was being said to him.

Those glittering eyes rose and fell upon Agricola. The teeth, white among the crimson blood, moved from a clenched grimace into a hungry grin, and the big warrior simply pushed down the man with the shattered arm and walked over him.

Another legionary tried to stop him, but the big warrior's shield slammed out, the boss catching the Roman in the chest and sending him reeling back. Soldiers closed the gap, preventing too many of the Ordovices from following and turning this one attack into a full-blown breech. Two of the enemy had managed to push in behind him, but quickly found themselves struggling, surrounded by angry legionaries.

Agricola watched the man approach. He took two small cuts from soldiers trying to stop him, but easily pushed them aside as though they were nothing. As the man broke through the last line, the tribune jumped from the saddle.

Behind him, he heard Luci cursing in a mix of Latin and his native tongue. Agricola felt the first moment of real nerves, then. Until that point, the adrenaline of the action had carried him along, but as he watched the man – a good head and a half taller than him – bearing down, he realised that he may have just bitten off more than he could chew.

'Concentrate.' He heard the voice of Gaius Suetonius Jovinus in his mind, echoing across a peristyle garden. 'Always be aware of your opponent, watch his eyes, his hands, his feet, anticipate every possible move.'

And he realised suddenly that he was. He'd made light of that with his friend, and it had sounded impossible, to be fully aware of everything about a man, yet as he watched the chieftain approach, he saw many things. The man was big and experienced, a fierce and tested warrior. But he was also thoroughly over-confident. He had absolutely no concept of failure. His eyes were on Agricola's head and shoulders. He'd killed two men while Agricola watched, and they were both blows to the upper body – instant-kill blows. He had no intention of duelling carefully and methodically. He just wanted Agricola's head. His feet were in boots, his lower legs wrapped in the pelt of some animal, wound around with twine. The Roman's gaze took in the boots. They were calfskin, he reckoned. They would be quite thick, would *need* to be, for the winter weather in these hills. A plan forming, he reached down with his left hand and pulled the pugio dagger – the one Luci had used to shave him – from his belt.

The big warrior roared and leapt.

Agricola had seen it coming, in the man's eyes and in his bearing. As the big man brought his huge sword down, intending to split Agricola in two, killing with his first blow, the Roman melted out of the way, allowing his knees to buckle, dropping to the soft, wet earth. As he dropped and the big man almost overbalanced, his victim no longer beneath the falling sword, Agricola's dagger slammed down, held reversed in his grip, punching through the leather of the man's boot, driving down so hard it sheared through the foot and jammed in the sole. Even as the chieftain screamed, Agricola was rising, but not too fast, for the second blow was struck even as he came up. Leaving the dagger jammed in the foot, his gladius came round behind the man and he pulled the blade hard, edge pressed against the man's legs behind the knee. He felt the hamstring cut.

As Agricola came to his feet once more, the chieftain was doomed. The man's eyes were wide with shock as he wobbled back and forth, struggling to stay up, his left foot and knee both crippled, putting all his weight on the right.

The chieftain roared, a chilling sound, managing with difficulty to remain standing, pulling his sword back for a second blow.

Agricola punched him in the face, not giving the warrior time to carry through his attack. The man reeled, sword held above his head. He tottered back from the blow and began to fall, his non-crippled leg no longer strong enough to hold him. Agricola looked at him. The man was done, but not dead. The enemy had to *see* him die. He had one chance before the warrior fell out of sight. His eyes picked out the targets on the man's body, remembering his earliest sword training, the standard fare of the army.

The three killing zones.

Groin, armpit and neck.

Each was a death blow. But the groin would not be seen. The man's armpits were protected by the chain shirt with its short sleeves. The only one of the three killing zones on display was the neck, though that was hidden behind the braided beard.

Agricola struck, hoping the beard did not hide some form of armour.

He was surprised at the resistance his sword met, and for a moment wondered whether the man wore a sort of collar, but then the resistance gave way and his sword plunged into the man's throat. The blood fountained, though fortunately it did not spray across Agricola, for the beard caught the flow and soaked it up as the man fell back with a gasp, the Roman's sword coming free.

Agricola stared, watching the man fall away.

He felt the urge to vomit. Somehow the sheer need and adrenaline that had been pushing him thus far washed out of him in a heartbeat as the danger passed, and the reality of what he'd done flooded in to replace it. He'd fought men on that charge into the bog, but that had been almost a passing thing, and he'd killed the druid, but that had been the druid's doing, pushing himself onto the blade. This was different. New. Now that it was over, it was hard to see it as battle, hard to see it as anything but murder. He had taken a life, deliberately, singling out his victim and almost tricking him into death.

He was shaking.

The blood was pumping fast through his veins, so fast it sounded like thunder in his ears.

Then he heard something else. He realised he was standing absolutely still, other than an unstoppable trembling, and staring at the space where the man had been. And there was a new noise. He blinked. He looked about.

The men of the Twentieth legion were cheering. No, not cheering. They were chanting. Chanting his name, even as they butchered and slaughtered. His sword was still held before him, blood running down the blade, pooling at the handguard, trickling slowly across his fingers, still warm.

He lowered the sword, almost dazed. The shock and horror of the kill were already beginning to fade, like a bad dream on waking. He had killed. It became a simple thing, and not murder. Not personal. It became...

War.

He even smiled.

The battle was changing as he watched. The enemy were still roaring, but there was more of an edge of panic and desperation about it now. Gone were the hunger and fury. The enemy were about ready to break, but they couldn't. The Romans had them surrounded, and now the edge in numbers had very much tipped in favour of Rome. Here and there an Ordovician warrior managed to escape through the press of the encircling Romans, but each and every one regretted it quickly, for Valda and his Batavians were waiting, ready to chase down survivors, and each was hungry to draw blood and to take a head as prize.

Agricola cleaned his sword and sheathed it, then slowly paced back to his horse and pulled himself up into the saddle. As he looked about, still slightly dazed, a legionary approached, head bowed in respect, holding Agricola's dagger by the tip, pulled free of the chieftain and cleaned, offering it to its owner. As the tribune thanked the man and took it, sheathing it, another reached up with a prize, offering it to Agricola: a torc of gold, taken from the dead chieftain. He could see the line across the decorative work caused by his sword, the source of that resistance he had felt at the man's neck. He looked at it for a long moment, wondering what to do.

'Take it,' murmured Luci close by.

He did so, thanking the legionary. He pulled it round his neck, then had to bend it slightly tighter to make it fit, for the chieftain's neck had been massive.

'You are mad,' Luci said.

'I did what needed doing.'

'Mad,' the slave said again.

'Would you have saved me this time?'

'Gods, no,' he replied with a surprising vehemence.

Agricola turned a frown on him. Luci smiled weirdly. 'Single combat? If I'd interfered you'd have been shamed. A laughing stock.'

'But a living one.'

'Better a dead hero than a live coward.'

Agricola's frown deepened. The man was right, of course, at least from a Briton's point of view. He felt he was slowly starting to understand the people of this island.

The two of them sat there and watched the battle finish. There was no doubt now. Rome had carried the day, and it was just a matter of finishing them off. Rising as high as he could in the saddle, Agricola looked this way and that. Of any relief force from the higher valley camp to the east there was no sign, but he could just see the distant mass of the shoreline force approaching.

His gaze jumped from them to the struggling last remnants of the Ordovician army, then to the hilltop fortress. There were some two hundred left in the hillfort, maybe a few more, but they would presumably not include the best, hardened warriors, who would have descended the slope for the fight. The army needed to finish mopping up here, for the battle was not over yet, but it would be nice to complete the victory before help came.

Four centuries of legionaries were committed here, and two centuries of auxiliary infantry, as well as two more of the

Batavians, the non-mounted contingent, who were still wading into what remained of the Ordovices. That left an ala of cavalry, some hundred and twenty riders, the Batavian horse who were waiting hungrily on the wings for any fleeing warrior they could catch. Agricola smiled. They wanted blood. He would give them it.

'Luci, we're going to take Bird's Rock.'

'What?'

'There can't be more than about two hundred up there, not their best. We have over a hundred riders, and they're Valda's Batavians. What do you think?'

Luci looked west, at the distant, approaching reinforcements. He grinned. 'Fuck 'em.'

'Quite.'

He gestured to a centurion. 'Finish them off. No survivors. We're going to take the fort.'

The centurion saluted, and Agricola, with Luci in tow, rode off out of the press, seeking the Batavians. Valda was easy enough to find, his riders gathered in small groups around the battlefield, some fifty paces back from the fighting, watching for anyone escaping. Half a dozen heads hung from saddles already, decapitated bodies visible lying in bloody grass here and there.

'Would you like a fight?'

Valda gave him a grin and followed his pointing finger up to Bird's Rock. In moments the orders had been given and more than a hundred Batavian riders were gathering on him as he led the slow ride across the valley. The Batavian infantry would certainly have their fill of blood back at the battle, but now the horsemen could finish bloodying their blades too.

With Luci and Valda around him, one to each side, and the rest of the Batavians close behind, he began the easiest route up the hillside, one they had followed innumerable times since autumn. The path worn up the slope began sharply, rising from the valley floor, heading south and curving around the rocky outcropping as it climbed. The horses plodded, the climb tough even for them, yet all present were expert riders, and all knew that the ascent had to be slow and gentle to save the horses. In tiring the horses on the slope, the men themselves were saved exertion, so they would be fresh at the top.

After what felt like an hour, with the valley floor looking like some distant world far below, they turned and moved onto the slightly easier, gentler uphill that crossed a low saddle and then ascended towards the gate of the hillfort.

'How do you want to play this?' Valda asked.

'You're the expert,' Agricola shrugged. 'I just want the fort taken.'

'Alright. Once we reach missile range, we charge and storm the fort.'

'What?'

'Minimal casualties on the approach. The horses can rest then, because as soon as we get near the ramparts we jump from the horses and rush the place.'

'That's what passes for a plan among Batavians, is it?'

Valda grinned. 'Complain if it doesn't work, sir.'

That made Agricola laugh, and so they closed on the hillfort, at the German's command, breaking into a gallop, racing up the last of the gentle slope. His assumption that the best of the enemy had committed to battle below seemed borne out, for the hail of missiles that greeted them was nothing compared to that which had turned away the initial attack months ago. A handful of arrows, bullets and rocks hurtled out into the air, and two riders fell on approach, one lying twitching in the grass, the other rising again close to his stricken horse, cursing and rubbing his head.

Then they were there, already, close enough to see the faces atop the rampart.

They were gaunt faces, ill and starving. They were the warriors no longer strong enough to take the battle to Rome, who had been left at the fort. With that realisation, any fear Agricola had over the assault evaporated. Indeed the Batavians, bellowing in their harsh native tongue, leapt from their horses and raced for the fortifications, swords torn free, pushing each other out of the way with the urge to fight. Agricola let them flood past him as he too dropped from his horse. This was their fight. They didn't need him, and he'd already had his fill of personal combat for the day. As the Batavians rushed the gate, Agricola turned to Luci. 'Best hold the horses. Theirs might not wander away, but ours might.'

Luci nodded. He was clearly far from worried about missing this fight. Instead, as the Batavians surged over the defences into Bird's Rock, Agricola and his slave looked about them and took it all in. The defenders were hopeless, ill and weak, but that did not seem to matter to the Batavians, who had the killing madness upon them now. Even as Agricola watched, the German auxiliaries forced the gate and clambered over the ramparts into the lower ward of the hillfort.

His gaze fell from the carnage there, down the vertiginous slope to the valley floor. Across the flat ground, the battle was over, the last survivors being butchered where they lay. The force from the shoreline had almost arrived, but by the time they did there would be no survivors among the Ordovices. With a blink of surprise, he spotted the legate's carriage bouncing across the turf. It seemed news of the fight had been sufficient even to bring the dying commander from his bed. Further up the valley, he could now see the force from the lake camp on their way too, not far from the battlefield.

Another glance at the hillfort, and he realised that the fight there would be over in no time. Already the Batavians were over the second gate and into the upper ward, rampaging among the native houses there.

Bird's Rock had fallen, and that meant that the resistance of the Ordovices in this coastal region was over. It was only a few short days now until Tubilustrium and the beginning of the campaigning season. By the time the trumpets were brought out and the war resumed in full, Geminus' force would be able to march north and meet the other legions with tidings of victory. The legate would be thrilled to be able to do so. Emeritus less so. He had missed it all. If he'd not hated Agricola enough already, this would be the nail on the crucifix to finish it.

'Let's go have a look,' he said, almost conversationally, taking the reins from Luci once more and pulling himself up into the saddle. The slave did the same, and in a few moments, the two men were walking their tired horses up towards the open, unguarded gate of the hillfort that had been denied them for a winter season.

The nature of the force that had taken the Ordovician fortress was plain to anyone who knew the Batavians, for the bodies littering the ramparts and the area around the gate were largely headless. Agricola moved among the decapitated shapes, noting the signs of illness and starvation evident on what was left of the bodies, climbing to the inner gate. Already, the last of the defenders were being overcome. As the two rode towards the centre of the fortress, where Valda sat tying a head to his saddle by the hair, two figures emerged from one of the huts, Batavians closing around it in a circle.

A man, already with a grey beard and thinning hair, but wearing expensive-looking clothes and a gold circlet about his brow. He was unarmoured, but held a good, gleaming sword. His face betrayed no fear – indeed, he looked almost serene, despite the fact that his death was clearly closing in around him. He lifted his sword and moved it back and forth, tracking the approaching Batavians.

Behind him, the second figure to emerge was the one that really caught Agricola's attention.

It was only the third time in all these months that he'd seen the woman in black, and the first time he'd seen her anywhere near this close. Her patterned face turned to him, as though she'd sensed his presence before even emerging, those tattoos or painted marks fascinating to the eye. She wore a robe and a dress beneath, both crow-black, both ragged, but not, apparently, through time and wear. Her ragged appearance was deliberate. She sent a shiver up the tribune's spine.

'No survivors,' Valda told his men, but Agricola found himself clearing his throat.

'Belay that. Kill the man. Bring the woman back to camp.'

The witch narrowed her eyes at him. Whether she understood, he could not say, but it certainly looked that way. Short of being able to interrogate a druid, he had a feeling that she might prove very informative. He watched as the starving king of the Ordovices met his end bravely, managing to convincingly wound one of the attackers before the first blow felled him. As he was repeatedly battered and hacked to pieces there was a brief argument over who got his head, but it was not long before they rose and the woman in black was surrounded. She hissed strange syllables at them, and pulled something from her cloak, a collection of bones and feathers that she crunched up and dropped before her.

The soldiers were on her then, grabbing her and binding her as she fought back, biting and scratching all the time. Agricola heard an indrawn breath and turned to see that Luci had gone pale.

'What is it?'

'She cursed you.'

'What *is* she? You know, don't you?'

Luci twitched. 'I've never seen her like. They say women like her live on Mona, in the sacred groves. They are sorceresses, they walk with the gods as often as they walk with men. They are the only ones who can refuse the druids.'

'What did she say?'

'I don't know. They speak their own language. I never believed they were real before. They are stories mothers tell naughty children. When I told you I didn't know who she was, it was true, really. I've never been sure the stories were real. And even then I've never heard tell of them leaving the island except in horror tales among kids, where they stalk the night, stealing children for their rites.'

Agricola watched the woman as the last of the buildings and bodies were looted, and the Batavians gathered ready to descend. Her eyes never left him, even when she was led with a jerk on a leash back down and through the two gates, out of the fortress. He became aware suddenly that he was wearing the golden torc of an Ordovician chieftain, and wondered whether that had helped to draw her ire. Outside, she was loaded on a horse's back, and they began to pick their slow way back down to the valley.

By the time they reached the lower slopes, crossed the fields and approached the site of the battle, it was well and truly over. The whole Roman force had gathered, the allied dead laid out in rows, the enemy heaped in a pile ready for burning or burial. The legate had not left his carriage, but the vehicle's door was open and the slaves were hurrying this way and that while two centurions reported in to the commander.

With Valda and Luci, Agricola had the horse with the witch-woman led forth, and approached the carriage. As they neared, Geminus appeared in the doorway, and Agricola's breath caught in his throat. Had the man not been moving, Agricola would have assumed him dead already.

'What is this?' the legate croaked, his voice little more than crackling parchment.

'A witch woman of the Ordovices, sir. A sorceress, apparently. I suspect she will have much information about what we will face on Mona.'

As a Batavian threw her from the horse to the ground, the black-clad woman rose slowly, her gaze, full of malice, sliding from Agricola to the legate. Her voice once again uttered something low and arcane in a vicious tone. Her hands were bound, but they came up together, forming shapes with her fingers, facing Geminus. Whatever she was doing, Agricola saw the legate's face fly into a rictus of horror.

'Get her out of here,' he hissed.

'Sir, she will know—' Agricola began.

'She curses me, like all her kind,' he barked in his death-close voice. 'She is why I die, tribune.' Then, to a centurion nearby, 'Crucify her.'

'Sir?'

'*Crucify* her. Now! And break off her fingers, cut out her tongue and fill her mouth with rags. She cannot make spells with no fingers and she cannot curse with no mouth.'

Agricola made to intervene, but held himself back at the last moment. It was infuriating to watch such a valuable source of information killed out of hand, but one glance at the terrified legate made it clear he would not be denied. As she was led away, the commander beckoned to Agricola.

'I know we have not seen eye to eye at all times, tribune.'

'Sir.'

'But this was a great thing. You have won me a true victory here. I shall be sure Suetonius Paulinus knows of your part in this.'

Agricola bowed his head in respect, and by the time he lifted it again the legate was already talking to someone else. Out of the corner of his eye he could see the witch being crucified, not even a whimper of fear or pain issuing from the woman. Though he did not look at her, he felt certain her eyes were on him. His glance moved to the legate again. The man planned to report this to the governor, but it was astounding he had made it this far from the coast. Twenty miles or more to the north, into the mountains? Geminus would never make it to such a meeting, Agricola was sure of that.

The legate was but a step from death, and Emeritus would be ready, desperate to fill his expensive shoes.

Now was the time to move.

15

The army lingered in the newly conquered region for twelve days, settling matters. Despite their clear and overwhelming victory, there was a great deal of administration to be dealt with in the aftermath, for remnants of the rebellious tribe lurked in valleys and settlements, hiding out from their new masters. The army split into units of two centuries and moved like ants across the land, into every hut and cave, every woodland and narrow valley, hunting the last resistance, burning farms and enslaving anyone they found. Only when Geminus was content that the whole area was trouble-free and conquered were they permitted to move on. Of course, the legate never left his tent by the coast, and so this decision was based entirely on the information he was fed by Agricola, Emeritus, Cornelius and a series of scout officers.

The time for a change of command was nigh, and at every turn, Agricola expected news of the legate's last breath, yet the man clung on with the tenacity of a cockroach. Despite the clear doom upon him and the cause that was blatantly obvious to everyone, Geminus laboured under the deluded belief that native druids and sorceresses were the cause of all his ills, that their magics worked on him maliciously. As such, he was managing to overcome his failing health through the desperate need to reach this island of druids, where he believed he could force them to remove their spells and heal him.

The opinion of every man from the lowest trench digger to the highest tribune was somewhat different. Still, it seemed to keep him hanging on, and the moment the land was settled, the legate gave the order to move, to travel north and meet up with the armies of Didius Costa and Suetonius Paulinus.

One thing had become rather clear as the army reassembled from its various winter camps around the peninsula: Emeritus had been far from inactive during his enforced separation. As the units rejoined one another, the three that had been based on the southern fringe, along the river valley on that edge of the hills, were clearly now partisans of the tribune's cause. He had absolute command of the unit that had been based with him all winter, and his influence had grown with those to either side. It infuriated Agricola in a way that while he had spent the winter pressing the Ordovices to their end, Emeritus had spent it bribing and lobbying the military to support him as a senior commander.

Indeed, though Agricola's reputation had grown to almost heroic proportions following his critical part in their victory, a rough estimate suggested that the army was more or less evenly divided in their support of the two tribunes. It mattered not that Agricola was the clear choice, for while he had given the men success and pride, Emeritus had given them gold and promises, and they were as important to the man in the field as pride and victory. Agricola still felt he had the edge, for Cornelius was the next most senior officer, and he was firmly in Agricola's camp, but when it came down to it, succession would go one of two ways. Either Geminus would admit that he was dying and would make some official announcement, or he would simply pass away and there would be a contest of wills, or perhaps even of arms.

The force began to move north one bright but chilly morning, crystal blue skies wafted with tiny fleecy clouds above hills of grey and green. The river that formed the northern edge of the region they had contested wandered inland and then turned sharply north, wending its way off towards the other Roman forces, and so they would follow that flow, along a valley that couriers and scouts had used throughout the winter to keep the armies in contact.

'We'll have a new emperor by the time we reach Costa,' Cornelius grumbled as they ambled slowly along the valley.

Agricola looked back. The going was, indeed, slow. The legions of Rome had an almost legendary marching speed. They had crossed Gaul under Caesar at an incredible pace, were able to race to trouble spots, to make good time even across snow-capped mountains, to shift from one end of the empire to the other readily. Yet here they were, moving so slowly that the soldiers kept having trouble maintaining the pace, often bumping into one another. The centurions had reacted to the laborious journey by moving their men into a much more open order, allowing room for them to mess up the march without causing knock-on effects. The legions could march fast, and they could do the difficult pace-and-a-half fairly readily – and double time and even the charge were second-nature to them, every man able to keep time well. What they *couldn't* do was one-third pace, which was what they were being forced to maintain.

'When will he give up and let go?' Luci snorted, eyes on the horse-drawn carriage that slowly trundled north, setting the pace for the whole army.

Agricola was about to tell the slave to keep such sentiments to himself but it was Valda, the Batavian officer, who spoke. 'It *is* ridiculous. Even the supply carts are having to struggle. When you're forcing the oxen to slow down, something is amiss.'

And it was true. An expert teamster had joined the legate's driver, and between them and two scouts picking the best route, they were trundling the slow vehicle along the least troublesome route they could identify. Even then, the commander now rested in the carriage upon a bed of fleeces and pillows two feet deep, taking out the last bumps and lurches of the vehicle. A small team of slaves moved ahead of the carriage on foot with hammers and a heavy roller made of quernstones, flattening the ground to remove every tiny obstacle.

Even then, they failed. Few knew it, but Agricola had seen first hand just how bad the dying legate had become. He'd been at the carriage door speaking to the legate when the vehicle had gone over a small stone, causing a wheel to bump and the carriage to buck slightly. The legate had shrieked as though run through with a blade, clutching his side with wide, pink eyes in his waxy grey face, and had immediately thrown up onto his fleece bed, the output more half-digested wine than anything else.

And so they progressed north at a snail's pace. They were now in the campaigning season, and the officers continued to wonder, sometimes vocally, how long they had before they received an irritated summons from the governor, wondering what was taking them so long.

As had become the norm, Agricola and his slave rode with Cornelius, Sabinus and Valda at the vanguard of the army, with the scouts and the Batavians, several centuries of the Twentieth following on closely, men who cleaved to Agricola's standard, having fought in the battle that had ended Ordovician resistance. Emeritus, with a small cadre of prefects and centurions from his favoured units, rode further back, close to the legate's carriage, where he could attempt to use a silver tongue to secure further power.

Somewhere behind, a horn blew a short, infuriating cadence.

'What the fuck?' Valda snapped, head jerking round.

'It's the call to fall out and make camp,' Cornelius put in, earning rolled eyes, for everyone knew the call well enough by now.

'But we've only been on the move for an hour since the noon halt,' Sabinus sighed. 'At our pace we could cover another mile or two before dark.'

Agricola snorted at the comment, but they were right. The army had covered half the distance to the site of Costa's winter camp, although the scouts had now reported that Costa had moved north to join up with Paulinus already. If they really pushed and moved at almost walking pace, they could overnight in Costa's abandoned camp, which would save the army having to erect defences for the night. Instead, here they were in the middle of nowhere, rolling hills off to the right, a wide valley ahead and the distant blue shapes of mountains to the left. The only signs of activity the scouts had picked out nearby were three farms and a native settlement, all cowed by the legions of Costa over the winter, and a set of broken kilns that men of the legions had used a few months back.

'I'll ride back and check,' Agricola announced, hauling on his reins and turning, trotting back along the line as the men came to a confused halt. No one argued. No one else wanted to go near the legate these days, apart from the ambitious Emeritus.

Past the Germanic cavalry and infantry, the lead centuries of the Twentieth, and the legionary cavalry, he passed the small command group where his opposite number was usually to be found and located him, finally, at the legate's carriage. The vehicle was at a halt, and the teamster and driver in front looked worried. Emeritus was at the open door, with two centurions attending him. As Agricola approached, the tribune turned to see him, his face taking on an almost unconscious sneer.

'Why has he called the halt?' Agricola asked as he slowed.

'*I* called the halt,' Emeritus replied, and for an instant that twitch and sneer dropped. For just a moment, Agricola could almost spot a different man beneath that veneer. Then the sneer returned. 'The legate is dying.'

'We all know that,' Agricola said, his voice low, trying not to be audible inside the vehicle.

'No, I mean now,' Emeritus replied, pointing into the carriage. 'Fuck.'

'Eloquently put.'

Agricola turned and gestured to a prefect from one of the auxiliary units, the most senior officer around. 'Have the men fall out and create two camps, one for the legions and one for the auxilia, with horse corrals and a supply compound. It's still early, so have riders sent to check out the site of Costa's camp a few miles north for our future use, and to locate Costa and his army. Despite any delay, our orders are to rendezvous with the other forces, and so we will do just that. For now, though, the men can have the afternoon free in camp once they're set.'

Emeritus listened to him, his expression suggesting that he was waiting for something to find fault with, but, since he didn't, he sniffed and returned to the carriage door. Agricola walked his horse over to join the man.

The stench from inside the carriage was overwhelming. Piss and shit and vomit all overlain with that strange sickly-sweet smell of the seriously ill. He was impressed at how the slaves inside seemed to be managing to ignore the smell and concentrate on their wailing and gnashing of teeth at the impending demise of their master. He wondered momentarily whether they might switch to joyful dancing were no one looking.

'Gric,' came a low, moaning voice from within. For a moment Agricola hardly believed it was Geminus. His lips hadn't moved, and surely he had one foot in Charon's boat already?

'Sir?'

The legate managed to open one eye. 'A... gricola. And Em... tus. Good.'

The two tribunes waited patiently, trying not to breathe too heavily as the legate gave a rattling cough and seemed to straighten a little.

'I die.'

Emeritus cleared his throat. 'I think this is just a bump in the road, sir. You'll be—'

'No. I die.'

Agricola had remained silent. If even Geminus had accepted the fact, there was little point in trying for fake hope.

'I wanted... wanted to see druids. Wanted them to pay. To save me.'

'Sir, it may be—' began Agricola, but the legate waved him to silence.

'I wish to be remembered... well. To be remembered for our victory, not... this.'

Still the other eye had not opened, and a fresh wave of

nauseating smell suggested that he had begun to leak. 'Command. I pass it. All orders in the chest,' he managed, though the last word was little more than a sigh, and one of the slaves had to indicate an iron-bound chest in the corner to clarify.

'I...' he began again, but this time it turned into a very long sigh, and all strength seemed to leave him. The legate appeared to deflate, turning into a waxy, vile rag of a man, draped over a pile of sodden, filthy pelts. His eye remained locked on them, and it took Agricola a few moments to realise that Geminus was dead.

'Open the chest,' Emeritus barked at the slave. Agricola turned. A number of officers and several signifers and musicians had now gathered close by. He noted the presence of the Twentieth's unit priest, dressed like all the other soldiers, but with his white cloak to hand for any official duties. A priest should be above reproach. Of course, most weren't, but that was Rome for you. Everything, from bread to honour, had a price. But in the army, where gods were closer and had a direct hand in your survival, the priests were known to be a little more pious and unbreakable than most.

'Sacerdos,' he called, beckoning to the priest.

Emeritus frowned at him.

'This is a man's will and of vital importance,' Agricola explained. 'Without his family present, it should be witnessed by a group of six or seven good men of outstanding character. These officers and the priest from the Twentieth would seem appropriate, wouldn't you say?'

Emeritus' eyes narrowed as he tried to work out what Agricola was up to, but the truth of it was clear. He was right. And Agricola knew that whatever was in the chest, it would need to be unarguable if they were to avoid a conflict between the two of them. He could not imagine Emeritus voluntarily giving way to him, and he had been appointed directly by the governor, so he was not going to back down to Emeritus unless ordered to do so.

Two of the slaves, still wailing dutifully, hauled the chest forward to the doorway while the others placed a coin under Geminus' tongue to pay the ferryman. One of the pair produced a hefty key ring and found the correct one, unlocking the chest. He then lifted the lid from behind so that the men outside could look in. Emeritus craned in the saddle, but would have to dismount to look properly.

'Sacerdos?' Agricola gestured at the chest.

The unit priest, still in his armour, dropped his shield and pilum and pulled the white cloak up and over his head in the age-old fashion, as though he were at a sacrifice. Appropriately and solemnly attired, he crossed to the carriage door and passed between the two tribunes, head bowed in respect.

'Find the will,' Emeritus commanded him. 'Break the seal and read it aloud.'

Agricola nodded. After a year of campaigning under Geminus, with Emeritus his direct opposition, everything was about to change. The priest, looking uncomfortable, stepped up to the carriage and lifted himself to peer into the container. He carefully and respectfully moved a few things aside until he found what he was looking for. He then lifted two ornate boxes, one in each hand, one of wood from the silver fir, one of local oak, each sealed with wax and an imprint of a ring. He looked at the pair, uncertain which he was supposed to be examining.

'Show me,' Emeritus said, and the priest brought the two over and turned them so that the seals were visible. Two different seals. Two different cases.

'The horse one is the legate's. The seal is healthy. Open it,' Emeritus commanded.

Agricola nodded. The other box, he'd noted, was sealed with the signet of the governor himself, Suetonius Paulinus. The priest placed the other box back in the chest and broke the seal of the fir wood one, opening the lid and lifting out the document within.

'Let it be known that the seal was recognised and subscribed.'

He opened the document, also of silver fir wood, coated with soot-wax and inscribed with neat writing. He took a breath.

'I, Lucius Valerius Geminus, son of Gaius Valerius Geminus, before I die, order that my nephew Gaius Valerius Flaccus be my sole heir. Let all other claimants be disinherited on no other terms than that I give here. Let Gaius Valerius Flaccus accept my estate within the next hundred days after my death and know that he is my heir, in the presence of witnesses. If he does not accept my estate and refuses to enter upon it, be he disinherited and my estate be granted to our beloved emperor.'

He turned that leaf over, completed, and Agricola could sense the impatience in Emeritus.

They listened on as the will continued, listing the specific aspects of the estate and certain conditions that the man's nephew was to maintain, passing some items and properties to loved ones. Agricola almost chuckled as the man posthumously freed his slaves and gave them a small fund with which to begin their new lives, for the slaves stopped wailing instantly, gasping, and finding their Phrygian caps of freedom in the chest. Good luck, thought Agricola. Of all the places for a slave to be freed, in a war zone on the most barbarous border of the empire surely was the least desirable. Still, better a free man here than a slave in the city, he supposed.

The priest finished the will. Emeritus huffed. 'That tells us nothing, other than that his nephew will be damned lucky to claim his inheritance within a hundred days. It'll take most of that for a message to reach Rome.'

Agricola pointed. 'He did not say necessarily that his orders were in the will. He just said in the chest.'

Emeritus thought on this for a moment and then reached out for the other box. Agricola swept it from beneath his fingers and held it out to the priest, levelling a meaningful look at his fellow tribune.

The priest took the box reverently and waited until both of them nodded to him, then broke the seal. Opening it, he lifted out a wax tablet of the variety used by military scribes across the empire.

'Gaius Suetonius Paulinus to Lucius Valerius Geminus, greetings,' the priest began, reading from the tablet. 'We are saddened to hear of your ill health, and we pray daily for your deliverance and continuation in the role to which you have been assigned. With the love of the gods, you will rejoin us in time for our greatest campaign. If, as you fear, your illness overwhelms you before that can happen, we hereby place that force under full command of the tribune Gnaeus Julius Agricola, based in no small part upon your own testament to his abilities. Let the other tribunes fulfil appropriate roles as assigned by Agricola until the forces are reunited and we are able to grant new positions. This I vow on this day, two before the kalends of Martius. Farewell, brother.'

Agricola tried not to explode with relief – joy, even. It would not be seemly, and certainly wouldn't go down too well with Emeritus, whose expression was unreadable, but whose eyes had acquired a gimlet gleam.

That was it. There could be no argument. The command had come down again from the governor with the blessing of the legate, sealed and irrefutable. Even Emeritus couldn't deny this. Still, there was something in his eye that said it might not be over. But not only had the governor confirmed Agricola in command, he had also acknowledged his part in their victory, of which Geminus had written. His mother would approve. A single year into his military and political career and he had been mentioned in dispatches. His future suddenly looked a lot brighter.

Without another word, Emeritus wheeled his horse and trotted off back to his more loyal friends. They would surely not interfere, though, for within heartbeats word of all this would be spreading through the army. Plenty of people were within straining earshot, and quite a few even closer. Agricola rode back to his friends and passed the news of everything that had happened to Sabinus, Cornelius and Valda. As he recounted the freeing of the slaves, he tried to ignore the pointed look Luci gave him.

'Do you think that's the last we'll hear of dissent, sir?' Sabinus asked.

'I hope so. Emeritus looked rather unimpressed by it all, but I doubt he will be stupid enough to go against the governor's orders.'

Luci cleared his throat. 'Have you ever heard the tale of Prince Danimacus?'

Agricola rolled his eyes. 'You know damn well that unless you told me it, I've not heard anything of your tribes.' He looked to the others. Sabinus and Valda shook their heads.

'Danimacus and his brother fought over the inheritance when the old king died. Then they found a will which named Danimacus the heir. He ruled for four days before he *accidentally* fell down a mine shaft and his brother claimed the crown.'

Agricola snorted. 'You just made that up.'

'If you say so.'

The tribune's brow furrowed. 'A cautionary tale?'

'Just look out for surprise mine shafts. That's all I'm saying.'

'I'm surprised you're not helping him, in case I free you in my will.'

'Personally,' Luci snorted, 'I'm more hopeful of my chances with you still around than with you gone and Emeritus in charge.'

Agricola mulled this over as the legions and auxiliary units settled into camp that afternoon. By the time he took a wander down to the river at the upstream end of the camp to splash cold water across his face, he noted that talk had begun among the men. The news of the legate's death was everywhere, of course, but there was more than that. He could almost feel a division growing in the camp between those who had fought with him this spring and aligned with his banner, and those who had been lobbied by Emeritus and stood to lose out with Agricola taking command. No matter what the governor commanded, it seemed the army remained divided. On his return journey, Agricola was surprised to find himself on the lookout for metaphorical mine shafts.

Back in his tent, he had Luci shave him and trim his hair again, and changed into just a clean military tunic, boots and his cloak. Thus subtly attired, he left the place and strolled across the camp to the other tribune's tent.

On the way, he could see the pyre being constructed near the river, where Geminus would be rendered down to ash at sunset. He would have to attend that particular ceremony, of course, but he had something to do first. He nodded to the two soldiers guarding Emeritus' tent and then stopped before them. One knocked, entered and spoke to the tribune, then returned and gestured with a bow for Agricola to enter. He did so. Emeritus was seated behind his desk, writing, but as Agricola entered, he dropped the pen and rose from the seat.

'Sit, man,' Agricola said. 'Let us not stand on ceremony.'

'It is the way things are done,' Emeritus said, rather aloofly. Still he was playing the superior role to this provincial who had muscled in on his life.

'We are alone, Tiberius Claudius Emeritus. Let us talk like men, not ranks.'

'A conversation with freedom to speak my mind?'

Agricola nodded. 'I am aware that you do not like me. That you see me as inferior and that you believe I have come from nowhere and taken what is rightfully yours.'

'I see no point in denying that,' Emeritus nodded.

'Similarly, I do not trust your strategic abilities. I fear that you, like so many of our peers, are more concerned with your own lineage and rights than the good of the army and the empire. That, I think, is what the empire gains from we new-bloods, we provincials.'

'So we see eye to eye that we do not see eye to eye, you might say,' Emeritus said, lip curling in dark humour.

'Quite. The situation is volatile now. Dangerous.'

Emeritus frowned. 'Oh? How so?'

Agricola sat on the edge of the bed and placed his hands on his knees. 'We cannot have division in the camp, nor the ongoing suspicion that the officers might attempt a coup.'

Emeritus suddenly shot to his feet, face creased into fury.

'Get out of my tent.'

Agricola lifted his hands, palms up. 'Wait. Don't fly off in anger.'

'How *dare* you?' Emeritus hissed.

'What?'

'You accuse me of forging some sort of plot against you? I am incensed to the point of apoplexy, Agricola.'

'Come now, I've seen you watching me. I've seen your face and listened to the men in the camp.'

Emeritus took two steps and thrust a finger so hard at Agricola's face he almost poked him in the eye. 'I dislike you, Agricola. I dislike everything you stand for, and I believe I would make a better commander of this army than you. But I am also a Roman of patrician blood, an officer in the emperor's legions, and I would put my own blade through my heart before I would betray my commander, my governor, my oath and the eagle. How *dare* you? You offend me.'

Agricola, forced almost prone by the angry pointing, reeled. How had he so misjudged this?

'You do not seek to replace me?'

Emeritus stepped back and folded his arms. 'I do not need to. The way you treat war like your personal playground, it will not be long before your ragged corpse decorates a Briton's lance. And when your hubris has killed you on the battlefield, the position will fall to me naturally. In the meantime, I will take whatever place you assign me, since the governor has made it clear that such a decision is yours, and I will perform my duties in said task to the best of my ability.'

He took a slow breath. 'But you will never again insult my honour with such base suggestions as this, or I will seek out a morning with swords drawn, and then only one of us will go on. Do you understand?'

Agricola nodded, still frowning, a little shaken by the outburst. 'You will play whatever role I assign without argument?'

'I should not need to repeat myself.'

'Then I would have you continue to lead the Fourteenth along with half the auxilia, with Cornelius leading the other half and the Twentieth. I would have you take the second in command position with Cornelius rising to third.'

Emeritus seemed a little surprised, but recovered quickly, nodding.

'You thought I'd shuffle you out of command?'

'But you want to keep your enemies close where you can see them?' Emeritus suggested.

'I thought you weren't my enemy?'

The two men stood in silence for a time and then, at length, the lesser tribune nodded. 'You say there is still division among the men? Some would stand against you?'

'I believe there are those who would make any move to support you, yes.'

'Then I shall speak to them and make the position clear. The command is yours, Agricola. What are your orders?'

Agricola rolled his shoulders as he stood and stretched. 'We should not delay. War is already underway once more, and at the pace Suetonius Paulinus moves, if we do not hurry, we might miss it. Tonight we burn the lamented Valerius Geminus, sacrifice, say our prayers and let the men mourn in the usual way, with wine. Then in the morning we gather his ashes, burn his stupid carriage, and move at a good pace north, marching to meet the governor.'

Emeritus nodded. 'Rarely do we see eye to eye, Agricola, but I also will be glad to see the back of that wagon and to move at more than a snail's pace.'

16

There had been a certain amount of settling into the role, not only on Agricola's part, but also on that of the officers and men of both legions and auxilia. Those who had been ready to support him continued to do so, while those who had fully expected Emeritus to step into the command position initially resisted the change. They had received promises of a bonus from the tribune, and a few had been vouchsafed new positions. By unspoken agreement, the two tribunes managed to sort the problem. While Agricola was a far from wealthy man and relied upon the funds that came with the army's pay wagons every month, Emeritus was clearly rich, and the next month an extra chest of gold arrived, which he liberally spread about the army, both those he had promised and those who had been Agricola's men, mollifying and pleasing all. In the meantime, Agricola had lived up to his second-in-command's promises, promoting all but one of those offered, and only refusing the last because his record showed he had arrived for duty drunk late in the winter. The man argued, but Agricola was adamant and, thankfully, Emeritus backed him on the decision.

On Agricola's part, within a few days of taking control and marching north at a now mile-eating speed, he found a new respect for the unfortunate legate who now travelled south and east in an urn with the couriers, heading to his family mausoleum back in Rome. He knew sufficient strategy and was familiar enough with the logistical side of the army to make what seemed important decisions, but he'd never expected the rest – had never seen what happened in the command tent when staff meetings *weren't* on. His free time seemed to evaporate in a matter of hours as clerk after clerk brought him lists, documents for countersigning and sealing, reports, headcounts, requisition requests from quartermasters, decisions to be made from the unit medical staff who had arms to amputate. It seemed to go on forever.

And then, in the few moments he *did* seem to get to himself, there were other interruptions.

The first morning, while Luci was shaving his neck, a knock and a respectful request for audience.

'Yes?'

A centurion. 'With respect, sir, I have a soldier I don't know what to do with.'

'What?'

'He was drunk the other night – off duty, mind, and no offence committed – but he fell into the full latrine and slept in it, with men shitting on him all night. He's bathed nine times in the river since then and changed his clothes, but no matter what he does, he still smells of shit. His contubernium won't let him sleep in their tent and no one wants to march beside him. I've tried transferring him to another unit, but no one will take him.'

Agricola blinked. Was this the sort of thing Geminus had had to deal with? He thought for a moment. 'Can the man ride?'

'I don't know, sir.'

'Find out. If so, make him a temporary scout. Give him a horse and send him a few miles ahead all day until the aroma wears off. Then he can return to regular duties.'

The centurion smiled. 'Very good, sir.'

As he left, Luci chuckled quietly. Nothing else needed saying.

That evening, Agricola finished working through the sick lists and had a bath-tub brought to his tent and filled with tepid water. He was about to take a few moments to relax, and had just unfastened his belt when the knock came.

'Yes?'

A Batavian officer, with a thick German accent. 'Sir, the cavalry of the Fourteenth have stolen a horse.'

'What?'

'My men went to check the corral, and one of our horses was lame. When its rider checked it over, he realised it was not his horse. It is extremely similar, but it is not his. He has found his healthy horse among those of the Fourteenth. Someone switched them in the dark.'

'Is he sure? Horses can look very similar.'

The man frowned as though Agricola had asked him if he might not recognise his own mother. 'Sir, we know our horses. Of *course* he's sure.'

Agricola sighed. '*How* lame?'

'Several days rest required.'

'Not critical, then. Deliver the lame horse to the Fourteenth with my compliments, identify the owner of the beast and send him to me. He will be disciplined and the horse returned.'

'Thank you, sir.' The man left, and Agricola heaved a sigh of relief. Barely had he finished his bath before the indignant rider was delivered to him, denying all wrongdoing. He managed to change into his sleeping tunic before the door knocker went once more.

'No. I'm to bed.'

'Sir, one of the pay chests has vanished.'

Agricola sighed and switched back to his uniform tunic. 'Alright, wait there.'

He was beginning to see how Geminus had been driven to drink.

And so it went on. A constant slew of paperwork with intermittent problem-solving. They passed Didius Costa's winter quarters the first day and, on the advice of scouts, marched north-east, crossing a range of hills and descending into a lush, green valley surrounded by woodland. They moved at speed, but with care. The area should be safe, for this region had been patrolled by Costa's army over the winter, but the woodlands on the hills to either side looked oppressive and could easily hide a warband.

As they passed the remnants of one of Costa's overnight camps a few days later, riders from the Twentieth arrived, bearing news from the governor. He had moved west at the start of the season, and Costa's army had now met up with him, close to the north coast and a little further west. Agricola was to make all haste to join them.

Despite arguments over the difficulty of the terrain, he decided not to continue following the gentle river valley north and then race along the coast. Instead, they would make directly north-west, through the mountain region. The going would be far tougher, and they may have to leave much of the supply train to catch up, but according to the scouts, they could turn a thirty-mile march into a fifteen-mile one.

That was their next day, then. With scouts leading the way and the advice of a few natives they could coerce into aid, they selected the best valleys and passes in the mountains and marched at speed. They departed as the first golden light of dawn brushed the peaks, and passed icy rivers, deep, serene lakes, grey scree slopes and snow-capped peaks, deep forested valleys and occasional settlements where natives watched them with resentment and fear. By noon the supply wagons were already miles behind, and Agricola had assigned four centuries – two legionary, two auxiliary – and a small cavalry escort, to keep them safe as they slowly followed. In the meantime, the bulk of the army pressed on. Fifteen miles in a day was nothing to the men of the army, but terrain changed everything, and even without the wagons it was slow and laborious going. Moreover, as they finally emerged from the northern edge of the mountains and into foothills, it had become clear that they had already done nineteen miles of the estimated fifteen. That was the problem with uncharted territory, even the best estimates were still just that: estimates.

Finally, they passed one long lake, marching along the shore line, crossing low, open hills, and Agricola reined in at the head of the army with the vanguard, eyes wide.

The island of Mona lay before them.

The mainland continued perhaps a mile further north from where they had emerged in the last hour of sunshine, green and verdant, then the grass dropped to a shoreline that marched east-west as far as the eye could see in each direction. Beyond that shore lay a channel perhaps half a mile across, and there, on the far side of that stretch of water, lay Mona, a flat green land with golden beaches, an attractive sight.

The vista provided by nature was enough alone to draw the breath. But to see the armies of Rome encamped upon the near shore was equally stunning. He'd forgotten just what it looked like when two whole legions and as many auxiliaries were gathered in one place. The camps stretched along the coast for some distance.

The army had reunited.

With the late evening sun in the west sending long spears of shadow from the column, Agricola led his men down to join the army. As they passed the first pickets and neared the lines, scouts enquired and reported in with the location of the headquarters. Agricola gestured to Cornelius.

'Find sufficient space to camp and get things set up. All the best spots will be taken but try and find somewhere flat and with a water source if you can.'

The junior tribune bowed his head and turned to give the orders to his men as Emeritus and the others sat ahorse beside him, looking ahead. He turned to them. 'Sabinus, Valda and Luci, as soon as my tent's set up, get in there and summon all the unit commanders for a meeting after the evening meal. I'll fill you in on everything then. Emeritus, you and I had best report in to the governor.'

Leaving the others to their work, the two senior tribunes rode on through the camps, making for the cluster of tents that marked the headquarters. It was clear that the army had been encamped here for several days, for they were settled in. Arriving at the tents, Agricola slipped from the saddle and handed his reins to one of the governor's bodyguards. As Emeritus followed suit, Agricola looked out across the north. The headquarters and the commander's tent had been pitched relatively close to the water, on high ground, offering an excellent view of the channel and the island beyond. There was a great deal of activity down at the waterline, and he could see timber being worked in vast quantities, fresh boles of trees being carried on carts through the camps and down to the shore all the time.

'The governor's taking this seriously,' he murmured. Then, with Emeritus at his shoulder, as the light began to glow red-gold with sunset, he approached the command tent. There was no need to request an audience. Their approach had been noted and reported to the governor, and as they neared the tent, a centurion gestured for them to enter.

The headquarters was an enormous place, and a dozen huge maps hung on the walls, etched on animal pelts, some of which were familiar, others far from it, describing areas Agricola's army had yet to visit. Three tables stood here, and a number of campaign stools were folded in one corner. Half a dozen clerks worked laboriously at one of the tables, while Suetonius Paulinus himself sat at another, a slave busily cutting the nails of his left hand with a small sharp knife, while he used his right to hold open a scroll and read. He looked up, marking his place with a finger, identified Agricola and Emeritus at a glance, and straightened. He placed a cup on the scroll to hold his place and waved away the slave.

'Good. I had feared you would be late, given your winter locations, but you are in excellent time. You are to be commended, especially dealing as you have with the loss of your commander. All is here? Nothing amiss?'

Agricola shook his head. 'Nothing amiss, Governor. I dispatched a group of soldiers to accompany the legate's ashes back south so they can be sent to his family. Our baggage train is not with us. We had to leave it behind to reach you before sunset. They are well protected, however, and will arrive at some point tomorrow.'

'This is good. I have had the reports of your legate over the winter. You've nothing to add since then on your journey north?'

'No, sir. We met no resistance following the fall of Bird's Rock, and between there and here have seen only cowed villagers. No armed enemies, no warbands, not even a bandit. The men are in good spirits and excellent condition, with a relatively small sick list. We are ready for your command.'

Suetonius Paulinus nodded. 'Good. You have done excellent work in the south, from what I understand. If Geminus' reports are accurate, we now have the Silures at peace, an alliance with the Demetae and all Ordovician resistance cowed as far north as Costa's winter position. For our part, while you have been at work in the south, we have taken full control of Deceangli lands back to the east, overrun all Ordovician territory from south to north, and beaten the Gangani on the western peninsula. With treaties now in place, that means the entire mainland as far north as my predecessor reached is fully under control. The only resistance now lies across the water.'

Agricola nodded his understanding, remaining silent. The governor leaned back in his seat.

'During the winter, I sent a summons for the fleet at Rutupiae, assuming we would need them to cross to the island. As yet we have had no sign of them, though reports confirm they passed Isca and Abona and so must be somewhere in the west, perhaps off the coast of Silurian or Demetae lands. It is somewhat irritating, but I am reliably informed that the waters in the west of Britannia can be treacherous in winter and spring, and so it is perhaps no surprise that they have not yet reached us.' He sighed. 'I had hoped to wait for them, but right now the occupants of that island have only what supplies they stored in previous seasons. Give them another month or two and forage will be good – they might even be able to manage early harvests of some crops. I would rather hit them while they're undersupplied, and so I fear we cannot wait for the fleet. Yesterday I gave the order for the army to start construction of large, shallow barges for the crossing. I am told there are places where the channel can be forded at the right times, but my own experts tell me that such an option is unpredictable and an unnecessary gamble when we can construct boats. As such, I think we should be ready to make the crossing in three to four days. Once your men are settled in, I would like you to detail them to join the construction crews, and then the individual vexillation commands will be dissolved now the army is whole again.'

This news came as something of a blow. Following Geminus' demise, he had been so concerned with who would take command, it had not occurred to him that said position would last only until the army recombined. It seemed his independent command had consisted solely of a few days of shepherding the army through the mountains. Despite his silence, the disappointment must have shown in his face, for Suetonius Paulinus paused and frowned at him.

'I realise that you have had precious little time to prove yourself in command, tribune, but rest assured that your actions last year have secured you a solid place on my staff. Though the three forces are no more, I will have positions and commands for you going forward.'

'Yes, sir,' he said, straight-faced. That was something, at least.

'The faster we assemble a flotilla, the sooner we can cross and finish this. Now to one other matter,' Suetonius Paulinus said, leaning forward. 'Druids.'

'Sir?'

'Have you seen druids in your campaigning to the south?'

Agricola shook his head. 'Only one, I would say, sir, and he allowed himself to be killed before we could interrogate him.'

The governor nodded. 'We have found similar. The druids, it would appear, have all moved to the island as Rome advanced across their lands. Indeed, I have sent out riders and made enquiries, and it appears that the druids even from the tribes who are our allies back in the east have gone. Their entire sect seems to have fled to their sacred island, and they have taken with them hundreds if not thousands of rebels, warriors prepared to defend their holy place from us.'

'We also encountered a woman, sir,' Agricola said. 'A seeress or some such.'

'Oh?'

'It would appear she had something of a similar authority to the druids. She certainly seemed to have the ability to curse, and the warriors of the Ordovices respected her. Unfortunately, just like the druid, she perished before we could learn more.'

It seemed unnecessary to explain *how* she had perished, and that it had been the legate's decision that had cost them such an opportunity.

Paulinus spoke once more.

'Tomorrow, I have arranged a number of sacrifices in preparation for the conflict, and auspices have been readied. I want a reading. The priests have assured me that we will anger no god of import in our invasion of their sacred place. They believe these druids are false priests, using religion like a political weapon to keep hold of their control over the tribes. They cite a number of examples of human sacrifice to support their claim. Still, it unnerves me to make war upon a holy place of *anyone's* gods, and I would like to be certain that Jupiter and Minerva and Mars are all with us on our journey.'

Agricola said nothing. He agreed entirely, though he was less inclined to write off the religious aspect of the druids or their seeress counterparts.

'Very well,' the governor said, 'I think you're caught up on the basics. There will be a full briefing an hour after sunrise when you will learn all the minutiae and have the opportunity to have your say and put questions forth. We will then discuss the invasion in detail and look at new assigned commands. After that there will be the sacrifices and the readings, while the engineers continue to work on the boats. In the meantime, I suggest you settle your force into camp and then relinquish command. Have you anything to add?'

Agricola shook his head. 'I do not believe so, sir. We have taken the liberty of arranging a number of internal promotions and transfers following our campaigns. They have not been over-costly, but naturally created a number of openings in the chain of command and among the excused-duty men.'

Suetonius Paulinus brushed that aside with a sweep of his hand. 'Good. Excellent, in fact. I would like a full breakdown of unit strengths, officer listings, medical section, artillery and supplies present and yet to arrive by the end of the day. That is all.'

And with that they were summarily dismissed. Agricola tried not to sag and sigh at the news that after that long, hard journey, all he had to look forward to was an evening of administration and numbers and then relinquishing his command, as he saluted and turned to leave.

Once outside in the fresh air and the rapidly purpling light of evening, he turned to Emeritus. 'In our new spirit of cooperation, I don't suppose you'd like to help with some unit listings?'

Emeritus gave him a look that was at one and the same time perfect innocence and wily smugness. 'With command comes responsibility, sir. If you need me, I'll be looking for the nearest dice game.'

Agricola gave him a bitter glance, momentarily considering making it an order before dismissing the idea as unnecessarily provocative. Besides, given what loomed on the horizon, he really should make the most of safe mundanity.

He returned to camp to find his tent already up, Luci overseeing the placing of furniture and gear. Hardly worthwhile since in the morning they would no longer be his army. He tried to fight down the bitterness creeping back in. There would be another command for him, the governor had confirmed. Sabinus and Valda stood outside, sharing a wineskin and watching the work. Agricola waited until things were ready and then settled in to wait for the others.

'The gods were on your side against the Ordovices,' Luci said as he began to polish Agricola's sword and his own knife.

'So you said.'

'This is different.'

'Oh? How?'

'What Paulinus is doing now is not war against a tribe. It is war against all the people, our history, our nobles and even our gods. What he does now will forever define this place, either as a free land or as your province. No matter what happens afterwards, if the gods allow Mona to fall to your legions, my people are done. It is the end of our world.'

'That need not be the disaster you seem to think. Rome brings greatness and order. Science and hygiene.'

'And absolute control.'

'Undoubtedly.'

'But Rome turns everywhere else into more Rome. Your people acquire our gods, as they did at Aquae Sulis, and just give them Roman names. Just as you do with slaves.'

'Not you. You still have your own name.'

'You are not every Roman master.'

'True. But we *respect* your gods. We may use our names for them, but we still do honour to them. Were it not for the druids stirring up trouble, we would be more than happy not to invade a sacred island. Unfortunately sometimes politics interferes. We are driven to it. Your druids advocate human sacrifice, and that is illegal in Rome.'

Luci took a deep breath. 'We shall see in the coming days whether it is just you the gods favour, or whether they extend their watch over the whole of Rome.'

That portentous comment stayed with Agricola throughout the evening as he worked on the lists required by the governor, and as he reported what he had learned to the officers still under his command for one more night. It stayed after he'd had his documents delivered to Paulinus, and even as he lay in bed and took precious time to get to sleep.

Rising the next morning, he was unsettled, a feeling that remained during all the sacrifices officiated by the governor, all the positive omens read in the flight of birds, the behaviour of chickens and the sticky, crimson innards of a pure white sheep. All portents had been pronounced good for the invasion, though Agricola privately wondered whether any priest with an eye on a continued career would ever dare offer up a bad omen to the governor, even if he found a diseased and corrupted liver in his lamb. Still, Paulinus was happy, the army was happy, and all seemed to be progressing with speed. Not for Agricola, of course, no longer in command and somewhat adrift.

From that morning, the men under his command joined in the felling and adzing of timber, the construction and caulking of rafts, and the flotilla that would carry them across the water grew rapidly. As he watched the work, somewhat bored after the busyness of command, he found Sabinus, Valda and Luci had all joined him.

'Bet you can't wait for another voyage,' Agricola said with a mean smile directed at Luci.

The slave snorted. 'This is not your southern seas and your great ships. If I fell in here, I could probably walk across.'

'Well, I for one will not need such a vessel,' Valda said dismissively.

'Oh?'

'You do not know our ways?' the Batavian queried.

Agricola frowned, recalling the stories that had circulated of these rugged, dangerous Germans. Back in the earliest days of the invasion, the Batavians had managed to cross the Vaga River in full armour, swimming alongside their horses, using them to stay afloat or, in the case of their infantry, crossing on their large body shields, using them as a form of raft. Of course, the Vaga had only been two hundred paces across and at low tide little more than a puddle, while this strait was half a mile wide and with unpredictable currents. But still, there was no lack of confidence evident in Valda. It also occurred to Agricola that, it only being sixteen years since that great battle at the opening of the invasion, Valda may well have been one of those very men who swam across that day.

That afternoon, the supply wagons began to arrive. At a loss for anything to do, Agricola stood and watched them roll into camp, men who had been his until so recently falling out and joining their own units under Paulinus and Costa.

The day ended as it had begun, a mass of boats on the shoreline, constant industry as long as the light lasted and, for Agricola at least, a whole lot of nothing. The next day brought more of the same, and the next too, though the morning after, the fourth day since their arrival, the engineer in charge of the fleet's construction pronounced the work complete. With no need to provide transport for the Batavians, the man had decided they had enough shallow-beamed, flat-bottomed vessels to ferry the army across in two waves.

Agricola looked up from the man as news began to spread across the army, his eyes falling on the far bank, wondering what awaited them and, still without a new command, wondering what his place would be in it all. As he watched, a figure in black, tiny at this distance, seemed to be looking directly back at him. He shivered.

Over the preceding days, figures had been noted from time to time on the opposite shore, sometimes alone, sometimes in small clusters. They were too far away to get much detail, but there had been white-clad figures among them, and it had not been the same people each time. As the days progressed, the numbers gradually increased, and as they were still different figures each time, the clear suggestion was that a large force of natives waited out of sight, not far from the water. They were being clever, Suetonius Paulinus surmised, not showing their numbers and therefore giving Rome no clear expectations to work with.

Not that that would stop them.

As the army began its preparations for the crossing, the governor called his staff together for the strategy meeting: two score senior officers, including all the unit commanders and several unassigned men, like Agricola.

The plan was simple. The Batavians would cross at the shallowest part of the channel, which was also one of the narrowest, just to the west of the camps. The boats would be filled with Suetonius Paulinus' shock troops, the heaviest of the legionary forces, and the strongest of the auxilia. They would make the first advance. It was assumed that the natives would form some kind of defence and attempt to stop the legions landing. The heavy infantry's job was to effect just that landing, then to forge up onto the sand and create a beachhead, holding it against the enemy long enough for the boats to cross twice and bring the rest of the army forward, which would include the cavalry, the light auxilia, the archers, artillery and so on.

With this second arrival, the archers and artillery would go to work behind the protective line of the legions and break the mass of defenders. When the natives gave way sufficiently, the order would be given and the army would move for a full engagement.

'I shall cross with the first wave, but in its last boat,' the governor explained. 'I want to be there as the beachhead is formed. The legates and tribunes of the legions and the prefects of auxilia will cross with their men of course, though their individual positions I leave up to them. I shall need several experienced officers for individual commands, though.'

Agricola's ears pricked up. At last.

'I need a man to take command of the second wave entire, one to take control of the artillery and archers, one the Batavian units that will cross separately, and one to act as a camp prefect here with the various sections not involved in the crossing. The three Batavian units have their own prefects, but I need a staff officer to coordinate their efforts.'

One of the governor's senior officers, an older man with greying hair and a pinched face that gave him a permanent squint, raised a hand. 'I would be honoured to take the second wave, sir.'

'Good man, Arruntius Pulcher.'

Before he realised he'd done it, Agricola found he had his hand in the air, even as other senior men opened their mouths to volunteer. Suetonius Paulinus looked across at Agricola, interested.

'Tribune?'

'I would like to lead the Batavian crossing, sir.'

'I called for *experienced* officers, Agricola. You are little more than one year a tribune, for all your laudable success and brief command. I had you in mind to take command here in the camp during the crossing.'

An honourable command, but a tedious one, and with little chance of glory. Agricola pushed away any disappointment, determined.

'Sir, I have come to know the Batavians, what they are capable of, how they work, how best to deploy then. Moreover, we have fought side by side for a season or more, and they trust me. For all my youth, there is no man here more conversant with them. No one better for the duty, sir.'

Suetonius Paulinus frowned for a moment, silent, then finally nodded. 'You had best live up to your reputation, young man. Over the past year I have been pleased with your progress, but this assault is critical. You will have much to prove. Men crossing in the manner of the Batavians will be slower than the boats, but I need them on the beach when the second wave deploys at the latest. We cannot wait for you once we are ready to advance. You understand?'

Agricola bowed his head. 'Perfectly, sir. We can do it.'

'We? Are you Batavian now, Gnaeus Julius Agricola?'

'Right down to the taking of heads, sir. For now, at least.'

This brought a rumble of humour around the room, and even Paulinus chuckled. 'Very well. Locate your three Batavian cohorts and prepare yourselves. You will not be able to begin your crossing before the boats, lest you give the enemy more time to prepare, but you cannot delay. You must move fast in order to be part of the landing. Very well.'

The governor continued to issue orders to the other officers, and once the briefing was over Agricola, content that he knew his duty and role in the invasion, hurried back to his tent. Luci was waiting nearby with Sabinus. The army may have recombined and been taken from Agricola's hands, but at least Sabinus and his riders, being part of the Second and not officially on the unit lists, remained tied to Agricola.

'Well?' Sabinus prompted. 'What news, sir?'

'We have the Batavians. Three cohorts. We cross with them and make sure they are there in time to join the advance up the beach.'

He was rather taken aback by the reaction from the others. Luci looked at him as though he was mad, and Sabinus recoiled.

'What is it?' he demanded.

'The Batavians might be renowned for swimming with their horses,' the decurion said quietly, 'but it's not something *we've* ever even tried.'

'No time like the present,' Agricola grinned. 'We learn by doing. I will be with you, remember? There's no other way for me to cross either.'

'I don't suppose you want me to wait in your tent with the wine?' Luci grumbled, eyeing the water warily.

17

Agricola gripped the horn of the horse's saddle with grim determination. He had to think continuously to remember everything the Batavian rider had taken him through the day before. It was a simple thing for them, whose horses had been trained with the water, who practised this technique even in peaceful garrison life. For someone new to it, there was a lot to take in.

Firstly, he'd been told in no uncertain terms to go and change everything. His tribune's armour and uniform were wholly unsuitable, apparently. No one could swim in a moulded bronze cuirass, as it left too little manoeuvrability. As such, he'd been given a shirt of chain like the ordinary Batavian riders, which moved with his own movements. It was heavier, for sure, but certainly more flexible. He changed into smaller boots, much less bulky. His tunic was altered by one of the Batavians, given ties that hung down from the hem, which he had no idea about until they thrust upon him a pair of the braccae, the knee-length trousers the Gallic and German auxiliaries habitually wore. These, he realised, had places to fasten those hanging ties to. Now he was in the water, he knew why. Had he been wearing his unaltered gear, the skirt of his tunic would now be billowing in the water and filling up, floating about, making movement difficult. With it tied to the trousers that encased his legs, there was little movement in the tunic, and he could paddle easily. Similarly, he'd had to swap his baldric for a sword belt that held the blade directly at his waist, for that prevented the sword from swinging around in the water. They were all small subtle changes, but every one made a difference, and every one made him appreciate all the more how clever the Batavians were, and how good they were at what they did.

If he'd thought that was all, he was wrong. His horse was taken away and put into a corral for the duration, and he was given one of the Batavians' spare horses. Their animals were trained for this. Agricola's wasn't.

He glanced round at a loud curse. Sabinus was having trouble. He and his riders, as well as Luci, had all been given the same training and kit, and it seemed Sabinus at least was having as much trouble as Agricola. Luci, of course, seemed to be a natural, damn the man.

He used his free hand and a few kicks of his legs to move his lower half a little further from the horse. That was one of their prime pieces of advice. Do not get in the way of a swimming horse's legs. The moment you get entangled, there is a high probability of both horse and rider drowning. *That* was a lesson he committed to memory from the start. Then there was making sure not to pull on anything that might drag the horse's head down. Hold on to the saddle. If you slip, try to grab the breast strap. If all else fails try for the girth, but that was a last hope, since it likely entangled you in the legs and led to a watery end. Pulling on anything that might drag down the animal's head would likely plunge it beneath the surface, and he was told that this must not happen under any circumstances, since horses could not hold their breath. Their head had to stay above the water, and try not to get any in their ears either.

The simple matter of trying not to get in the way of the horse's legs, making sure the animal was high above water, yet also to kick his own legs and keep a tight hold of the saddle, all was phenomenally difficult. And that was just the main rules. There were countless small ones, too.

The upshot was that even in the first hundred paces, he'd almost drowned twice, had accidentally let go of the saddle once in a panic, and then again when his hand slipped on the wet leather. Both times he'd only just managed to grab hold once more. He'd spent so much time and concentration on the horse that his own head had gone under more times than he could count, and all he could taste and smell was salt, which was in his eyes, ears, nose and mouth. By the time he was two hundred paces out into the water, he was regretting ever having volunteered.

Somewhere out in the middle of the channel, just when he was finally thinking he had the hang of it and that everything might be alright, the cavalryman from the Second off to his right, one of Sabinus' few remaining men, gave a cry of alarm and disappeared beneath the surface, gone for good, though his horse went on without him. Agricola concentrated all the more.

He could see the flotilla of boats out on the water, already much further ahead than the Batavians, closing on the beach.

And he could see the beach.

And what lay beyond.

The theory that a huge force of natives awaited beyond the trees, out of sight of the mainland, had clearly been borne out, for the moment the boats had moved off the shore, the enemy had shown their faces, and continued to do so throughout the action.

The lowest level of the beach remained clear, almost inviting, though it was an invitation only a madman would rush to accept. Further up the beach, defences were being assembled, piles of brushwood and sharpened timbers, dropped in a haphazard fashion, but enough to prevent the legions forming up and simply charging the enemy. These refugees had learned from their years of war, clearly. And beyond that hedge obstacle were the warriors, a mass of men, some in chain shirts and helmets, others in just a tunic, many bare to the waist, displaying their blue whorl tattoos for all the world to admire. They carried spears and swords and axes, waiting for Rome to come to them.

But to do so would bring them closer to the next line. Behind the mass of warriors stood rank upon rank of men with bows and slings, their position carefully selected to put them within range of the water. No man landing was going to be free of missiles. Behind them, up on the grassy sward, horsemen pottered about, waiting, spear points dipped, and between them chariots raced back and forth, two men in the back of each, a driver and a warrior holding high his spear and bellowing encouragement to their people.

The army of the Britons was quite something to behold, a greater force than any Agricola had ever seen levied. But between the desperate moments of kicking in water, slipping from the saddle horn, and dipping beneath the surface only to emerge again with an explosive breath, it was the others he could see that chilled the young tribune.

All along the beach and up onto the grass, those women in ragged black ran back and forth, throwing bones in the air, shredding birds, pointing at the approaching boats with curses and spells as they shouted words of war to the warriors.

And if those women were not bad enough, high up on the grass, just below the treeline, stood a massive circle of figures in white. Between the splashes and shouts, Agricola could hear them even from here. A chilling, moaning chant that rose and fell like the tide, somehow cutting through all the noise of two armies – prayers or magic, or perhaps both. And seeing them there, like that, suddenly Geminus' notion that it had been their spells that was killing him seemed a great deal less far-fetched. And there was some strange trick of the eye, too, for with every undulation of their chant, they seemed to move, stepping left or right in unison, and sometimes there seemed more of them and sometimes fewer. It was a little disconcerting. And if it felt like that to Agricola, who was busy struggling just to not drown, he could only imagine how the legionaries felt, sitting in their boats, crossing slowly towards that nightmare.

Indeed, as he watched, the boats slowed, almost imperceptibly, their pilots' nerves taking hold until grizzled centurions bellowed out commands and words of encouragement, pushing them into fresh action, speeding the advance up once more.

Agricola took a moment to look back. He was two-thirds of the way now, by some miracle, and the first wave of boats was approaching the beach. The Batavi would apparently make landfall sometime between the two waves of boats, just as the governor had hoped.

Once again, his world became a blur of salty water, thrashing legs, slippery saddles and shouting men as he struggled and forced his way on. Half a mile, he decided, was much further than it sounded.

By the time he next managed a good level of stability and control and had a chance to look at anything but his own body or that of his horse, things had changed significantly. The Batavi were bearing down on the beach at last. Off to the east, the first boats had landed. For a heart-stopping moment he noted the number of empty vessels still out to sea, a hail of sling stones and arrows falling like rain across the scene, bodies floating so numerous that they bumped into each other in the pink water, eddying aimlessly. It was not an encouraging sight, even though he could see heavily armoured legionaries, gleaming plate on display, forming up on the beach, shields high, arrows thudding into them with worrying monotony.

The boats were already turning and making back for the mainland, far speedier now without their burden of armoured men, skipping across the water like thrown stones.

Then his eyes slid to their own approach. The enemy had concentrated their forces directly opposite the main thrust of the advance, where the legionaries would land, but a smaller army had begun to form in front of the Batavians too, with its own infantry and missile troops.

A huge noise drew his attention once more, and he turned back to the main assault. It was faltering. The lines of forming legions on the beach were fragmenting as men began to back away towards the water. A huge moan of dismay from the Roman forces was audible, echoing out across the strait, strangely discordant when combined with that rhythmic chant from the druids and the strange sing-song cursing of the women in black.

The legions were breaking. And if they broke, the auxilia would collapse and the whole invasion would crumble. Rome's forces, and most likely her hope of full conquest of this island, would die on the beach.

Over the splashing and desperate sounds of his own men, he could hear a new voice, then. A quick glance, and he saw a single gleaming, colourful figure standing proud in one of the boats at the beach, braving the clouds of missiles that still flew, suicidally glorious. Suetonius Paulinus, governor of Britannia and general of the army, faced death as he urged his men back to the fray, reminding them of Jupiter's blessings, of Minerva's shield, of Mars' power that flowed through them all, reminding them that no force in the world could stand against the might of Rome, and the only enemy that could break them was their own doubt.

It was masterfully done, and rather put Agricola's little speech against the Brithii to shame.

With a roar, the legions began to reform and even as Agricola watched, began to move. They were on the beach but constantly battered by the hail of missiles, the spells of the druids and their seeresses tearing the courage from many a heart with every passing moment. The boats were back across the water already and beginning to load the second wave, but Suetonius Paulinus could not wait for them, and he knew it. He had halted the panic and put new courage into his army, but it would wane again if they waited there, dying, for the others. The governor gave the order. Without the light troops, cavalry and artillery, they were forcing battle already.

He turned back to their own beach. The Batavi were almost there. Their part in this had suddenly become a lot more critical with the absence of perhaps a third of the main army.

'Faster,' he bellowed, spitting out the mouthful of salt water that invaded on that single word.

They pushed on.

Arrows started to fall, and sling bullets. A man ahead of Agricola suddenly exploded, his head smashed with a stone half the size of a fist. The spray of unspeakable debris scattered across the water ahead of the tribune as the unfortunate rider slumped back, bobbing on the surface with what remained of his head slowly emptying into the water. His horse went on without him. A cry came from the right as a Batavian paddling along on his shield was suddenly pinned to it, an arrow through his calf that had penetrated into the shield beneath. The man was not done for yet, though, gritting his teeth against the pain and continuing to paddle. He made it another five paces before a second arrow took him in the back and he drifted to a halt, floating aimlessly.

Something struck Agricola's left shoulder. His flesh was protected by the chain shirt, but he knew in an instant that he was damn lucky not to have had his shoulder broken by the stone, and that he would suffer for some time from that. He could no longer use the arm to paddle, for it had gone numb.

Still the missiles came, still the Batavi swam and paddled.

The moment Agricola's horse touched the seabed beneath, the tribune found himself almost pulled from the water as the animal climbed to its full height. Around him he could see other riders pulling themselves up into the saddle, their horses finally able to stand. Shields were brought to bear, occasional men not fast enough, taking an arrow or stone shot. Men were falling, but the majority were at the beach.

They needed no command, no word of encouragement. For a moment, Agricola wondered why he was here as their commander, as they surged up the sand and bore down on the small force assembled to stop them. Compared with the boats full of legionaries, this unit of auxilia had seemed a small and unworrisome thing to the enemy. They had underestimated the Batavians, though, and that would be their undoing.

Even as Agricola pulled his sword from its sheath with some difficulty, the leather mouth of the scabbard clinging to the blade with the wet, his men fell upon the warriors and archers at the top of the beach. They had not waited to form up, but had charged individually, as soon as they were able to fight. The sooner they stopped that hail of arrows the better, after all.

Agricola kicked the horse into action and was surprised at how responsive it was, as it raced up the beach with little encouragement. He had only a moment to look about before he was into the fray, but in that heartbeat he spotted Luci not far behind him, and Sabinus, coughing violently, but climbing into his saddle.

Then he was at the fight.

It was, of course, not done for a tribune to fight in the front line, but then Suetonius Paulinus was in the press of it with his men, and if the *governor* could buck the trend, why not his officers. Besides, every man here made a difference, and if they could break this defence and hurry to the aid of the main landing, that might change the battle entirely.

He selected a small group of archers, two naked and painted, four in plain woollen tunics. All were still launching into the men in the water, while two men with spears stood to either side for protection. His left arm hanging by his side, throbbing and difficult to lift, he steered the horse with his knees, sword out and ready.

The archers failed to see the danger as they concentrated on the water, but the spearmen saw him coming. He veered slightly to the right, and as he closed on them leaned forward in the saddle and swept out with his blade. His sword knocked the spear aside just as it was being thrust at his horse, and he circled his wrist with the blow, bringing the weapon in an arc, sweeping down and back, where it bit into the spear's wielder. The man had tried to bring his spear back in time, but it was long and heavy and much more awkward than Agricola's blade.

Even as the man died in agony, Agricola was turning his horse, guiding it sharply left with his knees. It worked better than he could have hoped, and his respect for the horses of the Batavians, almost as clever and well trained as the men who rode them, deepened once more. The animal seemed to know instinctively what he wanted to do, and as the spearman fell back to the ground, gurgling and clutching the gaping wound in his chest, Agricola trampled the archers beneath his hooves, his horse almost dancing gleefully on their bodies.

He'd not counted on what he was going to do with the other spearman at the far end of the line, who was bringing his weapon round ready to deal with the attack, but fortunately he never found out. The spear flailed and fell and its wielder jerked and stiffened, and then fell forward. Behind him, Luci pulled back his sword, droplets of blood flicking through the air. The slave's eyes fell on Agricola.

'Funny. I didn't know whether I'd do that or not until it happened.'

Agricola gave a humourless chuckle. 'Well I'm glad you did.'

'Might want to give me a bonus for that?'

Now Agricola actually laughed. In the midst of chaos and carnage, he'd found himself saved from Briton warriors by a Briton slave. He took a deep breath and looked around. The fight was almost over already. The natives had totally underestimated the Batavians, and the result was charnel. Everywhere he looked, riders and infantry were hacking apart screaming Britons, sawing through necks, and not always of corpses, in order to carry the head as a prize. Those natives further back, who'd formed up to stop them but were yet to engage, broke in panic, turning and racing for the trees that promised relative safety from the cavalry.

Not from the infantry, of course.

The defence was broken, and the hail of missiles being launched at those still to arrive had slowed and almost stopped. Agricola wondered what to do next, looking to the prefects and decurions of cavalry, who had led this assault instinctively, without the need for orders. He was startled to see Valda looking back at him, waiting, as were a number of other officers. Thus far they had done what needed to be done to survive the landing, but beyond that they sought direction. This, he realised, was what he was here for. This was command.

He looked around him. The fight here was over. The Batavians were still chasing down those who fled and removing heads with glee and alacrity, but there was nothing to be done here but end the pointless slaughter. He looked east. The second wave of boats was now mid-channel. They would land soon enough, and the fight there on the beach was well and truly underway. The legions were wading into the defenders there, and the lines of the Britons had broken in places. But the battle was far from decided. The Roman forces had managed to advance and press the enemy, but they were greatly outnumbered and here and there their own lines occasionally buckled and broke as men died or stepped back in fear.

He could see the reason. The ragged, black-clad women, like Furies of legend, moved among the men on the beach, occasionally lifting pieces of a fallen Roman and tearing out bones, plucking pieces of flesh with their teeth as they cursed Rome and its armies, exhorting their warriors to ever greater frenzies of battle.

And it was working. Their warriors were showing no fear while, despite the governor's encouragement, the Romans were faltering once more, and might well break before the second wave landed to reinforce them. He could do little about the women, for they were all over the shoreline, working individually among their warriors. Then his gaze rose up the low slope to the white figures, circling and chanting. The very heart of the peoples of Britannia.

The druids.

He turned. Beside him Luci shook his head.

'I cannot.'

'I know,' Agricola said, not unkindly. 'Stay with the wounded.'

Perhaps he should have been more forceful. A slave should do what his master commanded, after all, but Agricola could not help putting himself in Luci's place, and knew that *he* could not have done such a thing, either. Besides, Luci had just saved his life, and that bought more than a little goodwill. He looked past Luci to Valda and Sabinus. The other prefects and officers would be watching too.

'We break the druids. Kill the druids and we kill their will to fight.'

Sabinus bowed his head, and Valda nodded. All around Agricola, Batavians saluted and turned their mounts, calling their men back where they were pursuing fleeing warriors towards the trees. In moments, three cohorts of Batavi, slightly reduced in numbers through their dangerous landing, but still fierce and craving the fray, were forming on the standards. A horn was blown, a strange melody that prickled the hair on Agricola's neck, and the officers issued their commands to the men in their native tongue. The Batavi may be a unit of Roman auxiliaries, but they were still very much German: only their numbers and strategy ordered by Rome, everything else their own.

Sabinus gave him the nod, and in moments they were riding once more, pelting across the grass, skirting the main battle on the beach and making for the circling figures in white.

For a moment, as they raced towards the figures, Agricola wondered about the wisdom of his plan. Tactically, it made perfect sense, of course, but how clever was it, really, to butcher priests in the holy places of their gods?

It was a question that was destined to go unanswered. The few remaining legionary cavalry under Sabinus saw only the enemies of empire, and the Batavians' blood was up, their lust for battle overwhelming all else. Only Agricola seemed to think beyond the now.

As they rode, they could see units breaking away from the rear of the native army, realising that the druids were now in danger. They were running to help but would not be in time, for the Batavi were fast, their cavalry racing out ahead, leaving the infantry cursing and demanding that their compatriots leave sufficient heads to take.

The druids, still chanting in their low tones, continually shifting and changing as they circled, somehow contrived to turn in the blink of an eye and were now facing outwards. Agricola's gaze fell on the man directly before him, but he found it hard to concentrate on the figure, for he seemed to blur and move, to change. His hands made shapes, the oaken staff he held whirling dizzyingly.

Something was happening to Agricola. He could feel it from head to toe, sinking into the very marrow of his bones: a dread. A deep feeling of fear and discomfort. Their magic at work? He had the urge to turn, to stop this madness and leave their gods untouched. His knees were pressing, trying to guide the horse to the left. A meaty hand reached out and clamped around his numb left wrist and he looked up to see a Batavian giving him a steady look.

The spell broke in an instant. The fear and uncertainty were gone, and the horse, Batavian trained, carried him forward even as his knees continued to urge it left. He realised then that the Batavian was speaking to the animal, telling it to ignore him, to ride forward.

The spell was gone.

As he looked up ahead once more, he did not see a blur, an ethereal white figure moving and undulating, casting spells. He saw an old man in a white robe, eyes filled with hate, swinging a stick wildly. That was all he was. Not a magician. Not a spokesman for the gods. A lunatic. A zealot.

A dead man.

Agricola swept out with his sword as they reached the circle of old men, and took the head from his target, something not easily done, and a tribute to the sharpness of his blade and the strength of the swing, backed by the speed of his horse. The druid's head tumbled through the air and fell to the centre of their great circle, where now Agricola's eyes fell upon the focus of their ritual.

Nine Roman captives knelt in a smaller ring within, hands manacled behind their backs, their innards in a tumbled mess, blood saturating the ring, their throats garrotted, their heads bashed in. Any lingering doubt in Agricola's mind evaporated at the sight. Human sacrifice was abhorrent. Even the senate said so, passing laws to prevent such horror. This must not be allowed to happen again, and any god that thrived on such rituals was not worthy of respect.

'Kill them. Kill them all,' he said, his words echoing out over the grass.

The Batavians needed no further encouragement. They'd planned just such a thing after all.

Agricola reined in as the slaughter began, for the druids relied upon power of the voice and the mind, while the Batavians trusted to muscle and iron, and it was this that was now carrying the day. He turned. Down towards the water, everything had changed. The legions had been struggling, but two things had given them a new chance: the druids, the very heart of the enemy, were dying, and the fight was going out of the rebels moment by moment. And those units who had pulled back to try and save them had left their own defences weak in places, which the centurions, knowing their battlefield well already, exploited, making inroads into the enemy lines.

The natives were broken. The battle was all but done. Even as he watched, the Batavians slaughtered with impunity, hacking free bearded heads, holding them aloft and whooping. The legions had broken the lines on the beach and the men of Britannia were now breaking into small units, some fighting to the last, others trying to flee the field. The second wave of Romans was beaching now, the artillery and archers falling into position too late to make much difference, though the cavalry raced forward to take part. He just caught sight of Claudius Emeritus amid the second landing, safely clear of any danger.

He watched the battle end, blood and harrowing screams the order of the day, and jumped a little in the saddle as a voice spoke nearby. He turned to see Suetonius Paulinus on foot, with a standard bearer at his shoulder.

'The gods are with us, tribune. And fortunately so are you. You are to be congratulated. I should not have questioned you when you claimed command of the Batavi. I knew your father and your mother. I should never have doubted the son that was the product of their blood.'

Agricola bowed his head. 'What now, sir?'

Suetonius Paulinus looked across at the mess of butchered Roman prisoners, surrounded by headless druids. 'Now, we finish this. No more druids. Every last one dies. I want their groves burned, their stones pulled down, and any man who calls them master clamped in irons and sent to Rome. This land is ours.'

Agricola saluted and turned to look at the carnage.

What next, though?

18

Agricola looked down at the water with some distaste. The shapes were clearly visible beneath the surface. 'These druids were a scourge,' he said.

Luci shrugged. 'You take the bad with the good. Whatever you don't like about them, they held the tribes together, guided us and kept the lore for a thousand generations. You don't understand.'

'I understand *this* well enough,' the tribune grumbled, pointing down.

Beneath the surface, five figures lay mouldering and bloated, each bearing those marks now becoming horribly familiar: a wound to the head, an opened throat and an opened belly. All five figures were chained together, each with a circlet of iron around their neck, echoing the rents in the flesh, the five rings connected by a strong chain. They had been sacrificed together, clearly led to this place as slaves. From the condition of the bodies, as best he could tell, the wounds were maybe half a month old. But these were only the latest victims, for Agricola could make out the shapes of skeletons beneath them and further out into the lake, and this was not their first find.

'Don't try to tell me the Romans don't kill their slaves,' Luci said.

Agricola shook his head, as though the question was ridiculous. 'Slaves die all the time, either because they have rebelled or disobeyed, or failed in their duties, or even sometimes because their owners are cruel, though that is so wasteful, I've never understood it. What Rome does not do is mutilate and butcher slaves for the love of a god. *Any* god. The gods of Rome would be appalled. Such were the abhorrent practices of the Carthaginians, and one reason their world was flattened and salted forever. Human sacrifice is an abomination. I had already taken against your druids for what I know them to have done, but now that I see it on such a scale, any indecision or hint of mercy is gone. They need to be wiped from the world entire. Only when that is done can your people hope to reach for true civilisation.'

Luci snorted. 'Romans. Always so superior.'

Agricola rounded on him. 'Remember your place, Luci the slave. I am a generous master, but never forget where we stand. Sometimes you overstep yourself.'

'Yes, master.' There was not even a hint of rebellion or bitterness in his tone, yet Agricola felt it there. Damn it, but he was coming to rely upon Luci, and moments like this did their relationship no good at all. And Agricola could have responded better than that, but the scene before him had robbed him of positivity for now.

'So this is a holy place even among their holy places?'

'So I'm told. I've never been here myself, but the captives explained it. This corner of Mona is an island within the island, the lake here is the home of all druidry, the surrounding groves as sacred as can be.'

Agricola looked up. 'Surrounding groves' was no longer an apt description. The surrounding groves had gone. What remained around this lake was a forest of low stumps and a carpet of ash ankle deep.

The victory at the beach had been complete and had given Rome control of the island, the last unconquered territory in the west. In the days that followed, Suetonius Paulinus had set about the complete rewriting of the island. Scouts explored the whole place, confirming that it was no more than twenty miles across in any direction. Complete control seemed a reasonable thing, then. The orders were simple. Any sign of druidry was to be utterly removed. Any stones to their gods could be left but would be consecrated by a priest from the army, given in honour also to a god of Rome. Their holy places were to be destroyed. Any man who was found under arms was to be killed on sight – no warrior would remain to challenge Rome here. The natives who had survived were to be allowed to live on under the Pax Romana in their own villages, but no fortresses, no druidic nemetons, no weapons. Nothing that challenged Rome.

The army had gone about it systematically. Any man they found with a sword was killed, any man who could be a druid questioned until the matter was confirmed one way or the other. The same for the women, for their seeresses in black were to be removed from history every bit as much as the druids.

Crosses dotted the island now, with old, bearded men or haggish women hanging from them, the last druids and witch women. So numerous were they that there were few places to be found on the whole island out of sight of one of the executions. Several times natives had been caught trying to save druids and bring them down to safety, but they had only earned a cross for themselves in the process, and so the attempts soon stopped.

Up on the mountain, on this separate holy island, the scouts had found a stronghold – a powerful hillfort, the centre of secular power on the island, inextricably linked with the sacred places that surrounded it. The place had been pulled down almost stone by stone, the buildings within demolished, the population scattered, the livestock slaughtered, anything else burned. Then – with the druids and their female counterparts sought out and removed, the population pacified and any potential redoubt of resistance removed – the army turned to the holy sites themselves.

This made a lot of them nervous. Killing druids was one thing. Burning woods sacred to a god did not sit well with any of them, and only discipline and the respect of their commander kept them at it. Nemetons were destroyed. The trees were felled and removed, the undergrowth fired and hacked away. The pools and lakes the druids seemed to favour for their sacrifices were dredged of long-mouldered bodies, the bones reburied elsewhere while Roman priests dealt with the waters.

This had fascinated Agricola as he watched the first time. The priest had invoked the goddess Salus as the antithesis of what the pools had been used for. They painted images of her on the druids' stones, with her staff and her snake, then began their rites of dedication, giving these waters now to the Roman patroness of health and well-being. The thing that really fascinated Agricola, though, was the venom. An integral part of the ceremony seemed to be cleansing the water of the druids' abhorrence with the venom of Salus' snake. Where the priests had suddenly acquired a few dozen snakes intrigued him: they must have had them with the supply wagons. He watched as a priest produced a snake, gripped tightly behind the head, and a bronze patera dedicated to the goddess. His assistant then covered the bronze bowl with a vellum sheet and the priest pressed behind the head, forcing the snake's mouth open. It was guided to bite the vellum, then the priest pressed on the snake's head, forcing a continuous flow of venom through the cover and into the dish. After this the spent snake was replaced in its basket and the dish of sacred venom placed in the tainted water to allow Salus to cleanse it.

That was yet to happen to this most sacred lake, of course, for each such pool had to be dredged of corpses first, and this one was the most packed of all.

Somewhere in the afterworld, he found himself thinking with a smile, legate Geminus was probably finally feeling satisfied.

'Come on. Let's head north.'

Luci nodded and turned as Sabinus and the other riders followed suit. It was a simple duty, and something of a relief after the fraught days of the invasion. Agricola was to tour the sites of occupation and check on the ongoing work. The war was over, and they had done as much in a season and a half as any governor had ever achieved on this island. Now, with war finished, came consolidation. Now their control had to be made absolute and the tribes brought into the arms of empire.

It began here on the island, but would spread throughout the west once they crossed back over that channel. Small garrison forts had been positioned at the eastern and western ends of the channel, another on the mountain with its own watchtower, close to the destroyed hillfort, and a last one up close to the north coast. Between them they could maintain complete control of the island as it began its journey from rebellious haven to peaceful province.

As the horsemen turned and rode away from the lake, a party of legionaries with ropes and grapples arrived, ready to remove the bodies and begin the process of purification.

'What's next, sir?' Sabinus asked as they made their way across the flat lands.

'The fortlet to the north, and then back to camp.'

'No, sir, I mean after all this. The governor's no more than another year in Britannia, unless he gets an extension, and it would be foolish, then, to begin another war in the north. But the west is done. All will now be consolidation and garrison. Once the west is settled, no more war. So what does that mean for us? Back to Isca and the Second? A new legate, sir?'

Agricola shrugged. 'I guess so. The governor will have sufficient achievements to gild his reputation in Rome. He will have advanced control further in one campaign than any man before him, so I presume he'll return to Camulodunum and settle into the role of governor. He won't need a military staff, so we'll go back to our own garrisons.'

Sabinus sighed. 'Mining duties again. Convoy protection. Tedious.'

Agricola gave him a sympathetic smile. 'You would think after what we've been through, the prospect of a year or two of peace would be something to look forward to. I know I came here hoping to make a name for myself and to live up to my family's illustrious past. I would say I've done that. Suetonius Paulinus will see me higher on the cursus now.'

'A year for you, sir. Then back to Rome and onwards and

upwards. I've another nine years' service to go yet before I get my diploma. That's nine years of sitting in damp mining settlements in the south-west or riding alongside ore shipments. Hard to achieve fame and gold doing something like that.'

'I've already seen to it that your name appears on dispatches with the governor, and back in Rome. I don't think your future will be all that poor and drab.'

'Ha. Thank you, sir. I just can't picture being back in garrison at Isca now.'

And in truth, neither could Agricola. In fairness, the only time he had ever spent in garrison had been last winter as they ringed in the Ordovices, so that hardly counted, and he couldn't imagine how tedious true garrison life might be. He'd find out, though, in due course. When Suetonius Paulinus had no need for staff officers anymore, a year in Isca definitely loomed. He wondered what it would be like. Until they had a new legate sent from Rome, he would effectively be in command of the legion.

He mused on this future for the two and a half hours it took to ride at a steady walk to the new fortlet on one of the rolling hills in the north, overlooking the blue waters beyond. He'd not been sure when he'd set out on this great adventure from Rome how he would deal with war, for it was his first time handling a blade in anything but friendly sparring, but it seemed on reflection that he had something of a talent for it, and gained great satisfaction from victory. He would miss campaign life when he returned to Rome, but perhaps a year sitting in a mouldering office in a fort would take the shine off the military life between now and then anyway.

It was as he glanced across at Luci that he realised he probably didn't have the greatest adjustment to make. Luci would come with him back to Isca, but there his use would end, his in-depth knowledge of these peoples. He would be just another slave in the fort, treated as such by all. And when that year was over, he would come back to Rome, and probably never see his homeland again. He wondered whether to grant the man his freedom before his term as a tribune was over, and let the man stay here in his native land. Agricola wouldn't have lost much over it, really, and the man had probably earned it. But somehow he didn't like the idea of not having Luci around. The very notion felt strange. The matter was something to ponder on, certainly.

It was early afternoon when they crested a hill and the small fortlet, as yet little more than a fresh rampart filled with lines of tents, came into view.

'I hope they have plentiful supplies,' Sabinus murmured. 'I'm hungry.'

'I'm sure they'll be able to spare us a meal, even if it's nothing fancy.'

'Something's going on,' Luci said, pointing ahead at the fort.

Agricola squinted into the sunshine, and realised that the man was quite right. A small group of riders had gathered at the gateway to the fortlet and there was a lot of activity.

'Trouble?' asked Sabinus.

'Hard to see how,' Agricola replied. 'This island couldn't possibly rise up now: the Demetae are our allies, the Silures at peace and the Ordovices so heavily beaten it will take some time for them to even remotely recover. What trouble can there be? More attempts to free druids from their crosses? But most of them are dead now anyway.'

And yet it did look like trouble.

With a fresh sense of urgency, the hair prickling on the back of Agricola's neck, they rode down the slope and across the valley towards the fort on the next hill. As they neared, he could see more of the riders there. Two native scouts and eight legionary cavalrymen from the Twentieth, led by a decurion. The question of why they were here was swiftly answered, as someone spotted the new arrivals and pointed at Agricola, the whole group turning their horses and riding to intercept.

'They're here for you,' Sabinus noted.

Alarms were going off now for Agricola.

'Tribune,' the decurion said, bowing his head as the two groups met on the lower slope of the fort hill.

'Decurion. You were looking for me?'

'Yes, sir. We knew only that you were somewhere in the north. The governor has called the staff to his headquarters, sir. As fast as you can. I have spare horses if you need them.'

Agricola shook his head. 'It's less than twenty miles and the horses are well rested. They've done nothing more than walk. What's happened?'

'I've only the basics, sir,' the decurion replied. 'Can we ride and talk?'

Agricola nodded and the two parties turned and began to ride south at a steady trot, saving the horses as much as they dared while maintaining good speed. They could canter for short bursts, trot for a while, and walk here and there to rest the animals.

'The Iceni have risen, sir. The reports are all a little confusing, but it sounds like the Trinovantes have joined them.'

Agricola shook his head. 'I have no idea what you're talking about.'

He looked to Luci, who shrugged. 'Not tribes I know.'

Sabinus leaned across a little to shout over the drumming of hooves. 'They're over on the far side of the island, right in the east, close to the capital. The Iceni have been one of our biggest allies. What could have happened?'

'That I don't know, sir,' the decurion admitted. 'I'm only repeating what I heard as I left camp to come and get you.'

Sabinus chewed his lip. 'It's over two hundred miles to Camulodunum. Even at the best speed it will take a message three or four days to reach us from there, and given how wild this place is, I'm betting a lot longer. The Iceni are only a day or two away from the bases of the Ninth legion. The Ninth have probably put down the revolt before the warning even reached us.'

Agricola shivered. The Ninth. Petillius Cerialis' legion. The man had been irritated at being left out of Paulinus' campaign. It seemed likely he would be having his fill of warfare now, regardless.

They questioned the rider as far as they could on the ride south, but it swiftly became clear that the decurion knew nothing more than he'd already told them. Sabinus was able to fill in a few blanks, but his own knowledge was sparse, for his legion had been based on the opposite side of the island. The Iceni were apparently one of the most powerful tribes in the east, close to the provincial capital at Camulodunum, but had become allies of Rome during the early stages of the invasion, their king invested as a client and friend of Rome. Something drastic must have happened to turn the tribe against Rome, though it was difficult to see what, given that the governor and the bulk of the army had been here in the west. Certainly the timing was about as bad as could be, with the majority of Rome's forces far from the trouble spot.

It was late afternoon as they spotted the large camp by the channel. Suetonius Paulinus and his legions were still based here on the island, but now several ships of the British fleet had arrived and had anchored at the western end of the channel. Agricola's level of alertness rose once more as he saw the camp and realised what was happening. Boats were in action, ferrying the men of both legions back over to the mainland. Whatever had happened, Suetonius Paulinus was mobilising his army, despite things here being unfinished.

As they entered camp, Agricola slid from the saddle and handed over his reins to Luci, telling him and Sabinus to go and get some food and stable the beasts. As they did so, he marched off towards the huge command tent at the camp's centre, the governor's bodyguard in position around it. One of the soldiers saw him approaching, noted his uniform and dipped inside for a moment before reappearing and gesturing for him to enter.

The command tent was almost empty, which surprised him. He'd expected a crowd of pensive officers, but realistically, of course, he was the last to find out. The rest had probably been briefed earlier and, if the transport of troops back across the channel was any indication, some *hours* earlier. With clerks hurrying this way and that, Suetonius Paulinus was busy applying his seal to documents, his signet ring sinking into the hot wax, as soldiers whipped the finished article out from under his nose, only to replace it with the next.

'Gnaeus Julius Agricola. It seems that somehow whenever I have an important briefing and somewhere to be, it is always you for whom I'm waiting.'

Agricola bit down on the irritation, saying nothing, standing at attention.

'I know,' Paulinus said, sagging a little. 'Not your fault that your duty took you far from camp. We must away, for there's much to do. I've no doubt you've already heard some of it, and you'll catch a lot of detail from the other officers as we move.'

Agricola nodded. 'I heard that the Iceni have revolted in the east.'

'And the Trinovantes. We move with all haste to deal with the matter. Another two months or more would have had this place nicely settled, but we will have to trust in the meagre garrisons I intend to leave, for the army moves at speed.'

'Sir, if the Ninth legion is based in the east, can they not deal with the revolt?'

The governor's face darkened. 'You've not heard much, then.' He leaned back, that statement filling Agricola with a sense of foreboding. 'Let me quickly give you the situation. The Iceni have risen against Rome. It seems the procurator and his people have grossly mishandled the matter of the king's will. Instead of inheriting half a kingdom from the dead king, we have inherited an angry queen and a rebellious tribe. I will have the full details when we reach the east, but it is looking very much as though the procurator, Catus Decianus, is wholly responsible for this disaster.'

'Disaster, sir? Surely the Ninth—'

He got no further, for the governor's hand came up to shush him. 'This is no small clash to be put down by a garrison, Agricola. Three reports reached us at the same time, the couriers having met up on the journey. Decianus has fled the capital and moved south to Londinium, protected by a small garrison. It seems he ran just in time, for Camulodunum is no more.'

Agricola blinked, shock rippling through him. 'Sir?'

'It seems the Iceni hit the capital unexpectedly and in force. The place had little more than a token garrison of retired veterans and a small unit brought by Decianus. In a single day the Iceni and their Trinovante allies overran the city. They destroyed the place entirely, throwing down every building. Every man, woman and child they found was put to the sword. The survivors fled for safety to the great Temple of Claudius, which was only recently finished, but the Iceni trapped them inside and burned the temple down with them in it.'

Again, shock took Agricola. The provincial capital, gone. Thousands of veterans and innocent civilians butchered and burned. Decianus, it seemed, would have a lot to answer for, but the mobilisation of this army so far from the trouble now made a lot more sense. Still...

'What of the Ninth, sir?'

The governor rubbed his forehead with two fingers, tired. 'Cerialis, it seems, continues to live up to his impulsive reputation. The man is nothing if not rash. As soon as news reached him about Camulodunum, he gathered every man he could and raced to stop the Iceni. Sadly, his legion is split between two main fortresses and a number of lesser forts, and it seems likely he managed to muster no more than two cohorts in time. According to our information, his infantry were overwhelmed instantly, and Cerialis managed to escape to Lindum with some of his cavalry. The Ninth are now depleted, scattered and of little use.'

'Gods.'

'Quite. The sheer scale of the uprising is impressive. If the numbers I've heard bandied about are to be trusted, this could be quite a problem and will require a military solution on a massive scale. We are on the brink of the worst defeat since Varus lost three legions in Germania, and I will not have that tarnish my reputation, especially when the blame is not mine.'

'It will take many days for the army to reach them, sir. We are as far from Camulodunum as you can get in Britannia.'

'Almost as far, yes. I have sent several messages. I have called your Second from Isca, with orders to march for Londinium and meet us. I've messaged Cerialis and told him to consolidate what's left of his Ninth and bring them to the edge of the trouble area without committing to battle until we meet. The rest of the army will march from here at their fastest pace.'

'Four legions, sir. That is a truly impressive force, especially with as many auxilia. But again, the timing…'

'Yes. The Iceni and their allies will be free to cause trouble for some time before we reach them. Also, our intelligence from the region is somewhat haphazard. I would rather know a great deal more about the situation before bringing my troops in. In the best possible outcome, we would combine the army and manage to draw the Iceni out to a field of our choosing.'

Agricola nodded. 'And there is always the possibility that in the time before we can face them, they will get tired and give up this fight and return home.'

'No. I do not believe so. And I do not want them to. They have burned the emperor's temple and destroyed the province's capital. They cannot be allowed to return to their homes without so much as a slap on the wrist. They must be taught a brutal lesson, and that is precisely what we shall do. I am gathering the staff first thing in the morning. We will ride as fast as we dare for the war zone, where we shall take stock of the situation. We will take only fast cavalry and let the army follow on in our wake. The various officers of the individual legions and auxilia will travel with their men, but the unassigned staff will come with me. It occurs to me, following your exploits these past two years, that you may well be a formidable strategist, young tribune, as well as an almost suicidally brave warrior. I may rely upon your talents in the coming days. Gather your men and be ready to leave at dawn.'

'My men, sir?'

'The Batavians seem to look to you as to their own general, and their riders will be of value. They come with us.'

Agricola nodded, threw out a salute, and turned to leave the tent. Outside, a respectful distance away, Sabinus stood waiting.

'Send word to Valda. I presume he knows the Batavi are coming south with us, but they're to be under my command again. I would like to meet with him and you in my tent. As soon as you send someone, come and find me. I'll fill you and Luci in on the situation.'

Two hours later, he had imparted to the others everything he'd learned from the governor. Sabinus and Valda had both left to brief their men and to prepare for departure in the morning, leaving Agricola and Luci in the tent. As Agricola peeled off his tunic, grunting at the pain in his slowly healing shoulder and noting with a sigh how damp and sweaty he felt, Luci busied himself with polishing swords and armour.

'What I would give for a civilised bath house right now,' he said, sniffing his own armpit and recoiling a little.

'Plenty of rivers to dip in.'

'That's not the same, and you know it. I would relish the opportunity not to smell like oxen for a change. And there's stuff under my nails so thick it could be Claudius Emeritus.'

That, at least, raised a small laugh from the slave.

'You're not talkative.'

'Slaves don't talk unless prompted.'

'Not something I've noted often in you. I've been giving thought to your status.'

'Oh?' the shush of cloth on steel halted.

'I bought you at something of a bargain price, I'll admit. You were intended to be a source of information on this campaign, and in that respect you have lived up to my intentions most excellently.'

'And, of course, I saved your life.'

'And that. The simple thing is that once we finish campaigning in the west, I'm not sure how much more you will have to teach me.'

'You're thinking of selling me on?'

Agricola frowned. Oddly, that had not occurred to him, despite being the obvious solution. 'No. Actually, I'm not. I'm toying with the idea of manumission.'

'I'm not familiar with the word.'

'Freedom,' clarified the tribune. 'Granting it to you, without all the tedious saving-up first. When I started back in Rome, I had very little money, and what my family put into my career was all we could spare from the estates in the north. I've had a year and a half as a tribune now, with monthly pay and nowhere to spend the money. I might say that when I looked to my accounts yesterday I realised that right now I have more gold than I have ever had.'

'Nice for you.'

'The point is that making a small loss on you is not the same burden it was a year and a half ago. I owe you, Luci of the Silures. When my term is over, I will return to Rome, and probably never come back here. If I grant you your freedom, right here, tonight, you are as close to home as you're likely to get. And then you won't have to come and face the Iceni.'

'Without me around, they'll probably skewer you.'

Agricola laughed. 'Perhaps. But it seems the elegant solution.'

'For you, perhaps.'

'Sorry?'

Luci leaned back. 'What do you think will happen if you free me here?'

'You'll go home.'

'To a people who are beaten and downtrodden, and who I've

not seen for a quarter of my life. My family will be long gone, even if they still live. And I will have served Rome twice now, once as a scout and once with you. How popular do you think I'll be among the Silures? Within the month I'd be hanging from a rope, blue-tongued. And even if I went elsewhere to another tribe, I have nothing. No money, no possessions, no home. I would be a vagrant. Would you wish that on me?'

Agricola frowned. 'What are you saying?'

'That being a safe and comfortable slave is not the worst thing a man can be. Freedom can just mean freedom to starve.'

'You're *refusing* manumission?'

Luci shrugged. 'For now. And here. One day I would like to be free again, but on my own terms. With a future. Until then I'll polish your armour and you can keep feeding me and popping the odd gold coin in my purse.'

Agricola stared for a long moment. And then he began to laugh again.

19

The lead riders reined in, exhausted and sore. Agricola stepped his mount an extra few paces to fall in beside Suetonius Paulinus as shouts echoed behind them down the line, calling the cavalry into their ranks. Light clouds scudded across the pale blue sky, the dust kicked up by their animals' hooves settling slowly in the warm, still air.

'Londinium.'

Agricola nodded at the governor's announcement, though this was the first time he'd been here, and he had no preconceptions. The city spread out before them, a marvel given its youth. Camulodunum was the capital, a Roman centre built upon the remains of the local tribe's own capital, while Londinium had been but a village before the invasion. In the intervening seventeen years, though, the place's critical position on the Tamesis River had seen it grow from a native village to a Roman commercial metropolis, with docks, ferries, a shipyard, markets and fora, temples and baths, and even the remains of an auxiliary fort, long since reduced in size and now housing a small garrison of part-time retirees.

'I had not thought to see a place of such size and complexity on the edge of empire,' Agricola murmured, taking it all in.

'In truth,' the governor replied, 'while Camulodunum is the capital, Londinium outstripped it in both size and value years ago. My predecessor had already mooted moving the governor's residence to this place, and the procurator holds office in both.'

'Now, the decision seems to have been made for you, sir,' one of the other officers noted.

A shadow passed across Suetonius Paulinus' expression. 'Perhaps. But not in this incarnation of the city.'

'Sir?'

'Londinium is doomed to the same fate as Camulodunum.'

'Sir? You can't be serious.'

Suetonius Paulinus sighed. 'Suro, what do we know of the enemy numbers?'

Agricola thought back for a moment. It had been something of a nervous ride from Mona, for there were a mass of confused reports concerning enemy numbers and movements, and the governor's relatively small force of cavalry was quite possibly riding within mere miles of the Iceni warband towards the end of their journey. As they had travelled, more and more information came their way, either in the form of sporadic reports from various overrun garrisons or of rumours spreading across the province. If the numbers were to be believed, they were facing the most significant uprising in a province since the Varian disaster in Germania half a century ago. Rumour put the forces of the Iceni and their allies at huge numbers, up to even two hundred and thirty thousand warriors. Of course, that was likely vastly overblown, but even the most conservative number that had reached them – coming from the survivors of the Ninth, now lurking in their fortress behind high walls – put the enemy at sixty thousand. Likely the truth was somewhere between the two, towards the lower end, but with every day of success for the Iceni, warriors would flood to their queen's banner from other disgruntled tribes.

Echoing Agricola's thoughts, Suro, an elderly officer, said 'Somewhere between sixty and two hundred thousand, sir.'

'And how many cavalry do we have with us, Suro?'

'A little over three thousand, sir.'

'And the garrison of Londinium?'

'A few hundred veterans.'

'How, then, do you propose we stop the Iceni doing to Londinium precisely what they did to Camulodunum?'

The officer had no answer to this, and sat silent.

'Precisely. The army is many days behind us. If we attempt to face the Iceni queen here and save Londinium, we will *all* perish. We must, by necessity, abandon this place to its fate, and potentially other local towns, too. We must delay the fight until we can begin it on our terms.'

He leaned back in the saddle. 'The army approaches along the military way to Viroconium, and it is somewhere along that route we need to meet them. We must bring them to us, to the best terrain on offer. And if we are to bring *them* to *us*, the prospect of battle needs to be enticing. The Iceni need to be overconfident and have a reason to come to us, else they may prefer to continue on a campaign of burning and looting and we would need to follow them and bring them down on *their* chosen terrain.'

'Letting them burn Londinium will certainly help their confidence,' Suro noted bitterly, earning a sharp look from Paulinus.

'Yes, I think being unopposed in their ravaging of the province will make them feel powerful. It will perhaps make them underestimate us. So, we need a reason for them to come to us, and we need a good location to which to draw them for the fight.'

'They may come to allies or lands in danger,' Agricola said out loud, surprising himself, as it had been meant only as internal musing.

'Go on.'

'One thing we learned from the Silures was that the tribes of this island can be prompted into action through alliances and feuds, if the prompter is clever or knowledgeable enough.'

'Keep going,' urged the governor.

'If only we could get near the lands of the Iceni or their allies the Trinovantes. If we could put their homes or allies under pressure, they would have to come to us. But if I remember the maps correctly, those tribes are even further west, and so not suitable.'

'The Coritani.' The governor smiled, wolfishly.

'Sir?'

'The tribe that covers the centre of this island, including the location of Cerialis' bases. I can send word to the Ninth to put pressure on the tribe, and if we can sow sufficient rumour here in the south that the Coritani are considering throwing their lot in with the Iceni, but that Rome is oppressing them, perhaps that will be sufficient to draw the enemy north and into battle. I will think on the matter. For now, we must seek out the ordo of Londinium and advise them to abandon their town.'

Leaving the majority of the cavalry at the city's northern edge, the governor and his staff rode south into Londinium itself with a small accompaniment of Paulinus' bodyguard cavalry. Agricola looked about himself as they rode into the street, clopping along the flagstones. Initially, he sensed something very wrong with the place, but could not quite put his finger on it. There were plenty of people, stalls selling food and knick-knacks at the side of the street, the usual drunks and ex-military beggars, cauponae with drink and food, bath houses churning out columns of black smoke, arguments between farmers with their wagons jammed up at junctions. It was all so perfectly normal, and yet there was something indefinable amiss in the air.

It took a while to realise that it was a sense of impending disaster. The people of Londinium were going about their daily business, but the ghost of what had happened in nearby Camulodunum haunted them, showing in their eyes. Voices were that little bit more subdued than normal, the streets that bit less lively. Camulodunum was less than a day from this place, and every day that passed must have been tense beyond belief as the inhabitants waited for the same fate to befall them, as befall them it surely would.

They rode through the streets, the people melting out of their way, arriving at the forum of the city, close to the great river. The city's curia was occupied, lights gleaming through the windows, two guards armed with clubs by the doorway. The council of Londinium, then, was in session, likely an emergency one called as the governor and his men had hoved into view.

Suetonius Paulinus dismounted near the government council chamber, allowing his cloak to settle about him as his five personal guardsmen also dismounted, drawing their fasces from the packs behind them and assuming the more standard guise of lictors, their presence and number making clear to all present that the man they attended was the propraetorian governor of Britannia. The two mercenary guards bowed respectfully as Agricola and the other staff officers dismounted and followed Paulinus over to the door, leaving the rest of the escort outside with the horses.

Eleven drawn and worried-looking old men in togas were scattered around the peripheral seating in the large, echoing chamber. Not the full ordo by any means. Were the others unable to be called at short notice, or had they fled the coming cataclysm already?

'Great Gaius Suetonius Paulinus,' said the nearest, rising to his feet as they entered and beginning a wave of senators coming to stand in respect. 'Our noble governor, may the gods be thanked.'

'Do not be overhasty, master curiale,' the governor replied, coming to a halt and standing before the meagre council, folding his arms.

'Our plight is great, Suetonius Paulinus,' the man said. 'Fresh reports reached us this very morning. Boudicca approaches the city.'

'Boudicca?' Agricola frowned at the unfamiliar name, turning to the others.

'The rebel Iceni queen,' Suro hissed back, indicating that he should be quiet. Agricola did so, watching carefully.

'I come some days ahead of the army,' the governor said. 'The legions remain a distance away. Londinium cannot be saved.'

'But you must!' The councillor who had spoken thus far approached now, stepping around the seats, eyes wide. 'Londinium cannot be allowed to suffer the same fate as Camulodunum.'

'You are listening to me, but you are not hearing me,' Suetonius Paulinus said in flat, emotionless tones. 'The forces to repel the Iceni and their allies are simply not here. The Fourteenth and Twentieth legions march from Mona but are a number of days away yet. The Second have been summoned from Isca, but they have just as far to travel. That leaves just the Ninth, who have already come off the worse of a clash, and sit in camp licking their wounds.'

'But Londinium is the heartland of commerce on the island,' another councillor put in, panic edging into his tone. 'If the city burns, Rome loses all the island's profitability, probably for years.'

Even Agricola could see through those words to the personal investment the man likely had in the city's commerce and industry. All these men would have enormous sums tied up in Londinium. No wonder they had not fled yet.

'I will not sacrifice a small force to save what cannot be saved,' the governor said. 'Any troops I can call upon to help will be vastly insufficient to face the Iceni, and would perish along with the city they were sent to save. *No* strategist would send help. All available forces have to be consolidated to form one large army that can meet the enemy in the field and best them there.'

'But—'

'That is the end of the matter. I am not here to save anyone, nor to negotiate. I am here to advise you, and through you the entire city, to abandon your homes and flee the coming disaster. Flight is your only hope.'

As this sank in, Suetonius Paulinus' expression took on a hard edge. 'Where is the procurator, Catus Decianus?'

A third man, less taken by panic than his companions, cleared his throat. 'He took ship for Gaul two days ago, governor, along with his *familia* and his entire entourage.'

'Then that would appear to be the first thing the man has got right since his appointment,' the governor snarled. 'I will have his head for what he has caused here, but for now we have more to deal with.'

'Like the Coritani,' Agricola said suddenly, filling the odd silence.

Everyone in the room turned to face him. Suro was angry, the ordo confused, Suetonius Paulinus frowning with a question. Agricola swallowed. It had seemed a sensible time to introduce the subject, though speaking out of turn in a conversation between the governor and the council was not something a polite man would do. Paulinus' brow flickered as he considered what should follow.

'The Coritani?' asked one of the ordo. 'What have they got to do with this?'

The governor threw a carefully contrived look of feigned disapproval at Agricola, as though he had revealed some great secret, then turned to answer the man.

'With the failure of the Ninth and their huge losses, control over Coritani lands is wavering. We have good intelligence that the tribe are considering throwing in their lot with the Iceni. Needless to say, if they do so, then others will follow. While we wait for the army to arrive, we must now move north and do what we can to prevent the Coritani from rising to join the enemy.'

Agricola tried not to smile. The governor had picked up, precisely as he'd hoped.

'But they are too far north to be important,' one of the councillors wailed. 'We have homes, and families, and businesses.'

'Families can be moved, homes and businesses can be rebuilt. I say again, leave Londinium for a place of safety and do not come back until we have put down this insurrection.'

Suetonius Paulinus turned and strode from the room, still devoid of visible emotion, his lictors around him, the others following on as the eleven present members of Londinium's ordo hurried after them, clawing at their togas that unwound and threatened to fall to the ground, continuing to plead and implore, wailing and panicking, desperate for the governor's help.

Even in the open air, the men continued to follow, shouting and begging. The governor's lictors formed a rearguard, holding off the councillors who clawed at them. Once mounted, they turned and began to ride north through the city once more. Once they were out of earshot of the panicked politicians, Suro leaned across, throwing Agricola an angry look.

'Why did you interrupt with that Coritani comment?' he hissed.

Before Agricola could reply, though, the governor spoke. 'He saw the opportunity to sow the first seed, and good that he did, for I had missed it.'

Suro's perturbed look switched from Agricola to the governor. 'Sir?'

'Those men are terrified, and they are the very centre of power in this city. Before we even reach the countryside, they will be spreading word of everything we said, including that little gem about the Coritani. By the end of the day every household in Londinium will know it. It would appear that the Iceni are a day or two away from here at most. When they come and do to Londinium what they did to Camulodunum, they will inevitably learn all of this. This is how they will first hear of the danger to their new potential ally. This is what could turn their heads and make them abandon their looting and come north.'

Suro frowned, but accepted it, for that was a clear and concise summation.

'I have a new assignment for you, tribune,' Paulinus said, turning to Agricola.

'Sir?'

'Your position in the army is moot until the Second reach us. Until then you are on my staff, and I have a job for you and your Batavians. I must ride back up the military way, make contact with the army, appear to be concentrating on the Coritani, and seek the perfect ground to bring the Iceni to battle upon. You will take your riders and remain in this region, just ahead of the enemy. I want you to watch and judge. You have a good military eye. Watch them fall upon Londinium and send me your best estimates of what we face, so that I have a good accurate figure from which to work. I want to know rough numbers of cavalry, infantry, archers, chariots and the like, and how they deploy. Everything we know in advance gives us a better chance of success when we meet.'

'Of course, sir.'

'And have word sent to me regularly. I want updates at least daily, preferably more often than that. And if you have any more brilliant ideas for drawing them north, feel free to act upon your notions with my blessing. Stay ahead of them, though, and out of sight if you can. As soon as they commit and move north, pull away and return to join the main force, leaving only fast riders behind you to monitor their progress.'

Agricola saluted.

An hour later, he was watching the governor and half of the cavalry riding off to the north. The other half, the five-hundred-strong horse contingents of the three Batavian cohorts, remained with Agricola.

'What now, sir?'

Agricola chewed on his lip. The presence of one and a half thousand German cavalry was extremely comforting in the circumstances, but they would be hard to keep hidden. They might provoke something of a reaction should the rebel forces become aware of them. It would be easier for a small number of riders without all the pomp and glory to keep an eye on the situation, and to move fast when needed. He took a breath.

'What is the first settlement on the road between here and the army, towards Mona?'

Sabinus, thinking back on the places they had passed on their approach, frowned. 'Sullo-something or other. Little place. Derelict fort from invasion days and a couple of streets of housing.'

Agricola shook his head. 'Too close. Too small. What was the bigger place a bit further north-west?'

'Verulamium?'

'About twenty miles from here, yes?'

'I'd say so, sir.'

'That's the direction we need to draw the Iceni. Have the Batavi ride for Verulamium and camp there, pending further orders. Here, we'll keep just Sabinus and his three legionary horsemen. There's a hill with some woods over there, maybe a mile and a bit from the edge of the city. We can make camp there. We should be able to see the enemy, and gather intelligence for the governor, and we should be able to do it without being noticed. The Iceni will be busy anyway.'

The small force rattled away along the road to the north-west. As they neared the hill Agricola had indicated, Valda and the Batavi, disgruntled at being kept out of things and in reserve, rode on, heading for the town of Verulamium, while the six riders who were to stay made their way up to the trees and found a position with a good view over Londinium's northern edge.

Agricola located a grey, lichen-covered stone, brushed the worst of the muck from it, and sat down, peering off at the city. Luci tethered their horses with those of the cavalry, close to the treeline where they would be hard to spot, then found a tree stump not far away and did the same. As the two of them examined the landscape, Sabinus and his three riders hacked an easy path into the woods and began to set up a temporary camp in a clearing close by.

'No cook fire,' Agricola called into the wood.

'Sir?' a voice hollered back.

'Not until nightfall. At night the fire will be hidden by the trees, and the smoke by the darkness. In the day, though, the smoke column would give away our presence.'

Then they settled down to wait. He watched the city for the rest of the day, with Luci and Sabinus often in attendance, and occasionally other riders. Londinium, it seemed, was preparing for the worst, but not as much as Agricola would have expected. He thought the situation should be perfectly clear to the city's residents, and yet it seemed the panicked exodus that was the only rational response was not happening. As the day wore on he did see a steady stream of citizens leaving their homes and making for relative safety in the country, and he fancied he could even see the various commercial ships abandoning the city's wharves and sailing away down the channel, but they were relatively small in number. A family on foot, a businessman with his cart of valuables, a nobleman in his carriage with a small gaggle of slaves around. They exited the place all afternoon, but not in such great numbers. For all this abandonment, the vast majority of the population would still be in the city.

Why?

Were they in denial? Did they not believe the ordo when they'd been told to flee? Had the ordo themselves stayed and not bothered to give the warning to the city? Despite everything, were they all still labouring under the impression that Roman forces would sweep in and save them? Perhaps, he thought, the story they had spread about the Coritani had taken such hold that the locals believed the Iceni would run north now and not bother with Londinium. Indeed, as the sun set on that troubled day, he himself was beginning to wonder whether that was the case.

Darkness came, bringing with it a chill, the myriad stars glittering up above, and moonlight giving the world an eerie silver glow. In the woods, the riders began a fire and cooked up a meagre stew with some bread for the evening meal. Lights began to twinkle all across Londinium in mockery of the sky, and

Agricola scoured the landscape away to the east, searching for any sign of a vast army. He could identify distant glows, but they could easily be the lights of towns and cities, for no one on this hill had any great knowledge of the local area. Clearly nothing was going to happen that night, and once dinner was underway the tribune abandoned his backside-numbing rock and joined the others. Though they were content nothing would happen during the night, Sabinus set a rotating guard duty anyway, with himself and the other three riders each taking a two-hour watch stint through the hours of darkness.

Despite any fears to which they clung, the night passed without incident, and it was as the first golden rays of morning pierced the woodland that Agricola was woken. He had been dreaming of the most luxurious bath house imaginable, and the disorientation as he woke to Luci's gentle shake left him blinking wildly for a moment.

'It's morning?'

'It is, and you're needed.'

The slave's tone carried a certain gravity and Agricola, alert already, slipped from his blankets and rose, stretching momentarily before walking away. He had slept the night in his uniform for speed and ease, just his armour and sword settled off to one side. This last he grabbed, just in case, before making his way out to the open. Sabinus and one of his riders stood near the treeline and as Agricola emerged, the decurion pointed off to the east. Agricola's gaze followed the gesture, and his pulse quickened at what he saw.

The army of this Iceni queen had clearly been moving since before dawn, for they were already closing on Londinium even as the light of morning came up. It had to be them. They could not be mistaken for anything else.

'I find it rather difficult putting a number on such a rabble,' he muttered, eying the distant warband, which seethed like a landslide across the green fields towards the city. 'How many did we face on Mona?'

Sabinus tapped his lip. 'The estimate was twenty thousand or so, I think.'

'This has to be three times as many. Maybe four.'

The decurion nodded. 'That's a pretty good estimate. Closer to four times, though, I'd say.'

'So we're looking at a force of seventy or eighty thousand. That's quite an army.'

They all fell silent, each of them doing a brief mental calculation of their own numbers. Even if both the Second and what was left of the Ninth managed to reach the field of battle, and Suetonius Paulinus managed to gather up every garrison in his path, they would still number at most thirty thousand, and half of those would be auxilia.

'I hope the governor's found us an excellent place for the battle,' Sabinus murmured, his tone taut, worried.

'Two to one odds, perhaps. *Three* to one, even,' Luci added.

'With the right terrain, that's fine,' Agricola said, drawing surprised looks from all around. 'Suetonius Paulinus is a master strategist. Once he knows what we face, he will use our numbers and the ground to great effect. Our men are still feeling the exultation of their victory in the west. They will be in good spirits, and they are well trained, very experienced, and well equipped. I understand the tribes in the east were disarmed some time ago. Even allowing for them re-equipping as they go, they will be relatively poorly equipped, overconfident, and lacking the discipline of legions. Even three men to one will not buy them victory unless something goes horribly amiss.'

'I hope you're right, sir,' Sabinus replied. 'They seem to have battered the Ninth with little difficulty.'

Agricola nodded. 'But Petillius Cerialis is rash. My uncle always said so. The man is brilliant, but unpredictable. They say he wins wars more often than he loses, but when he does either, he does it in a big way. This time, he led an army far too small against an unknown foe, and did so with towering confidence. The Ninth's defeat was not Iceni success, but Roman failure.'

'I hope you're right,' Sabinus said again, eying that vast tide of humanity rolling across the green landscape towards the city. The enemy's approach had clearly come to the attention of someone in Londinium now, for bells and horns began to ring out across the city, warning of the imminent danger.

Finally, the reality of the situation had dawned on the people of Londinium, albeit too late. What had been a steady trickle of refugees pouring from the edges of the city yesterday afternoon became this morning a panicked torrent of humanity, flooding from the place as fast as they could, taking only what they could carry.

Agricola watched in fascination. Part of the approaching rebel army broke off from the whole now and skirted the outside of Londinium, bearing down on the fleeing locals. They were moving at a much greater speed than the main force, and he squinted into the distance.

'Cavalry?'

Sabinus was silent for a moment as he pondered the new force. '*Some* cavalry. Not many. Chariots, though. Quite a few chariots.'

'Estimates. The governor will want estimates.'

'In that lot, maybe three hundred horse and fifty chariots.'

Agricola nodded. 'Good estimate, I'd say. I concur. And now we know what we're looking at...' he mused, his gaze straying back to the rest. 'I can see very few more with the main force. What, maybe another hundred horse and a few chariots bringing up the rear. The rest just a mob of disorganised infantry.'

Sabinus nodded. 'I'd say as much, sir. Yes.'

'So we're facing a force of seventy to eighty thousand, but with no more than about five hundred horse and certainly no more than a hundred chariots among them.'

'Quite, sir. I would say that this is a result of their lack of resources. The disarmament of a few years ago will also have robbed them of trained war horses and most chariots, let alone good iron or bronze weapons. I see what you mean, tribune. I think, for all their numbers, they will come off worse against our legions.'

'We must keep them in sight still, in case things change. Then, only when they are ready to leave Londinium, do we move.'

'And then?'

'And then, if they move north, taking the bait we left, we ride ahead of them and pick up the others at Verulamium. If they do not, we may have to show ourselves and tempt them.'

They sat for the whole day and watched the fall of Londinium. It was a soul-destroying thing to view, but Agricola felt he owed it to the victims of the Iceni to at least bear witness to their fate, even from such a distance. The riders and chariots rode into the fleeing citizens and butchered them mercilessly, looting their goods as they went. The rest of the Iceni and their allies tore through the city, occupying every street like a tidal flood. Wherever they went, buildings began to burn. The screaming was audible even on this hill, so far away, such was both the volume and quantity. Even when Agricola closed his eyes, he could see the slaughter still, in more personal and gory detail behind his eyelids, the distant noises given ample grisly shape by his imagination. He saw the forum begin to burn, with its grand temples. He saw a great building that may have been the procurator's residence fired, and found it hard to feel sorry for the man who had apparently started all of this.

All day they watched, and the slaughter, rapine and destruction went on into the hours of darkness. As they ate an evening meal that tasted of ashes in their mouths, they watched what was left of Londinium burn. In the darkest part of the night, when the entire region was adequately lit by the burning city, the Iceni finally left the last meagre pickings and camped on the green lands outside the city.

The Roman observers suffered a poor night's sleep, once again with men on careful watch. In the morning, as Agricola rose, rubbed his face with cold water and noted with some irritation the light misty rain that began to fall, he made his way to the hillside and watched once more.

The Iceni and their allies were preparing to move. He stood, tense, with the others, watching, waiting. Much rode on what happened next. If they moved away south, Agricola would have to come up with some desperate last-moment plan. His sense of relief, when the lead elements of the rebel army moved off and made for the hill on which the watchers waited, was profound.

'To Verulamium, next, to gather the others. The Iceni have taken the bait.'

20

A gricola stood, stony-faced, in the governor's command tent.
'Needless to say,' Suetonius Paulinus announced, 'we have received the reports from your riders over the past few days. I am grateful for every morsel of information you've gleaned and passed on to us, for they are all of value. I would like you, however, to give a brief summary for the benefit of those officers present who, like you, have only just joined us.'

Agricola nodded. 'Of course, sir. The Iceni and their Trinovante allies form a force some seventy to eighty thousand strong, with negligible mounted contingent. We estimate around five hundred cavalry and perhaps a hundred chariots. We have yet to estimate their missile capabilities as we've not seen them in combat, but the general feeling is that the recent disarming of the tribes will have left them as short of bows as of warhorses and other weapons. What bows and slings they do have will belong to hunters or have been taken as spoils of their campaign so far.'

'And that campaign?' nudged the governor.

The tribune took a breath. He'd relived a few scenes of that campaign in the darkness of dream the past two nights, and was not overly keen on recalling any of it on purpose.

'Everyone is presumably aware of events leading up to the fall of Camulodunum. Following that, we watched the army reach Londinium. From a distance we watched the city fall and burn. It took a whole day, and unfortunately many of the population had decided to stay, against our advice. As with Camulodunum, rebuilding in Londinium will be a task from the ground up. We seeded rumours there beforehand that the Coritani were considering joining the revolt, but were being pressured by the Ninth and the rest of our forces. It seems the Iceni took that bait, for they arrested their southerly advance at the river and turned north-west, following the route of the military road.'

Flashes of that day whipped through his mind. The speedy race for Verulamium, a rider sent on ahead with orders for the Batavi to form up ready. They rode ahead of the Iceni army, out of reach and out of sight, but paused at high points to check the enemy were still in pursuit. When they reached Verulamium, the Batavi were already mounted and sitting waiting, atop the high slope on the far side of the river to the town.

In fact, 'town' was perhaps too grand a term. Verulamium was no Camulodunum or Londinium. It retained many of the features and structures of its past as a stronghold of the Catuvellauni, many native houses and farms scattered around a central enclosure of more recent date. At the heart of the place, Roman forces had constructed a ditched and walled enclosure and a causeway across the marshy ground near the river. Perhaps a dozen new Roman buildings, so recent that their tiles still gleamed, the paint still crisp white and blood-red, were clustered at the centre of the town. It was, in essence, a native township that was in the slow process of becoming Roman.

Or, it *had* been.

Arriving at the place, Agricola had ordered the Batavi on once more, sending them along the military road some ten miles, out of sight and reach of the enemy and with orders to camp there and wait for him to catch up. Once again, he waited as they had on the hillside near Londinium.

'While the Batavians moved on at my command, I remained in the Verulamium area with my close guard. It occurred to me that we needed to be certain the Iceni were following the bait and heading north, and so we would wait and watch again. We observed the Iceni army reach Verulamium, and I saw that place sacked and burned.'

And saw more. *Much* more. He would not tell the officers the details, but they stayed with him. They had lingered too long there, and by the time they needed to move on, the Iceni had moved between Agricola and his route. The Iceni were indeed continuing north-west, but he would have to find a way around them to move on. As the Iceni left the smouldering remains of Verulamium and surged away towards the waiting forces, Agricola and his companions had ridden down into the ruins, seeking a safe way to skirt around the enemy and get ahead once more. What he had seen there had made his gorge rise. The Iceni had not merely killed and looted. They had mutilated and murdered with glee. Bodies left in the open, some burned, some not, bore the clear visible marks of the most appalling tortures visited upon innocent civilians, most of them not even Roman, but Catuvellauni. One street, such as it was, had been lined with dead women, each impaled on a sharpened pole standing wedged into the ground, where they had clearly slid agonisingly down the shaft until they hung there, bleeding their last in intense pain. What the bastards had done to the babies he had found, he couldn't even begin to describe.

He had been noisily sick before they emerged from the far side of the place, and he had not been alone in that. It had changed things for him, though. From the moment they had marched back from Mona, he had viewed this whole revolt as a war. It was two enemies facing one another, and the Iceni needed defeating, but it would be battle, and there would be chances for personal glory that could echo through command and all the way back to Rome, securing a man's career. What he had seen in Verulamium, however, had thrown aside all notions of a normal war. The disgust and horror he had felt at what the druids had done in the west had come back in force. The Iceni could not be allowed to do such things anymore. This whole problem may well have been caused by the procurator, but the Iceni had not just risen against Rome, they had become monsters. They had to be stopped.

'We were almost caught by them at Verulamium, but managed

to slip around them and get ahead. From there, we made sure to let the Iceni know we were there. We made ourselves visible to their scouts, always at a distance, luring them on, enticing them. We wanted to avoid the fate of those three settlements happening to anywhere else on the way. It seems to have worked. The Iceni have followed us all the way here. They are but three or four hours behind us.'

The various officers digested this, most nodding at confirmation of reports they had already received, others with grave expressions as they heard it for the first time. Agricola looked around the gathered faces and noted for the first time the absence of Petillius Cerialis, and of Poenius Postumus who, in the absence of Agricola and Geminus, was the senior commander of the Second. The presence of Claudius Emeritus, giving him the usual superior glare, did *not* escape his notice.

'Might I ask of our forces, sir?' Agricola hazarded. 'I saw a sizeable camp on the way in, but perhaps not as large as I had expected.'

Paulinus' expression darkened a little. 'Cerialis cannot spare men for the fight. He has his legion in garrisons all across the lands of the Coritani and the edge of Iceni territory. He fears that removing his boot from their neck will allow a new enemy to rise while we deal with this one. It is unfortunate, but he may well be right. We cannot afford to concentrate on the Iceni and allow their neighbours to rise in revolt at the same time. The Second legion are a different story.'

'Sir?'

'We have had no word as yet from Poenius Postumus, but if he has left Isca, there is no evidence of it. Messengers from as far south as the Aquae Sulis mansio confirm no sign yet of the Second. There are faint rumours of troubles in the south-west, so it is at least remotely possible that Postumus has his hands full and cannot spare the men, but some word would have been useful. And I was rather relying on the presence of the Second as a fresh and rested unit.'

Paulinus blew out a loud breath. 'So our force consists of the Fourteenth and the Twentieth, minus the casualties of the last two years' campaigns and those men we've left in garrisons. And, of course, the various auxiliary units. Current records put the headcount at just over six thousand legionaries and just under five thousand auxilia, including those Batavi you've just brought in.'

Agricola's eyes widened. 'Eleven thousand men, sir?'

'Yes.'

'Can we beat them?'

'Of course we can, tribune. Their superior numbers can be countered with adequate strategy and planning and suitable terrain. You believe the enemy are three hours or more away?'

Agricola nodded. 'Yes, sir. They're moving slowly, keeping their wagons and baggage with them. We've counted them at a steady two miles per hour all the way, and we lost sight of them at the eight-mile marker as we sped up to get here.'

'The day is still young, with many hours of daylight left. Plenty, even allowing for three hours to reach the field. From all I have seen it seems unlikely that the Iceni will delay when they come upon us. With adequate light, the advantage in numbers, and the presumably high morale that their repeated depredations will have bestowed upon them, they will undoubtedly make their attack without delay. We will need to be prepared. With the correct conditions, good Roman discipline, and the favour of the gods, we can end this today and settle the province once more.'

The governor rose, clapping his hands together and then rubbing them vigorously. 'Each of you with a command of your own, send word to your men to fall in at the standards and move off to prepare. Most of you know my chosen terrain already and can fall in and accompany your units into position. Those of you freshly arrived, issue the orders and then join me. The field of battle lies but a mile to the south of here, in the direct path of the enemy. They cannot fail to come upon it.'

With that, the officers were dismissed. The vast majority saluted the governor and then hurried off to their units, ready to prepare for the coming conflict. One tribune and three prefects joined Agricola as they followed Suetonius Paulinus from the tent. Outside, at a respectable distance, Sabinus, Valda and Luci stood waiting, a gathering of officers from other units all around, attending on their commanders. As Paulinus paused to speak to a cavalry prefect, Agricola motioned to his officers. 'Have the men fall in and follow along with the rest of the army. We deploy a mile south. Individual unit positions will be assigned on arrival.'

Valda and Sabinus saluted and turned to ride away. Luci lingered for a moment, perhaps wondering where his place was, but then turned and followed them. Once orders had been distributed, Agricola motioned for his horse as the governor's was brought for him. The small gathering of men climbed into the saddle, joined by a number of senior officers, mounted messengers, signallers and bodyguards, and then rode off on the governor's signal.

The camp was in a state of ordered turmoil as they passed. The orders had already been disseminated through the army, and every unit was abandoning its tents and cook fires, falling in in battle-ready condition as officers and signifers strode around bellowing orders, musicians blowing cadences on cornua and buccinae, the shrill din of a hundred centurions' whistles carrying commands across the massive camp. The army was moving to battle.

With a small group of guards ahead, they moved south from the camp, heading for a ridge that ran parallel to the military road, roughly north-west to south-east. They were still but a quarter of a mile from camp when a weary and dusty rider reined in ahead and saluted.

'Report, soldier?' the governor called.

'The lead elements of the enemy force approach the six-mile marker, sir.'

'Cavalry?'

'They appear to move in no order, sir, horse mixed with infantry, chariots visible here and there.'

Suetonius Paulinus nodded his thanks, and the picket hurried off to join his unit. They moved on, following the line of the road and the ridge, travelling between the two now. At roughly a mile's distance from the camp, the governor gestured towards the ridge.

'Here is where we make our stand.'

Agricola peered off to the west. Several times on the journey he had seen gaps in the ridge line, where valleys or defiles opened up, though this one was both wider and more pronounced than the others. The various officers murmured their appreciation as they left the road behind and moved into the dip. The flat plain of the region met the ridge with little interruption all the way along, and so here, the ground continued into that defile with no obstacle. Agricola looked this way and that. The flat ground between the valley sides, including the lowest slopes, which would still be suitable for infantry, stood some quarter mile across. Not much space. A line maybe three hundred men long would fill the defile from side to side. Two-thirds of a cohort. He made a mental calculation. Of the heavy infantry that would make a line twenty men deep. Not bad at all.

'The enemy will, of course, be restricted,' Paulinus said. 'We form up across the defile. They will not have easy access to the upper slopes,' he added, pointing up to each side. 'We shall put small units up there just to be sure we maintain control of the heights, but it is my contention that they will be so over-confident that they will look no further than a direct, headlong attack.' He pointed away up the valley. In the distance, where it narrowed and sloped upwards they could see forest. 'The treeline should similarly prevent them pulling any crazed flanking manoeuvre, should they be that inventive.'

'Deployment, sir?' a prefect asked.

'I am putting the two legions in the centre, occupying two-thirds of the valley width. Flanking them will be the auxiliary infantry. We do not have many archers or slingers with us, but those we have we will place on the heights with the small defensive units. I have given orders that every pilum available is to be brought here. Every man in the pilum lines will have plenty of opportunity to split a few of the enemy.'

Agricola gave a grim smile. He could see it now, the mass of the Iceni, jammed up in the narrow valley, arrows and shot falling on them from the sides, volley after volley of pila from the legions in front. For the first time, he began to see the possibility that the huge discrepancy in numbers between the two armies might not be the problem it had appeared.

'Where will we deploy the cavalry, sir?' he asked. 'The Batavians are quite agile.'

Suetonius Paulinus nodded. 'Yes. The lower slopes should not present too much trouble for the horse. They will be deployed on the wings but a little back, almost in a reserve position. I have a plan for this battle beyond simply restricting their numbers.'

The others fell silent again, as the governor gestured to the position in which his front line would deploy. 'You say they have their wagons with them, which means they will have to deploy them. The only feasible place will be at their rear, and that is a Celtic tradition, as we've seen from both the Cimbri and the Suevi. The difference is that those two battles were fought on the open plain, and so their wagons presented no great obstacle. Here, I intend to use them as an anvil to my legionary hammer.'

The officers turned intrigued looks on the governor. 'We will hit them hard with every missile we can muster, from three sides. Ideally, I would like to spend every last arrow, pilum and bullet before a single native gets within sword range of our men. I want to thin out their ranks thoroughly, begin the process of demoralising them.'

'And then we set to work with the meat grinder, sir?' the tribune asked.

'Quite. We let the legions and the heavy auxiliary infantry do their work. The weight of numbers will be rendered moot by the narrowness of the front. It will come down to man on man, and in those circumstances I have no doubt that our men will prove more than equal to the task. There is always a moment in battle when the enemy are on the verge of breaking, and it takes only one strong blow to tip that into rout. I intend to capitalise on that. I will be at the rear of the army, keeping an eye on things from the lower slope, sending in reserves where necessary. But I will be only one observer. I will also have two of my most strategically talented and most observant men watching for that moment. Servius Didius Costa of the Fourteenth will take position on the heights to one side of the valley, and Gnaeus Julius Agricola of the Second will do the same on the other side.'

Agricola fought a welter of conflicting emotions that flooded him at the decision. He had assumed that his command of the Batavi would continue through the battle and that he would be with Valda and his men. That would, of course, be horribly dangerous in such circumstances, but he had rather become accustomed to the press of battle now. To learn that he was going to sit this out and play little more than the role of a watcher was disappointing. Yet the recognition of his value, ranking with the impressive legate of the Twentieth, was what he had come to Britannia hoping for. He could have had a safe posting in a quiet province, where he could make money and relax in a sinecure, but there would be no glory, no place to make a name for himself that would propel him up the cursus honorum back in Rome. His selection here was confirmation that he had achieved a place of note in the army of the province, that the governor valued him. And as such, details of his achievements would be spreading through Rome already, long before he returned there and needed such fame to propel his career.

'You look disappointed,' Suetonius Paulinus noted.

'No, sir.'

'I owe your family, Agricola, and securing your position here paid an old debt, but it would be a poor repayment if I had to return to Rome and inform your noble mother that you now lay mouldering in a provincial grave because I misused you. You are young, tribune. You have many years of attempting battlefield suicide ahead of you. If you are lucky, you'll serve with Petillius Cerialis. I doubt you'll ever find a better opportunity to be foolishly heroic than with him. For now, your place is on that hill. You and Costa, as well as I from the rear, will watch the enemy for that breaking point. When you judge the time is right, you will give the signal. If it is echoed by one of us, that means at least two watchers have decided the future of the battle is in the balance. When that happens we end our simple butchery at the lines.'

'Sir?' One of the prefects frowned. 'Wouldn't it be better to keep fighting the way we are at that point, to be sure of victory?'

Paulinus rubbed his chin. 'To do so is to drag out the battle, and given the difference in numbers, every heartbeat the battle goes on thins this province's military. With the Ninth already now heavily under-strength and the circumstances of the Second unknown, we cannot afford to keep abrading the Twentieth and Fourteenth. There will be little value to winning this battle if afterwards we have too few soldiers to maintain control over the island. No. We watch for that "breaking" moment, and we act. We want them to break. To flee.'

'Sir?'

'As soon as the signal goes up and is echoed by a second, the two legions will move into the wedge formation and push forward. While they do so, the auxilia on each flank will do the same. Three spearheads of men will launch into the enemy force. And if that is not enough to break their will, the cavalry,' he turned a smile on Agricola, '*including* your precious Batavi, will advance around the flanks and try and hem the enemy in, flaying their ranks to either side. It is my hope that their wagons will be formed up behind them in the manner of the Cimbri and the Suevi. Where those two tribes fled past their baggage in the open, here the wagons will, hopefully, form a wall. Between the valley sides and the cavalry, the advancing wedges, and the wagons to the rear, they will be trapped, with nowhere to go. Fear and hopelessness will do the work of our missing legions then. If we play this battle correctly, we can utterly annihilate Iceni resistance here with the least possible damage to our own numbers.'

'And if they surrender, sir?' the other tribune prompted.

'Surrender will not be acknowledged. We are not here for clemency. We are here to make the rebel tribes pay for what they have done to three cities and countless Roman civilians. I want what we do here to send such a clear message to every warrior on this island that it will be centuries before any tribe even dares pick up a sword in anger. You understand?'

They all nodded. By now, stories had reached them of families who had travelled nervously to the ruins of Camulodunum, with the enemy long gone. The things they had found had torn the glory of any of this war from anyone who listened. Acts of individual barbarism aside, everyone shuddered at the descriptions of the charred corpses that had been found amid the ruins of the great Temple of Claudius, many captured in their dying poses, clawing at doors and walls in the desperate hope of getting out of that oven even as the Iceni fed the fire and fanned the flames outside.

No mercy.

Ever.

'If everyone is happy with their roles, prepare yourselves. I can already hear the distant calls of the legions on their way, and they come battle-ready with no baggage or excess kit. Within the hour, the army will be in position. I want not a man out of place when the enemy come into view.'

As the other officers broke up into small groups to discuss the coming confrontation, Agricola found himself standing out, alone. He had an important role to play, yes, but it was a small one, and a quiet, lonely one. As Paulinus had noted, in the distance Agricola could hear the army of Rome approaching. In an hour or two he'd be able to hear the Iceni, too. Leaving the others to their business, he kicked his horse into motion and rode a little further up the valley, into where the Roman forces would be deployed.

The governor had certainly chosen his ground well. The slope was negligible for some way, making it ideal for fielding the heavy infantry, but also for cavalry. The slopes enclosed the valley, and the woods to the rear were thick and dark, and would protect them from attack from the rear, for it would take many hours for any army to force its way through all that. Agricola reached the upper end of the valley, some way from the others, and found a small track, perhaps forged by animals, or perhaps once used by native shepherds. This he followed as it slowly climbed the sloping valley side, heading back the way he'd come, but bringing him to the heights that looked down upon the small gathering of officers with their entourages and bodyguards.

In no time, he found himself at the top of the hill. From here he could see how the ridge ran on, south-east, until it was punctuated by another narrow defile. Some way south, he could see the silent and still remains of an ancient hillfort, though there was no movement or smoke there now, the original occupants long since displaced by Rome. His gaze drew back to the immediate vicinity. He tried to picture the legions and auxilia in position in the valley below, tried to imagine the sheer mass of the Iceni and the Trinovantes flooding into the narrow defile, their wagons to the rear. He would certainly have a good vantage point here and, looking across at the far side of the valley, he could see where Costa would be positioned, echoing his own placement. Both of them would have a clear line of sight to the governor at the rear, too, as well as out across the plain as far as the road and the river beyond it.

He was still contemplating the landscape when the army began to arrive, the distance between here and the camp negligible. That they were in high spirits was both visible and audible, even from here. Either they had no idea of the numbers racing to face them, or they simply had sufficient confidence in Paulinus and in each other to consider the battle a done thing. Oh, for such confidence.

A tiny spot of rain patted the back of his neck and he looked up. The sky was a pale grey. It didn't *look* like rain waiting to happen, but was that one drop a warning? He waited for another, face upturned, but none came. For a moment, he wondered whether a very small bird had shat on him. That was said to be lucky. Rain would not be good. Rain would turn the turf of that valley into thick, churning mud under the countless boots of Roman and native. It would quickly turn into a swamp that would make any attempt at organised charges unpredictable. Moreover, it would dampen the strings of any bow exposed to the air, allowing stretch. Rain was anathema to archers, and would allow only a few accurate shots.

'Jupiter Pluvius, I pray you give us dry, good weather for this day.' He faltered for a moment, his fingers twitching as he counted how many altars he now owed the gods. In his defence, the only time he'd not been marching, riding or fighting this past year and a half had been the winter among the Ordovices, during which there had been no chance to organise such ordinary things as altars. When this was over, someone in Isca was going to be very busy carving. Ah well. In for a sestertius, in for an aureus, eh? 'Great Jupiter Pluvius, I vow you an altar in hope for your benevolence and care this day.' He wondered whether one to Mars might not be a bad idea too, but at that moment his eyes fell on a small cavalry group out to the side of the main column who were making directly for this hill: Sabinus, Luci and the other legionary cavalry. They circled the main force and searched for some time before finding a feasible route to the top on horseback.

'Seeing the sights, sir?' smiled Sabinus.

'This is the battleground,' Agricola replied, gesturing to the valley.

'Good ground.'

'Quite. I'll give you the complete rundown of the plan in a moment. Our job, though, is to be no part in the battle.'

'The Batavi?'

'Back into the direct command of the governor today. We are to be part of the observers, here at this viewpoint, with legate Costa opposite, and the governor at the top end of the valley. It is our task to identify the moment the Iceni are on the verge of breaking.'

'Exciting stuff,' Luci murmured, with an odd smile.

'The plan, sir?' Sabinus put in, and Agricola took a breath and settled back in his saddle. For the next half hour, as the army assembled below, he ran through the governor's grand plan, what he hoped, and the individual unit positions. Within the hour, the last of the army had arrived and the legions and auxilia were already moving into their blocks and lines. Agricola was impressed with how many pila had been brought, strapped to pack horses like sheaves of iron stalks. Thousand upon thousand of the throwing javelins were moved into place, most of them stored between the fifth and sixth lines, where they could easily and quickly be passed forward to the men of the second and third ranks, who would throw them. On the hillside they were swiftly joined by a unit of archers and one of slingers, taking up position carefully to grant them the best range over the valley while not obscuring the view for Agricola.

Finally, everything in place, the valley settled into a strange, expectant silence. Time crawled by, the only noise the cawing of birds above.

A drop of rain struck Agricola on the forehead, and he looked up, but any rebuke or plea he might level at the great god went unspoken, for a new sound drew his attention.

Carnyx calls, discordant and eerie, like some metallic, echoing dragon.

The Iceni were here.

21

'Look at them,' came the voice of the governor, echoing around the defile. The legions and auxiliary forces of Rome stood silent, pensive, watching the Iceni and their allies approach, every man down there emitting an aura of nervousness at the sight of the massed forces of the enemy. It may have been a trick of the terrain, but somehow the words of Suetonius Paulinus reached almost every ear – caught, amplified and returned by the slopes around him. Even Agricola, high on the peak, hardly had to strain to catch them.

'Look,' the man repeated, 'and cast fear from your hearts. They are a massive force, and we can all see that, but do not let the sight unman you. Look and see how few are warriors. How few wear iron or bronze, how few have good swords. There are farmers there, women, wives and youngsters. This is not an army, but a rabble. Let them come and fall beneath Roman blades. Let us build a rampart of their dead.'

Looking down from the hill, Agricola could see the shape of the governor, gleaming and proud on his horse at the rear of the lines, at the centre, behind the legions. As he watched, Paulinus began to walk his horse forward, the loose ranks stepping aside to open a passage for him. The tribune shot a look the other way. The mass of the Britons was now approaching the entrance to the defile. Soon they would be close enough to engage, but there seemed no plan to their attack. Warriors surged forward, horsemen among them, chariots here and there struggling to manoeuvre in the press. Their confidence was high. They were singing, chanting, bellowing prayers to their gods, and brandishing their weapons – swords, spears and axes, but also hay-forks, sharpened poles, cleavers and the like.

His gaze snapped back to the Roman lines. Suetonius Paulinus was only three rows back from the front line now, as he reined in. From somewhere he'd acquired a weapon, and Agricola had to smile. Paulinus, it seemed, was something of a showman, a fact he'd first suspected with that rousing speech during the crossing to Mona.

The governor lifted the weapon, a slim javelin with a narrow tip, and hefted it. Agricola saw what he thought was a flicker of droplets spray from the tip as it was brandished, and certainly those close by would have seen it clearly. The spear of a fetial, dipped in the blood of a sacrifice, cast into the territory of the enemy to declare war.

'Butchers,' the man shouted. 'Monsters. Enemies of Rome.'

And with that, he gave the javelin a massive overarm throw. Agricola was impressed. The man clearly had a strong arm, for the javelin flew high, straight and true, high over the heads of the ranks before him, plunging down, tip first, to thud into the turf some ten paces in front of the legions.

A roar arose from the ranks in response to this imitation of the traditional declaration of war, the throats of thousands of soldiers creating a din that encompassed and drowned out the songs of the Iceni. By the time the roar began to wane, the governor was back-stepping his horse through the ranks with the skill of an expert horseman, the lines closing up again as he passed, and he was chanting, a chant that was taken up by the soldiers around him and gradually rippled outwards until the entire army was bellowing.

'For Rome. For Rome. For Rome.'

The nerves the army had been showing were gone. The governor's little display and his words of fire that filled their bellies and ran through their veins had replaced fear with righteous determination. The army was ready for the fight. As the chanting continued unabated, Agricola looked back at the enemy. Their singing had stopped, the melody buried beneath the chanting of the soldiers of Rome.

Agricola watched. The enemy might have lost the war of volume, but they were still supremely confident as they came on at a steady walking pace, infantry, cavalry and chariots mixed. They were approaching optimum pilum range.

His gaze snapped back to the Roman forces. The front line, the heaviest-armoured legionaries were braced ready: banded plate covering torso and sword-arm, heavy helmet with a reinforced brow low over their eyes, left leg forward, covered with a greave of leather or bronze and pressed against the lower edge of the huge body shield, an impressive wall of metal and flesh, swords out, ready to wreak havoc. The second rank had left three feet between that wall and their own, the third a whole six feet gap, allowing the second rank the space they needed to go to work. The fourth rank had done the same, and spare pila occupied every hand, row upon row.

The chanting of the Romans ended now at some unheard command, and the army fell silent, allowing the disordered din of the approaching Britons to rise once more and fill the quiet. Now, Agricola thought.

Yet still nothing happened as the enemy approached. Surely they must be in javelin range now?

He started slightly as a sudden blast of whistles shrieked out across the valley, every centurion giving his order simultaneously. Agricola watched with the interest and satisfaction of a Roman officer seeing his men execute a drill perfectly. On the first whistle, the second rank pulled back their arms, steadying the pila. At the second, two heartbeats later, they released their weapon in a strong throw, while the third row pulled their own weapons back ready. Two more heartbeats brought the third whistle blast, and the third rank released their weapons.

The result was impressive. Two hundred pila had been launched on a low trajectory, just over the heads of the front rank, plummeting into the advancing line of Iceni warriors, while a moment later two hundred more had been released on a higher arc, and fell beyond the enemy front line, plummeting into the press. Hundreds of warriors fell, and their songs and chants rippled into silence beneath the screams of the slain and the wounded.

Already, though, even as the enemy advance faltered, pila had been passed forward from hand to hand, and now the second and third ranks prepared themselves once more. As the triple whistle began the next volleys, extra signals were given higher up the slopes, even in front of Agricola. While pila continued to shred the advancing Iceni, now arrows and sling stones dropped on the mass from the heights to either side. There was no real need for the missile troops to aim, either, for the seething ranks of Iceni and Trinovantes were simply so tightly packed that any missile falling among them would inevitably find a target.

The enemy were no more than fifteen paces away now, as the third set of pilum volleys was prepared, the whistles going in their triple bleat, the legionaries now releasing on a much lower arc, aiming for the closing enemy.

'Now's your time,' a voice murmured at his shoulder.

Agricola turned with a frown. Luci was standing behind him, his expression taut, his lips pressed together tight.

'What?'

'You wanted the moment they could be broken. Now is your time.'

'But the fight's hardly begun. Just a few pila. We can make the most of the narrow defile and butcher so many.'

Luci shook his head. 'Your javelins are getting used up, and the enemy have slowed. Look.'

As Agricola turned back to examine the fight, Luci stepped forward, pointing. 'See how they've slowed? They're having to climb across the piles of their own dead, but that's not why. The front ranks are nervous. Fear is doing half your work now. And that's rippling back. Look at how they falter here and there. But if they manage to engage your men properly, they'll recover. You have a dozen heartbeats to act. Twenty, maybe. Then they'll close up again, but right now you can break them.'

Agricola peered. He just couldn't see any real change in the mass of warriors. They were slowed, slightly, he would admit, but that was surely just the difficulty of climbing over their own dead. As he watched, the next volley of pila struck, yet another being readied.

He was about to deny Luci's appraisal when his gaze caught an odd movement.

One man on a horse in the press of warriors, one of so many, but this one, a nobleman armoured in bronze and holding aloft a long sword, was going the wrong way. It was hardly noticeable, and in the press of men it could even represent nothing more than one noble trying to reach another, or repositioning himself in the army.

One man riding against the tide, and a slowing that could easily be nothing more than difficulty of terrain. It was not a lot on which to base a move that could win or lose a battle. Tense, he looked up at the hill opposite. He could not see Didius Costa himself, of course, at this distance, but he could make out the standards that marked the second most senior officer on the field's position, on the crest, above the units of archers and slingers. There was no signal being given there.

He breathed heavily, bit into his lip. Looked again. Yet another volley issued, the enemy almost too close for pila now. He'd lost that lone horseman in the press, and it looked like the speed had picked up a little. The front lines were closing now, shields up, weapons swinging and thrusting.

'Are you sure?'

'You're losing the moment,' Luci said.

Agricola looked the slave in the eye. There was no doubt in the man's expression or manner at all. He was confident, and apparently truthful.

He is a slave Agricola reminded himself, weighing up a moment that could define his career one way or another.

But Luci was also a warrior who knew tribes and battles, tactics and logistics. He was an expert horseman, who'd taken to the specialised skills of the Batavi as though born to them. He'd been a scout for Ostorius Scapula, and a warrior in the warband of Caratacus. He was a slave, but he had decades more experience of battle than Agricola.

If he got this wrong, it could lose them the battle. To lose this battle was to lose the war, and to lose Britannia in all probability, to lose a province of the empire, to become the author of the worst defeat for Rome since Varus. But if he didn't act...

'Now,' Luci said, and there was an urgency to his voice.

Agricola felt a moment of panic pass through him. When he called for the signal, it surprised him, for he hadn't really made the decision. Something in his subconscious had driven him to it without the need for conscious thought. His hand had shot up and then dropped. He stared at that hand as though it had betrayed him even as the men behind him reacted. The musician put the tuba to his lips and blew a cadence of five short blasts. Beside him, the man with the vexillum of the Twentieth dipped it three times in the direction of the enemy.

The signal had been given. Agricola felt his bowels shift uncomfortably. The onus was entirely on him now. He could hardly blame a slave. His gaze shot to Luci. He'd come to trust the man – but really, how far could *any* man trust *any* slave, especially one watching his own countrymen being beaten?

He shuddered.

He looked up. There was no reply from across the valley. He could not see their faces, but he could just make out that legate Costa and his men were all facing this way. Beside the bright figure of Costa on his horse, he could see another gleaming officer, which could be none other than the man's senior tribune, Claudius Emeritus. He could imagine the mix of astonishment and anger on their faces. Emeritus, in particular, would be livid. Very likely the tribune was busily persuading his commander that Agricola was wrong. He turned to look up the valley. No signal had gone up in response from Suetonius Paulinus either. No one was confirming Agricola's order.

His eyes fell back to the front lines of the army. The pila had stopped moving forward, but then they'd only have managed one more volley at most anyway. The front line was braced and already fighting off the few enemy warriors who'd broken into a run and pulled out front. By the time Agricola counted to ten, the entire line would be engaged and there would be a full press of battle.

Luci had to be right.

Had to be.

Agricola took two steps and grabbed the horns of his horse's saddle, pulling himself up with the speed and strength of an acrobat, and before he was even fully settled had urged his horse into movement.

'Repeat the signal,' he bellowed over his shoulder as he urged his mount into an almost suicidal canter down the steep slope of the valley side. He'd not got far before he heard, over the top of the repeated cadences, more hooves racing to join him. Luci, Sabinus and the other horsemen. Arrows and stones continued to arc out over the top of him, falling into the press of the enemy.

His horse was struggling to stay up on the slope, close to panic, but he ignored that, trusting to the animal as he looked out over the Roman lines. Centurions and legionaries were looking to him, uncertainty etched in every face.

'Form cuneus,' he bellowed. 'Wedge formation, *now*. Charge!'

A strange noise echoed along the valley side, at once chilling and wholly welcome. He looked back past the lines of legionaries to see horsemen climbing the slope to skirt around the front lines and surge out on the flanks. Batavian riders, obeying the command, regardless of the lack of confirmation elsewhere.

He felt the whole field change in that moment. As a stone rolled down a scree slope would jostle other pebbles into flight, so his command had its effect. As his signallers up on the hill continued to issue the call, he had thrown himself into the fray.

That had galvanised Valda and his Batavi into movement, and they had broken their ranks to move along the flank, ready to commit. Their movement had triggered the same thing on the far flank, where more Batavi led a cavalry charge around the other slopes of the valley.

And because the Batavian cavalry had committed, now the Batavians among the auxiliary infantry were moving, and as they moved, inevitably the other auxilia joined them. Only the legions at the centre were not yet moving, though they fought hard against the lead elements of the enemy force.

Then the dam broke.

Aware that the charge had already been committed to by part of the army and that delay now would only lead to confusion, Didius Costa had relented and let blast his own command, which was being picked up at the rear of the army. The legate remained on the hillside, but some of his officers were even now picking their way down the slope opposite Agricola, Claudius Emeritus at their fore.

That was all the centurions needed. Unwilling to move without confirmation, still they had been ready to give the commands at a moment's notice. Now that confirmation had been given, in a heartbeat the legions were re-forming, a centurion of the Twentieth smacking an Iceni warrior around the face with his vine staff as he settled behind his shield, the wedge falling into place behind him. As that native went down in a heap, his face smashed into a bloody pulp, the centurion began the push.

Agricola was still on the lower slopes, some two dozen paces from the fray, watching the Batavi race to catch up with him, and saw the whole army surge forward, then. The enemy might outnumber the army of Rome by a huge difference, but very little could withstand the push of a legion in wedge formation. Thousands of bodies, heavily armoured and bristling with weapons, hammered their way forward at a quick pace, the weight of every man pressing into those in front, adding their own momentum to the irresistible whole.

To each side of that massive push, the auxiliary forces had achieved the same formation, albeit to a lesser extent, with roughly half the manpower and many of their number lightly equipped. Still, their sheer ferocity was sufficient to grant them the force they needed to pierce the frontage of the enemy.

From his slightly elevated position, Agricola watched with a new appreciation. The three wedges slammed like living spear-points into the flesh of the native army, driving deep. The centurion who'd led the charge lived long enough to fall in the press, cut down by desperate Iceni even as their force was driven back, split into panicked groups and brutalised. The centurion was replaced in an instant by the next man in the wedge, himself falling in behind his heavy body shield, heaving forwards, sword stabbing again and again, seeking victims constantly in the press forwards.

Agricola looked to the Batavi, who were closing around him now, and saw them lowering their spears like lances. Turning, he kicked his horse into movement, falling in on their flank, ripping his sword from its scabbard. Ahead, across the enemy mass, he could see them faltering.

Luci had been right. He had seen it where Roman strategists had not. Had they had sufficient time to truly engage at the front lines, the Iceni would have fought there until all was over, for they had the numbers. It was under the merciless hail of pila, arrows and bullets that their morale had faltered, and that was the moment, despite Paulinus' grand plan. The critical point was when they were still reeling from the missiles and before they were fully committed to the fight. That was when they had been vulnerable.

And now they would never recover.

The mass of Iceni surged this way and that, many still trying to bring the fight to the Roman lines, despite the fact that the Roman army was now in among them, pushing, scything like blades into the body of the tribes. Though battle had only just begun, Agricola could now see how simple a thing it could be to end it. The Iceni had walked straight into their ruination, confident after their unopposed ravaging of Roman cities, totally underestimating what awaited them, despite the lesser numbers. Their courage had faltered as hundred upon hundred died in the crush, felled by pilum and arrow and stone, and with Luci's insightful call, the army had capitalised on that and broken into a series of charges that pushed deep into the heart of the enemy, refusing to allow them time to recover. And that was the crux of it: the Iceni must be kept off balance, unable to regain their wits, for they still vastly outnumbered the Roman force, and the moment they realised that and stopped panicking, the whole fight could easily go the other way.

The Batavian riders had their own idea, though. Ordered to commit to the wings when the signal was given, with the simple command to 'engage the enemy', they had been given a certain free rein as to how to do that. Where the traditional role of Roman cavalry on the field of battle was as a light skirmishing force used to harry the flanks, Valda clearly had other plans. His five hundred riders, backed by almost as many from another Batavian cohort, had lowered their lances and now, once they had passed the front-line clashes, pulled in and aimed directly at the flanks of the Iceni force.

They had been racing along the sloping side of the valley, and as they angled for the mass below them they kicked into a charge, their momentum only increased by the gradient. They hit the flanks of the Iceni force like a tidal wave over crumbling insulae. The spears killed plenty, but many more were simply churned and broken beneath the hooves of the charging horses. As spears smashed in torsos, men pulled their swords free and began to lay about them as they rode, the blades finding victims with ease in the press. Indeed, it was impossible not to hit someone, and the only skill required was to make sure it wasn't an ally.

Looking out across the surging battlefield, given a clear view across most heads by his horse, Agricola could see the officers of the Fourteenth, now down from the hill, joining their spearhead of men. Claudius Emeritus was there among them, sword out, though as yet unbloodied. Agricola was forced to pay attention to his close surroundings then, as flailing spears and lancing swords came his way. The next time he had a chance to look up he was just in time to see Emeritus torn from the saddle, across the field, disappearing beneath the mass of brawling humanity.

Then his attention was pulled back once more by immediate danger before he could decide whether or not to mourn the tribune. Swords slashed and men bellowed, and Agricola found himself truly fighting for his life.

The churning blur of warfare became an all-encompassing thing, and the next time he dragged his mind out of the to-and-fro of blades was when he felt a white-hot pain across his thigh and looked down to see that his tunic was torn and bloody, a furrow of crimson across his leg. Out of the corner of his eye, he saw the blood-soaked spear tip responsible, wavering in the air for a moment before disappearing into the press.

He looked from the wound to his own sword, running with blood from two or three victims in the roiling mass. He felt faintly stunned, and it took him moments to recover. Staring at his leg again, he wiggled his toes within his boot. He felt them moving. Surely, if he could feel that, the wound was not bad. Was he going to be the echo of his counterpart, Emeritus, felled on the far side of the field?

Suddenly he was aware of shouting, and drew his attention back, focusing, turning. Luci was busily batting away spears and swords, along with two legionary riders, while Sabinus was bellowing at Agricola.

'... to safety.'

'What?'

'Come on!' the decurion shouted, a touch of desperation in his tone.

Still a little stunned, Agricola allowed Sabinus to lead them back out of the press, though the Batavi continued to push forward, the only pause among them brief delays as warriors hacked free heads with a whoop.

In moments, Agricola was part-way back up the slope with his guards.

'How do you feel?' Sabinus was asking.

'Eh? Oh, it's fine.'

'Not broken?'

'No. It was a spear, not a sword.'

'I think it'll stitch up neat, sir,' another rider announced, peering at his thigh. Agricola looked down. How the man could tell, he had no idea. There was so much blood he couldn't really make much out himself. Now that the numbness of the initial wounding, compounded by the shock and the adrenaline, was wearing off, the pain of the wound was starting to make itself known. A hot pain, accompanied by a throb so heavy he wondered briefly whether everyone else could feel it through the soles of their feet.

Before he knew it, Luci had dismounted and was beside him, pulling off his scarf, hooking the brooch from it into his tunic and then tying the scarf tight around Agricola's leg just above the wound.

'Why?'

'Because, knowing you, it'll be some time before you get round to seeing a medicus, and if you die of blood loss before then, I'll get sold to someone else.'

Agricola snorted a little laugh, then took a deep breath and turned his attention to the fighting again. He walked his horse a little further up the slope, the others with him, and turned to get a better view.

The three columns of infantry, led by wedges, were causing chaos and bloodshed in the midst of the enemy force, and no Iceni front could be brought against the legions and auxilia, for they were in among them. Indeed, any time it looked as though some small part of the native force was gathering, recuperating and readying for some solid action, they were scattered by yet another push. It seemed the Batavi were expertly identifying the places where resistance was in danger of re-forming, and hitting them hard, cutting down the nobles and the heroes and liberally taking heads, a practice that seemed to shock the Iceni almost as much as it had Agricola when he'd first seen it.

His eyes widened in alarm as he turned further, looking back along the lines of the enemy towards the rear of the mass, for five chariots had broken free from where they had been circling at the back, and were racing towards the small group of horsemen on the slope, having spotted a wounded senior officer among them. Each chariot held a driver, whooping and bellowing as he held the reins and the rail of his wicker vehicle, and a warrior in the rear, gripping spear or sword as he also held tight with the other hand against the possibility of being thrown from the platform with the many bumps and jolts.

Agricola looked about. The bulk of the military were committed deep in the fight. The Roman reserves were pulled up in ordered rows, holding that narrow defile against the sporadic bursts of Iceni aggression that escaped the massacre and bore down on them. A small cavalry reserve remained with Suetonius Paulinus, but none of these, horse or foot, were going to be able to help in time, for the chariots rattled their way closer at an astonishing and highly dangerous speed. Indeed, their number was swiftly whittled down to four as one hit a dip in the ground and the wheel exploded, the whole vehicle, lightly constructed, shattered and strewn across the grass like so much kindling. The driver and warrior aboard were killed instantly, smeared across the landscape with a variety of broken bones, crushed and torn by shattered timbers.

Still the other four were a worry, for Agricola, Luci and Sabinus were accompanied only by the remaining two legionary riders, and one of those was nursing his sword-arm, which hung bloody and limp. Agricola himself could feel the pain in his leg beginning to overwhelm him.

They turned, bracing, ready to face the onrushing nightmare, but the chariots never reached them. As the vehicles closed across the grass, suddenly the air was filled with a cloud of arrows so thick it almost darkened the sky. Drivers and passengers alike screamed as they were thrown from their vehicles, punched through with half a dozen arrows each, as were the horses pulling the chariots, which bellowed and fell, ploughing gouges across the earth with their bodies and the wreckage they dragged behind them.

Agricola stared, then turned to see that the missile units that had been based with him at the apex of the slope had descended, unseen, during the action, for their lobbing of missiles into the press had had to stop the moment the Roman forces had pushed among them. Even now, as the prefect of the archers threw him a grin, the bowmen were moving again, using a slightly elevated position, closer to the enemy, to pick out individual targets with careful aim, usually horsemen or chariots for the size of the target, or men in gleaming armour and colourful crests, for such figures were the leaders of the army.

The fight, for Agricola at least, was clearly over, although he felt it safe to say the battle *entire* would be over soon enough now. The enemy had never once had the upper hand, for Rome had pounded them with missiles and then, before they could recover, cut deep into their ranks, hacking bloody swathes through the mob. The enemy was demoralised, disorganised, and failing. Many were already trying to run, but they had, just as Paulinus had anticipated, brought their wagons to the rear, covering the plain in a wide arc, and as they tried to clamber under, over, or around those wagons, the auxiliary horse of the Roman forces, including the vicious Batavi, cut or chased them down.

Agricola's group was no longer alone on the slope. The Roman reserves were moving forward, joining the fray, killing with impunity, and a small group had gathered around Agricola and his riders. From among them, a capsarius appeared, unshouldering his leather satchel, opening it and finding his medical supplies within. He took a sharp blade and cut away the tunic from around the wound on Agricola's leg, then tipped water from a flask across it. The blood cleared for a moment before it welled up afresh from the cut. Agricola was surprised. Cleaned, it looked a lot deeper than he had thought.

'Ach,' the combat medic snorted. 'Hardly worth a stitch, sir.'

Agricola blinked. It looked worth a stitch to him.

'Still, let's make it a pretty leg again, eh, sir?'

The man graced him with a sly grin, then produced a needle that looked rather large for Agricola's comfort. He looked down at the wound, at the smiling medic, and bit down on the sleeve of his tunic. He sat like that, chewing rich wool to prevent crying out as the man put in three stitches, repeatedly pulling at his leg to close the wound as he did so. The worst of it over, Agricola spat out the sleeve and blinked away tears while the capsarius applied a salve of honey and then wrapped his leg in bandages before pinning them tight.

'All done, sir. You'll have a nice scar to show the ladies, but nothing more.'

Agricola wondered for a moment whether he should really be snapping angrily at the easy manner the man displayed towards a senior officer, but brushed it off. One thing he'd learned already among the legions was that engineers and medics were both breeds apart from normal soldiers, and one had to accept their idiosyncrasies if one wanted the best of their abilities.

'What in the name of all gods was that?' a voice asked.

Agricola turned in surprise. Gaius Suetonius Paulinus had reined in close by, a small gathering of officers behind him. Agricola saluted weakly. The governor's eyes slid down to the bandages on his leg, where blood was already forming a pink blossom. His eyebrows rose in a question.

'You tasked me with spotting the moment the battle could turn, sir. It was, in fact, my slave, Luci, who brought it to my attention. As soon as I realised he was right, I knew there was no time to lose. The Iceni could be broken straight away, but if we didn't act, then the battle would press on and become harder and harder to end. Legate Costa seemingly couldn't see it the same, and if we'd waited for confirmation, we might well have lost, sir.'

'And it was such a pivotal moment that it even required your own sword?'

Agricola tried not to look abashed at the hinted admonishment. He gave that weak smile again. 'It seemed appropriate.'

'I have half a mind to put you and Cerialis in a fight somewhere and watch to see which of you gets himself killed first.' Paulinus sighed and leaned back in his saddle. 'You did well, tribune. I will bring your contribution to the attention of the authorities when I complete my campaign reports for the senate.' He looked out across the battlefield. 'For now, I think the day is ours. I only hope this queen can be found. I think she would look good leading the emperor's triumph, don't you?'

Agricola made a noncommittal noise. Paulinus had already turned away, and no answer was really expected.

That was it. The battle was over. The *revolt* was over. The danger to the province was gone.

He was done.

22

F*rom Gnaeus Julius Agricola to his mother Julia Procilla, warmest greetings.*

Agricola paused, looking around the room. All was silent in here, bar the rhythmic scrape of Luci running a whetstone down the tribune's sword. Where to begin? He'd not written since that brief break in Mona.

> *I presume that by now the Acta Diurna is filled with news of the end of the revolt in this province. The rebel queen Boudicca and her Iceni were a fearsome enemy, but with the gods on our side, as well as the redoubtable Suetonius Paulinus, her forces came to nothing in battle, and the province settles once more.*

It seemed such a small description for such a massive thing. With the Iceni broken, the governor's forces had overrun them easily. The wagons had prevented most of the natives from fleeing the field, and the butchery had been unprecedented, the Batavi gleefully riding down anyone who managed to escape, and removing their head. Rome had most certainly claimed vengeance for the three burned cities that day. No quarter had been given. No slaves were taken, no clemency granted. Any native who cast down his weapon in hope was cut down to fall beside it. It had been simple slaughter. The queen herself had not been among those on the field, for she had somehow managed to escape before the rout had truly begun. She had not lived long, though. Her trail was picked up by the scouts and followed by

Batavi and legionary cavalry, and she was found the day after the battle, dead by her own hand, laid in state in some native mound in the hope that she would not be found. They cast her body out for the crows. Her daughters had seemingly escaped. Whether or not they might cause trouble in the future nobody knew, but it was the considered opinion of all that the lesson taught that day by the Viroconium road would loom in the mind of any potential rebel for many years.

He paused again, wondering what to say. Luci had finished with the sword and was now polishing it with a rag, little more than a linen whisper, which allowed the muted sounds of fort life to reach his ears through the shuttered windows. The most insistent sound out there was that of the stonemason working late.

That brought a smile to his face. The courtyard of the Isca fortress headquarters was home to a row of altars that had been raised by various tribunes, prefects and legates over the decade or so of the fortress's life. What might it say of a three-year tribune's appointment that Agricola's contribution had almost doubled the number of altars in such a short time. He'd kept the fortress masons busy, and had paid them a healthy bonus atop their wages for their work. The last altar would be finished in a few days: all Agricola's promises to the gods paid in full, since they had lived up to their side of the deal on every occasion.

I am in winter quarters once more. I cannot lie that, despite having endured two years of campaign living, hardship and almost continuous danger, I quickly tire of the ennui of garrison life. That being said, until spring comes around, I remain the acting commander of the Second Augusta, pending the arrival of a new legate, sent from Rome. Suetonius Paulinus is happy to leave the legion in my hands and not interfere with the running, for he too will return to Rome next year a celebrated general.

Should he mention the prefect? Agricola found that one a tricky subject, for he felt a distinct sympathy for the man. Poenius Postumus, camp prefect of the Second, had refused the order to march against Boudicca. His message had reached the governor only after it was all over, and Paulinus had been furious. He had given orders for the prefect to attend the governor's temporary headquarters at Corinium, for that was a good central position from which to govern until Camulodunum or Londinium could rise from the ashes.

Agricola had personally hand delivered the governor's summons to Poenius Postumus on his return to Isca. The prefect had said little, acknowledging Agricola's return and his taking command, accepting the governor's letter, and then excusing himself for a time. He had been found that evening in his house, amid a veritable lake of blood. The man had dismissed his slaves and guards, jammed his sword in a crack and thrown himself upon it.

The ignominy of having refused the governor and missed such an important battle had been too much for the man, and he had taken his own life in quiet solitude rather than live in public disgrace. Within a matter of days, Agricola had caught up on the reports of local disturbance, of unsettled tribes in the area tentatively supporting Boudicca, and of the widespread nature of the Second. He had swiftly concluded that there had been no way Postumus could realistically have marched to war with more than a few centuries of men, and might well have been destroyed in detail en route, suffering the same fate as Petillius Cerialis early in the revolt, had he tried.

With Geminus dead, back in Rome in a jar, and Poenius Postumus gone, Agricola was now the sole senior officer in the Second, though there was little enough to do other than oversee ongoing operations, and next summer he would be recalled and return to Rome. Still, he had decided he needed to look at the legion's deployment and see if he could improve things while he was here. After all, one day he would have a legion of his own, and then he would need such skills.

Sabinus had been equally 'thrilled' to return to regular duty, but Agricola had at least softened the blow for his friend. Whatever troops could be spared from the Second were to be sent to the governor to distribute among the units left understrength after the war, and Agricola had managed to send the centurion in command of the Second's cavalry contingent to be reassigned and promoted to prefect of an auxiliary cavalry unit, which had left space to promote Sabinus to command of the Second's horse in his place. Not a lot more exciting as positions go, during winter garrison, but it did at least carry a healthy pay increase and more authority.

The subject of reinforcing the army brought back something.

The governor has sent to his peer in Germania, asking for any recruits he can spare from the province to bolster the forces on the island. It seems a sizeable vexillation is to make for Britannia on the first sailing after winter, and the man who will bring them is Titus Flavius, son of Vespasian, currently serving in the same position as I, but across the water. I shall be interested to make the acquaintance of Titus, since you always spoke so highly of his father. Please do pass on to Vespasian my compliments and this little titbit of information, which I'm sure will please him, if Titus is so honoured as to be given such a task.

Because when Titus came, Agricola would be there. In fact, it rather looked like not a single month would pass over the winter without at least one summons to the governor's office. He'd already been back several times, the first within just a few days of his return to Isca, though at least the journey from the fortress to the temporary capital could easily be managed in three days with stops at Lindinis and Aquae Sulis, so there was little disruption, really.

The governor was making a habit of calling on his military commanders, particularly Agricola, Cerialis and Costa, since the arrival of the new procurator of Britannia. The disgraced Catus Decianus had retired to his family estates in Umbria and there hid and made no waves, hoping not to draw the attention of the emperor after his utter failure on the island. The replacement, Gaius Julius Alpinus Classicianus, had taken immediately against Suetonius Paulinus. He had declared the governor a blunt hammer, useful in putting down insurrections, but too violent to attempt to impose the Pax Romana. He had already demanded that Paulinus be withdrawn from the island early. The two men had almost come to blows several times, and Paulinus regularly sought the support of his officers in keeping the new procurator out of his business.

On the second visit to Corinium, Costa of the Fourteenth had also been present, and Agricola had enjoyed a stifled and uncomfortable three days in the presence of Tribune Claudius Emeritus, whom Costa had brought with him. Emeritus had not only survived the fall during the battle against the Iceni, but had somehow contrived to come out of it as some kind of hero, mentioned in dispatches by the governor in the same breath as Agricola, something he tried not to feel too bitter about. The tribune of the Fourteenth had acquired a pronounced limp and was still using a stick to walk.

'My, but you were lucky,' Emeritus had said, upon his meeting with Agricola.

'Oh? How?'

'You and I both know your slave could have been mistaken, and you could have cost us the battle. How lucky you are the gods were with you and it all worked out in the end.' He nodded in the direction of Didius Costa, engaged in conversation with the governor. 'The legate is of the opinion that Petillius Cerialis is too rash and unpredictable to be left in charge of any force greater than a cavalry patrol, and he's right. And I see in you exactly that. A foolhardiness. A need to prove yourself so strong that it drives you away from your allotted place. I dread to think what it will be like when you have a legion of your own.'

'Likewise,' Agricola had countered. 'Ingenuity wins wars, not routine.'

The two had gone their separate ways then, and avoided one another for the rest of the visit, but Agricola had a horrible feeling they would be seeing more of one another in future. If they were serving as senior tribunes together, then they would be on parallel career paths, with other commands coming simultaneously in future. Moreover, since Agricola would now have to take a more active and high-profile place in the political circles of Rome, he and Claudius Emeritus might very well find themselves working together at any time.

That realisation had rather soured the meeting.

He sighed and reached to the letter once more.

I shall ride out this winter in camp and return to Rome in due course. I have acquired no small amount of savings during this time, some of which I have forwarded with this letter, in the sure knowledge of its safe delivery in the hands of the cursus publicus. I pray you put it to use for yourself and the house and estate. Too long have we languished in impoverished obscurity thanks to Father's stance against a cruel emperor. But the blessed Nero is not Caligula, and so it is time we stood proud once more.

He paused, wondering whether to tell his mother about the one other curious event this winter, but decided that perhaps some things were best left unshared. His mother would undoubtedly worry. It had happened only half a month ago, long after the dust of battle had settled. A unit of scouts had found a woman lurking around the outside of the fort, watching like some sort of spy. She had been brought in for questioning, and had asked to see the commander. When Agricola had been brought to her, something about her had made him shiver. She had looked him straight in the eye and nodded as though confirming something to herself.

'The butcher of Mona,' she had said quietly. 'The threefold death of my people. I had expected more of a monster.'

He'd frowned. Somehow, though she wore a plain, dun-coloured tunic, he could imagine her in ragged black, cavorting and pulling birds apart. 'The *butcher* of Mona you seek would be the governor, I suspect. I was but an officer.'

'Not all worlds have been, for some have yet to come,' the woman replied mysteriously, again sending a shiver up Agricola's spine.

'Shall I have her flogged, sir? Interrogated? She was watching the fortress.'

Agricola shook his head. 'Send her on her way.' Before he turned, he narrowed his eyes at the woman. 'Your time is done, witch. Find a quiet corner of the island and mourn your losses.'

With that he'd turned and walked away, though she spent some time that night bothering his dreams too. He shivered even now, remembering the encounter. Taking a deep breath, shaking off such dark portents, he put pen to paper once more.

I bid you enjoy Saturnalia and the winter, and I will see you again in the late spring.

With that, he dabbed at the ink and let the scroll furl, leaning back.

'You know you talk aloud while you write?' Luci murmured.

Agricola silently cursed himself. He'd not realised he was doing that. Swiftly, he ran back over his thoughts, hoping he'd not said anything out of place.

'Where will your career take you next?' the slave asked, without even a hint of deference. If he was not going to be freed yet, then he would have to adopt a very different stance when they were back in Rome, moving in important circles.

'I shall have a short time in Rome, building a network of contacts, and then, once I can secure a position, a quaestorship. If I cannot attract the eye of the emperor, then I will have to become very good friends with one of the better-placed senators. The last thing I need is to be given a quaestorship with little promise.'

'What's a quaestorship?'

'A sort of administrative and financial officer for a province, supporting the procurator and the governor in fiscal and administrative duties, and as a military officer if required.'

'A posh slave, then.'

Agricola rolled his eyes. 'Will you accept manumission back in Rome? The strange relationship we've developed here will never work in the capital.'

'I might.'

'I've been thinking about your future, Luci. I can't see you as a house slave, folding washing, or a personal slave, up to the elbows in massage oil, and I dread to think what your culinary skills are like. But a man of means in Rome needs a bodyguard. Hand-chosen mercenaries, ex-gladiators and retired soldiers, that sort of thing. Rome's streets can be quite dangerous even in the most peaceful of times. And any such bodyguard would need a leader.'

The polishing stopped for a moment. Luci made a noise that sounded carefully noncommittal, before it began once more, but Agricola found himself smiling. He knew Luci well enough now to know what the man was hiding behind that noncommittal noise.

'That's enough polishing for now, Luci. Shall we surprise everyone? I'm in the mood for a snap parade. I wonder how many soldiers are still sleeping off the Armilustrium celebrations last night.'

'Can I blow the horn?'

Agricola laughed.

Historical Note

All source materials in this note are in the public domain, drawn from Bill Thayer's LacusCurtius website or the Perseus Digital Library:

Dio Cassius, *Roman History*, trans. by Earnest Cary and Herbert B. Foster (Cambridge, MA: Loeb Classical Library, 1914–27).

Cornelius Tacitus, *The Life of Cnaeus Julius Agricola*, trans. by Alfred John Church and William Jackson Brodribb (NY: Perseus, 1942).

Cornelius Tacitus, *Annals*, trans. by John Jackson (Cambridge, MA: Loeb Classical Library, 1931–37).

Of Agricola's three sojourns on the island of Britain, this, the first of them, occupies but a single chapter in Tacitus. Of the tribune's activity in this tumultuous time, we are told only this:

> He served his military apprenticeship in Britain to the satisfaction of Suetonius Paulinus, a hard-working and sensible officer, who chose him for a staff appointment in order to assess his worth. Agricola was no loose young subaltern, to turn his military career into a life of gaiety; and he would not make his staff-captaincy and his inexperience an excuse for idly enjoying himself and continually going on leave. Instead, he got to know his province and made himself known to the troops. He learned from the experts and chose the best models to follow. He never sought a duty for self-advertisement, never shirked one through cowardice. He acted always with energy and a sense of responsibility.

Neither before nor since has Britain ever been in a more disturbed and perilous state. Veterans had been massacred, colonies burned to the ground, armies cut off. They had to fight for their lives before they could think of victory. The campaign, of course, was conducted under the direction and leadership of another – the commander to whom belonged the decisive success and the credit for recovering Britain. Yet everything combined to give the young Agricola fresh skill, experience, and ambition; and his spirit was possessed by a passion for military glory – a thankless passion in an age in which a sinister construction was put upon distinction and a great reputation was as dangerous as a bad one.

I could, of course, do worse here than point you to my own non-fiction biography of the great general, published in 2022, but for the benefit of those who'd prefer not, I'll summarise here the parts of it that are relevant to this novel.

Of Agricola's family and youth we are told quite a lot by Tacitus, much of which can be confirmed by cross-referencing with other writings and epigraphic evidence, from his father's viniculture that was lauded by the writer Columella to his senior education in Massilia (modern Marseilles). I have in this book worked directly from the portrait painted of the man and his formative years by Tacitus who, being Agricola's son-in-law, knew the great man personally. I will not therefore delve into that history. If you are interested in Agricola's history, again, I would point you to my other work, and to the writings of Tacitus. And so we leap forward to the start of his adult career.

The various luminaries who attend the dinner at the start of the book are speculative. We have no such dinner recorded, but Rome's military appointments were largely the province of favours granted by powerful patrons, and each of the names I include would have been in a position to have personally known, and likely served alongside, Agricola's father Graecinus.

As such, this scene is far from unlikely as a background to his appointment as tribune.

Luci is an entirely fictional character, created for this story in order to help both Agricola and the reader with the complex geographical and political situation in Britain. His background, however, is quite plausible. The Romans had a habit of using native scouts. Scapula had campaigned against the Deceangli, and then the Silures had risen and backed the charismatic Caratacus, who in the end was betrayed by the Brigantes and sold to Rome where, by some miracle, he is recorded as ending up living rather well as a free man. Caratacus's family seem to have shared in his luck, but *only* his family. The same was likely very untrue of those warriors who were captured with him. Hence: Luci. The name, I have drawn from a name referenced several times in Roman Britain, specifically from *RIB* vol. 2 2501.301, where it is stamped on a Samian ware bowl that was found in Caerleon, deep in Silurian territory.

The name and nature of the legate of the Second Augusta is also my own creation. We know nothing of the man other than that he cannot have been with the Second during this period, or it would have been he who responded to the call to arms and not the camp prefect, Poenius Postumus. Postumus, however, is drawn from the historical record, as is his refusal to move against Boudicca.

Of Suetonius Paulinus and his Welsh campaigns prior to the druids in Anglesey, Tacitus tells us only this: 'Suetonius Paulinus enjoyed two years of success, conquering fresh tribes and strengthening forts.'

As such, it's very easy to see how little information we actually have about the campaigns. Before this time, the Silures had been an almost constant thorn in Rome's side, even after Scapula's brutal campaign, and after this time they seem to be settled and quiet, and so it is reasonable to assume their suppression was part of the campaign. Rome had met the Silures and the Deceangli, and even the Ordovices, and so the fresh tribes very likely included both they, the Gangani of the Llŷn Peninsula, and the Demetae in what is now Pembrokeshire. The nature of the campaigns, the routes they took and even the formation of the Roman army is all open to interpretation, and so I have here put together a plausible route, taking into account a number of sites that would have been occupied and perhaps even important at the time.

From Viroconium, which is the modern Wroxeter, and the earlier camp a couple of miles away near Eaton Constantine, I send the army south to the camps of Clifford and Clyro, and then west into Wales. Agricola's branch of the campaign first meets the natives at my imagined nemeton. The army follows a valley north of the village of Abergwesyn and climbs a road known now as the 'Devil's Staircase', then down into a valley far from the built-up lowlands.

It is becoming clearer with time that many of the tribes the Romans name were, in fact, their own labels for what may actually have been confederations of smaller tribes. The Caledonii and the Maeatae in Scotland were just such groups, and it seems quite possible that the Silures were the same. As such, I have made much of the subdivision of tribes in this work, giving us a more complex and probably realistic socio-political ancient Wales. To that end, I have created terms for subtribes, partially based on local place names, since tribal appellations often live on in the landscape. The Brithii I named for a village on the map in the rough region for the tribe, for example.

The Caron Bog, which I have used for the first real fight, still exists, and is an impressive sight. Parts of it can now be explored thanks to engineered walkways, and it remains a protected landscape and habitat. The hillfort where the Brithii are overcome is the hillfort of Pen y Bannau – an impressive sight when viewed from Agricola's position, which would be coming from the east, across the high range around the Teifi Pools. Pen y Bannau lies just outside the village of Pontrhydfendigaid, just a few short miles from the north-east edge of the bog.

From there, we move south and west into the lands of the Demetae. Their early interaction with Rome is entirely unknown, but since they are never mentioned in a martial context, it seems more than possible that they were peacefully assimilated and possibly even survived for a time as a client kingdom, such as was happening elsewhere in Britannia. I mention their gold riches. These can still be found today in the Roman gold mines of Dolaucothi. The first and second forts I introduce among the Demetae are the Cefn Llan hillfort near Llandysul and 'Merlin's Hill' near Carmarthen, which I have named Morida in a foreshadowing of Moridunum, the Roman name for the town.

We then move into war once more. We can safely assume that many of the natives fled to Anglesey along with the druids, and must have been doing so for some time under the pressure of the advancing Roman forces. As such, I have described a near depopulation of the region. Some areas must have resisted strongly, for Tacitus to mention that Paulinus achieved success, and so I created a winter of warfare in the hills between the Dyfi and Mawddach rivers. Here there is something of a profusion of hillforts, standing stones, circles and an ancient trackway, the Ffordd Ddu, and that seems likely to point to something of a power centre. I spent a week exploring the hillforts and sites and tracks in the region, and it was Bird's Rock in the Dysynni valley that struck me as the most impressive defensive fortress of the region, a place to which the tribes might fall back when faced with Roman aggression. Thus it is Bird's Rock on which I centred my war.

It is my own opinion that Ostorius Scapula placed a specific line of forts to block native access to good land and starve them into submission. I believe that it was this Agricola saw, and this that influenced his own policy later in Scotland. As such, I have had him use the very same principle during that winter. Forts still exist at Brithdir, Cross Foxes and Pennal, which largely surround the area. Add to this Roman finds near Llys Bradwen on the Ffordd Ddu, and a number of other small finds, and it is possible to imagine a Roman noose of powerful forts closing on this region. Thus my war takes place.

The death of legate Geminus occurs on the march north once more, in the wide valley south of Trawsfynydd. Two sites in the area have produced Roman tile works, and one of the most impressive Roman forts in Wales, Tomen y Mur, lies to the north (the site at which I had Costa wintering). The reason for the funereal location, given that the man and the event are both fictional, is pure serendipity. In the collection of the National Museum of Wales lies the only surviving Roman will in Britain. The name is illegible, but some of the text is not. Geminus' will in the book is taken from the wording of this find, and the find was made near Trawsfynydd, right on the route my dying legate would take, heading north from the Mawddach to Tomen y Mur.

Anyone conversant with Welsh geography will not find it difficult to trace the route from there to the coast opposite Anglesey, right across the Snowdonia National Park. The precise site of Suetonius Paulinus' crossing of the Menai Strait has never been confirmed, though tradition places it at Llanfair-is-gaer, and certainly the terrain there is suitable, and the place name translates as 'the church of Saint Mary beneath the fort'. Should you find yourself in the area, make your way down to the shore below the church and look out at Anglesey across the strait. It is immensely hard not to picture the whole thing. Once again, it is Tacitus who gives us the entire invasion in beautiful Tacitus-O-Vision:

> He prepared accordingly to attack the island of Mona, which had a considerable population of its own, while serving as a haven for refugees; and, in view of the shallow and variable channel, constructed a flotilla of boats with flat bottoms. By this method the infantry crossed; the cavalry, who followed, did so by fording or, in deeper water, by swimming at the side of their horses.

On the beach stood the adverse array, a serried mass of arms and men, with women flitting between the ranks. In the style of Furies, in robes of deathly black and with dishevelled hair, they brandished their torches; while a circle of Druids, lifting their hands to heaven and showering imprecations, struck the troops with such an awe at the extraordinary spectacle that, as though their limbs were paralysed, they exposed their bodies to wounds without an attempt at movement. Then, reassured by their general, and inciting each other never to flinch before a band of females and fanatics, they charged behind the standards, cut down all who met them, and enveloped the enemy in his own flames. The next step was to install a garrison among the conquered population, and to demolish the groves consecrated to their savage cults: for they considered it a duty to consult their deities by means of human entrails.

As you can see, my account is lifted more or less directly from sources, though I have given the cavalry, who are so impressively mentioned in their crossing, more of a part in the actual fight. The Batavi, incidentally, are renowned historically for this method of transport, having been noted doing the same in sources numerous times, from the days of Caesar right to the end of the western empire and beyond. Over the book, I have forged something of a link between Agricola and the Batavi. While the reason for this might yet seem unclear, given their lack of recorded involvement in the Battle of Watling Street, I would invite you to read on in this series, for there are ties that will become clear much later.

With regards to the events after the battle, the bodies in the water are my explanation for the finding of a pre-Roman five-person slave chain that was spotted in the lake Llyn Cerrig Bach, on Anglesey's Holy Island. The chain is now in the National Museum at Cardiff, along with numerous votive offerings found in the lake. For some time there was a belief that the only Roman site on Anglesey was the small late Roman fort and signal tower on Holyhead mountain. The forts I have mentioned in my text include the recently identified fortlet in the north, in the farmlands above Cemlyn Bay, the fort beneath the village of Aberffraw, and a fictional one at Beaumaris, though there may yet be a fort to be found in the area, since a Roman coin hoard was unearthed at Baron Hill there.

Before Anglesey could be dealt with in any greater depth, however, one of the most infamous events in Romano-British history occurred. Tacitus tells us, 'While he was thus occupied, the sudden revolt of the province was announced to Suetonius', and then goes on to detail the revolt of the Iceni under Boudicca.

We know that Petillius Cerialis came to grief with a vexillation of the Ninth, that Boudicca's army burned Colchester (Camulodunum) and that Suetonius Paulinus raced south-east, with his army following on slowly. We know from sources that the Second legion refused the summons to war, and are told that later Poenius Postumus threw himself on his sword for having done so. We know that Paulinus abandoned London to its fate because he had not the forces yet to save it. We do not have any detail as to why the Iceni, having burned Londinium, then moved north-west to burn Verulamium (St Albans) and continued in that direction to meet the Romans. It is possible that they were simply so confident of victory that they couldn't wait to get stuck in to the Romans that were marching their way. I have simply manufactured a plausible reason for their turn to the north and march via Verulamium. I have not described in this text the horrors of the fall of three cities to Boudicca. If you wish to read fictional accounts of those disasters, I would point you for Colchester to the excellent *Hero of Rome* by Douglas Jackson, and for the other cities – and, indeed, for the whole uprising – to *A Year of Ravens* by various authors, including myself in a section which tells of the revolt and of the fate of London and St Albans.

The location of the revolt's final conflict is still a subject contested and with no clear resolution. Locations along Watling

Street from just north of St Albans right the way into Wales have been proposed. The most convincing argument by far, in my opinion, places the battle midway between the last town burned, St Albans, and the Welsh border, namely around Mancetter, a known Roman town. The ridge I have described follows the same line as Watling Street (the A5) south of the town, between Mancetter and Hartshill/Oldbury. There are signs of valleys such as I have described, though sadly much of the terrain has now been quarried away.

Of the actual Battle of Watling Street, our primary and most trustworthy source, Tacitus, actually says surprisingly little. In his *Agricola* he tells us only that 'By one successful engagement, he [Suetonius Paulinus] brought [the province] back to its former obedience.'

And in his *Annals*, he gives only a little more detail. Of the terrain, he says, 'He chose a position approached by a narrow defile and secured in the rear by a wood, first satisfying himself that there was no trace of an enemy except in his front, and that the plain there was devoid of cover and allowed no suspicion of an ambuscade.'

And of the fight itself:

At first, the legionaries stood motionless, keeping to the defile as a natural protection: then, when the closer advance of the enemy had enabled them to exhaust their missiles with certitude of aim, they dashed forward in a wedge-like formation. The auxiliaries charged in the same style; and the cavalry, with lances extended, broke a way through any parties of resolute men whom they encountered. The remainder took to flight, although escape was difficult, as the cordon of waggons had blocked the outlets. The troops gave no quarter even to the women: the baggage animals themselves had been speared and added to the pile of bodies. The glory won in the course of the day was remarkable, and equal to that of our older victories: for, by some accounts, little less than eighty thousand Britons fell, at a cost of some four hundred Romans killed and a not much greater number of wounded.

The numbers here, of course, are clearly enormously exaggerated. Cassius Dio gives us more detail of the battle, though while Tacitus would have been alive at the time and spoken to men who had been there, Dio was born a century after the event, and could only be learning of the battle himself through extant sources, so should be treated with less certainty. Dio, in fact, assigns the figure 230,000 to the size of the Iceni army, which has to be a truly outlandish whopper. Dio's account of the battle is:

the Romans silently and in order until they came within a javelin's throw of the enemy. Then, while their foes were still advancing against them at a walk, the Romans rushed forward at a signal and charged them at full speed, and when the clash came, easily broke through the opposing ranks; but, as they were surrounded by the great numbers of the enemy, they had to be fighting everywhere at once. Their struggle took many forms. Light-armed troops exchanged missiles with light-armed, heavy-armed were opposed to heavy-armed, cavalry clashed with cavalry, and against the chariots of the barbarians the Roman archers contended. The barbarians would assail the Romans with a rush of their chariots, knocking them helter-skelter, but, since they fought with breastplates, would themselves be repulsed by the arrows. Horseman would overthrow foot-soldiers and foot-soldiers strike down horseman; a group of Romans, forming in close order, would advance to meet the chariots, and others would be scattered by them; a band of Britons would come to close quarters with the archers and rout them, while others were content to dodge their shafts at a distance; and all this was going on not at one spot only, but in all three divisions at once. They contended for a long time, both parties being animated by the same zeal and daring. But finally, late in the day, the Romans prevailed; and they slew many in battle beside the wagons and the forest, and captured many alike.

Agricola's part in the battle is unknown. He must have been there, having been on Paulinus' staff for the past two years. As such I have given him a part in the action as suits the character we have come to know.

The aftermath is well known. Poenius Postumus (Heaven help the man for nominal determinism) was probably perfectly sensible in refusing the summons to battle. A camp prefect is a very senior and very experienced and capable officer, who has worked his way up through the centurionate in his career. If Postumus would not move, you can bet your life's savings he had a damn good reason not to. Still, Tacitus brushes him aside and notes the prefect's suicide, putting it down to his embarrassment at having missed all the fun and chance of glory. The visit of Titus during the following winter is not directly attested in sources, but is hinted at very thoroughly, and I have mentioned it, given the future links between Agricola and the Flavians. The arrival of Classicianus and his arguments with Paulinus are well attested. For those with an interest, the massive, imposing tombstone of Classicianus is on display in the British Museum. We also do not know where the provincial administration was based immediately after the revolt, given that Colchester and London, the two prime sites, had been razed to the ground. I have selected Cirencester as one of the older surviving sites, but that is simple conjecture.

We know virtually nothing of Agricola's remaining months in Britain. As the senior tribune of the Second, though, and at a time when military campaigning had ceased, he was likely stuck back in camp in Exeter for the rest of his service, barring visits to the governor.

Agricola, then, is done with Britannia for now – although, as portents above suggest, this will not be his last visit to the island. In the meantime, a political career in Rome and abroad awaits, along with a period of vast upheaval and change in Rome. His fictional companions are all in this text for a reason, so look for them going on to new things in coming volumes – not just Luci, but Sabinus and Valda too.

See you in Book 2.

Simon Turney, November 2022

About the Author

SIMON TURNEY is from Yorkshire and, having spent much of his childhood visiting historic sites, fell in love with the Roman heritage of the region. His fascination with the ancient world snowballed from there with great interest in Rome, Egypt, Greece and Byzantium. His works include the Marius' Mules and Praetorian series, the Tales of the Empire and The Damned Emperor series, and the Rise of Emperors books with Gordon Doherty. He lives in North Yorkshire with his family.

Follow Simon at www.simonturney.com and @SJATurney